Blood Reins

Other Detective Sandra Cameron Mysteries by Michael Joens

An Animated Death in Burbank

Blood Reins

MICHAEL JOENS

THOMAS DUNNE BOOKS
ST. MARTIN'S MINOTAUR
NEW YORK

This is a work of fiction. The names, characters, horses, and events in this book are fictitious, and are the product of the author's imagination. Any resemblance to actual persons or animals, living or dead, is purely coincidental.

THOMAS DUNNE BOOKS.
An imprint of St. Martin's Press.

www.minotaurbooks.com

Library of Congress Cataloging-in-Publication Data

Joens, Michael R.
    Blood reins : a detective Sandra Cameron mystery / Michael Joens.—1st ed.
        p. cm.
    ISBN 0-312-32105-8
    EAN 978-0312-32105-5
    1. Police—California—Los Angeles County—Fiction. 2. Horse trainers—Crimes against—Fiction. 3. Los Angeles County (Calif.)—Fiction.
4. Policewomen—Fiction. I. Title.

PS3560.O246B57 2005
813'.54—dc22

                                                                      2004054943

First Edition: February 2005

10 9 8 7 6 5 4 3 2 1

To my beautiful daughter, Stephanie, my joy
and crown, lover of horses and big dreams

Acknowledgments

My heartfelt thanks go to the following men and women for their valuable help in the making of this book:

Deputy Sharon Falbisaner, Los Angeles County Sheriff's Department (retired), and Detective Matthew Miranda, Burbank PD.

I would also like to thank Dr. Gary F. Hathaway, M.D., Dr. Wayne D. Marteney, DVM, and Dr. Larry J. Connelly, DVM. Also, a thank-you to David Nilsson.

A big thank-you to my wife, Cathy, and to Kathie Huenemeier for their inexhaustible knowledge of horses.

Also, thanks to Brandon Joens for his creative design on the cover.

Any errors in police, medical, or veterinary protocol or procedure are solely mine.

Once again, I would like to thank Natasha Kern for her investment of time, energy, insights, and moral support.

Many thanks to Marcia Markland and the kind folks at St. Martin's Press for believing in this work.

Blood Reins

Chapter One

Detectives Thomas Rigby and Dan Bolt heard the "man down" call as they headed down Alameda in their unmarked sedan. The location given by the radio dispatcher was the Cottonwood Equestrian Center, a destination to which the detectives were, coincidentally, already heading.

Dan made a noise in the back of his throat. "That's cozy." He reached for the radio and keyed the mike. "David one-sixteen responding. ETA in four minutes." He took his thumb off the mike button.

The radio squawked. A woman's voice repeated: "David one-sixteen responding."

Tom turned on the flashers and rolled Code Two past apartment buildings and older bungalows on a blacktop street that was lined on either side with mature sycamores and parked cars. He turned left onto Main, drove past more apartments on the left, and came to a stop at Riverside Drive. The equestrian center was directly ahead, across Riverside. Tom made for it.

The gateway was made of twelve-by-twelve wooden posts that were painted white, the name Cottonwood Equestrian Center written in forest green block letters across a wide transom that had a western look about it. As Tom drove through the gates a short, heavyset man wearing blue jeans, a paisley, short-sleeved shirt, two sizes too small, and a straw cowboy hat waved him to stop. Tom rolled down his window, felt a wash of hot air on his face, a dry smothering morning heat that promised a blistering sun later.

The man made quick gesticulations with his hands and face as he briefed the detectives on the man down, pointing in the direction of the scene with a thick forefinger. "A black-and-white unit got here a couple minutes ago," he said excitedly.

"Paramedics arrive yet?" Tom asked.

"No, I'm waiting for them. I think he's dead, though."

"Oh?"

"He looks dead," the man said with a sharp nod. "I made the nine-one-one call—gave my name and number to the officers."

"Okay." Tom drove on into the center, wheeled past the white stucco clubhouse on the right, the sun glaring on its terra-cotta tiled roof, then headed west toward the far end of the compound. He turned down a dirt road, past rows and rows of dusty green-and-white stables where horses poked their heads out of stalls and followed them with curious eyes. Turning a corner, slowing to allow the passage of a horse and rider, Tom saw the flashing lights of a Burbank cruiser parked in a wide dirt area by another row of stables.

"Over there," Dan said, pointing.

Tom angled toward a crowd, turned into the shade of a giant cottonwood, and parked. Dust followed them and hung motionless over their vehicle in the dead air. From where they sat Tom could just see through the crowd a man lying on his back in the middle of the dirt road. He wasn't moving.

"Horse accident, maybe?" Dan speculated.

Tom said nothing.

"Horses are stupid." Dan called in their ten-twenty, fished a Snickers bar out of his coat pocket, and tore off the wrapper. "You know they got a brain the size of a walnut?"

Tom looked at him.

The detectives got out of their vehicle and badged their way through the crowd. The man in the dirt appeared to be dead. His left hand was gripping his chest, the knuckles white; the fingers of his right hand were dug into the dirt, as if clinging to the earth. "What've we got, Kyle?" Tom asked the nearest uniform.

Officer Kyle Platchett, a beefy, simian-browed man with a crisp flattop, sunburned where the scalp showed, shrugged his big shoulders. "Looks dead to me."

Dan, chewing on his Snickers bar, cast Platchett an ironic sneer. "What was your first clue?"

The man in the dirt gazed unblinking at the sun in a dull, expressionless, half-lidded stare. His lips, slightly parted, showed the bluish effects of cyanosis. His skin color was a bloodless dusty pallor. He didn't appear to be breathing, which was a pretty good indicator that he was dead. Tom stooped and felt his carotid artery. He was. Dead maybe ten, fifteen minutes. "Any ID?"

Kyle raised his eyebrows without emotion. "Just got here."

Tom patted the body for a wallet. There wasn't one. He looked up at the crowd. Some were dressed in cowboy hats, boots, and jeans; others were wearing touristy outfits—shorts, Hawaiian-style shirts, sandals—turf meets the surf. "Anyone know this man?"

Heads craned to better see the dead guy. Shoulders shrugged, lips pursed. A woman covered her little girl's eyes.

"He came crashing out of that trailer," a man in an Australian bush hat said, stepping through the crowd wagging a knobby finger.

The heavy woman in shorts and tank top beside him nodded seriously. "Next to the Sundowner."

Tom followed their points to a long white aluminum-sided trailer angled against a curb of railroad ties, beneath a row of giant cottonwoods, about thirty feet from where the dead man lay. There were RVs and horse trailers parked on either side of the one of interest, the latter being the kind that held both horses and humans—an RV setup in front, horse stalls in the rear. The door leading into the living quarters was open. Tom could hear the air conditioner running.

"Came busting out like a crazy man," the man in the bush hat said. "Like his hair was on fire."

The dead man's shirt was open, revealing a bare torso. There didn't appear to be any signs of foul play. No bullet holes or knife wounds visible. No horseshoe prints tatooing his forehead. He was wearing faded jeans, cowboy boots, and a silver belt buckle, AQHA World Champion written on it. A MedicAlert bracelet gleamed on his right wrist. Tom checked the backside. "Has a heart condition," he said. "He's also a diabetic. Insulin dependent."

"Not anymore," Dan said, reaching for his cell phone. "What's the one-eight-hundred number?"

Tom read the number.

Dan dialed it, waited, then identified himself to the MedicAlert dispatcher. "Need an ID on one of your clients," he said. He listened, looked at Tom. "That bracelet have an ID number?"

Tom waved a fly from his face, read the number across the bottom of the tag. Dan repeated it into the receiver and waited.

Tom stood, looked across the compound, past the clubhouse, and could just see the dull green metal roof of the arena through stands of giant eucalyptus and sycamores. He assumed that that's where Sandy was right now (it's where she'd said she would be). He checked his watch—10:33 A.M. Sandy's event was supposed to start at 10:30. She'd asked him to come watch her compete, something she had not been able to do since the shooting, two months ago. She needed his support, something Tom was happy to give her.

Dan folded his cell phone, snapped it into its little belt holster, then scribbled in his notebook. "Name's Chester Gundry," he said. "Type one diabetes. He also had a bad heart . . . weak lining in his aorta. . . . He was a walking time bomb. Dispatcher said they'd contact the next of kin."

Tom looked at him. "Chester Gundry?"

Dan read his notes. "Yeah, Chester Gundry. Lives out in Acton."

"*Chet* Gundry?"

Dan shrugged his notebook back into his coat pocket. "Chet's short for Chester. Why?"

Tom felt something move inside him as he looked at the dead man with heightened interest. The man had square rugged features and wavy black hair, swept back off a tanned brow that hooded deep-set indigo blue eyes. He was good-looking, shaped in the Tom Selleck mold, except that he was dead. Flies, testament to the fact, were finding their way from a nearby manure pile and working him over pretty good. Still, Tom felt the movement. He felt it deep inside his chest; a movement of tides—the marly confluence of thoughts and feelings, churning, and a prickling of doubt, like a slow-moving propeller, dredging through it.

"What is it, Tommy?" Dan asked, taking another bite of Snickers. "You know him?"

Tom shook his head.

"What is it then? You look like you've seen a ghost."

"If he's who I think he is then Sandy knew him. Used to be her trainer."

Polishing off the candy bar, Dan crumpled up the wrapper, looked for a place to toss it. He shoved it in his coat pocket. "No kiddin'?"

Tom did not mention that Chet Gundry had also been Sandy's one-time significant other. "Best call the coroner."

"You bet. In this heat that boy's gonna ripen real quick."

Sirens mounted in the distance. Minutes later, a second cruiser and a paramedics unit rolled toward them amid a boil of dust. Horses in nearby stalls kicked and whinnied. Both vehicles cut their sirens and lights before they came to a halt at the periphery of the crowd.

"Cavalry's arrived," Dan said needlessly. "I'll send them away. Nothing more they can do for our boy here but send flowers."

Tom nodded.

Dan started toward them, waved his arms as he walked through the crowd. "Okay, folks, show's over. Let's get on with whatever you do here."

The crowd backed away a little, allowing Dan to pass, and then closed back over the opening he had made. Dan talked to the paramedics.

A vague curiosity spread through Tom as he studied the dead man's face. Sandy had told him one night over a good steak and a bottle of merlot that Chet Gundry was one of the better horse trainers in the business. Tom didn't give a rip about her past heart throbs, but they had recently entered the I-tell-you-you-tell-me phase of their relationship, so Tom had listened politely. Gundry was well liked, apparently, a man's man and a lady's man, the latter being the source of Sandy's breakup with him close to a year ago. She had gone over to his house one night and discovered Gundry in his barn with a brunette Barbie doll. They weren't talking horses.

Dan made his way back through the crowd. Dan was built like a small black bear wearing a shapeless brown-on-brown suit. He had no taste in clothes; wore the same two suits year after year, rain or shine. One basic blue, the other one he was wearing, the color of his Snickers bar. Both were made of polyester. There was a man with him. "Gentleman here says he saw women coming and going from the trailer. Isn't that right?" Dan smiled at the man, a little sheepishly it seemed.

The man appeared to be in his late seventies. He wore a sweat-lined, beat-up felt cowboy hat pushed back off his deeply lined forehead, showing the white beginning of his tan line. His face, darkly weathered and craggy, had the look of beef jerky; likewise his hands that seemed all knuckles. He reminded Tom of an iguana. His legs were slightly bowed, which completed the stereotype of an old cowpoke in off the range. "That's right," he said. "A blonde and a brunette."

Dan stood eyeballing the man like an idiot, his high round forehead and red and balding scalp beading with sweat from the sun that was already well into the nineties. Tom thought that maybe his partner had been out in the sun too long, but then Dan sweated in air-conditioned rooms.

The cowpoke leaned over, angled his head to better view the dead man. "Whaddya know—Chet Gundry." He turned sideways a little and spat a brown stream into the dirt, making a dust crater.

"You saw women enter his trailer?" Tom asked.

"I was unloading my horse." He fanned a thumb. "That's my rig over there."

Tom followed his point to a one-horse trailer hitched to a beat-up '70s faded red vintage Chevy pickup parked alongside a practice arena where several riders had reined their horses to the rail to look over at the spectacle of the dead man.

"There were two of them," cowpoke said. "A blonde and a brunette. Blonde went in first. Good-looking. Both of them. All decked out."

"Decked out?"

"Show outfits. Good-lookin' broads," he said, showing a rake of old brown crooked teeth as if watching the women cross through his mind. " 'specially the blonde. Left when the brunette arrived."

Tom felt a sudden tingling over his scalp. "How long ago was this?"

The man shrugged. "I don't know. Could've been a half hour."

"You don't know their names?"

"Nope. Was I younger, I'da got 'em in triplicate." He spat again then, grinned for effect.

Tom wrote down the man's name and phone number, his mind on the dead man. "Thanks for your help."

"You bet."

Dan watched the man leave. "You know who that was, Tommy?"

Tom looked at his notebook. "Yeah, Jim Dakota."

"That name don't ring any bells for you?"

Tom shrugged absently. "Should it?"

Dan removed a bag of beer nuts from his coat pocket. "Guess you didn't watch TV growing up. That was Dakota Smith. Character actor—played bad guys mostly. You've seen him. Been in every B Western since Gene Autry. I musta shot him a million times with my Mattel Fanner 50."

Tom watched the man untie a high-withered swayback palomino from a trailer hitch and load him onto the trailer. The horse looked like it was two steps from the glue factory. "Looks like you hit his horse," he said.

Just then the crowd opened up to allow the coroner's wagon to pass through. Phil Carlton, a thin, hunch-shouldered man in his early fifties, and a tall black man with a head of cornrows, stepped out of the vehicle.

Carlton, wearing blue jeans and a banana yellow polo shirt, took a deep breath. "I love the smell of Bandini in the morning," he crowed, à la Robert Duvall in *Apocalypse Now*. He walked over to the detectives, took one look at Chet Gundry, and said, "Looks like a dead guy to me."

Dan popped a handful of beer nuts into his mouth. "That was scholarly."

"Thank you."

Dan briefed Phil on Gundry's age, medical status, and approximate time of death as the coroner and his assistant made a cursory examination of the body. Dan said, "From his history I'd guess he suffered insulin shock—maybe a grand mal seizure. His heart couldn't take it."

"Grand mal, huh?"

Dan indicated the crowd. "Man says he came staggering out of his trailer like his hair was on fire."

"Maybe." Phil shook his head. "I don't know, though."

"What?" Tom asked.

Phil pointed at the dead man's exposed abdomen. "Either of you crime fighters see this?"

Tom stooped, saw a small black-and-blue area to the left of the man's navel. "Looks like a recent puncture mark. Insulin injection?"

"Perhaps."

Tom looked at him, looked back at the dead man. "What are you thinking, Phil?"

"You tell me. Man in his midthirties drops dead after injecting himself with insulin—assuming he injected himself with insulin."

"He had a bad heart."

Carlton raised his wispy eyebrows. "Why the seizure?"

Both men stood. Carlton looked at Dan. "Could you have his medical files sent to the morgue?"

"You want to open him up?"

"I would recommend it."

Tom considered that for a moment. He went over to their vehicle, opened the trunk, grabbed the digital camera, and came back and clicked off several shots of the body. Finishing, he said, "He's all yours."

Carlton and his assistant loaded Gundry's body onto a gurney, rolled it into the wagon, and closed the doors. People glanced at the vehicle as it drove away quietly, their faces registering disappointment. The show was over.

With the excitement of death removed from the scene the crowd dispersed, leaving Tom and Dan and the four Burbank officers sweating bullets in the sun.

"Need us to secure the trailer?" Officer Platchett asked Tom.

"No, Dan and I will take care of it."

The officers waved, got into their cruisers, and drove away, a fine haze of dust lifting behind them.

Tom and Dan were alone. The air was thick, hot, dusty dry, the pungent smell of horse manure clinging to the insides of their nostrils. "Whaddya think, Tommy?"

Tom kept his thoughts to himself.

"Pretty screwy if you ask me," Dan said. He started to pop another handful of beer nuts into his mouth when a fly the size of a Cessna 150 buzzed out of the bag. He frowned, eyed the nearby manure pile, then tossed the bag onto it.

Tom glanced in the direction of the covered arena. He hated missing Sandy perform; she needed his support, especially now. He could hear a loudspeaker in the distance, a man's voice rasping through it: "Riders, trot your horses."

"Maybe her event's still going," Dan said. "We can toss the trailer afterwards."

Tom looked at the trailer, shook his head at a troubling thought that was fingering into his mind. "No, let's do it."

•

The living quarters of the trailer were eight feet in width, and twenty feet in length, about the size of a small RV. A pop-out wall containing a Navajo-patterned sofa and a white oak dining table on a chromium pedestal added an additional four feet in width to the living area. Bluebottle flies flickered in and out of bars of light falling down through skylights and slatted wooden blinds, the buzz of tiny irridescent wings muffled by the garrulous hum of the air conditioner that was working overtime to cool the heat. Maroon-and-gray indoor-outdoor carpet, color coordinating with the other furnishings, covered the floor. Other things covered the floor, too.

Dan looked around. "What a wreck."

A vertical cupboard stood open next to the refrigerator. There were cans and boxes of cereal and flour dumped out, their contents spilled. A bathroom was opened to the left, a small leather bag on the floor, along with other toiletry items. Over on the right wall, occupying the space made by the gooseneck, was the sleeping quarters, viewable through open curtains that coordinated with the sofa and rug. Blankets and sheets appeared to have been clawed off the mattress and hung down in a tangle over the light-colored half-wall paneling.

"Looks like your time bomb went off in here," Tom said.

Along the inside right wall there was a small kitchen area,

complete with refrigerator, three-burner gas stove, oven, oak counter with an inset aluminum sink. Dust blown in from outside covered their surfaces with a powdery film. A bottle of Jack Daniels, half full, stood beside a glass tumbler on the dining table, the cap off the bottle. There was a small bottle of insulin standing about six inches to the left of it. No sign of a syringe.

"Since when do diabetics drink alcohol?" Dan asked.

Tom gave that some thought. He took several pictures, set the camera down on the counter, pulled out a pair of latex gloves he kept in the side pocket of his navy blazer, and got to work. Dan did likewise.

A magazine lay open on the sofa. The page on the left showed a full-color bleed of a stallion, the name "Ideal's Bar Zhan Zee" splashed across the bottom of the page. Tom shook his head. He thought it weird the names people gave their horses. Names like Spot and Fido wouldn't cut it in the horse world. He whistled when he read the standing fee.

"Got anything?"

"Thirty-five-hundred-dollar stud fee."

"I'm worth it," Dan said, opening a kitchen drawer.

The page on the right showed the same horse, standing in front of rich blue drapes, a gold cup the size of a fire hydrant at his feet. Mounted on the horse was a raven-haired beauty in show regalia: Angelina Montoya, according to the copy, the stallion's owner. Standing on the ground beside her was the trainer, Chet Gundry. Tom looked closely. It was the dead man.

"Here we go," Dan said, still going through the drawers. He pulled out a little red book and thumbed through it. "Address book of some kind." He whistled. "Talk about your studs. This guy's got a mess of fillies in his stable."

Tom let it pass. He opened the refrigerator. It was fairly empty except for three cans of Coke, a plastic gallon jug of water, and a stalk of celery.

Dan stepped over to him. "Look at this, Tommy. What's Sandy's name doing in this guy's little black book?"

Tom shut the refrigerator with a muffled thump, took the address book, and read where Dan pointed. Sandy's name, address, station and home phone numbers were written in neat printing. He looked at the cover. "It's a little red book."

"That why it's got a little star next to her name?"

"Gundry used to be her trainer. I told you that." There were scores of names in the book, mostly women, but there were men's names as well. Tom figured they were business acquaintances, not consorts. He thumbed over to the M's, found Angelina Montoya's name and address. The address was off Sand Canyon, in Santa Clarita. She wasn't too far from where Sandy lived. There was no star next to her name.

"You gonna tell her?" Dan asked.

"Tell her what?"

"About Gundry. I mean, if he used to be her trainer—"

"I'll tell her." Tom handed the address book back to Dan, looked at the opened bathroom door in the wall to the left of the dining table, and went over to it.

The bathroom was about the size of a broom closet, large enough to contain a dinky fiberglass shower stall, porcelain commode, aluminum corner sink, and a tiny skylight that shed a blaze of sunlight on the white oak paneling. A room designed strictly for business. A burgundy leather case, about the size of a large hardcover novel, was unzipped and opened and lay on the floor. Gundry's insulin works, Tom guessed. The bag contained several needles in plastic containers, glucose test strips, a small bottle of rubbing alcohol, cotton swabs, bottles of Mercurochrome, hydrogen peroxide, and on the top half there were elastic loops for three small insulin bottles. There were two insulin bottles in the loops, both empty; their labels listing Gundry's name and the name of the pharmacy—a Rite-Aid out in Palmdale. The third bottle was probably the one on the dining table. There was no syringe in the case.

Tom's mind was working on two levels. The first level was that of the detective, that of collecting forensic data, bagging and tagging it, storing it into mental compartments to be retrieved later, in case it was discovered that the man's death was due to something other than natural cause. The second level was a bit murkier. There was no data collected on this level. No hard data. On this level Tom's mind fingered through a green mist of emotions, inchoate thoughts, oily suspicions (hunches, in cop jargon) whispered in his ear by demons from his past, real or imagined. Then out of the mist the dead man's face rose: the death grimace frozen in a kind of mocking smile. Mocking Tom.

Once again he felt the movement in his chest.

Chapter Two

Detective Sandy Cameron couldn't get the image of the gun out of her mind. The killer pointing it at her chest. Every detail of the face and gun in pristine clarity—the two-inch blued barrel, the muzzle oscillating in midair as the killer thumbed back the hammer, the sun glinting off the cylinder as a bullet wheeled into place. She tried to focus on what she was doing—sit erect, poised, maintain Buster's steady, fluid gait—but she kept seeing the gun, the green slits of madness behind it, narrowing, the bloody index finger squeezing the trigger, the knuckle whitening, all of it there in her mind uninvited.

"Riders, lope your horses."

In response to the judge's command, Sandy spurred her quarter horse gelding into a lope. Doing so, she felt her pulse quicken, her heart racing, not because Buster had somehow gotten onto the wrong lead but because she felt the onslaught of another attack. She grimaced. *Not now.*

The attacks were brutal. They came without warning, jumped her with fang and claw. In the refuge of her home she could cope; she could lock her doors and windows and crawl into bed, pull the covers over her head and ride it out. She could call a friend—call Tom. But now, competing before a grandstand of spectators, she felt terribly exposed, vulnerable. Naked. A part of her mind told her to fight it, to relax, slow down the breathing, focus on what she was doing. Another part screamed at her to flee, screamed that a killer was watching her—a crazy in the crowd with a gun.

There was no sound in the attacks, except a guttural chuckling in the killer's throat, the soft click of the locking hammer, and then the wicked flame tongue lashing out from the muzzle an instant before the hollow-point struck her chest with the force of a pile driver. She never heard the shot, one that, even now, shook her body with its phantom impact.

Buster must've felt her wince through her legs, for he raised his head, as though inquiring if it was some new signal she was teaching him. "Easy, boy," she whispered, fighting back a nauseating tremor. She tugged gently on the reins with the third fingers of each hand to bump his head back down, to steady him, slow down his gait to a crawling fluid lope, barely faster than a human walk. *There we go. Focus. Breathe deep.*

She had thought that getting back into competition would be just the thing to get her mind off the shooting, get her back on an emotional center. Her therapist thought it might be a little soon, but Sandy had insisted, had trained hard for it during the past month. It appeared that her therapist had been right, after all. The tremor gripped her.

Sandy rounded the far turn of the circuit feeling light-headed, when the judge, mercifully, called the riders to jog, then walk, horse hooves padding softly in the sand, then called everyone to the center of the covered arena, where they were asked to line up abreast in front of the judge's stand. There were twelve riders in all, most of whom Sandy knew and had faced in competition before. There were a couple that she didn't know, one, in particular, a girl of seventeen or eighteen, riding a spirited bay that had shied at the sight of a child holding a silver balloon and nearly thrown her.

Bespangled in show attire, both riders and mounts shone and sparkled in resplendent glory. There was enough silver gleaming in saddles, bridles, and belt buckles to float the economies of most Third World countries. The riders sat motionless, eyes straight ahead, pretending not to notice the man and woman judges in white Stetsons and clipboards eyeing their mounts and writing down scores. These two met in the center, compared notes, and then walked over to the elevated booth where the announcer, wearing a black Stetson and smoking a cigar, sat waiting.

Sat waiting. Coping. Sandy's hands trembling on the reins, forcing the gun from her mind. She looked for Tom's face in the crowd, didn't see him, started as the loudspeaker broke silence, a low, gravelly drawl that said, "The judges' results for the Western Pleasure class . . ."

Six numbers were called in ascending order, and as each was called the rider wearing that number spurred his or her horse forward amid the applause of the crowd to receive the appropriately colored ribbon. Sandy did not place. She didn't care. She just wanted to get out of the arena as quickly as possible.

She reined Buster toward the gates, glanced quickly into the thinning bleachers once more for Tom's face. It wasn't there. She was certain that his duties must have kept him away, and was glad now that he hadn't shown. She had shown miserably.

Bud Nichols was standing at the gates on one foot, the bootheel of the other hooked over the lower white rail, his elbows bent over the top one, one hand folded lightly over the other, a twist of smoke rising from the brown cigar angling from a leathery knuckle. He was staring down at the tip, thinking, maybe—Bud was a thinker. He looked up as a horse pranced through the gates, looked it over in a glance, the points of a horse. Caught it all in a languid sweep.

As Sandy approached, he looked up, same look as always—dark gray eyes, almost charcoal—looking at you but thinking horse. That's all he ever thought about, horse. That's all he ever talked about. "I missed his lead," she said. It was a mea culpa. Sandy could hear the flutter in her voice, the two parts of her mind—fight and flight—crashing in her throat.

Bud flicked the ash off his cheroot, took a drag. "Yes, you did," he said, blowing a cloud of smoke into the hot, dead, moistureless air.

"I'll do better next time."

Bud didn't comment. He looked away, removed his blue ball cap, and ran his fingers through a longish thatch of black hair, slapped the cap back on his head and adjusted the bill over his eyes. Bud didn't fit the image of a world-class trainer. Wearing faded Wrangler jeans, Budweiser T-shirt, a pair of well-worn packer boots, and a Pro Rodeo baseball cap, the bill creased lengthwise— he looked like anything but a trainer. Bull rider, maybe. He had the build for it—lean, sinewy, five-tenish. However, Bud was a trainer, one of the better ones in the business. A rival of Chet Gundry, Bud understood horses from the hooves up, inside and out, better than anyone Sandy had ever worked with, perhaps even better than Chet Gundry.

"You looked like a novice out there," he said.

"I felt like one. This mean you won't train me?"

He shrugged noncommittally.

"It's been a while, Bud. What was all that commotion earlier? I heard sirens."

Bud watched another horse exit the arena—the spirited bay whose young rider, clearly a novice, appeared on the verge of tears. He shook his head, a deprecating dismissal of novices. "You up for Equitation?"

"I don't know."

He looked up at her, the light slipping under the bill of his cap, catching the deep-set gray that was dangerous to women as well as men, but for different reasons. He chuckled. His chuckle, though outwardly friendly, masked a sneer. "You don't *know*?"

She didn't. Equitation, as opposed to the Western Pleasure event she had just competed in, was where the *rider,* not the horse, was judged for poise and control, neither of which Sandy possessed at the moment. Right now she only wanted to put Buster in his stall, enter her trailer, and retreat from the world. Uncomfortable with the flow of conversation, she changed leads. "Sorry to hear about you losing the Sorrel West deal," she said.

Bud's eyes caught a flash of light. "How do you mean?"

"I heard Chet got it."

"He tell you that?"

Sandy felt her cheeks redden. "Well, yes, as a matter of fact."

Bud grinned.

Sandy frowned. "What? Chet *didn't* get the deal?"

Bud pulled on his cheroot, blew a cloud to one side. It hung motionless in the air a few seconds, then slid off in a seductive curl of breeze. "If that's what Chet told you, I'm sure it's true. He say anything else?"

"He told me about your new mare," Sandy said. "I'm so sorry."

Bud gave no indication that he'd heard her. He was looking at something behind her.

Sandy turned in her saddle to see what held his attention.

Angelina Montoya, the last competitor to exit the arena, was riding toward them on her chestnut stallion, a blue ribbon pinned to his bridle.

"I gotta go," Bud said, eyeing the woman's horse. He patted the top of the rail, tipped his cap to Sandy, and left. Sandy watched him walking away, a bit puzzled.

Angelina reined to a halt beside her. "Hey, Sandy," she said.

Sandy turned her head, smiled at Angelina, then eyed the blue ribbon. "Congratulations on your First. You looked great out there."

But then Angelina Montoya would look great mucking out the corrals in burlap. "Thanks," she said, a diamond-studded brooch flashing at her throat. Wearing a black high-crowned Stetson set squarely on a mane of black hair that was secured in back by a purple bow, black chaps, and a purple vest over a black slinkie, with swirls of dazzling rhinestones over the vest and cuffs, she sparkled like a diamond tiara set against a field of jet velvet. "Sorry you didn't do better. You seemed a little jittery out there."

"I was," Sandy said, still hearing a residual flutter in her voice.

"It's hard getting back into it, isn't it?"

Sandy smiled. She didn't want to go there.

"What's ol' Bud up to?" Angelina said, taking the hint. She turned in her saddle to watch Bud heading toward the clubhouse. "Didn't want to talk with the competition?"

Sandy laughed. "Bud doesn't miss a trick—not when it comes to horses." She admired Angelina's horse, a magnificent liver chestnut with four white socks and an S-shaped blaze on his forehead. Ideal's Bar Zhan Zee, winner of the World Championship two years ago. His coat gleamed in the sun. "He sure is a beauty."

Angelina leaned forward and patted the stallion's thick muscled neck. "He's a good boy, aren't you, Zee-Zee?" she said with a girlish lilt in her voice.

The stallion stamped his foot at Buster.

"I saw your spread in this month's *Western Horseman,*" Sandy said. "I see you raised Zee-Zee's standing fees."

Angelina laughed, her startling blue eyes catching flashes of violet light beneath the shade of her hat. "Why not? His babies are winning big shows. Strike while the iron's hot."

It made sense to Sandy. She'd heard that several of Zee-Zee's babies were winning big shows—the AQHA Congress, the Pacific Coast Firecracker—others racking up championship points in halter and yearling classes. The proof was in the pudding, as they say—*blood* pudding, in this case. A champion stallion was worth his weight in gold, but a stallion that passed on his good genes to second and third generations was priceless. "I read that you're only shipping his semen now?"

Angelina nodded, the new leather creaking as she sat upright in her saddle. "That's right. I don't want to risk some hormonal mare kicking him when he's trying to mount her—maybe breaking a leg." She smiled. "Besides, I can hardly keep up with the orders as it is."

Sandy admired the sheen of the stallion's coat, the shape of his head and neck. He was truly a magnificent horse. "You and Chet have done a super job with him."

"Thanks. It's all Chet's doing, of course. He's the best trainer in the business. Well—you know that." Angelina smiled.

Sandy nodded. She had introduced Angelina to Chet several years ago at a barbecue at her house. Owner of a twenty-acre horse ranch just down the road from where Sandy lived, Angelina had come with her husband, Julian, to meet him. Not a good idea. Julian, a man with a Latin temper, glowered at Chet from beginning to end. Sandy had no idea why, since Chet had been a perfect gentleman to Angelina, talking only about her horses. "Chet's the best," Sandy agreed, feeling a twinge of remorse.

Angelina crossed her hands on her silver saddle horn, the reins held loosely in her fingers. "You should've stuck with him. Your personal life is one thing. Your professional life is another."

Sandy smiled politely. She definitely didn't want to go there. "How are things with you and Julian?"

Angelina made a so-so gesture with her hand. "Spring is still in the air and the grass is greener."

Sandy was sorry she asked.

Angelina patted her stallion's neck. "I've got my Zee-Zee," she said, the girlish lilt returning to her voice. "Don't I, boy?" She glanced over at the bleachers where there were still a few people left from the crowd. "You haven't seen him, have you?"

"Julian?"

"No . . . Chet."

"I saw him earlier with Vern."

Angelina grunted. "He and Vern, huh?"

Sandy chuckled. "They were having a spat."

"Oh?"

Sandy screwed her face up into a dismissive smile. "You know Vern."

Angelina made a face back. "Yes, I do. What was it this time?"

"I didn't hear." Another prick of conscience. She'd actually heard the tail end of their argument but saw no reason to burden Angelina with it.

Angelina looked at Sandy for a moment, probing, it seemed, then glanced over at one of the nearby practice arenas where riders were putting their horses through drills. "Well, if you happen to see Chet, could you tell him I need to talk to him?"

"I sure will."

"I can't believe he didn't come watch the event."

"He'll turn up."

Angelina smiled knowingly. Chet was most likely observing a horse of a different color, one with two legs. "I'm sure he will," she said. "Take it easy, Sandy." Angelina started to spur her stallion forward, then drew up on the reins and glanced back. "By the way, are you competing in the Equitation class tomorrow?"

"I don't know yet."

"I wish you would. You always do well in it." She smiled, her eyes dipping to admire a splash of rhinestones across Sandy's breasts, then gazed probingly at her. "Getting back into competition— especially after what you've been through—is difficult I'm sure. But you need to do it. A horse throws you, you get right back up on it, as the saying goes. It sounds corny, I know, but it's true."

Sandy smiled appreciatively. Once again she felt vulnerable and didn't like it. "We'll see."

Angelina nodded, clucked her tongue, and rode away in a glittery flash.

Sandy sat for a moment listening to the drone of nearby Ventura Freeway, thinking, her gaze absently following riders threading quietly along trails through the trees of adjacent Griffith Park. The park, with its golf course, zoo, jogging and riding trails, belied busy L.A. hidden behind the mountains that rose a drab green slash against the sun-leached southern California sky, a smudgy brown haze that one could taste around the edges. Sandy wasn't thinking about the park, however; she was wondering how many people besides Angelina could see that hidden behind the glitzy veneer of her outfit a scared little girl was doing her best to cope.

She glanced around the center once more, hoping to see Tom. No Tom. Not one to break a promise, she guessed he must be on a call.

She spurred Buster along a broad dirt road toward the rows of stables at the far end of the forty-acre stable and arena complex. Her intention was to find Chet and finish the conversation she'd had with him in his trailer, a conversation that had been interrupted by a very unpleasant scene. A line of cottonwoods, thick trunked and proud in summer leaf, threw mottled shade patterns across her path. A breeze lifted, the leaves trembled, then hung still on the dead air that would soon give way to a punishing June sun. She smiled at a cooling thought.

This past Saturday Tom had taken her sailing to Catalina, a fair wind aft, dolphins splashing alongside the bow like children racing just to race. That evening he had fixed dinner on the boat—filet with rock lobster, steamed wild rice, stir-fried vegetables, and a bottle of Chablis. Tom's culinary skills bordered on the gourmet; strange, considering he was a tough homicide cop. Afterward they had walked through Avalon, sampled shooters at a local brewery, then set sail at sunset, the horizon blood red and shimmering as if the great red ball had actually fallen into the Pacific. By the time they motored into his slip it was who-knows-what-time in the morning. It didn't matter. She wasn't the least bit tired. Not once during the entire day did she feel threatened. The thought of Tom was a healing balm.

Sandy reined Buster down a wide alley between two long rows of wooden stalls, white with green trim, most of which were occupied by horses trailered in from all over the North American continent. When she came to the end of the stalls she turned right, and there, parked by the mouth of yet another row of stables, she could see Vern Wieder's dusty blue Chevy truck. Vern was rummaging through a compartment in the dirty white Porta-Vet perched in the bed. A pretty red roan was tied to a hitch rail next to him.

Sandy reined Buster toward him. "Hey, Vern, you seen Chet?"

Vern Wieder was a wide-shouldered man in his early fifties with a balding, disproportionately large head set atop a stringy neck. His face looked as though it had been flattened in a vice. It was a red face, the kind that doesn't tan, just blisters in the sun. He wore a beige straw hat, old blue jeans, roper boots, and a blue-and-white striped short-sleeved shirt that revealed blotchy red arms. Without looking at her, he held a small clear bottle to the light, angled his big head back to read the label through half-glasses perched on a small raw nose, then jabbed a syringe into the stoppered mouth.

Sandy figured that either he didn't hear her or he was ignoring her, which would be typical for Vern. "Vern?"

"What's that?" He drew back on the little plunger, eyed the syringe filling with clear fluid.

Sandy guessed he was about to give the horse a sedative so he could work on her, one of the reasons she didn't use him. She thought Vern overdrugged his horses. "You seen Chet lately?"

"Haven't seen him all morning."

She laughed in astonishment. "What're you talking about, Vern? I saw you talking to him earlier. It looked like you were having a friendly argument, so I kept riding by."

Wieder lowered the syringe, dipped his head to look over the top of his glasses at her with pale blue eyes. "I'm sorry, Sandy, what did you say? My mind's elsewhere."

"I just asked if you'd seen Chet. I need to talk to him."

"Why?"

Sandy frowned. "Why? I just need to talk with him, that's why. Nothing special. Have you seen him or haven't you?" she said, tempted to take off without hearing his answer.

"You try his trailer?"

"Not yet."

"Try his trailer." He winked. "I'd knock first."

"Thanks, Vern." I'll be sure to knock first. Sandy rolled her eyes, started to leave.

"And Sandy . . ."

She turned in her saddle, saw Vern's round unblinking eyes gazing at her over the withers of the red roan.

"We weren't arguing. Chet and me. We weren't."

"It's no big deal, Vern. So you were having a spirited debate."

He shook his head fast. "I just don't want you thinking we were arguing when we weren't. We were discussing how to keep horses from colicking. Chet has his opinion, I have mine."

Sandy felt suddenly light-headed. Vern was lying. Not only were they not discussing colick prevention, but she'd distinctly heard Chet arguing with him about something Chet called a federal offense. In fact, when Chet approached her later with a question requiring her police expertise, she thought it might have something to do with their argument. "My mistake," she said, reining Buster away.

Vern smiled. A fake, irritating curl of the lips that never reached his eyes. "Just didn't want it getting around that we were arguing."

"You made your point, Vern." Sandy wished now that she'd just kept riding past him. Angelina Montoya swore by the guy. She put up with his eccentricities because she thought he was one of the better vets in the business, good with semen shipments, anyhow. Good vet or not, Vern gave Sandy the creeps. She knew that if she turned around she'd see his pale blue moons staring coldly at her.

She did.

They were.

She felt a shiver of revulsion, bumped Buster up into a trot.

By the time she reached Chet's trailer, it felt as if the temperature had risen another ten degrees. Sandy could feel sweat collecting in her armpits and along her sides. So far, southern California's legendary June gloom had been nonexistent, except for a vague feeling of failure, and something akin to dread that cooled her thoughts.

Sandy dismounted, felt the solid certainty of ground as she stood, her legs feeling a bit rubbery in the knees after being so long in the saddle. She tied Buster to a trailer hitch at the rear of the trailer, then walked back around to the side door. As she was about to knock, the door opened, startling her. Tom Rigby stood in the doorway, a look in his eyes that she had not seen before.

A puzzled laugh bubbled out of her throat. "Tom! What're you doing here?"

Chapter Three

They were sitting in a quiet booth in the dining area of the clubhouse that was cool and well lighted and not too crowded, considering that it was a big show. Large multipaned windows went along the wall above the booths. Sandy was sitting across from Tom. She was looking out of the window on her left that offered views of the courtyard and the covered arena. Indirect light slanted in under the arcade, showing the soft hollows beneath her wonderfully high cheekbones, the smooth, articulate line of her profile and neck, and a spectrum of copper highlights in her creamy blond hair that was as thick as a young Latina's. She seemed pensive, her mind fixed on a point seemingly miles away.

Tom had never before seen her in show attire. She was wearing a pair of cream-colored suede chaps with fringe lining the outer seams, the cut accenting the curve of her hips and long-striding shapeliness of her legs in much the same way as a French-cut bathing suit might. A cream-colored knit shirt with rhinestone cuffs—a slinkie, she called it—and a silver brooch beneath a blue suede vest clung to her wondrous shape and sparkled in a rhinestone star pattern over her breasts. Tom could not take his eyes off her.

A waitress with a long hard face, cynical blue eyes, and tight platinum curls stepped over to their table and Tom ordered a club sandwich and iced tea. Sandy asked for water only, removed her hat, and set it on the green vinyl seat beside her. Her hair was tied back with a blue silk bow that matched her vest, so that her ponytail fell below her shoulders. The hat made an indentation in her hair and a red line across her forehead, which she scratched vaguely with a fingernail.

"Should we order something for Dan?" she asked absently.

Tom shook his head. "I wouldn't worry about Dan's stomach. He's worried it into pretty good shape by himself."

Sandy smiled down at her hands folded on the Formica-topped table.

Dan Bolt was hunting down someone named Kate Bledsoe, Chet Gundry's on-again, off-again girlfriend, according to Sandy's initial report at the trailer. Bledsoe was a pretty woman in her early thirties, five-seven, light brown hair, green eyes, and was wearing an outfit that resembled an American flag. She was the woman who'd interrupted Sandy's meeting earlier with Chet Gundry. Sandy's report had been brief, shock-edged, and a bit vague, which was understandable in light of her relationship with the dead man.

Tom could see Sandy's thoughts sailing off again on the ebbing drift of her smile. Once again she looked out the window, light flickering in her clear hazel eyes that were fixed on a faraway point. Watching her, Tom imagined her on his sailboat, looking out over the bow as mist-shrouded Catalina rose in the distance, her hair lying flat on the wind, her face braced forward with the promise of happiness in her eyes, and he felt again the thrill that had gone through him then. A thrill now tempered by a somber mood. He reached across the table and took her hand. "Are you all right?"

No response.

"Sandy?"

"He was thirty-six," she said quietly.

Tom could feel her hand trembling. There was something in her tone, a tone that Tom had not heard during the past two months of their relationship, and once again he felt a prickling of doubt. "Tell me about it."

Sandy looked at their hands, smoothed her thumb over Tom's long, square-tipped masculine fingers. "It doesn't make sense. He took his insulin."

"When?"

"This morning. In his trailer."

"You didn't tell me that before."

"I just now thought of it."

Tom looked out the window automatically, but from where they were sitting he could not see the trailer. He could only see the covered arena. "What were you doing in his trailer?"

"He wanted to ask me something. I told you already." She looked at him suddenly, her eyes sharpening. "What do you *think* I was doing?"

Tom didn't answer at first. He realized then that he'd been pumping her for information. It had not been his intention to do so. Maybe it had been. Sandy was, after all, a witness. He was, after all, a detective; that was his job. "You say he's had these grand mal seizures before?"

"I told you about Chet."

She had told him that she'd had a brief relationship with a horse trainer named Chet Gundry. She'd told him that it was over before it ever really got started, and he believed her. She had never mentioned that she still kept in touch with him. She had never mentioned that he was a diabetic, and it made him wonder if there weren't other details she had failed to mention. "And you saw him inject himself?"

She shook her head. "No. He was about to when Kate busted into the trailer. Kate was his girlfriend."

"The Barbie doll," Tom said, glancing at his notebook.

"That's right." Sandy made a noise in her throat. "She took one look at Chet's shirt unbuttoned and went ballistic. I left. I assumed he injected himself. That's all there was to it, Tom. Chet gave himself injections three times a day. Sometimes in his stomach, sometimes in his thigh. It was common knowledge."

"Was his heart condition common knowledge?"

Sandy gazed probingly at him. "I don't know. I suppose most of his friends knew about it. Chet may've looked healthy, but he was not a well man."

Tom thought about that. "Maybe with his girlfriend's interruption he forgot to take the insulin."

Sandy waved it off. "Chet kept a strict regimen. He was as regular as a clock."

"Clocks break."

"Not this clock. You didn't see his syringe?"

"No."

"He was holding it when I last saw him." Sandy shook her head in amazement. "It doesn't make sense."

"You think there's maybe more to it?" Tom asked.

She shrugged her eyebrows.

Tom glanced out the window on his right as a horse and rider walked past, the horse lifting little puffs of dust with its hooves. "His girlfriend shows up and twenty minutes later he's dead."

"I'm not saying there's a connection." Sandy looked at Tom. "Could she pick up a frying pan and lay it across his skull? In a heartbeat. She's got a temper."

The waitress brought Tom's sandwich and their drinks. Tom sprinkled a little salt over the turkey, and took a bite. He looked at the sandwich as though it had just bitten him on the upper lip, set it down on the plate, and washed it down with iced tea.

Sandy turned her glass of water between her long, slender fingers, a thoughtful gaze in her eyes.

Tom said, "You mentioned before that Gundry wanted to talk to you about something. A police matter."

"That's right."

"You can't think of what that might be?"

"No. Just the federal-offense comment I heard him mention to Vern."

"The vet."

Sandy nodded, peering at Tom over her glass as she took a sip of water. Then she repeated, almost verbatim, what she'd told Tom earlier about an argument she'd overheard between Chet and Vern, how Vern had denied it when she mentioned it to him later. "That's all," she said, setting the glass quietly down on the table. "When you cross a state line it's a federal offense."

Tom looked up from his notes. "When you cross a state line?"

She nodded. "That's right, I told you."

"No, you didn't."

Sandy looked at him for a moment, then glanced over the empty tables in the restaurant, a pensive cast in her eyes. "This isn't easy to talk about, Tom. Can't we leave it alone? Chet probably forgot to take his insulin, went into shock, and had a heart attack. He's dead."

Tom gave her a moment. "Did he have any enemies?"

She chuckled ironically.

"Something funny?"

Sandy kept turning her glass. "Chet was in and out of so many things. A real wheeler-dealer." There was a slight acerbic tone in her voice. "No, he was a good-natured fool. He wasn't the kind of guy you could stay mad at."

"That include you?"

She looked at him, her eyes misty. "Especially me." She started to look away then glanced back, her eyebrows furrowing. "There is one thing," she said. "Something Chet started to tell me but never got around to finishing." She told Tom about a "ruffled feathers" comment Chet had made earlier in his trailer. "It had something to do with his deal with Sorrel West Outfitters."

"That some kind of clothing line?"

She nodded. "You see their ads in all the big magazines— runway models wearing cowboy duds. Chet said they wanted to add credibility to the line by using professional horse people. Kind of like how Wrangler uses rodeo stars to advertise their lines."

"Pretty lucrative?"

"Could be. We never discussed his deal."

"Whose feathers got ruffled?"

"I don't know. I know he beat out Bud Nichols on the deal. Least that's what Chet told me. I mentioned it to Bud this morning and he seemed to have a different take on it."

Tom wrote in his notebook. "Bud Nichols?"

"Another trainer. A good one. We went to one of his clinics three weeks ago, don't you remember?"

Tom thought back. "Oh, right." He had been there physically, if not mentally. A lot of women and men on cranky horses; plenty of dust, no shade, lots of flies. Not Tom's idea of entertainment. "I remember."

Sandy shook her head. "He and Chet have been rivals for years, but it's always been professional. Shoot, they'd drink beer to- gether and swap horror stories about their clients. No, I can't see Bud doing anything to hurt him."

"Any horror stories come to mind?"

Sandy shrugged. "The usual. This owner doesn't know one end of a horse from another. That one can't ride to save her soul. Typical. Chet did turn in a client once to the American Quarter Horse Association because he used steroids on his halter horses."

Tom looked up from his notes.

"Horse class where the points of a horse are judged," she said. "Head size, general conformation, its stance. That kind of thing."

"Anything there, do you think?"

"It was years ago." She smiled sadly. "For all his faults, Chet did retain a thread of integrity."

Tom showed her the little red book.

Sandy thumbed through it. "I know a lot of these people," she said. "Most of them are friends or clients."

"Your name is in there."

"We're friends." She reprised the smile, then the corners of her mouth began to tremble. "Were," she added, lowered her head, and brought her left hand up to her face.

Tom saw that she was crying.

Her right hand was stretched languidly across the table, palm up, the little red book held loosely between the tips of her index and middle fingers. The book slid to the table. "I don't believe this," she said, throaty emotion in her voice.

Tom took her hand and patted it. "It's okay. You've been through a meat grinder."

Sandy, shielding her eyes, looked around for her purse, then realized she didn't have it with her.

"Here," Tom said, offering her a napkin.

"Thanks." She dabbed beneath her eyes. Her eyes were normally bright hazel in color, sometimes aquamarine, sometimes sea foam green, depending on her mood, lighting, and the colors of her clothes, always with flecks of coral and driftwood in them. Right now they had the gray watery look of a desert grotto, a sad melody drifting over their quiet surfaces. She was hurting. "I keep seeing it over and over."

Tom stared at her a moment, not sure what she meant. Then he knew she was no longer talking about the death of Chet Gundry but about the shooting. "It will pass in time," he said.

"And you? Did you keep seeing the crazy who shot you?"

"No, but the circumstances were different. Mine was more like combat." Tom had taken two 9-mm slugs in his chest and one in his thigh while saving a woman and two kids in a drug bust gone bad. "There was less intimacy. I had quite a lot of support afterwards, too."

"Your wife?" There was a fluttery edge in her voice.

"Yes." Tom thought about Carolyn. They were newlyweds at the time and, yes, she had been supportive, despite her later failings. "That's right," he said. "And I had my partner. I was fortunate."

Sandy did not respond. Her eyes flickered in a mist. She seemed lost in a fog of emotions, groping for handholds.

Tom patted her hand. "You've got me."

Sandy's expression came alive as she studied Tom's face, her eyes again probing, searching for light, for truth perhaps. A safe haven. "I must look a sight," she said, once again dabbing beneath her eyes.

"You're beautiful."

She gave Tom an ironic smirk. "And you're not a very good liar." She looked out of the window, took a deep cleansing breath, and blew it out hard, as though blowing away all the dark clouds. Looking back at Tom, her face cleared with a smile that was as convincing as a bright yellow "happy face." "Are you going to go through Chet's trailer again?"

"Would you like to come?"

She shook her head. "You finish your sandwich while I go repair my face," she said, her voice sounding a bit more confident. "I'll be back in a few minutes."

"Okay."

Sandy slid out of the booth. Tom watched her walk across the clubhouse, admiring her until she disappeared behind the counter into a hallway, where he guessed the rest rooms were located. He checked the time on his wristwatch. It read 12:05.

He picked up the little red book, thumbed through it, and found Sandy's name, a little star next to it. He put the book back into his blazer pocket, took another bite of sandwich, immediately regretted it and set it back down on his plate. He took a sip of tea and stared out the window. They had capped off the evening in a little bistro overlooking Avalon harbor, holding hands, stealing kisses, talking about everything under the sun: the death of Sandy's brother Paul; Tom's failed marriage to Carolyn; Sandy's faith, Tom's doubts—talk that had moved them to a more intimate level. A level of growing trust.

Of hope.

"There, all better," she said.

Breaking from his thoughts, Tom looked up and saw Sandy standing beside their table, beaming radiantly. She had definitely repaired something. "That was fast."

She smiled. "We should probably get going," she said, reaching for her hat. "I've decided to pack it up and head home."

"Home?"

"I need to think through this. Get some perspective."

"Okay." Tom stood, dropped a couple bills on the table. "You gonna be all right?"

"I'll be fine." She put on her hat. "You didn't eat your sand-wich."

"Let the cook eat it." He took her arm and led her out of the clubhouse and stood in the cool shadows of the arcade. "We still on for tomorrow night?"

"We better be."

"I'll pick you up at six, then." They kissed. "Sandy?"

"I'll be okay, Tom." She gave him a peck on the corner of his mouth. "Really."

Tom watched her walk away beneath the shade of towering cottonwoods, walking erect in her boots with the chaps accenting her length of stride and womanly shape, until she disappeared around a corner of the building. Even then he could still see her in his mind. He thought about her for a moment, thinking of what she meant to him now and what was happening inside him; his once-dead affections coming alive after the divorce, and the death of his baby boy. He did not think he could grow a new heart so soon after his former heart had been so unexpectedly and brutally torn from his chest.

He brought his hand up, absently, and scratched his chest, as though scratching the itch from a wound, still seeing Sandy in his mind as he looked over at the row of trailers parked in front of the clubhouse. He started toward Chet Gundry's.

•

The single, monotonous note of the air conditioner masked the outside world. It was a calming, almost peaceful sound that provided an odd counterpoint to the tossed magazines, broken lamp and spilled items that evidenced a brawl of some kind.

Tom glanced around at the mess and speculated a likely scenario: Gundry had made a mistake in his insulin dosage and, some time later, succumbed to a grand mal seizure and trashed the place. Nothing unusual about that. People die. It was the man's time. *C'est la vie.* What was unusual was the fact that the owner of the trailer, the victim of the seizure, had once been Sandy's trainer, and who knows what else he had been?

Tom had never considered himself a jealous man until one day, less than a year ago, his wife, Carolyn, someone whom he deeply loved and trusted, left him for another man. It had blindsided Tom, opened in him a dark fissure that cut him in half, cut deep down into the bedrock of his soul where the ideals of virtue and love formed the basis for his worldview. Out of the fissure came the green thing, Jealousy, like a wraith rising through the mists of suspicion and doubt, bringing with him its twin brother, Hate. Women were not to be trusted. Maybe they could be trusted in the world of Ozzie and Harriet, but not in today's world, where words like *faithfulness* and *commitment* and *for better or for worse* seemed to have fallen from the American lexicon.

Then he met Sandy. Beautiful Sandy. A woman who was morally upright, a woman of integrity, good, decent, honest; a woman who went to church every Sunday. A woman who had renewed a sense of trust in him. Day by day the fissure began to close, the twins sent packing. Light filling his soul. But standing in the dead man's trailer, he once again felt the green thing moving deep inside him. He hated it.

He suppressed it.

He was a detective, secure behind a gold shield.

The smell of whiskey drew Tom's gaze to the bottle of Jack

Daniels sitting on the dining table. He looked at the small bottle of insulin beside it, started to look away, then looked back at the insulin and frowned. Something was different. He recalled the insulin bottle sitting about six inches to the left of the Jack Daniels. Now it seemed closer. Either his mind was playing tricks on him, or someone had moved the bottle since he was last in the trailer.

Tom stepped over to the table. A thin film of dust covered its surface; no doubt blown in from when the door had earlier been left open. He leaned forward to catch a better view of the light over the surface, and saw what he was looking for. About six inches to the left of the whiskey bottle, barely visible, was a small, dust-free circle the same diameter as that of the insulin bottle. His mind had not been playing tricks; someone had moved it. Someone had moved it since he and Sandy had gone into the clubhouse, thirty-five minutes ago.

Then as he straightened upright a gleam of something caught the tail of his eye—a small cylindrical object protruding from behind the left forward foot of the sofa. Tom bent down to get a better look, removed a ballpoint pen from his inside breast pocket, and nudged the object with it. It was a hypodermic syringe. He had missed it in his earlier sweep. Tom stood frowning. There were two possibilities for that: either he was getting sloppy or the syringe had not been there before. He looked back at the insulin bottle on the dining table, his brows pinched in thought. If someone had gone to the trouble of moving it recently, perhaps they had also put the syringe where it now lay. Why?

Tom clicked off a shot of the syringe with his camera, then put on a pair of latex gloves, picked it up near the bottom of the tube and held it to the light. It was empty. Sandy said she saw Gundry fill the syringe with insulin; if so, it appeared as though he injected himself with it, then dropped the syringe as he went into shock. Tom thought about that. Why would he go into insulin shock? Assuming it was insulin shock. Assuming Sandy was telling the truth. Of course she was telling the truth. He had no reason to disbelieve her. No rational reason.

Dan Bolt appeared at the door, stood framed in a rectangle of glaring light, his face flushed; his forehead beaded with sweat. He was holding a half-eaten hotdog in his hand. "Figured you'd be in here," he said stepping up into the trailer. "Brother, is it hot! You'll never guess who I just saw."

"A woman wearing an American flag outfit?"

Dan shook his head. "Bill Everwood. You remember—Steeler's quarterback. He's a horse lover, apparently. Saw him talking to that guy used to play on *Dallas*—what's his name. . . ."

Tom could've cared less. "In all your hobnobbing with the stars, you didn't happen to see Kate Bledsoe, did you?"

Dan polished off the last of the dog, crumpled the wrapper. "Nope," he said, tonguing the food into his cheek so he could speak. "Not a sign. I asked around, but she took off, apparently."

Tom looked once more at the bottle of Jack Daniels, eyed the insulin bottle beside it. He looked out the door and could just see the entrance of the clubhouse, set back in the cool arches of the porch, about fifty yards away from Gundry's trailer. A dark thought wormed its way into his mind.

"What is it, Tommy?"

"Nothing."

"Don't tell me nothing. I can hear you thinking. You're coming in loud and clear."

Tom did not respond. He could still see her walking away from him, her gait a long-strided loveliness that reminded him of a morning mist gliding soundlessly over a deep water calm.

"You're thinking we should maybe get a team over there, right?"

"What's that?" Tom said distractedly. "No. We need to move this rig over to the impound lot. The FETs can take it from there. I want the place dusted, the residue inside this syringe checked," he said, handing it to Dan. "The insulin bottle too."

"You think there's something fishy going on?"

Tom said nothing.

Chapter Four

Sandy drove her F-250 diesel and horse trailer down Sand Canyon, a narrow tree-shaded road at the northernmost edge of Santa Clarita. She turned left at her street and wound up a moderately winding, oak-lined grade past several upscale custom homes; some ranchettes on two- to five-acre parcels, others larger, until she came to her own house; a three-bedroom contemporary single-story with pale yellow siding, white trim, and forest green shutters. With its concrete-tiled roof steeply pitched and accented with dormers, the house sat well on the property, commanding killer views of the San Gabriel Mountains to the south and north, and distant views of Santa Clarita sprawling to the west.

Slowing past her cement driveway, Sandy turned right onto a gravel drive at the far end of her property that wound through massive heritage oaks dotting the sun-dried gold of the hillside to the east. Their dark burly limbs reached over the drive, branches touching, the house showing through to the right, cool in afternoon shadow. Then the trees opened and she drove past the sand-filled arena on the right lined with mature California peppers, and then up the slightly elevated rise of the barn, nestled amid stately cottonwoods and a variety of ash and flowering pear at the rear of her ten-acre estate.

The barn was an eight-stall, raised center-aisle metal prefab, with tack room and washing area, the breezeway and wash area made of rough-finished concrete. Sandy drove her rig through the open breezeway and stopped when the rear of the trailer had cleared the far bay doors. She lowered the ramp, opened the top left door of the three-horse slant trailer, then clucking her tongue, said, "Come on, boy. Here we go."

Buster backed off the ramp nervously, his feet blindly stamping the slanted floorboards for footing. Once finding solid ground he blew a snort of contempt and settled down. Leading him to his stall, Sandy noticed that his front left shoe had come loose.

She frowned. "How'd you do that, boy?"

She gave Buster carrots and some hay and stood in his stall brushing his neck, trying not to think about Chet. She swept out the trailer, closed and secured the ramp and outer door, got into her truck, drove into an open-walled metal-roofed shed behind the barn where she unhooked the trailer, set the socket hitch on a block of wood and kicked the wheel blocks into place.

Retrieving her show chaps, she left the truck parked where it was and walked down the gentle slope to her house, fifty yards away. She kept her eyes downcast, not seeing the stands of hardwood and flower grottoes planted for beauty and color, nor seeing the orchard that she so loved to walk through at night as she prayed; not seeing or thinking of anything but Chet now, and of how her unspoken anger toward him earlier in the day was no longer relevant.

Stepping into her house was like entering a fortress of quiet and peace. She took off her boots and set them on a mat by the French doors. The house was cool. The grandfather clock clicked a welcoming salute. She was safe, the world locked outside.

She padded across the rust-colored carpet of the living room in her stocking feet, smelling the sweet, floral potpourri that reached her from the foyer, went past the raised formal dining room on the left, until she stepped up onto the hardwood floor of the kitchen and entry. These areas formed one great room, perfect for entertaining, with coffered ceilings in the kitchen and dining rooms, and in the sunken living room cathedral ceilings that seemed impossibly high and grand for a single story. She and her father had designed it together, and it was as a home should be—beautiful, solid, and full of light, a personal statement. A place of refuge.

Sandy poured herself a glass of white Zinfandel and took a sip, felt its cleansing fruitiness cooling down to her toes, then taking a larger sip, stepped back down into the living room, sat in the upholstered love seat beside the stone fireplace and put her feet up on the distressed-wood coffee table. She loved the look and feel of distressed wood, decorated her home with several pieces. She also liked the more traditional pieces, blended these into an overall southwestern look that all worked together somehow. But she wasn't thinking of her decorating acumen at the moment. She was thinking about Chet.

She turned her head at the sound of a tinkling bell. A smile tugged at the corners of her mouth as she watched Sylvie batting a rubber ball in the hallway, the ball rolling and tinkling from the direction of the three back bedrooms.

Tom had given Sandy the black-and-white kitty to comfort her during her convalescence, as well as to replace the loss of Rhubarb. Although she was grateful for Sylvie, grateful to share her home with another living creature, she found that she had not grown as attached to the kitty as she thought she might. She reminded her too much of Rhubarb, not of Rhubarb herself but of the brutal wickedness that had taken her cat's life. Sylvie was a constant reminder of the shooting—of the killer.

Sandy took another sip of wine. As she set the glass down on the side table she noticed her hand trembling. In her mind she imagined Chet staggering toward her, his eyes wild, his face contorted; one hand clutching his chest, the other reaching toward her, pointing at her it seemed with an accusing finger.

She shook the image from her mind, looked up at the ceiling as if to pray. Praying would help. She focused her mind on God, on His kindness, words rising into her throat only to die as they reached her lips. Those which escaped seemed to ascend as far as the ceiling, then bounced back onto her, lamely, dead, as though God had turned a deaf ear.

She sat for the longest time staring at nothing, listening to the ticking of the grandfather clock, the incessant tap of the sculptor's chisel cutting away little increments of time. Finally she reached for her journal and pen on the side table, dated her entry in the upper-right corner of a clean page. She glanced up at the Crow war shield over the fireplace, thought for a moment, then wrote:

Dear Paul,

I must talk to someone. I tried praying but the ceiling was like brass. It's as though God stepped out of the room. I feel as though He has abandoned me to stumble through an insufferable isolation. How I wish you were here, Paul. Even though I was your kid sister I could always talk to you. You would always listen.

Sandy released a deep, aching sigh, then wrote: "I thought that time would heal the pain of your loss, but it hasn't. Sometimes . . ."

She paused, lowered pen to paper, but found she could not write further because of her trembling fingers. She closed the journal over the pen and set it back down on the table. She stared across the room at a Bev Doolittle print, unaware of the tears leaking down her cheeks.

The ringing of the telephone startled her. It rang four times before her answering machine picked up—Sandy's recorded voice asking the caller to leave a name and short message at the tone. *Beep.*

"Hi, Sandy, it's Tom. Are you there? I'll wait a second for you to pick up if you are."

Sandy did not pick up. She sat listening, waiting; for what, she had no idea. A part of her wanted to leap up and answer the phone, beg Tom to not wait until tomorrow but to come over now. Hold her in his arms. Another part of her seemed paralyzed, as though sinister forces had knit her limbs and torso to the sofa cushions with invisible steel threads; malevolent Lilliputian forces working to keep her isolated from the world.

"I guess you're not home yet," Tom said. "Anyway, just thought I'd call to see how you're doing. You seemed pretty shook up earlier. I was thinking I could come over tonight after my shift. Let me know, okay? Take care." His tone seemed reticent, his words carefully chosen, as though freighted with hidden meaning.

The brash sound of the line disconnecting sent a jolt through Sandy's body, followed by a shiver over her limbs. She felt an isolation closing around her, as though the walls were pushing inward, the ceiling lowering, the floor rising to meet it. Sandy brought a hand up to her face, wiped tears away with the heel of her palm. "What's wrong with me? Dear God, what's wrong with me?"

Sylvie leaped up onto her lap, again startling her. Sandy felt a jangle of emotions, her nerves raw and fragile like live wires protruding through frayed insulation, sparking against each other.

She shooed the kitten onto the floor, gulped down a mouthful of wine and stood, glass in hand, and padded down the hall into her bedroom.

Sylvie ran into the room after her, leaped up onto the large trunk at the foot of her bed, jumped off and raced in circles around the room, darted up into the sitting room and disappeared behind the love seat facing a gray stone fireplace.

Sandy allowed a smile, then stepped into the arched alcove separating bedroom and master bath. There was a mirrored vanity on the left, a walk-in closet opposite, the closet hidden by a mirrored slider. Sandy opened the slider, stepped inside and undressed. A bath would help. As she came out of the closet she saw herself naked in the vanity mirror. With the slider behind her, her image was multiplied back into infinity.

Her hand rose automatically to the scar over her right breast, a look of astonishment filling her eyes as she beheld the wicked purplish lump made by the bullet, the stitch marks still visible. It had the appearance of a spider. Her fingers gingerly touched its jagged edges as though to coax the thing off her breast. It didn't move. Then she saw the scar made by the knife in her left shoulder, a vertical ridge about an inch in length, stitch marks on either side. She saw the bullet scar in her right thigh and, once again, she saw the gun—the green slits behind it, a guttural chortle rattling in the killer's throat as the bloody finger closed on the trigger.

Bang!

Sandy wheeled as she felt the phantom impact of the bullet, the sledgehammer blow knocking the wind out of her lungs. She staggered backward, her pulse suddenly racing. Her eyes widened in terror. She looked at her image, saw a thousand pairs of green eyes leering at her, and gulped back a shriek.

Running back into the bedroom, she jerked open the top drawer of the nightstand, nearly knocking over Tom's picture sitting on top, and grabbed the .357 magnum Smith and Wesson she kept there. She snapped open the cylinder and made sure it was loaded. Of course it was loaded. She checked it each night before retiring to bed. Checking the gun had become a ritual. A compulsion.

She spun the cylinder, clicked it shut, turned the gun over in her hands, smoothing her fingers over the cold nickel plating to feel its solid heft, to feel a steeling resolve moving through her arms. A feeling of power, of control. She clasped the wooden grips with both hands and stepped warily toward the trunk at the end of her bed.

The trunk was the thing.

She stored extra blankets in the trunk, but it was large enough for a small person to hide inside; which is exactly what the killer had done that day, waiting there in the trunk, crouched, watching her like some voyeuristic ghoul.

Fear mounting in her throat, vibrating through her teeth, Sandy sighted over the gun barrel at the trunk as though she expected the killer, like some Jack-in-the-box to pop up any moment, a crazy look in its eyes. She reached out a hand and took hold of the trunk lid, touching it warily as though the trunk contained a nest of coiled rattlesnakes, then threw it open and stood back pointing the gun at . . .

Blankets.

Her breath caught in her throat. Quickly she tore the blankets out of the trunk, one at a time, and tossed them carelessly to the floor until she got to the bottom. The trunk was empty. No rattlesnakes. No ghouls.

She looked under the bed, stepped up into the sitting room and made sure the window latches were secured. She checked the dead bolts on the French doors, looked out at the patio through the wooden blinds. Reason dictated that it was a fool's exercise, a chasing after the wind, but once a compulsion gripped her Sandy felt powerless to stop its momentum. Reason disintegrated. A tempest of fear and anger blew her from room to room.

She was crying.

Tears streaming down her cheeks, her eyes blurred with tears, she stalked through the two spare bedrooms down the hall, making sure the windows and doors in each room were locked or bolted shut, searching under beds and in closets, checking the adjoining bathroom, checking behind the door, and in the shower stall. She checked the kitchen pantry, looked in the cabinets under the sink, beneath the granite counter, anyplace large enough for an intruder to hide.

Sandy checked places impossible as well—stooping to look under sofas, under chairs. She found nothing. Still, it did little to abate the tempest raging through her.

She stepped down into her living room, stood in the middle of the room, sunlight streaming in through windows and doors, uncovering her, revealing her. She felt as though she were in a dream, a dream in which she stood naked in a city square in which a million pairs of eyes leered at her from behind walls of mirrored windows. Feeling shame, unable to flee as terror spread over her body.

Sandy raised her revolver, biting her lower lip as she turned in a quick circle, then a slower one, her arms outstretched in a white-knuckled, double-fisted point, expecting someone—some *thing*—to pop up from behind a chair, or slide out from behind the drapes, or swing down from the ceiling—a target—like a silhouette on a combat course.

A crazy with a gun.

There were no targets. There was only Sylvie sleeping in a shuttered square of sun on the floor, her motor running.

Sandy stood glaring at the kitty, her chest heaving, her lips drawn back over her teeth, the corners of her mouth twisted outward into an appalling grin—her attempt at a smile. *Sylvie. Beautiful Sylvie.* A feral sound bubbled in the back of Sandy's throat—a laugh, a sob.

An airy giggle fluttered through her teeth like a release of butterflies. She gave her head a little shake. Immediately she felt something give way in her chest, a movement like a glacier shelf giving way, a sliding, cold, dead numbness moving over the warmth of her body. She swiped a palm over her wet cheeks, stood looking over the cool, quiet, isolation of her living room.

She lowered the gun to her side, felt the cold metal barrel against her bare thigh. Lifting her other hand, she gripped the upper arm of her gun hand, and stood looking down at the floor. After a while she sat down on the armrest of her sofa. She stared at the gun. Feeling a surge of helplessness mounting in her chest, of anger, of a host of indefinable emotions, she lifted the gun, opened the cylinder, spun it and clicked it shut. Again she smoothed her palms over the nickel plating, gripping it. Feeling it. Feeling nothing. She opened the cylinder a second time, spun the wheel, clicked it shut, hefting its weight—opened the cylinder, clicked it shut. Opened, clicked shut. Emotion bled out of her like an opened vein until she felt completely empty inside. Clicked shut. Staring at nothing, holding the loaded gun in her hands.

The tempest spent.

Chapter Five

"That's Chet. That's my boy," the woman said, looking at the Polaroid taken at the scene. "Where is he now—down't the morgue, you say?"

"That's right," Tom said.

"When can I see him?"

"Right away, if you'd like."

They were standing in the open lobby of the station, a shiny new building shared by the fire department, located on the corner of Third and Orange Grove. Dan was off getting something for the woman to drink.

Gundry's mother looked to be in her late sixties. She was a sharp-featured, sharp-boned rail of a woman, with short wiry hair the color of turpentine, fierce gray eyes, skin as tough looking as rawhide, and a thin, tight, no-nonsense mouth that turned down at the corners like Katharine Hepburn's. She was wearing a loose-fitting cotton print shirt over faded blue jeans, snakeskin cowboy boots with pointy toes and silver caps, and looked as if she could whip half a dozen detectives in a bare-knuckle brawl. Her face was expressionless, no indication of emotion or tears.

It was difficult to tell which way it would go when telling a parent or a spouse of the death of a loved one. Sometimes there would be plenty of waterworks, at other times nothing. Flatliners. Sex was not a determining factor. Often it was the man who would break down.

"We're real sorry about this," Tom said, feeling a sense of emotional detachment from his words. It wasn't that he was cold-hearted, or oblivious to the sufferings of others. He meant what he said; he just felt nothing when he'd said it. Tom was a flatliner. It was a behavioral trait he'd learned at an early age. Raised by an alcoholic mother and a string of garrulous stepfathers, young Tom had learned to detach himself and float, mentally speaking, outside of his body while undergoing emotional and sometimes physical abuse. He would not let pain touch him, touch his core. That part of him had learned to escape it, deflect it, or to insulate himself from it.

Mrs. Gundry shook her head at the photo. "It's hard to believe. Chet gone. Thirty-six."

"Is there anyone we can call for you?"

"No, it's just me now."

She handed the photo back to Tom. "You think insulin shock?"

"That's what the coroner speculated at the scene." Tom slipped the photo into his blazer pocket. "We won't know for sure until we get the autopsy report. Let's not talk here."

Tom led Mrs. Gundry down the hall into an interview room, pulled out a straight-backed padded chair for her. "Thank you," she said, adjusting herself in it.

Tom took the chair opposite her, took out his notebook and pen, and set them down on the faux wood table. "You don't mind answering a few questions for us? We'd like a little background."

"Not at all." Mrs. Gundry glanced around the room that was bare except for a couple of black file cabinets that stood in the far-right corner, and a blackboard that took up most of the left wall. There were words on the blackboard that had been erased. Incandescent lights glared down at them from the ceiling. There were no windows. "Doesn't feel like a police station," she said. "Feels more like an insurance building."

Tom's sentiments exactly. The old station on Alameda and San Fernando fit like an old shoe: cigarette burns on tables, coffee stains on the lobby furniture, the ghosts of good busts past haunting the halls. He smiled. "We'll break it in. Your son was thirty-six?"

"This past April."

Mrs. Gundry settled in her chair, patted her hands on top of the table as she looked across the table at Tom, and then folded them. Her hands were arthritic, sharp-knuckled and disfigured, the index and middle fingers of her right hand stained from nicotine. "Insulin shock, huh?"

Tom nodded.

"I find that hard to believe," Mrs. Gundry said, once again adjusting her seat. She appeared uncomfortable. "Not Chet. Heart attack maybe—him and his father had bum tickers."

"Oh?" Gundry's medical file made no mention of his father's heart condition.

"Didn't die from it, though, if that's what you're thinkin'. Got run over by a train. Metrolink. You mighta seen it in the news a few years back. Fell asleep on the tracks in his pickup—drunker'n Who's-on-first. Didn't know what hit him, I expect." Her gray eyes blazed, the right corner of her mouth jerked upward in a wicked smile. "Waste of a good Chevy."

Tom smiled. He figured she might be doing her best to deflect pain. Humor was a good deflector. He figured that's why the Irish held wakes. Laugh it up at the old boy's sendoff; drown it with booze, save your tears for the wee hours of the night when the leprechauns came with their sad songs.

Dan walked into the room with a can of Sprite, and some other goodies, set the Sprite on the table in front of Mrs. Gundry. She frowned at it like he'd just put dog doo in front of her. "Ain't you got anything stronger?"

"We got Coke. You want a Coke?"

She waved him off, popped the lid and took a swallow, made a face and set it back down on the table. "You boys said you had some questions?"

It fell to Tom. "We'd like to get a little background about your son, "if you're feeling up to it."

"I'm fine." She crossed her legs, man style. "What can I tell you? Chet's a good man. *Was,* I mean." She chuckled. "He was the best horse trainer in the business. Best there ever was."

Tom compressed his lips together into a grim smile.

Dan, sitting at the head of the table, nodded in agreement as he peeled a banana. "That's what we hear."

"It's no lie." Mrs. Gundry pulled a pack of cigarettes out of her breast pocket, tapped one out and grabbed it with her thin lips. She leaned on her hip, hooked out a Bic lighter from her jeans pocket with a clawed forefinger and started to light it. Her hands trembled. She looked around for an ashtray, saw none and gave Tom the eye. "You allowed to smoke in here? Don't matter." She slapped the cigarette and lighter onto the table with a grunt. "I'm tryin' to quit anyway." She took another sip of Sprite, grimaced, set it down and pushed it away. "Let me see that photo again."

Tom slid the Polaroid across the table.

The hard lines of her face softened as she looked at it. The faintest color blue edged into her gray irises. "He was a good-looking boy, don't you think? I always thought so."

Tom watched her closely.

She chuckled humorlessly, buttoned it with a grunt.

"What is it, Mrs. Gundry?"

"Myrtle. Call me Myrtle."

"All right, Myrtle. Did you have a thought about something?"

Myrtle Gundry shook her head, a look of incredulity squinting in her eyes. "It's hard to believe he died from insulin shock."

"Why do you say that?"

"Chet was very strict about his insulin regimen. He monitored his glucose levels constantly."

"Maybe he gave himself the wrong dose?" Tom suggested.

She blew a noise through her lips. "No."

"Maybe he got a bad batch of insulin?"

She tossed the photo down on the table without looking at it. "Chet's been at this since he was a boy. He knew the drill, inside and out. To my knowledge he's only had one close call."

"Oh?"

"Baseball game," she said. "The game went into extra innings, apparently—threw his timing off. Had a grand mal seizure, three rows back from third base. Fortunately, the woman with him knew a little about diabetics. She poured a can of Coke down his throat—managed to bump his glucose levels up. Saved his life."

"Lucky for him."

"I thought so. Sandy's her name in case you're interested. Sandy Cameron."

Tom looked across the table at her.

"They were dating," she clarified. Her eyes widened. "Hell's bells—Sandy. I expect I'll have to let her know about this. They were quite serious."

Tom ignored Dan's eyes boring into his temple. "Can you think of any other reason that might account for your son's death?" he asked. "You said yourself you don't believe it was insulin related."

Myrtle Gundry seemed to study him a moment. She rolled the unlit cigarette back and forth over the table with a crooked index finger. "You think there might be some hinkus going on?"

"We won't know anything until we hear back from the medical examiner," Dan said, noshing on a Baby Ruth. "We have to ask these questions whenever there are unusual circumstances connected with a death. Strictly routine."

"Chet was well liked," Myrtle said, the hard lines back in her face. "I can't think of anyone who'd want to hurt him."

"No enemies?"

"Not that I know of."

"Nothing troubling him lately?" Tom asked.

She looked at him, blinked a couple times, and then stared at a blank wall. She shook her head. "Nothing concrete."

"Anything that comes to mind may be helpful."

She picked up the Polaroid, glanced at it briefly, then fanned it a couple of times. "Last night," she said, dropping the photo onto the table, "Chet came over to my house. Out of the blue. Just came over."

"That's in Sunland?" Dan asked, reading his notes.

"That's right. I just figured he wanted to get away from all the hubbub at the equestrian center, so I fixed him supper. He never spoke two words. He was bothered by something. After supper he went out to the barn. He'd do that as a boy. If something was eating at him, he'd head to the barn and work it out his own way. His 'cave mood,' I called it."

Tom was familiar with cave moods, only he called them his boat moods. Whenever he needed to work something out of his system, he'd take his forty-two footer out on the water and, as the song goes, let the canvas do miracles. "Any ideas what was troubling him?"

Myrtle Gundry shook her head. "No, and I didn't ask him, either. Chet was not one to open up. But I could tell. A mother can tell—" The words caught in her throat. She looked quickly down at her hands, rubbed the trembling out of them, glanced up at the detectives, smiled embarrassedly, and then looked back down at her hands.

Tom and Dan gave her a moment.

Myrtle rolled the cigarette some more. "About an hour later he left," she said, talking through gravelly emotion. "Said he had a meeting at the center he had to attend. It was the last time I saw him." She smiled at her hands.

"Any ideas who he was going to meet?"

"Nope. I just figured it had to do with a horse," she said. She laughed, picked up the cigarette, tapped the tip against the table, lit it, and blew a cloud of smoke at the ceiling. "That's all he ever cared about, horses. Cared more about horses than he did people. Horses he could trust."

Tom glanced at Dan, who had made the same inference Tom had made apparently. He looked back at Gundry's mother. "Any people he didn't trust come to mind?"

Mrs. Gundry's eyes flickered in the harsh overhead light. "Nope. Chet was in a competitive business. I suppose there were people."

"To your knowledge was Chet involved in any kind of deals? Business? Horse? Something that may have upset anyone."

She pursed her lips. "Only deal I can think of was some clothing line that wanted him to endorse their product." She thought for a moment. "Sorrel Something-or-other."

Tom glanced back through his notes. "Sorrel West Outfitters?"

"That's it. A big deal, I hear. Chet seemed to think so."

"Do you know a Bud Nichols?"

She took a drag of her cigarette, squinting sharply at Tom through a curl of blue smoke. "Why?"

"Your son beat him out of the Sorrel West deal. Maybe he got his feathers ruffled a little."

Mrs. Gundry tapped the ash against the Sprite can, blowing smoke at the table, the smoke flattening over the surface. "What're you saying?"

"I'm not saying anything, Myrtle," Tom said, waving smoke from his face. "Just spitballing some ideas."

"Bud Nichols is a good trainer," she said. "Him and Chet were friends. Don't get me wrong, Bud ain't no choirboy; neither was Chet, but you're dancin' with no music if you think Bud would hurt him."

"What can you tell us about Kate Bledsoe?" Tom asked, changing tacks. "I understand they were seeing each other."

Mrs. Gundry made a rasping noise in her throat. "I don't know what he ever saw in that woman. She's nothin' but a tramp with a short fuse."

"Why do you say that?"

"Fly off the handle at nothing. Maybe she caught Chet looking at another woman."

"Was there another woman?"

Mrs. Gundry smiled, an impish wink crinkling the corners of her eyes. "Chet was a rake. Just like his daddy. Didn't want to waste his good looks on one woman." She tapped her cigarette against the Sprite can opening, looking beyond it at a spot on the table. "I do wish he'd stuck it out with Sandy. She's the one I told you about. Sandy Cameron," she repeated for the benefit of Tom's note taking. "Ain't you gonna write that name down?"

"I know about her," Tom said, once again feeling Dan's eyes on him.

"She was prettier'n a mare in foal. Smart too. Friendly." She shook her head at a thought. "You'd never know she was a cop."

Tom ignored the comment. "Was Kate a drinker?"

Mrs. Gundry gave him a level stare. "Kate Bledsoe could drink a fish under the table."

"That may account for the bottle of Jack D in the trailer," Dan said, tearing the wrapper off a Milky Way.

Mrs. Gundry looked sharply at Dan as he was about to take a bite. "You just ate one of those."

The Milky Way froze. Dan blinked. "I got low blood sugar."

"You should eat fruit. Fruit's a good sugar." She eyed Dan's ample stomach, his shirt buttons straining against their holes. "Fruit won't make you fat," she said, took a long pull of her cigarette, blew out a lung full of smoke, then dropped the butt into the Sprite can with a sizzle. "I'd like to see Chet now."

Chapter Six

Sandy's residence. Thursday morning

The sound of a garbage truck clanking heavily up the street woke Sandy from yet another fitful night's sleep. Her bedcovers were soaked with perspiration. Same as the night before. And the one before that. She was glad for the morning light streaming in through the French doors and windows. The clock on the nightstand read 6:25. She glanced sleepily at the picture of Tom, Tom smiling at her. Such blue eyes, sunset eyes that, though outwardly cool, seemed to glow with inner heat. She regretted not calling him back last night. She needed him.

She swung her legs out of bed, waited a moment for her blood to circulate, then padded down the hall into her kitchen and started a pot of coffee. A cup of coffee would help. She looked out her kitchen window as the truck pulled up to her rubber refuse container and, accompanied by pneumatic whirring and whining sounds, hooked its huge metal tines into the side slots and lifted it up and back, emptying its contents with a loud metallic clatter.

Sandy frowned. It was a blue truck, different from the usual garish orange one that had picked up her garbage for several years now. There was a different logo on the truck as well—a lightning bolt with the name Jiffy Trash over it. She thought that maybe the old company had been bought out by this new one; the latest salvo in a trash war that seemed never-ending. She didn't care about that—who cares about trash?—as long as it didn't affect service or price.

As the garbage truck pulled away, she saw Ozzie's white pickup and trailer turning into her gravel road then drive up through the trees toward her barn. She frowned at the kitchen clock—6:30. No one ever accused Oswald Ramsey of keeping banking hours.

Sandy went back into her bedroom, shrugged on a pair of blue jeans, threw on a blue-and-white striped T-shirt, and a pair of white cotton socks. She went back out into the kitchen, poured a second cup of coffee for herself, poured one for Ozzie, and went outside onto her patio. She stepped into her mucking boots that she kept by her back door, and headed up to the barn, holding the cups steaming in her hands.

The sky was a clear blue with the sun low behind the trees. The air, though presently cool and sweet, smelling of wet grass and foliage, held in it the threat of another hot one. A flock of rosy-headed birds picked at the ground, lifted as a sheet as Sandy approached, scattering and alighting farther ahead to continue pecking the ground. They lifted once more and disappeared into the oaks as Sandy caught up to them.

Ozzie was opening the back of his trailer that was backed up to the barn entrance. He looked over as Sandy approached and waved. "Hey, girl!"

"Up with the birds, I see," Sandy said, smiling.

Ozzie flashed a big grin, slapped his dull blue ball cap back on his shaved head. "Gotta get a jump on the day." He reached into the trailer and removed a leather tool belt that resembled the kind carpenters wear.

Ozzie was a black man in his late thirties, his skin the color of well-oiled saddle leather, his bare arms smooth and muscled. Built like a middle linebacker—broad shoulders, narrow hips, good running legs—he was wearing a yellow T-shirt, leather farrier chaps over blue jeans and ropers. He had followed the rodeo circuit for years, rode saddle broncs mostly but did some calf roping and bull-dogging as well, but gave it up six months ago when his wife, Melanie, was crushed by a horse, leaving her a paraplegic.

"Brought you some coffee," Sandy said, lifting a cup.

Ozzie finished buckling on the tool belt, and extended a big callused hand. "You're an angel."

"Didn't know how you took it, so I left it black."

"Black's fine with me. Always has been." He winked at her, took a sip. "Oh yeah." He set the cup down on a bale of hay, then began removing tools from the trailer.

Sandy watched him. Ozzie was her friend, had been for many years. Smiles came easily to his strong face, but lately behind the smiles she caught glimpses of sadness, of a simmering rage, malevolent ghosts that hid in the corners of his eyes, or along the edge of a remark. "Thanks for coming on such short notice," she said.

"No problem."

"Need me to hold Buster?"

"We'll just crosstie him—he's a good boy. Not like Bud Nichols's mare—she won't let me touch her hind feet."

"I know what you mean." Mares could be temperamental and fractious, and liable to kick without warning—especially if they were in season. She smiled. Not unlike many of the two-legged variety.

"Shame about that one of his dying. D'you hear about that?"

Sandy nodded.

"Heart attack, I hear." Ozzie shook his head.

Sandy set her coffee down next to Ozzie's, went into the barn and led Buster out of his stall, the horse, curious, swinging his head to look at Ozzie. Sandy attached leads to his halter, one on each side, and fastened the ends to D-rings on opposing walls near the barn entrance.

Ozzie was busy removing an assortment of tools from his trailer, slipping them into belt loops. The trailer was really a small workshop on wheels. Inside were tools hung on the walls—tongs, nippers, rasps, hammers. A workbench went along the left wall. There were drawers under the bench that contained horseshoes and nails. A butane forge, attached to the trailer door, was already swung out and the door anchored into the dirt with a metal rod.

Ozzie lifted an anvil off the floor and set it outside atop a metal stand beside the forge. He took a plastic bucket over to a hose looped on the barn wall, turned on the tap and filled the bucket with water, he turned off the tap, carried the bucket back and set it down beside the forge. Everything set, he stepped over to Buster, put his hands on his waist and, tilting his head to one side, looked down at the horse's front right hoof. "Now what'd you do, big fella? I just gave you a brand-new set of shoes not two weeks ago, and here you go throwing one. Make me look bad."

"He probably stepped on it, the big goof," Sandy said, patting Buster's neck.

Buster blew out a snort.

Ozzie clucked his tongue. "What are we gonna do?" He stepped closer to Buster, leaned his weight against the gelding's right shoulder, forcing the horse to shift his weight to the other foot, then rubbed a hand down the leg and picked up his hoof. Ozzie inspected the shoe. "Nail come loose," he said.

He removed a pair of tongs from his belt, pulled off the shoe and gave it a look-see. "No need for a new one," he said, tossed it into the dirt and slipped the tongs back into his belt. "That's somethin' about Chet, huh?"

Sandy nodded. "I didn't know if you'd heard."

"In this business?" He shook his head. "I can't get over it. Just up and died. What was he—thirty-something?"

"Thirty-six."

Ozzie shook his head. "Thirty-six." With a hoof pick he cleaned around the frog, dusted it with his thick fingers, then rasped the bottom of the hoof flat. He did this all in a few seconds. He set the shoe against it, testing it for fit. "Might need a little reshaping," he said. He stepped over to the forge, lit it and, holding the shoe with the tongs, passed the shoe through the flames, back and forth a few times. He was looking at the shoe, but Sandy could see his mind was elsewhere. He set the shoe on the anvil, tapped it with a hammer; the *tink . . . tink . . . tink*ing of hammer and iron ringing against the morning quiet. "Diabetes, huh?"

"Had a seizure."

Ozzie worked on shaping the shoe. "I had an aunt once died of it."

Sandy listened politely, picking up her cup and taking a sip. Horseshoers were talkers. Talk about anything to pass the time. Like hairdressers.

"She came to live with us before she passed on," he said, tapping one end of the shoe. "We had to give her shots. She kept forgetting, so me and Melanie took over. That was a couple years back. Her heart gave out."

Sandy started to voice her condolences.

"She was eighty-two," Ozzie said, lifting the shoe with his tongs to inspect it. "Fine one day then up and died the next. Just like Chet. Just like Bud's mare. Just goes to show you, we got nothin' but the air in our lungs."

Sandy did not want to discuss Chet's death—or anyone's death for that matter. "How's Melanie doing? Last you told me, she was having another MRI. Any results?"

A shade crossed over Ozzie's face, the ghost of sadness and rage surfacing in his brown eyes as if they had been awaiting a cue. "Doesn't look good."

Sandy groaned inwardly.

Ozzie smiled humorlessly. He plunged the shoe into a bucket of water, the water spitting and hissing, then once the shoe was cooled he stepped over to Buster, picked up his foot, and held it against the hoof.

Sandy watched him work, wishing there was a magic button she could push that would make people well, bring them back to life.

Ozzie stepped back to the anvil and tapped one end of the shoe with the hammer. "Don't guess we'll ever have children," he said, examining the shoe. "Melanie will likely be confined to a wheelchair the rest of her life. Other than that we're in good shape." His grin never reached his eyes.

"I'm real sorry to hear that, Ozzie."

He grunted. "Wasn't your fault." He grabbed a handful of nails from his belt bag, held them between his lips like toothpicks. "Good old Vern," he said around the nails.

Sandy took a sip of coffee. It had happened six months ago. Melanie's horse had gone lame. She suspected navicular, a crippling hoof disease, so she called for Vern Wieder to come out and x-ray the foot. Vern didn't like horses too alert when he worked on them, so he'd sedate them. Melanie was holding him, and when the horse started to walk, she pulled on the lead to steady him. The horse stumbled and fell on her, crushing her pelvis and back. It ended her career as a barrel racer—as a mother, too. Ozzie claimed that Wieder overdrugged the horse. Wieder disagreed.

"What's your lawyer got to say about it?" Sandy asked.

Ozzie spat into the dirt. "Lawyers. Said it'll be real hard to prove malpractice, seein' as how the horse had a game leg to begin with. Ol' Vern claims Melanie shouldn't have pulled on the lead. Can you believe that?"

Sandy could believe anything about Vern Wieder.

"Shoot, kids, ain't nothin' but trouble anyhow," Ozzie said, dropping a nail from his mouth. He picked it up, set the shoe against the hoof, angled the nail in one of the shoe holes and hammered it into place. The nail point protruded through the outer wall of the hoof. Ozzie tapped each of the nails through the holes in the shoe. "Gonna use four on each side," he said, tapping in the last nail. "That should keep him from losing it."

Ozzie took a pair of nippers, pinched off the points, and with a rasp filed off the remainder until the ends were flush with the hoof wall. He smoothed his hand over the hoof as though he were admiring a fine piece of furniture. "That's okay, we'll get by. Got me an agent now. A real Hollywood agent."

Sandy watched the ghosts clear from his eyes, descend back to the dark place in his soul they inhabited. "Hollywood Agent, huh?"

"Sure. They always lookin' for extras—folks know how to rope and ride. Bein' black don't hurt neither. Not that many black cowboys." He grinned. And me bein' so handsome and all. Don't you think I look like Brad Pitt?"

Sandy smiled. "With a suntan maybe."

Ozzie laughed, set the hoof down, ran his hand over Buster's leg and patted his shoulder. "There's a boy, good as new."

Buster tried to nibble on his shirt, but was restrained by the crosstie. "None of that now," Ozzie said, patting Buster's cheek.

"I appreciate this, Ozzie," Sandy said, unhooking one of the ties from his halter. "How much do I owe you?"

Ozzie put his hands on his hips, arched the kinks out of his back. "Let me see now. That'll be one cup of coffee."

Sandy started to object.

He put up his hand, picked up his coffee cup off the bale and sipped. "Paid in full."

"Ozzie—"

He shook his head. "Don't want to hear about it, girl. That's my price." He unbuckled his bags, set them in his trailer.

"Let me give you something."

Ozzie lifted his cap by the bill, scratched his head with the same hand, then slapped the cap back in place. "Tell you what, you hear of anyone needs a black cowboy, expert roper, bronc rider— not to mention real good-looking—you tell 'em about me."

Sandy smiled. "I'll do that."

Ozzie closed up his trailer, frowned suddenly. "Shoot, I was going to shoe Chet's horses today. Don't guess I'll need to do that, will I?" He looked over at the mountains, "Gone, just like that." Shook his head.

"Ozzie, you knew Chet pretty well."

He looked at her. "As well as most, I suppose."

"Did he ever mention anything he might have been involved in—some business deal that may have been a little shady?"

"Shady?" Ozzie grinned. "I thought you were supposed to be giving that detective mind of yours a rest."

"Maybe something he and Vern were involved with."

At the mention of Vern's name Ozzie looked away, a little too quickly, Sandy thought. "Not that I know of," he said. "No, he never mentioned anything to me. Then again, he wouldn't— knowing how I felt about Vern."

Ozzie took a sip of coffee, slung the remainder into the dirt and handed the cup back to Sandy. He checked his wristwatch. "Gotta go," he said. "A couple snooty mares are waitin' for their pedicures."

Sandy smiled.

Ozzie climbed into his truck and started the ignition, the diesel engine pinging as he hooked his elbow out the window. "If you're trying to make heads or tails of this, girl, you'll only frustrate yourself. Chet had diabetes. It was his time." He gave her a supportive smile. "Put whatever you're thinking out of that pretty little head."

Sandy raised her chin in a parting gesture, then watched as Ozzie backed away from the barn into a turnout, stopped then, turning his wheels, drove forward down her gravel drive. He turned left onto her street, and finally disappeared around a bend in the road. She could hear the sound of his diesel a long while after he was gone.

She looked down at the cups in her hands, hefted them, thinking about Ozzie and his wife. Thinking about Chet. She couldn't put it out of her head. Once a thing took root that's where it stayed until there was some kind of resolution. She walked back to her house, already feeling the heat of the day.

Chapter Seven

Tom and Dan were sitting at their desks in their shared office. The desks were pushed against the left wall as one entered the office, with both their front edges abutting the other so that the detectives faced one another. Tom's back was to the door. A four-feet-wide walk space separated the two desks and the right wall, the wall holding a large rectangular cork-filled bulletin board. There were two beige filing cabinets in the far-right corner; some law books sitting atop them collecting dust.

Tom had just finished reading through the toxicology report and handed it over to Dan. He opened his bottom desk drawer, removed a copy of the *Physician's Desk Reference*, thumbed to the index and found what he was looking for.

Dan looked up from the report and frowned across the desks. "What's Xylazine?"

Tom read. "It's a sedative."

"A sedative?"

"A muscle relaxant used by anesthesiologists to knock you out. How much does the tox report say was in his system?"

Dan glanced over the report. "Twenty milligrams."

Tom frowned. "What was Gundry's normal insulin dose? It mentions it on the front page."

Dan flipped back, read: "Twenty units of insulin, injected three times daily."

Tom thought about it a moment, made some calculations on a

sheet of paper. "There are one hundred units in every cc. Twenty units would be—"

"Twenty milligrams." Dan thumbed back through the report. "Kind of odd he'd inject himself with the exact same dose, don't you think?"

"Yes indeedy," Tom closed the reference book, put it back in the drawer and shut it. "You didn't notice any bottles of Xylazine in his trailer?"

"Nope. Curiouser and curiouser, don't you think? Who'd have access to that stuff?"

"Someone in the pharmaceutical industry—doctors—"

"A vet?"

Tom looked at him. "Sure. He'd have to sedate dogs and cats."

"And horses," Dan said. "What was that vet's name who was arguing with Gundry?"

"Vern Wieder."

"Probably ought to ask him a few questions."

Lt. Joe Stenton entered the detectives' office holding a manila file. Joe was wearing a crisp navy-on-white pin-striped button-down shirt, with a navy tie with maroon stripes that went well with his sharply creased camel-colored trousers and Armani loafers. A good-looking man with intense cocoa brown eyes and short, close-cropped hair, he looked like Shaka, sans spear and loincloth, about to step into an *Ebony* ad. "Got the technicians' report on the trailer," he said. "It appears we've got a murder on our hands."

Dan opened a bag of beer nuts, leaned back in his chair, and popped a handful into his mouth. "We're miles ahead of you, Lieutenant."

Stenton eyed him, opened the file. "Says here there were trace amounts of something called Xylazine in the insulin bottle."

"That's an anesthetic," Dan said, crunching loudly. "Anesthesiologists use it to send you to la-la-land, before poking around in your guts. They didn't teach you that in lieutenant school?"

Stenton ignored him. Recently promoted to lieutenant, he was growing weary of Dan's playful digs. "There were also trace amounts of it in the syringe," Stenton said. He closed the report, handed it to Tom.

Tom opened the file. "Yeah?"

"Like someone emptied out the Xylazine with the syringe then filled it back up with insulin."

Tom glanced through the file. "Trace amounts, huh? That confirms where we were heading."

Stenton shot a look at Dan. "Miles ahead of me, huh?"

Dan shrugged. "We'da got there."

Stenton put his hands on his hips, his elbows at sharp forty-five-degree angles. "Doesn't make sense that Gundry'd go to the trouble of removing the insulin from one of his bottles, then fill it with Xylazine."

"Doesn't make sense, either, that he'd empty out the Xylazine, then refill it with insulin." Tom thumbed through the technician's report, thinking through a possible scenario. "Killer steals into Gundry's trailer, empties one of his insulin bottles—" He broke off from his thoughts. "Any sign of tampering on the bottle, Lieutenant?"

"Report doesn't mention any."

Tom thought about that. "Probably sucked out the insulin with his syringe, refilled it with Xylazine. Beat-feets it to wherever to establish an alibi." He frowned, shook his head.

"What's wrong, Tommy?" Dan asked. "Makes sense to me."

"The killer could've made the switch anytime."

Dan blinked, crunched loudly on another handful of beer nuts.

"There were two empties in his medical kit," Tom said. "The third one had the payload. If someone has a habitual regimen, like Gundry, all the killer'd have to do is lace one of his insulin bottles and sooner or later he's going to get to that bottle."

"Kind of like you and your beer nuts, Dan," Stenton added with a grin. "Someone could lace one of your bags with cyanide or whatever, and—crunch, crunch—you're history!"

Dan looked at him, looked down at his bag of beer nuts.

"Yesterday his number came up," Tom said.

Dan tossed the bag on the desk. "Like Russian roulette."

"Exactly. One thing we know though. The killer was at the equestrian center yesterday, between eleven-thirty and a little after twelve."

"How do you know that?" Stenton asked.

"I was in the clubhouse questioning Sandy at the time. Dan was off hunting down Kate Bledsoe, the other woman who visited Gundry in his trailer," Tom added. "When I got back to the trailer I noticed that the bottle of insulin had been moved. Not much. But enough to get me thinking that someone had come in there after I'd gone."

"You left the trailer unsecured?"

"I locked it before I left. Any sign of forced entry, Lieutenant?"

Stenton shook his head. "None."

"Killer had a key," Dan put in.

Tom thought about that. The killer—someone with a key, maybe—stole into the trailer while Tom and Sandy were in the clubhouse, used Gundry's syringe to empty out the Xylazine, then refilled the bottle with insulin and returned the bottle to the table. Why? To cover the murder, of course. Maybe the killer was thinking that with Gundry's medical condition there might not be an autopsy, or a police investigation. A cursory examination of the bottle and syringe would show that they contained insulin, missing the trace amounts of Xylazine in each. Maybe that's as far as it would go: Chet Gundry died from a heart attack, induced by insulin shock. Death by natural causes. End of story. Still, if there was an investigation; if Gundry's death was ruled a criminal homicide, then the killer, presumably, would have made provision for an alibi. Not hard to do, considering the Russian roulette angle of the killing. It could be anyone.

"The killer had to know about his diabetes, he said. Had to know about his weak heart, too. What's the report say about it, Dan?"

Dan read. "Bzzz . . . bzzz . . . bzzz. Here we go: congenital heart disease. Lining of the aorta weak . . . bzzz . . . bzzz . . . bzzz . . . susceptible to dissection under stress." He looked up. "Dissection?"

"Ruptured aorta," Tom said. "Boom! Like you said, he was a walking time bomb. The seizure set him off."

"A friend might know his medical history," Dan said.

"Maybe a business associate or someone he was intimate with," Stenton put in.

Tom thought about the last possibility. "The FETs catalogue all the latents?" he asked.

"It's all in the report."

Tom turned the page. The field evidence technicians were thorough. Digital photographs detailed every corner of the trailer; the contents of bottles and containers lab tested; every surface, movable and immovable, dusted for fingerprints.

"Several latents unaccounted for," Stenton said. "Place was like Grand Central Station."

"We get all the easy ones," Dan said, reaching for a banana in his top drawer, eyeballed the skin as though inspecting for needle holes.

Stenton indicated the file on Tom's desk. "There's one set of prints we were able to positively identify," he said.

"Yeah?"

"Sandy Cameron's."

Tom nodded. "She told me she'd gone in there to talk with him. It makes sense she might've touched something."

Stenton shook his head. "Maybe so. Just the same, I'd like to know why her prints are all over the tainted insulin bottle."

Tom looked at him.

"Check it out," Stenton said. He started to exit then looked back from the door. "You should've posted a uniform on the trailer. You know that though. 'Nuff said." He walked down the hall.

Dan polished off his banana, tossed the peel into the trash receptical beside his desk. "I'll be sure and say an extra Act of Contrition before I go to bed tonight."

Tom stared down at the file for several long quiet moments. He wasn't thinking about Stenton's rebuke. In fact, he'd never even heard it. The dark thought that had wormed into his mind yesterday in Gundry's trailer was once again spitting venom.

"Can't let Stenton get you down, Tommy. It was an honest mistake."

Tom closed the file, picked up his car keys and stood. "I'm heading over to Sandy's. Alone," he added, and headed out of the office.

•

Sandy was walking down from the barn as Tom turned his Bronco into the gravel driveway of her property. He parked in the shade of a huge oak, got out and stood in front of his vehicle. When she saw him she waved, "Tom!" and picked up her pace. She was happy to see him.

Tom felt lousy.

Sandy was wearing faded blue jeans, a blue-and-white striped knit shirt, and a pair of goulashes—mucking boots, she called them. Her hair was pulled back into a ponytail that poked through the back opening of a blue Dodgers cap. "You're here a bit early," she said, still smiling; her ponytail bouncing jauntily. "You're not supposed to pick me up until six."

Tom looked down at his feet.

As she drew closer to him, close enough to read his eyes, the grim line of his mouth, her countenance fell. "What is it, Tom?" She slowed to a stop. "This is about Chet, isn't it?"

"He was murdered."

Sandy took a step backward, gave her head a little shake of denial. "Murdered?"

"That's the way it looks. Someone filled his insulin bottle with Xylazine. Horse tranquilizer."

"Yes, I know what it is."

"He apparently injected himself with it—thinking it was insulin, of course. Knocked himself out."

She shook her head incredulously.

"He went into insulin shock—had a grand mal seizure. It was too much for his heart." Tom saw that her hands were shaking. She clasped them together. "Here, let's have a seat," he said. Taking her arm, he guided her to the brick-and-flagstone patio where they each sat in iron chairs covered with flower-print cushions.

Sandy stared blankly at the pool, its surface a mesmerizing play of light that reflected over her face, the antiseptic smell of chlorine now and then lifting on a prowling finger of dry hot air. "Why would anyone kill Chet?" she asked remotely, rubbing her hands between her legs.

"That's what we're trying to figure out. Are you okay?"

"No, I'm not okay. This is horrible."

Tom gave her a moment, allowing her time to process the

news. "I have to ask you some questions, Sandy. I need you to put on your detective's cap for a few minutes."

She nodded absently.

"You said he'd mentioned something about a federal offence," Tom said. "When you cross a state line it's a federal offence. Can you think of anything more he might've said."

She shook her head.

"He was talking to Vern Wieder. Nothing more there?"

"No."

"Have you ever see them argue before?"

"No, but Vern—" Sandy looked at Tom quickly, shook her head. "He isn't the easiest man to get along with. But still—" She didn't complete her thought. She continued rubbing her hands. Then: "If anyone had access to Xylazine it would be Vern Wieder."

Tom nodded. "I thought about that."

"But—?"

"Your prints are on the bottle not his."

"My prints?"

Tom felt a sudden vague floating sensation, as though a mooring had come loose between them. He did not know if it had been a conscious effort on his part or if it was his subconscious mind distancing itself to protect him from the emotional confrontation he knew was coming. "That's right,"

She frowned. "What are you saying?"

Tom felt his eyebrows drifting upward. "Nothing. It just raises some questions."

She laughed, a nervous flutter of disbelief. "Because I handed his insulin to him?"

"Why'd you do it?"

"Because he asked me to," she said sharply. "He couldn't find his bottle. I saw it on the counter and gave it to him."

"It was on the counter?"

"Yes." She inclined her head toward him with an unbelieving smile. "*Tom*—?"

"Did you know that the bottle contained Xylazine?"

"What? No, I didn't. No—" Her smile metamorphosed through a range of expressions—surprise, shock, hurt—finally settling upon a dead level glare. "Is that what this little surprise visit is about?" she said evenly. "You think I had something to do with Chet's death?"

Tom didn't know what to think at the moment. He felt numb. Then he felt the old swelling floating movement, a drifting-away movement into cold protective detachment. "Sandy, you know I have to ask you these questions."

Sandy looked at him, pain in her eyes, disbelief furrowing her brow. "If I wanted to kill Chet Gundry, do you think I'd leave my prints all over the bottle? For heaven's sake, Tom."

"Why didn't you tell me you handed it to him?"

"I thought I did." She stood angrily. "I was pretty shook up at the time, in case you hadn't noticed. A good friend of mine had just died. I'm sorry if I left out a detail or two. Now I hear that he was murdered, and that I'm the prime suspect. Got any more questions?"

Tom stood, fingered the edge of his blazer. "No, I—"

They stared at each other for several moments, an unspoken conversation taking place on a mental plane: thoughts touching, circling, assessing the other. A man and a woman drifting apart.

"I'm not a killer, Tom."

"I believe you."

"Do you?"

Tom felt powerless to halt the widening gap. "I'm sorry, Sandy."

"I am too." She started to walk away, stopped and turned, sadness and hurt and anger straining her features. "You might try talking to Kate Bledsoe," she said. "Chet's *girl*friend. She was in the trailer *after* I left, in case you forgot. Talk to Vern. Talk to—shoot, I don't care who you talk to." She continued into her house and shut the door behind her.

Tom stood on the patio for a long while, listening to the obnoxious caw of a crow behind him in the oaks, somewhere in the distance the sound of a diesel tractor, the muted roar of an airliner, twenty-five thousand feet above, making its long descent into LAX. He looked south across the valley stretching from the edge of her property to the San Gabriels, proud against the hazy L.A. sky, looked once more at Sandy's house.

"Nuts," he said, then turned and headed toward his vehicle.

●

Kate Bledsoe lived in a small stucco and wood-shake house, off Saddlehorn Lane in Shadow Hills. Tom parked his vehicle on a curbless strip of weedy ground in front of the house and got out. It was a quiet older neighborhood, adjoining Sunland, where Gundry's mother lived, most of the homes situated on large lots with small pools and horse facilities in back. Mister Ed homes, he called them. Homes of the California dream.

He was about to head up the broken cement walk to the front door when, looking to the left of the house, he saw a woman at the rear of the property working a horse in an arena. He assumed it was Bledsoe. She was a brunette, which fit her description.

Tom headed toward the back. The place was an eyesore. Weeds crowded neglected flower beds. Tumbleweeds grew along the chain-link fence. The unmowed scrabble of front lawn had long ago surrendered the fight to dandelions and crabgrass. A single pathetic white birch stood in the center, abandoned, waterless; its leafless limbs, withered and drooping to the ground, rattled plaintively in the smothering air. It reminded Tom of an old coverless umbrella, its ribs bent and twisting.

The California dream gone to seed.

A faded blue barn dominated the rear of the property. A giant sycamore shaded one side. Horses, standing in individual corrals, hips cocked, heads lowered, tails flicking flies, turned their heads slowly as Tom approached. They seemed bored. Probably were. Tom wondered if horses thought about anything, or if they just stood around staring at the ground, their minds flatlining. Occupying the remainder of the property were a small, sand-filled pipe-railed arena and round pen.

The woman riding the horse in the arena seemed oblivious to his approach. She had changed out of her American flag outfit and was now wearing a lemon-colored sleeveless shirt, blue jeans, and boots, her long dark brown hair pulled back into a ponytail. There were dark circles under her arms. A black-and-red trimmed Angels cap kept the sun off her face.

Tom hooked his elbows over the top metal rail of the arena, waited for the woman to look in his direction. She didn't. "Kate Bledsoe?"

She kept riding. She loped along the far rails, the sound of the horse's footfalls muffled in the sand. As she made the right corner, rounding it and loping toward him, the sound of the approaching footfalls growing louder, louder, Tom knew she could clearly see him. "I'd like to talk to you," he said.

The horse thundered past Tom so that he stepped back automatically from the rails to avoid having his elbows hit by the horse's left flank.

"Who are you?" the woman demanded in an acerbic tone, her back to him as she rounded the left corner.

"Detective Rigby." Tom flashed his badge in the sun. "Burbank Police."

She didn't look, didn't seem to care.

Tom put his badge back into his coat pocket.

"This about Chet?" she asked, her eyes focused on the ground between the horse's ears.

"That's right. I have some questions."

"I'm busy right now."

Tom bristled. "So am I. I understand you were seeing each other, is that right?"

She continued around the arena without a word. Tom figured she'd answer his question as she rounded the corner but she kept riding past him, close enough so that Tom could smell the sweat foaming on the horse's neck. He didn't step back this time.

"Watch yourself," she said.

Tom was half tempted to pull out his Glock .45 and drop the animal. He said, "We can either do this civilly, here, or we can do it down at the station. Your choice."

Bledsoe pulled back on her reins. "Whoa!"

Immediately the horse stiffened its front legs, its buttocks lowering as it skidded to a halt. As the horse straightened, Bledsoe immediately tugged back on the reins, causing the horse to tuck down its head as it stepped backward. Bledsoe relaxed her grip, the horse shuddered and stood still.

"Good boy, Jewel," she said, leaning forward and patting its neck. She walked the horse once more around the arena.

The horse was some kind of reddish brown (Tom didn't know the first thing about horse colors), with three white socks and a white blaze on its forehead. From where he stood he could not see if it was a male or female. With a name like Jewel he figured it was a female. Good-looking horse: big chest, big rump, small head. Then again, Tom was no judge of horseflesh. He was a pretty good judge of human flesh, though, especially female human flesh. Kate Bledsoe was fairly attractive if you liked the type—hard, angular features, high cheekbones, dynamite in her eyes.

Bledsoe reined the horse toward the entrance where Tom stood. "Open the gate, could you? It swings inward."

Tom really felt an itch in his trigger finger. "You didn't answer my question."

She smiled. "Yes, we were seeing each other. What of it?"

Tom opened the gate and, as she passed, closed it behind her and followed her to the barn. Once there she swung out of the saddle, walked the horse onto a cement pad to one side of the barn and tied it to a metal hitch rail. She was about five-seven, curvy. A garden hose was coiled at the foot of the rail. Beside it stood a bucket containing a brush and squeegee. Tom guessed they were used for washing the horse.

"We looked for you at the center," he said.

Bledsoe removed a halter from a wooden dowel just inside the barn. Without looking at Tom, she said, "You didn't look very hard, did you?" She put the halter on the horse, removed the bridle, and retied the horse to the rail. "Is this going to take long?"

"You saw Chet Gundry yesterday morning?"

She loosened the cinch. "That's right. Before my Western Pleasure class. Why?"

"He seem all right to you?"

"His normal perky self." She removed the saddle, showing its dark wet imprint on the horse's back, and carried it into the barn.

Tom followed her into a twelve-by-sixteen-foot tack room. The room smelled of saddle leather and horse sweat, mixed with the smell of hay and manure that drifted in from adjoining stalls. A window in the center wall opened onto the arena. Flies crawled over it. Flies spotted the pressed-wood drop ceiling. Dirty brown-and-white linoleum tile squares covered the floor; horizontal tongue-and-groove paneling covered the walls. A desk stood against the inside-right corner, pictures of Bledsoe winning various horse events crowding it. Tom didn't recognize any of the people in the photos, most of whom were men. A horseshoe-shaped wall clock hung over the desk, the hands of the clock ending in horse shapes. To the left of the desk a small refrigerator hummed a sad note. Trophies and ribbons took up most of the wall space on that side. Layers of dust covered everything. Bridles and tack hung from pegs on the opposite wall. A row of saddles went along the same wall. These were clean.

Bledsoe placed the saddle on an empty rack, laid the saddle blanket, sweaty side up, on top of it. To air it out, Tom guessed.

"You don't seem to be too broken up about his death, Ms. Bledsoe," he said.

"I don't wear my emotions on my sleeve, Detective." She smiled as she gave him a quick once-over. "The name's Kate, by the way."

The color in Bledsoe's eyes changed from an dusty oleander to the color of morning grass, dark, long-bladed and glittering with dew. In them was revealed a deadliness Tom had recognized, even as a boy, as both desirable and dangerous. She might not wear her emotions on her sleeve, but she wore something else there; something that sent tiny red spiders up his spine. "Where were you when you heard about Gundry's death?"

"I was here."

"Eyewitnesses put you at the equestrian center when he died."

"You asked me where I was when I *heard* about his death. I was here." She gave Tom a sharp smile.

"All right, then," Tom said. "You were at the center and you didn't hear anything?"

"I heard sirens."

"There was quite a buzz. You must've been the only person not to know what had happened."

"Then I was the only person."

Tom raised his eyebrows. "I find that hard to believe."

"Believe what you want. I came straight home after my event. My trailer was on the opposite end of the center to Chet's. Didn't hear a thing but sirens, and you hear sirens all the time in L.A. I swear I didn't know about his death until I got home."

She walked out of the tack room, her boot heels striking the floor with impertinent jabs. Tom started to follow but she came back holding the bridle and hung it inside on a wooden dowel. "Is that all you wanted to know?" she asked.

"How'd you find out then?"

"About Chet's death?" She nodded toward a grimy white phone on the desk. "A friend called me. These are awfully strange questions, Detective. Is this normal procedure when people die?"

"What friend?"

"Is it important?"

"What friend?"

Her fingernails clicked against a saddle horn. "Bud Nichols. Bud called and told me."

Tom made a mental note to check her phone records. "What time did he call?"

She shrugged, glanced up at the horseshoe clock. "Around eleven-thirty or so. I'd just gotten back from the center." She crossed the room and headed back out of the barn.

Tom followed.

Bledsoe picked up the garden hose coiled at the foot of the hitch rail, turned on the spigot, twisted open the brass hose nozzle and began spraying the horse from stem to stern. The horse shuddered. It was a stallion, Tom could see now. A stallion named Jewel.

She slanted her eyes toward him. "What was your name again?"

"Detective Rigby."

Bledsoe looked him over pretty good this time; her eyes, sharpening like saw grass, slashed slowly over him, down and up. "Detective Tom Rigby, by any chance? Of course you are," she said without waiting for his answer. "Sandy Cameron's been seeing a Detective Rigby. You look like her type."

Tom said nothing.

"There aren't two of you, are there?" she asked, a mild come-on in her voice.

Tom ignored the question. "You said you saw Gundry before your event. Was that in his trailer?"

She chuckled, an empty rattle. "I think you know the answer to that question, Detective Rigby."

"Would you mind telling me?"

"What—don't trust your girlfriend?" Bledsoe twisted off the

hose, then squeegeed the water off the horse's flanks and buttocks, untied and walked him toward a lonely-looking hotwalker machine that stood about fifty feet off the corner of the barn.

Sandy had one just like it. The hotwalker had four metal arms radiating up and outward at forty-five-degree angles from a vertical axle that rose from a central machine, encased in sheet metal that was corroded around the edges. The machine and arms, painted rust red, were bleached by the sun. A lead line dangled from the end of each arm, a chrome clip attached to the line.

Bledsoe clipped a line to the horse's halter, then walked back to the barn and hit a switch on the inside wall of the barn. The machine hummed plaintively, the arms began to turn slowly, like helicopter rotors, walking the horse in a clockwise circle. The horse didn't seem to mind.

"I'm still waiting for an answer, Ms. Bledsoe."

"Yes, I was there," she said, coming back outside. "No need to be coy, Detective, I'm sure Sandy told you that. She was there, too, you know?"

"You all have a friendly chat?"

"She left as soon as I got there. Had other fish to fry, I suppose." The corners of her mouth jerked outward into a sarcastic smile. She turned on the spigot once again and began hosing off the cement pad.

"I'm told you went ballistic."

"Is that what she told you? My—" She continued hosing the pad, the spray forcing Tom to keep his distance. "I didn't go all that ballistic. Just a little ballistic. Watch your feet."

Tom sensed she was hiding something. "Do you have a key to his trailer?"

She turned off the nozzle. "You certainly are nosey."

"I'm paid to be nosey. Key—?"

She rolled up the hose. "No."

"How about a key to his house?"

Bledsoe shook her head, set the hose down on the ground beside the hitch rail. "Didn't need one. Chet never locked it."

Tom made a note of that. "Didn't he inject himself with insulin while you were there?"

She leaned back against the rail, folded her arms across her chest. "No. Why?"

"You're sure?"

"Yes, I'm sure."

"Did you have a drink together?"

"No. Why?"

"Didn't notice a bottle of whiskey in the trailer? Jack Daniels?"

"I don't know whose that was. It wasn't mine, I hate the stuff."

"The way I hear it you can really put it away."

"Whoever told you that is a liar." Bledsoe straightened away from the rail, started toward the barn.

"His mother."

Bledsoe wheeled at the barn's entrance, grinned back at Tom. "That woman wouldn't know a drunk if he tripped over her," she said, laughing at her joke. "She's pie-eyed half the time herself. What's with all these questions, anyway, Detective?" She went into the barn without waiting for an answer.

Tom followed her and stood at the tack room door.

"Chet and I were friends," she said, taking another bridle off of a peg. She walked across the room and laid it across a saddle. "We had a lot of laughs together, but now he'd dead. I'll shed a tear for him later. Right now I've got to get ready for my next event."

Tom watched her closely.

Bledsoe lifted the saddle off the rack, stiffened when she saw Tom's face. "Why are you looking at me like that?" she asked. "You act like *I* had something to do with his death. Chet was a diabetic. He was a high risk. He knew it. Everyone knew it. He didn't beat the odds."

"Is that what Bud Nichols told you?"

"Yes. Why?"

"Did you know that he had a bad heart?"

A flicker of light in the oleander greens. "No, I didn't."

"You were his girlfriend. He never told you that if he were to ever have a seizure the stress on his heart could kill him?"

"I never knew anything about his heart. Why?"

"Someone spiked his insulin with Xylazine."

Bledsoe's eyes flattened, turned a gunmetal gray. She lowered the saddle. "Xylazine?"

"That's right, Ms. Bledsoe," Tom said, taking a step closer to her. "He was murdered, and so far from what we can ascertain, you were the last person to see him alive."

Bledsoe blinked, raised a hand into the air and made a meaningless gesture. Tiny beads of sweat glistened on her upper lip. She did wear her emotions on her sleeve, after all.

"You said you got home by eleven-thirty." Her eyes had drifted away from his. "What?" She asked, looking back. "Yes. I told you."

"Did you kill him, Ms. Bledsoe?" Tom asked. "Kate?"

Bledsoe's mouth parted slightly, as though she were going to release a word. Nothing came out.

Tom stood looking at her, hearing the rusty squeak of the hotwalker outside, the lazy clop of hooves making mindless circles in the dirt, hearing the flat dead drone of a fly hunting manure in a smothering stillness. "Kate, I'm waiting for an answer."

Chapter Eight

Valencia, the office of Dr. Claire Evans.
11:45 A.M., Thursday

"I keep seeing the gun. I keep seeing the killer's eyes, narrowing—wicked green slits—and that chortle, deep in the throat, sounding like something from hell. I see the bloody finger squeezing the trigger. The knuckle white as it squeezed. Whiter—" Sandy, relating the scene, once again felt the phantom impact and shuddered.

The therapist gave her a moment.

Sandy stared vaguely at a potted palm in the corner of the room, reached across her chest with her left hand and rubbed her other arm, massaged the muscles up around the shoulder. It gave her a sense of security. She knew it was a false security, like a child ducking beneath bedcovers at the thought of monsters. "It felt like somebody hit me in the chest with a sledgehammer," she said, feeling a twinge of pain in her upper chest.

"I see," the therapist said, watching Sandy rub her shoulder. Claire Evans was a middle-aged soft-spoken woman with salt-and-pepper hair, a pleasant oval face, with large doe eyes the color of Godiva chocolate, and a pear-shaped body. Wearing a flower-print blouse over pastel green pants, she was soft looking and nonthreatening.

Still Sandy felt disquieted.

For over a month now, since becoming ambulatory, she had been seeing Claire, two sessions a week; each session lasting forty-five minutes. It was department policy for officers involved in a shooting, whether on the business or receiving end of it, to see a therapist. Getting the officer back on duty as quickly as possible was the main objective. Claire, having worked with the department for several years, had a good success record. Most of her patients made it back okay. Some didn't. Those who didn't left the department under a cloud, broken, shamed, wounded souls struggling for a sense of normalcy. For a night without terror. Some sought it in multiple relationships, others in a bottle or in pills or a needle. A few ate their guns. "Is there anything else you can tell me about the shooting?" Claire asked Sandy in a soothing voice.

Sandy glanced quickly at her, looked back at the palm tree and shook her head. "That's about all," she said, picking absently at the frayed edges around a knee hole in her jeans. "I keep having these attacks." She had gone over this material with Claire several times now, had covered essentially the same ground to a point that she thought the sessions were not accomplishing anything. She felt like she was going around in circles, going nowhere. "How long am I going to have them?"

Claire smiled, a sympathetic softening of facial features designed, no doubt, to put one at ease. Sandy wasn't sure if the smile was genuine or a professional affect learned at a head-shrinker's school. "It is difficult to say with PTSD."

Sandy knew that, of course, from her police training. Posttraumatic stress was a psychiatric disorder that often followed traumatic events, where life and limb are threatened: military combat, severe accidents, violent assaults such as rape or battery, to name a few.

Claire shook her head thoughtfully. "Your body and your mind have been brutally assaulted," she said in a gentle, comforting tone. "Your body will heal itself quickly. But your mind—"

Sandy looked at her. "You're telling me that I'm a nutcase?"

"Of course not," Claire said, a mild rebuke in her voice. "I'm saying that it may take a little longer, is all. Healing the mind is not quite the same as splinting a broken arm, or taking two aspirin for a headache. People respond differently to trauma. And you've certainly had more than your share of it, Sandy. Now the death of—" Claire read her notes. "Chet Gundry. He was your trainer?"

Sandy nodded vaguely. "A while back."

"I don't know that much about trainers." Claire smiled. "But

I'm sure that you must have worked closely with him. Developed a certain closeness, perhaps."

"We were friends."

Claire's soft brown eyes probed gently. "Were you more than friends?"

"We were friends," Sandy repeated, not very convincingly. "That's all."

"I see," Claire said, her expression sharpening.

Sandy was forced to avert her eyes from Claire's penetrating gaze. She looked out the second-story window at the trees lining Valencia Boulevard, at the birds flitting playfully. She wished she could escape and join them, hide amid the dark leaves.

"Still, his death," Claire said, drawing Sandy back. "Now. Two months after the death of your partner. It's a tremendous load for anyone's mind to process."

Sandy did not want to process it. She did not want to think about Chet at all. It was too recent, too painful. Her mind drifted back to thoughts of Nick, instead, her partner of five years. Big Nick Ivankovich. Ivan the Terrible Nick. Fingers that could crush walnuts between them Nick. Nick with a heavy Russian brow that could intimidate the hardest criminal or wrinkle with humor. Devoted husband and family man Nick. Five kids Nick. She'd read in the ME's report that the blade had penetrated his broad back and punctured his heart. Big Nick was brought down with a single blow. Sandy lowered her eyes. "I should've seen it coming," she said quietly.

Claire lay her head on one side. "Should've seen what coming?"

"Nick's killer. His death could have been avoided."

"Do you feel responsible for it?"

Sandy was quiet a moment, noticed that her hands were trembling slightly. That was happening a lot lately. She rubbed a thumb over the nail of the other. "I should've seen it coming," she repeated.

"Nick didn't see it coming either. Why not share the blame with him?"

Sandy raised her eyes.

Claire smiled. "If Nick had seen it coming he would be alive, wouldn't he? The killer would have been apprehended and everyone would've gone home happy. Justice would have won. We wouldn't be having these sessions. But that's not what happened, is it? You didn't see it coming. Nick didn't see it coming. Here we are."

Sandy said nothing.

"Justice is not always something we can have," Claire said. "Criminals sometimes outfox the authorities. Sometimes they manage to get off on technicalities. Innocent people sometimes go to jail. We live in an imperfect world."

"I know."

"Why do you keep flogging yourself, then?"

"It's just the way I'm wired."

Claire raised her eyebrows. "I can see we have to do a little work in that area." She took a sip of tea, set the cup back down on a coaster, and then flipped back a few pages in her notebook. "How are you sleeping?"

"Fine," Sandy lied, smiled to cover it.

"Are you sure?"

"Pretty good." Sandy did not mention that she drank a large glass of wine before bed each night to knock her out, only to wake up at one or two, shivering with fright, her bedsheets wet with perspiration. Or that she would sometimes shut herself in her walk-in closet, back against the corner, gun in hand, pointing it into the darkness, her mind filled with dark thoughts. Sure, she slept pretty good.

She averted her eyes from Claire's scrutiny to the shade patterns on the wall, made by the single shuttered window to her left. She was sitting on a padded sofa in an office designed, like Claire's smile, to put one at ease—soft complementary wall and carpet colors—peach, dusty rose. Flower-shop prints hung on the walls. No desk. Nothing threatening. Two women facing each other in an informal setting, sipping chamomile tea.

"You were wounded in your chest and thigh?" Claire asked.

Sandy reached over and lifted her cup off the end table, took a sip and set it back down. "I've told you before."

"Repetition is good." Claire glanced back at her notes, tapped the armrest with her pen. "You were stabbed also, weren't you?"

Sandy nodded absently, touched her left shoulder where the blade penetrated her rib cage about an inch. Same blade that had killed Nick.

"You're lucky to be alive," Claire said.

"I wouldn't be, except for Tom." Sandy thought about Tom for a moment, how he had made an airtight bandage from a cellophane wrapper to stop the sucking wound in her chest, kept her breathing until the cavalry arrived. Once again she rubbed her left arm.

"Does it make you feel a little guilty?"

Sandy looked at Claire, frowned. "Guilty?"

"That you survived and your partner didn't."

Sandy shook her head. "I don't think so."

"Tell me about Tom," Claire said. "You've been getting close these past two months?"

"Close?" A smile tugged at Sandy's mouth. "When he puts his arms around me it's—I don't know." She shrugged, smiled full flower. "It's like God holding me."

Claire looked at her over her reading glasses. "This is new."

It had only just occurred to Sandy as well. "I've never felt this way about a man before. It's a little—" She struggled to find the word.

"Frightening?"

"Yes, I suppose it is." Sandy looked down at her hands, held her fingers to keep them from trembling. "I—" She smiled back at Claire. A fake smile.

"What were you going to say?"

Once again Sandy felt Claire's eyes boring into her, probing around inside her tender places. Like the blade had done.

"You need to talk it out, Sandy. You can do this."

Sandy felt her eyes water. She didn't want Claire to see her cry, so she looked out the window at the trees once again, the leaves dark green against the glass buildings, the buildings cool in shade and lush landscaping, people walking in and out of shops. A world at peace.

"Sandy?"

She shook her head.

"I'm here to help you through this. What is it about Tom?"

The room fell silent, a taut, whining silence. Sandy reached for a tissue on the side table and dabbed her eyes. "Nothing. I'm fine."

Claire looked at her for a moment, wrote something in her notebook, then turned a page. Sandy was certain she had written the word *liar.*

"Let's put Tom aside for the moment," Claire said, shifting the tone of conversation. "We talked about your brother in our last session. Care to talk about him some more? It may give us a baseline, or context, for some of these other things."

Sandy shrugged. Her brother's death was still painful. The adage "Time heals all wounds" was a lie. "I don't see how talking about Paul helps any of this."

Claire folded her hands on her knee, leaned forward slightly. "Sandy, three men in your life that you cared very deeply about have been taken from you. I think that you are harboring a deep-rooted guilt that will eat away at your insides until you are no longer able to cope. It's important that we talk about your brother. You have to trust me in this."

Sandy looked at her. "Trust?"

"Yes, trust. It's the basis for all successful relationships. Without it there's no hope." Claire's features firmed slightly, took on a professional tone that said, *I'm going to be quiet now and let you talk. Talking is important.* She leaned back in her chair.

"I've told you everything," Sandy said after a few moments.

"I'd like to hear it again." Claire smiled. *Trust me.*

Sandy sat back in the sofa, opened the tissue and smoothed it over her leg. "Where to begin?" she said, feeling the dampness of the tissue beneath her fingertips. Paul was a major pillar in her life. Her brother. Her friend. Her confidant. Now he was gone. How does one describe a hole in one's life as large as the Grand Canyon? "He was a great brother," she said quietly. "I loved him dearly."

She felt silly saying it, since it was probably in every one of Claire's session notes. Still, obediently, she told her about the things they did together; how they went to movies and ball games; how they went on horseback rides together. Paul was a fine horseman, although he had no love for horses. Still, he liked to take Sandy up into the mountains and teach her about wildlife and nature; they represented "God's handiwork," as he used to say. "We ought to be good stewards of the earth."

"A wise brother." Claire smiled. "Generous, too."

Sandy looked at her, returned the smile, and continued smoothing her palm over the tissue. "I think because he was quite a bit older he could afford to be generous." She frowned. "That's not exactly true. He was generous by nature."

Sandy went on to describe how civic and socially minded Paul was, taking on this cause or that one, large or small, politically correct or incorrect. He wasn't a Leftist or Rightist; he simply loved people and hated injustice. Didn't matter if the injustice was against blacks, browns, reds, yellows or whites; he simply could not tolerate the various "breaches in human protocol." Paul was the real deal. He ran for city council and was elected, hoped the office would give him a platform from which to effect positive change in the Santa Clarita Valley.

"Someone shot him?" Claire asked.

"He was gunned down in front of city hall," Sandy said, once again feeling a pang of sorrow that she knew would never go away. "Sitting in his car. The killer got a few dollars and a Rolex. The department said it was a robbery homicide. Paul was at the wrong place at the wrong time."

Claire looked up from her notes. "The crime remains unsolved?"

Sandy nodded. "There was nothing to go on except the slug that killed him. It was a nine-millimeter. Ballistics didn't turn up anything on the slug, either. Nothing traceable. And, no, there weren't any witnesses." She shook her head. "Five o'clock in the afternoon. Broad daylight. People coming and going and no one hears or sees a thing."

"No one had a grudge against him?" Claire asked, giving her shoulders a little shrug. "Maybe someone didn't like that he won the election."

Sandy raised her eyebrows, thinking as she once again rubbed her thumbnail. "I thought about that—still think it's a possibility. But after ten years the trail has gone cold. Most everyone on the council back then has since moved on."

"That certainly makes it difficult. Did you interview any of them?"

"Yes, but nothing came of it. No one really knew Paul; he was a bit of a dark horse." Sandy laughed weakly. "If there's no link between killer and victim," she said, "if the killer doesn't strike elsewhere—establish an MO or pattern—then it's next to impossible to build a case."

"There were no other robberies at the time?"

"There were robberies, sure. But none where a gun was used. Someone robbed my brother, killed him, then disappeared without a trace."

"Incredible."

"I thought so." A dark thought entered Sandy's mind, an old bitterness. "Didn't stop Lieutenant Ubersahl from retiring my brother's case to the open-case file though."

Claire looked down at her notes. "Lieutenant Ubersahl is your watch commander?"

Sandy nodded. "He was a sergeant then," Sandy said, trying to disguise her feelings toward the man. She and Ubersahl were not on the best of terms. He was a good cop—good arrest record, smart, fearless, the kind of cop you'd want covering your back in a shootout. But they never really clicked personality-wise. He was the one dissenting vote at her first sergeant's oral. She wrote it off to the "boy's club" mentality that still existed in some quarters of the department. There'd been a bit of an edge between them ever since.

"You sound bitter," Claire said.

Sandy looked at her. "Do I?"

"You think Lieutenant Ubersahl was wrong in retiring your brother's case?"

"I think he quit too soon."

"And that's why you joined the sheriff's department. You wanted to catch the bad guy?"

"That's me." An ironic smile twisted across Sandy's mouth. "Superwoman. Righter of wrongs, champion of outcasts, defender of the downtrodden."

"Like your brother."

Sandy took a sip of tea, set the cup down on the coaster. "Like my brother."

"But you haven't solved the case either."

"No."

"How does that make you feel?"

"Lousy."

"Maybe a little guilty?"

Sandy said nothing, once again smoothed her palm over the tissue.

Claire said, "You are a very bright and caring person, Sandy. Like your brother in many ways, I'm sure. You hate injustice. You want to make things right, and when you can't you take it upon yourself—something inside you demands its pound of flesh."

Sandy thought about that for a moment. "You think that's why I keep seeing the gun?"

"It's really hard to tell." Claire shook her head. "The best thing you can do is to talk it out, like we're doing right now. Run it into the ground. You've got a good support group in place—your parents. Your church. People you can trust."

Sandy nodded. Yes, she had a good support group. The best.

"And there's Tom, of course," Claire said.

Sandy looked at her quickly, looked away at one of the floral prints. A Paul Landry, she saw now. She looked out the window, the sun bright, intense, like Claire's unrelenting stare. She fiddled with the tissue, crumpled it into a fist, pounded the fist against her leg. She could feel a lump the size of a baseball in her throat.

"Tell me about Tom," Claire said.

Sandy shook her head, felt her eyes water. She cleared the emotion from her throat, twisted the tissue around her fingers, and then raised a hand to her face. She was crying. "Oh, God. God. He thinks I killed Chet."

Claire waited a moment. "Did you?"

Sandy lowered her hand, blinked at Claire in the silence that filled the room.

Chapter Nine

Chet Gundry lived on a twenty-acre horse ranch in Acton, a country town nestled in the foothills of the San Gabriel Mountains, about an hour's drive northeast of Los Angeles. The house was a three-bedroom Spanish custom, with a red tile roof and arched patio overlooking the grounds that were well kept. There was a large red center-aisle barn about a hundred yards from the house, outbuildings and horse facilities—two arenas, round pen, and hotwalker. Mature desert willows lined its several graveled drives crisscrossing the ranch. Liquidambar, modesto ash, and rock pines provided shade and windbreak and relief from the view of Gundry's nearest neighbor. A scraggly orchard stood to the south side of the property, boughs heavy with early fruit. Horses grazed in an open pasture, a three-rail white fence enclosing it. Mount Gleason provided a spectacular relief against a cloudless sky.

The house inside was masculine in its furnishings: heavy leather-covered chairs and sofas, oak tables and hutch, brass and wrought-iron table lamps and ceiling fixtures. Saddles on racks lined one wall of the living room, along with a couple of old flintlocks; their powder horns dangling from the gun supports. Remington and Russell prints hung at various focal points. There were quite a few Remington bronzes, one on the coffee table; a couple on the fireplace mantel. A masculine smell in every room.

Field evidence technicians went from room to room, bagging and tagging, dusting for latent prints. Because Gundry's death had been upgraded to murder, they would draw a tight net in hopes of finding evidence or clues that would point to a motive, an opportunity, a "crime print" that would identify the killer. So far, there was nothing outstanding, no smoking gun, no grainy convenience-store video of shadowy figures; no tape-recorded conversation between killer and victim; no letter of confession. The clues were probably there, though. A man does not pass through time and space without stirring up a mess of molecules.

Tom and Dan busied themselves in the study, both detectives wearing latex gloves. Dan was going through the dead man's financial records he'd gotten out of the desk, a heavy-legged piece with carved feet and molding that went around the base and desktop. Tom was over by a pinewood gun cabinet built into the wall, the cabinet lined with hunting rifles and shotguns. Nothing fancy, mostly over-the-counter field-grade weapons—Winchester, Browning, Ithaca, Ruger. Tools of a hunter, not a collector.

There was a fine elk mounted above the fireplace, to prove the point, its head lifted to one side in a bugling challenge. A mule-deer rack was mounted beside a black bear head on the wall opposite. Male and female pheasants were perched on a credenza behind the desk, beside some architectural plans. Afternoon light streamed in through the room's only window above the credenza, washing over the hardwood floor and knotty pine walls that were stained a honey color. Tom felt a twinge of envy for the man's outdoorsy lifestyle. Chet Gundry had clearly been a man's man.

Bookshelves took up the wall space on either side of the gun cabinet. Horse trophies, silver belt buckles and books filled the shelves; framed photographs lined one of the shelves. They were mostly photos of Gundry at various equestrian events, several of Gundry with Angelina Montoya, the dark-haired woman that Tom had seen in the *Western Pleasure* magazine in Gundry's trailer. There was one of Gundry with Kate Bledsoe at a social event; Bledsoe, cocktail in hand, wearing a red dress with a plunging neckline, laughing at who-knows-what, Gundry grinning knowingly at the camera.

Tom picked up a photo sitting on a separate shelf and stared. Gundry was holding a trophy of some kind. Sandy Cameron, looking radiant in western show attire, was leaning against him, her arms wrapped around his neck as she kissed his cheek. Tom felt suddenly hollow inside.

"Got anything, Tommy?" Dan called from the desk.

Tom shook his head. Gazing at the photo, it was clear that Gundry and Sandy had been an item at one time. How much of an item, he could only speculate from Sandy's bright-eyed expression in the photo, and from bits and pieces he'd gleaned from her description of their relationship. He set the photo back down on the shelf.

The mantel clock sounded the quarter hour.

"Looks like a hefty chunk of his income came from someone named Angelina Montoya," Dan said.

"Horse breeder," Tom said vaguely, walking over to the desk. "He trained her horses."

Dan glanced over the room. "He'd have to have other income to support this place."

Tom agreed. The house and grounds, though simple in its furnishings, would've cost at least six hundred thousand in current California real estate values. "He got a mortgage?"

"Pays about two thou a month. Don't know if that includes taxes, though. Got to be more dough coming in."

Tom noted a wall calendar behind Gundry's desk. "Horse clinics," he said, glancing over the calendar. "Three in this month alone."

Dan looked at the calendar. "Horse clinics? He some kind of a vet or something?"

"Horse school. People want to brush up on their horsemanship skills come to his clinics. Sandy told me about them. People pay big money—four, five hundred bucks for a three-day clinic. Depending on the trainer, of course. Multiply that times twenty, thirty students. Not bad for a weekend's work."

Dan shook his head, grinned. "Horse school, huh? Maybe one of his students didn't like how he graded."

Tom looked at him. It was meant as a joke, but Dan had, intentionally or unintentionally, just opened the door to hundreds of possible suspects. Three weeks ago Tom had attended a clinic with Sandy, who said she needed a tune-up before the Burbank show. Bud Nichols, a well-known Western Pleasure trainer, was brutal in his public critiques of students, reducing more than one woman rider to tears, and belittled a man to the point where Tom thought it might come to blows. He could very well see how someone might want to cut someone like Nichols down to size. He made a mental note to inquire about Gundry's ringside manner, see if perhaps he'd had any recent altercations with students. "No clinics this weekend," Tom said, once again looking at the calendar.

"Probably because of the horse show."

"No doubt." Tom turned the page. Three of the weekends in the upcoming month of July were set aside for clinics, one down in Norco, one in Temecula, one up in Santa Barbara. Flipping back to the month of May, Tom saw that three of Gundry's weekends were, likewise, set aside for clinics, two in Acton, one in Santa Clarita. The words "Pacific Coast Congress" were written across the fourth week that included the weekend. Tom guessed it was another horse show of some kind. "Any sign of a day planner on the desk?"

Dan shook his head.

Tom started for the door. "I'll see if there's one in the kitchen."

The kitchen was wide and open, with big square terra-cotta tiles covering the floor, and a butcher-block-topped island in the center. Tom found what he was looking for on a small phone desk next to the breakfast nook. A heavyset black woman with olive brown eyes and a generous smile was dusting items from inside the refrigerator. "Okay to take this, Sheila?" Tom said, holding up the Day Planner.

"Sure, Tom. Already took care of everything over there."

Tom quickly thumbed through the calendar, saw names penciled in time slots.

"Found a couple large bottles of insulin in the fridge," Sheila said. "We'll check 'em out."

"Okay." Tom headed back to the study, paused briefly in the hallway to look at a Terpning print hanging there. Terpning was one of Sandy's favorite painters, a man who specialized in Native American subjects. This particular one was titled "Crow Pipe

Ceremony," a council of Crow warriors passing the pipe. Tom wondered for a moment if Sandy had bought Gundry the painting, or if he had given her the three Terpnings hanging in her house. It made him think about his own apartment; its walls bare except for a couple of framed photographs. No art prints. No bronze sculptures. Sandy's house was full of art—paintings, bronzes, Indian artifacts; in many ways a feminine version of Chet Gundry's house. It seemed cut out of the same cloth, an observation that made Tom wonder what he and Sandy really had in common. She was a horse lover. He loved sailing. She was raised in a nurturing Christian home, secure in her beliefs. He had no idea what religion he was—a spiritual mongrel by all reckoning. He was a dog lover; she loved cats. They were polar opposites in so many ways.

"See something there, Tom?" a man said, jolting him from his thoughts. Hal Peters was a tall, lanky evidence technician with a lantern jaw and hands too large for his arms. He reminded Tom of Lurch in the old *Addams Family* TV series.

"Dust it for prints, will you, Hal?"

Peters raised his dark eyebrows. "Sure thing, Tom. Want us to dust the rest of the wall hangings?"

"Wouldn't hurt. Make sure you get this one." Tom headed down the hall without giving the reason.

As he entered the study Dan was poring over some papers, his nose sweeping inches from the desk so that his bald spot, gleaming on the back of his head, reminded Tom of a searchlight. Dan looked up as he crossed the room. "Find it?"

Tom held up the day planner, chose a comfortable-looking red leather reading chair facing the hearth. As he settled into it he felt his pager buzz. He looked down, angled the little window to the light, but didn't recognize the number. He ignored it.

He flipped the Day Planner open to the day of Gundry's death, Wednesday, and found a single name written there: Abbe Newton. Tom had no idea who she was (assuming Abbe was a she). That the appointment was penciled in for 7:45 A.M., two and a half hours before Gundy augered into the dirt, piqued his interest. There was a telephone number written next to the name.

Tom looked down once again at the number that had just buzzed his pager. "Whaddya know," he said, flipped open his cell phone, and dialed it.

Dan looked up from a pile of papers, a look of inquiry widening over his amiable round face.

Tom made a "we'll see" gesture with his eyebrows, looked at the beady eyes of the black bear mount as a woman's voice answered.

"This is Abbe," she said. It was a young-sounding voice with a southwestern twang. Texas or Oklahoma maybe.

"Did you just put in a call to someone?"

"Yes. To Detective Rigby of the Burbank Police Department."

"What can I do for you?"

"Detective Rigby? Lucky me. Thank you for getting back to me so soon. You must be busy."

"I am."

"I won't keep you, then. I understand that you are investigating the death of Chet Gundry."

"Who told you that?"

She giggled. "I'm a reporter, Detective. I find things out."

"I see." Tom didn't like reporters. He considered them carrion crows—same level, socially speaking, as bottom feeders.

"I was wondering if there was a time when we could get together and talk."

"About what?"

"I work for *Journal West Horse*—an equestrian magazine out of Austin. I'm doing an article on Chet Gundry. The lead feature, actually."

"Oh?"

"I mean I *was*." Newton chuckled dryly. "You know . . . his techniques as a trainer." There was a pause. "I suppose I'll have to change the focus of the article now that he's dead, won't I? He was murdered?"

Tom frowned. That little detail was known only to a handful of people. "Where'd you hear that he was murdered?"

"De*tective*—" A playful scold in Newton's tone—*I just got finished telling you I was a reporter, didn't I, sugar lamb?* "That's why I wanted to talk with you—get the inside scoop. You know."

"No, I don't know. Ms. Newton, did you meet with Gundry on the morning of his death?"

Silence.

"Ms. Newton?"

"Who told you that?" The playful charm had sharpened with suspicion.

Tom noticed the single yellow eye of a stuffed red-tailed hawk, perched on a dowel over the door, glaring at him. "I'm asking the questions now," he said evenly. "Did you or didn't you?"

"Yes. We met briefly."

"What time?"

"I don't know—sometime in the morning."

"You don't remember what time?"

"It was early, I know that. My appointment book would give the time. Want me to check?"

"That would be helpful." Time for her to regroup, Tom thought. He heard a voice in the background, a loudspeaker voice announcing the results of a halter class for yearling fillies. Tom had no idea what that was, but guessed that Newton was at the equestrian center.

"Says here seven-forty-five," she said, coming back on the line, pleasant as ever. She giggled. "Must've been seven-forty-five, then. I live by my appointment book."

"Where did you meet?"

"At the Cottonwood Equestrian Center. In the clubhouse," she added quickly. "We had coffee. Why?"

"You didn't meet in his trailer?"

"No-ooh." One syllable drawn out into two, with a playful little tail on the end. "Why?"

"Didn't have a drink with him after your coffee?"

"A drink?"

"Bourbon."

"At seven-forty-five in the *morn*ing?"

"Did you?"

"No. I have a snort now and then but never before lunch. Is that some sort of clue or something? The bourbon, I mean."

"I would like to meet with you, Ms. Newton," Tom said. "Where are you staying?"

"At the Holiday Inn."

"How about we meet you there in an hour or so?"

"Let me check my schedule." Tom waited while she presumably checked her schedule. "I'm covering an event in about a half hour. Shouldn't last too long."

Tom checked his watch. "It's twelve-thirty now. How does twoish sound?" Twoish, California time, meant anytime after two and before three. This allowed a margin of time for freeway snarls, earthquakes, or the occasional drive-by shooting.

"Twoish? Sure, that would be fine. Can I ask what you want to talk about?"

"I'm a detective, Ms. Newton. I find things out." Tom had to grin. "We'll call before we come."

"Okay, sweet pea. Twoish then."

Tom folded his phone back into his coat, glanced over at Dan who looked up from a pile of papers. "Abbe Newton," Tom said. "She's a reporter with some western magazine. Had a meeting with Gundry a couple hours before he jackknifed into the dirt."

"Interesting."

"We'll meet with her in an hour and a half," Tom said. "That should give us plenty of time to finish up here, as well as a stop at Angelina Montoya's on the way back to Burbank."

"Who? Oh, right, the horse breeder." Dan nodded, aimed his searchlight at the ceiling.

Tom flipped back a page in the day planner, the day before Gundry's death. The only entry was a note that read: "Talk to Sandy tomorrow!" Tom thought about that. The word "tomorrow" was underlined, suggesting urgency. He wondered if it might have something to do with a federal offense. Something that crossed a state line. Something that required Sandy's police expertise, perhaps. He could only guess.

"I'm going to get a box," Dan said. "No way can I go through all this junk here." He stood and left the room.

Tom thumbed back through the calendar. He recognized a few names. They weren't names of people but of western apparel companies: Wrangler, Dan Post, Stetson, Roper. Tom guessed they either sponsored Gundry or that he endorsed their products (he'd have Dan check Gundry's financial records).

There were a couple of recurring names he didn't recognize that were sprinkled through the past several weeks. One of the names (or initials, in this case) was S.W. (Tom thought it might be Sorrel West), and the other was a man named Max (assuming it was a man, and not short for Maxine or something). The last entry for S.W. was the night before his death, 8:00 P.M. Tom guessed it was the meeting Myrtle Gundry had told them about, the one that her son, deep in a cave mood, had left her house to attend. Prior to that entry the initials appeared in the Day Planner at two-week intervals, sometimes in clusters of two and three days (and nights). Once, back in May, S.W. appeared on the weekend.

Tom stood, walked over to Gundry's wall calendar behind the desk, flipped down a page and saw that the entry would have coincided with his Acton horse clinic. S.W. met with Gundry at his clinic. Business, maybe (if S.W. was Sorrel West). There were no S.W. meetings scheduled after Gundry's death. Tom found that interesting.

The "Max" entries began back in January, but were mostly grouped in the months of February, March, and May, none (according to the wall calendar) coinciding with a clinic. There was only one entry for the month of June, two days before Gundry's death, and none afterward.

He returned to the leather chair and sat there thinking. Neither S.W. or Max, apparently, had scheduled any further business (or pleasure) with Chet Gundry after his death. Coincidence? Or was it because they knew he wasn't going to be around?

The planner contained no entries for Angelina Montoya or Kate Bledsoe. That made sense. Gundry trained Montoya's horses and probably saw her every day (assuming horses needed to be trained every day). No need to keep a record of their meetings. Bledsoe had been Gundry's lover. Lovers don't usually keep appointment books, unless, of course, one has many lovers. Tom guessed that the day planner was used to track his business appointments only.

Once again Tom thumbed forward to the day before Gundry's death, reread the entry: "Talk to Sandy tomorrow!" He wondered if there was a connection between S.W., Max, and a federal offense of some kind? No way to tell at the moment. He'd have to give it some thought. Later. The mantel clock struck the quarter hour—12:45.

Tom closed the calendar, stood, and walked over to the credenza. He was curious about the set of plans he'd seen there earlier. The plans were about three feet by four feet in dimension and appeared to be some kind of real-estate development. The development was in Agua Dulce, a small bedroom community between Acton and Santa Clarita, about forty minutes from Burbank. Very horsy.

Dan came back into the room holding a cardboard evidence box. "The FETs are just about finished here, Tommy. Whaddya got?"

"I don't know."

Dan set the box down on the desk, stepped around it to the credenza, and looked at the plans. "Some kind of real-estate development?"

"Sweetwater Equestrian Estates," Tom said, reading the legend in the lower-right corner of the plans.

"What would a horse trainer be doing with those?"

Tom shrugged. "Maybe he was interested in real estate." He turned a page. A lot map showed about fifty home sites, each lot ranging from five to ten acres, the lots radiating out from a hub that included a huge covered arena, clubhouse, stable complex, and a two-acre lake that curved around the clubhouse. Riding trails wound through the estates. A horse lover's paradise.

"Looks like quite a setup," Dan said.

"Sure does." Tom flipped back to the front sheet, looked at the legend in the lower-right corner, and stared.

"What is it?" Dan asked.

Tom indicated the name of the developer.

Dan read the name. "Maxwell Cameron. Isn't that—?"

"Sandy's dad. Max."

Dan raised his eyebrows. "Whaddya know."

Tom looked out of the window at Gundry's long red horse barn, suddenly feeling a knot in his stomach.

Chapter Ten

A thought had been working on Sandy's mind like a woodpecker ever since she left the therapist's office. It wasn't an epiphany, it was a notion. Not even that much of a notion. Still, it moved her from gazing at her navel to more of an outward perspective, and for that she was grateful. She had fully intended to head home after the session; perhaps make a pot of tea and curl up in an easy chair with a good book. Retreat into solitude. Raise the drawbridge against the world. Instead, driving through Burbank, she turned off the southbound Golden State at Alameda, "This Kiss," by Faith Hill, blowing through her truck speakers as she headed west toward Main. After a couple of turns through an older residential area, she crossed Riverside Drive and wheeled her F-250 through the gates of the equestrian center, parked in front of the clubhouse, got out and walked over to the covered arena, the thought, or notion, or inkling—or whatever it was—tap, tap, tapping on her mind.

Wearing faded blue jeans with tears in the knees, a "Cowgirl Up" T-shirt, boots, and a blue Dodgers baseball cap, she was dressed for comfort, not style, dressed to sit back in the bleachers and enjoy the show, unobserved, and without competition concerns. She was in time to catch one of the halter classes.

Sandy loved the event because here was where the horse's conformation was judged: the size and shape of its chest and hip, its head and neck shape, stance, temperament, and something indefinable—call it chemistry between judge and horse. Sandy liked to pit her own eye against the judge's, see if her choices matched. Most of the time she was spot on; however, sometimes—Sandy wrote it off to the chemistry thing—the judge appeared to have walked in from a dog show.

Instead of finding a seat in the bleachers, she went down into the staging area behind the judge's stand where the air was cool, a welcome relief from the outdoor heat. Owners or handlers stood holding their horses—yearling colts, by the look of them. Sandy went over to the rail, leaned her elbows on it, and watched the weanling class in progress—colts or fillies under a year old. There were eight horses in the class.

Bud Nichols was standing a bay colt, presently being looked over by one of two judges. Sandy knew the colt, had gone over to Bud's ranch the day it was born and watched it wobble about on uncertain legs. His sire was Mister Dobbins; his dam, Brownie's Luck; each horse the result of years of careful breeding. The colt had a nice chest and hip, a shapely little head that fit well on a graceful neck. With straight legs, neat feet, and a solid square stance, he was a good-looking young quarter horse. The best on the field, if Sandy were to judge.

The judges, a man and a woman in western-cut coats and white hats, walked over to the elevated booth, handed in their scores to a craggy-faced man seated behind a microphone. Moments later, the loudspeaker squawked, followed by the announcer's easy voice: "And we have a decision for the colt weanling class. First Place goes to number one-forty-seven: Mister Dobson's Brown Boy, a handsome colt owned by trainer Bud Nichols."

A handful of spectators applauded, a few hooted, as Bud walked over to the booth, received a blue ribbon, then headed toward the gates.

The announcer called out the place awards in descending order.

"Lookin' good, Bud," Sandy said as he led the colt into the staging area. She meant the colt, not Bud, though Bud was easy on the eyes himself. Dressed in a navy western-cut jacket, blue pinstripes on white shirt opened at the neck. Wrangler jeans, and rattlesnake boots, he looked like he'd just stepped out of a *Drysdales* spread. An oval silver belt buckle and black Stetson completed the ensemble.

He acknowledged Sandy with a sharp nod.

"Beautiful little colt," she said, rubbing Brown Boy's cheek. "You heard about Chet?"

"It's a lousy deal."

"It hasn't hit me yet." Sandy continued stroking the colt's cheek, trying to picture Chet's face. She couldn't. "Can you believe it? Chet gone."

"Ain't none of us gonna beat the odds."

Sandy stopped what she was doing and looked at Bud. He was watching a buckskin colt, the last of the Halter class, exit the arena, his charcoal gray eyes making a thorough appraisal. "You know what I mean, Bud."

A tired smile spread over his face. "Good old Chet," he said, laughed, then clipped it short with a grunt of contempt. "It's a lousy deal all around." He shook his head, and then looked at Sandy. "Let's not talk about it, okay?" The remnant of a smile lurked in the corners of his hard, thin mouth, but his eyes were void of expression. It made Sandy think of a sunrise without the slightest bit of warmth or hope in it.

"Okay, Bud. Here comes Ramon."

A round-faced Mexican youth approached Bud with a magnificent-looking red roan yearling stallion; no doubt Bud's entry for the next halter class. Bud handed Brown Boy's lead to the youth, and took the other lead. The yearling colt snorted, stamped a front foot.

Sandy looked him over, liked what she saw. "Is this one of Mister Dobson's babies?"

Bud grinned. "Dobson's Lucky Boy."

"He's wonderful, Bud. Really." Sandy smoothed her hand over the colt's sleek neck. "Mister D's sure throwing some fine babies."

Bud removed a round tin of Copenhagen from his coat pocket, opened it, took a pinch of snuff and inserted it between his lower lip and gums. "You bet," he said, tamping the snuff with the tip of his tongue. "I'm up against two of them in this event." He jerked a thumb at two colts entering the staging area—one sorrel, the other gray—each a near copy of the colt Bud was holding.

"Looks like Lucky Boy's got some stiff competition."

"Bring it on. The better Mister D's babies do, the more I can charge for his standing fee."

Sandy smiled, glanced down at Bud's trophy belt buckle. "Winning the World last year didn't hurt."

"Bumped his standing fee up to twenty-five hundred," Bud said. "Got some semen orders coming in too."

"That's great." Mail-order grooms, as Sandy called the practice. She waited a moment, rubbed a hand over the colt's cheek, then tried a different approach. "It's a shame about your mare."

Bud looked at her.

"The one that died," she clarified. "You just bought her?"

"That's right."

Bud had lost two mares in the past few months; one to HYPP, a killing disease, and now this recent death. "Were you going to breed her to Mister D?"

Bud shrugged noncommittally. "What can you say?"

"I'd be heartbroken." Sandy shook her head thoughtfully. "It's strange. A heart attack, huh?"

Bud stared at her with a calculating gaze. "Where'd you hear that?"

"Chet told me." Sandy felt as though she'd touched a nerve. "Chet must've heard it from Vern," she said carefully. "Vern did the vet check, right?"

"Vern's got a big mouth." Bud leaned to one side and loosed a lipful of brown juice into the sand, then straightened, wiping his mouth with a flick of his forefinger. "Why all the sudden interest in this?"

"No reason. It's the kind of news that gets around." Sandy smoothed her hand over Lucky Boy's neck some more. "I just find it odd . . . a young mare."

"Let's drop it, okay?" Bud grinned. End of discussion. He removed a white card from his coat pocket, the number 187 written on it in black, and turned a shoulder to her. "Here—would you mind?"

"Not at all." Sandy took the card, held it in her teeth as she unpinned the existing number 147 from Bud's coat back. She pinned the new card in its place, handed the old one back to him.

"Thanks."

Lucky Boy stamped his feet, tossed his head, and screamed a challenge as another yearling entered the staging area. Bud patted the colt's muscled neck. "Easy, boy."

"Looks like one of Zee-Zee's babies," Sandy said.

Bud turned and watched the incoming horse, his eyes narrowing with interest. The colt, a light chestnut with two white socks and a blaze on his forehead, looked a lot like his sire, Ideal's Bar Zhan Zee—Zee-Zee as he was known—Angelina Montoya's World Champion stallion, a horse that was presently siring numerous World Champion hopefuls.

Sandy smiled. "Looks like the competition just got stiffer."

Bud made a noise in the back of his throat. "Standing halter's one thing. You got to train 'em, don't you?"

"Yes, you do." Sandy thought about that. "I wonder what Angelina's going to do now that Chet's gone."

"Chet wasn't the last word on horses," Bud said. "She'll find someone."

"Oh, I'm sure of it. But Chet was the backbone of her training program. His fingerprints are on every one of her horses. It'll be hard to fill his boots." She patted the colt's cheek. "I guess it opens the field for everyone else, though, doesn't it?"

Bud slid a steady look at her. "I don't follow you."

Sandy adjusted her cap on her head. "Now that Chet is gone it kind of changes everything around—some stand to lose, some stand to benefit. That's all."

Bud shook his head, shrugged, as if to say, *I still don't follow you.*

"Angelina will need someone to train her horses," she said. "It'd be a great job."

"If you say so."

Sandy smoothed her palm over the colt's shoulder that seemed alive with burnished red highlights. "What a beautiful coat. You give him flax seed?"

Bud seemed lost in thought; his eyes fixed on a point over Sandy's left shoulder. He came back from wherever he'd gone. "What?"

"Flax seed. To get his coat so shiny."

"Flax seed—sure." Bud loosed another lipful into the sand. "You think that's why he was murdered—for his lousy trainer job?"

"Who told you he was murdered?"

Bud stared at her a couple of moments as if he needed time to think of an answer. "His old lady," he said. "She called me up yesterday afternoon—said she'd just heard about it from the Burbank police. Thought I'd like to know since we were friends. Xylazine, huh?"

She nodded.

"That's a dirty trick. Is that what's eatin' you?"

Sandy stopped petting the colt.

Bud grinned. "I figured you didn't come down here to shoot the breeze about my dead mare or anything else. You wanna know if I spiked his insulin."

She eyed him for a moment; no point in denying it. "Since you brought it up—"

"You think I'd kill my friend so I could be second banana at Montoya's? I'd have to have a better motive than that."

"There's the Sorrel West deal."

"What about it?"

"Now that Chet's gone it'll most likely fall to you, don't you think?" She let Bud make the inference.

"You're chasin' your tail, Sandy," he said with an arrogant chuckle. "I haven't thought about it for a couple of weeks. Not since I last met with Sorrel."

"Sorrel West?"

Bud shook his head. "Sorrel Rose . . . owner of the company."

Sandy could usually tell if someone was lying. He'd either blink, or cough, or avert his eyes from hers; anything to avoid the finger of guilt. Some went pale as sheets, others perspired, made sweat circles under their arms—"Sweatin' BBs," as Nick Ivankovich used to say. Bud, though a bit defensive, was either the best liar she'd ever met or he really hadn't thought about a deal that could potentially net him an enormous sum of money. "Can you think of anything he and Vern may've had going?" she asked. "Something shady, maybe?"

Bud frowned. "What kind of shady?"

"Something that might be considered a federal offense. I heard the two of them arguing about it the morning Chet died." Just then she caught a subtle flicker of light around his dark gray irises. The light steadied into something flat and dull, without depth. There was no ill-will behind the eyes, no rancor, but they were wolf's eyes, set with a predatory detachment.

Bud grinned. "A federal offense, huh?" He leaned to one side and spat. Then he hooked out what was left of his chew into the sand. "I wouldn't put anything past Vern," he said with a dismissive sneer. "It don't sound like Chet, though."

Sandy didn't think it sounded like Chet either. But Chet had known something; something that may have gotten him killed. "No ideas, huh?"

"Nope."

Just then the throaty drawl of the announcer's voice came through the loudspeaker. "The next class will be for yearling colts. Yearling colts. Handlers."

"Gotta go," Bud said, and walked out into the ring with the other contestants.

Bud stood holding his colt, looking at the judges walking out onto the field. However, watching him, Sandy got the feeling that for once he was not thinking about horses, or breeding, or winning events in shows. She felt that he was thinking about Chet Gundry, about matters that may or may not have something to do with his death. It was just a notion she had, not even that much of a notion. But the thought kept tapping against her mind.

●

Sandy left the staging area, felt the air warming as she made her way up the cement bleacher steps and found an aluminum seat in the shade near the top. The bleachers were about a quarter filled. Halter classes weren't usually the biggest draw for spectators (not enough action). Most of the people there were trainers or buyers or horse lovers, and were sitting down in front where they could better see the horses. Sandy could see them fine from her seat. She wasn't looking at the horses, anyway; she was watching Bud.

"Sandy Cameron?"

Sandy turned. A woman with a camera was standing in the aisle. She had a cute angular face with a sprinkling of freckles over a pert nose, the face framed by springy yellow curls. Petite in build—a pixie in blue jeans—she wore a blue vest with fringes over a red-and-white broad-striped shirt and buckaroo boots with heels a mile high. Perched on the back of her head was a red felt hat, like a buffalo gal might wear at an Old West show. The hat looked as if it might sail off its perch at any moment but for the red leather stampede string, cinched at the throat with a brass horseshoe-shaped clasp that kept it tethered there. She looked vaguely familiar. "Yes," Sandy said. "Who are you?"

The buffalo gal appeared not to have heard Sandy's question; instead she seemed to be giving her the once-over lightly—a woman-to-woman appraisal—leaving Sandy's question drifting slowly skyward like an abandoned balloon. Suddenly a grin spread across her face like a prairie fire. "Where's my manners? Abbe Newton," she said, an amiable Texas twang betraying a rasp usually associated with cigarettes or booze. She stretched out her hand. "I work for—"

"*Journal West Horse*," Sandy said, shaking her hand. "I thought I recognized you."

Newton grinned even more broadly, her eyes crinkling up into little crescent blue moons. "You've read it, then?"

"I've got a subscription." *Journal West Horse* was an equestrian magazine with wide circulation that catered to the serious horse lover. Abbe Newton was a respected journalist whose articles profiled celebrated horsemen and -women, trainers, horses, and events, such as the one presently at the equestrian center. Her photo accompanied each of her articles. "You here covering the show?"

"That's right," Newton said, indicated the empty seat next to Sandy. "Mind—?"

Sandy would have preferred to sit by herself, but yielded to social etiquette. "Not at all."

Newton sat down, set a black leather satchel the size of a small horse down on the cement floor in front of her feet. Through the open mouth of the satchel Sandy could see more camera equipment, a laptop computer, magazines and books. Newton clicked off a couple of shots of a big man wearing a white hat who had just taken a seat along the rail. Sandy had seen him before at other events—a rancher out of Bakersfield, no doubt looking to pick up some breeding stock.

"How'd you know who I was?" she asked Newton.

Newton pulled out the laptop, opened the lid, and turned on the machine. "I watched you in the Western Pleasure class yesterday," she said.

Sandy gave her a deprecating smile. "I haven't competed in a while."

"You did fine." A gravelly chuckle rattled in Newton's throat as she began typing. *Ticka-ticka-ticka . . .*

Sandy watched her for a moment. "What are you writing?"

"Oh, just a couple of articles. This horse. That rider. You know."

"Interesting work?"

Newton smiled. "You meet all kinds of people."

Sandy looked down at the horses.

Newton stopped typing and adjusted the telephoto lens on her camera. "There's some good-looking horseflesh down there," she said, snapping a series of photos as the judges headed toward the booth.

Sandy was once again watching Bud Nichols. He must have felt her eyes, for after a moment his wolfish grays swept up into the stands, hunting, and locked when they found Sandy's. She nodded. He looked away.

"Some fine-looking horseflesh," Newton repeated, clicking away. After each shot the camera advanced to the next frame with a whirring sound. "I like Bud Nichols's colt, but I think that chestnut has the edge on him, don't you think? Who's he belong to anyway?"

"What's that?" Sandy asked distractedly.

Newton removed a show guide from her satchel and read: "'Ideal's Gold Bar, sired by Ideal's Bar Zhan Zee.' Well, no wonder, that's one of Zee-Zee's babies."

Mike feedback clawed the air, followed by the announcer's drawl: "Ladies and gentlemen, for the yearling colt halter class, First Place goes to number one-thirty-eight. Ideal's Gold Bar."

Click—whir.

"Hard to beat Zee-Zee's bloodline," Newton said.

Sandy roused from her thoughts. "Zee-Zee? Yes, of course." His babies were consistently good-looking, consistent winners. Money in the bank.

The Second Place went to Mister Dobson's Lucky Boy, Bud

Nichols's colt. The Third and Fourth went to Lucky Boy's siblings. With these it could have gone either way, as each was a fine-looking colt. Sandy wrote the results off to chemistry. She watched Bud leave the arena. He did not look back at her.

Newton dug around in her satchel for another camera, flipped out a little viewing screen on the side panel, and aimed the lens at Sandy. "Mind if I take your picture?" she asked. "I like to keep a record of people I meet at the shows." Not waiting for Sandy's reply Newton pressed the shutter release. *Click.* "You're very pretty," she said, adjusting the lens for a second shot.

Sandy frowned.

"I mean it. You've got cheekbones to die for." *Click.* "I bet you have to chase the men away with a stick."

Suddenly Sandy heard something slithering through her mind with a vague rattling sound. She smiled cautiously. She didn't trust flattery. People used it either as a feint to divert your eyes from the point of a hidden dagger or as a gambit to put you off-balance; to extract something from you, sexually or monetarily; to gain position; or to lay a trap. It was always used as a means of control.

Click.

Newton lowered the camera, closed the view screen, and put the camera back into the satchel. "You're the police detective, aren't you? The one that was shot a couple months back."

Sandy turned her head to see what Newton was writing but the computer screen was tilted away from her view. "You couldn't have learned that from watching me ride," she said.

"I'm a reporter, Ms. Cameron," Newton responded with a quick smile. "I find things out. Read about that nasty business in the papers. You're lucky to be alive."

Ticka-ticka-ticka.

Sandy didn't believe in luck. Furthermore, she had no intention of talking about the shooting with a stranger, respected journalist or not. She'd already seen one therapist today, and that was enough, thank you very much.

Newton lifted her fingers off the keyboard, slid her eyes toward Sandy. "Mind if I ask you a couple of questions?"

"What kind of questions?" Sandy asked, her tone flattening. She felt suddenly like raising the drawbridge.

"I'm thinking of doing an article on Chet Gundry. A biography of sorts. Both his professional life as well as his personal—his relationships. What made the man tick kind of thing. You know—?"

The rattling sound in Sandy's mind was more articulate now. "I don't see how I can be of any help."

"Is there another time that would be more convenient for you? Perhaps I could buy you a drink in the clubhouse. Get out of this heat."

"No, thank you."

"You sure?"

"I'm sure." Sandy looked down at the staging area where the next class was gathering. Bud was nowhere in sight.

"I met with Chet yesterday," Newton said.

Sandy looked at her. "Oh?"

"Before he died, of course. Like I said, I'm doing an article on him—his philosophy of training horses. His life and times. He talked about you. A lot."

"We were friends," Sandy said guardedly.

Newton smiled as she typed. "I got the idea from him that he had carried the torch for you."

"Without a flame." Sandy immediately regretted saying it.

Newton lifted her fingers off the keyboard, a puzzled look on her face. "Funny. It's my understanding that you dated steadily for about six months." She shrugged her shoulders. "I don't know, but that seems a little more serious than just friends."

"We were friends," Sandy said evenly. She looked back down at the horses.

Newton typed something. "All right. Friends. I guess Chet saw it a little differently, is all. How would you characterize the man? What was he like?"

"He loved horses," Sandy said, not looking at her. "That's all I care to tell you about Chet. Now if you don't mind, I'd really like to watch this class."

"Of course." Newton clicked off a couple shots. "Just one more thing before I go. Chet mentioned he had a story for me," she said with a cryptic edge. "One that would blow the lid off the equestrian industry."

Sandy looked at her.

Newton smiled knowingly. "Those were his exact words," she said. "Don't ask me what he meant by them. He was almighty tight-lipped about it. Said he wanted to talk to you first—get your advice on a matter before letting the horse out of the barn."

"No idea what it was about?"

Newton shook her head, her yellow curls bouncing like weighted coils. "You can imagine my interest."

Sandy thought about it a moment, figured it might have had to do with the federal offense business. That was an assumption, of course. Chet never actually said what he wanted to talk to her about, only that it was important. Something that required her police expertise. Knowing Chet, he might've wanted her to fix a traffic ticket. "And you think I know what it is?"

Newton shrugged. "He said he was going to talk to you about it. I figured maybe—"

"Sorry. Never did."

"Hmm." Newton took a couple more photos. "That gray has a nice chest—little thick in the neck, though. A bit bulldoggy, don't you think?"

Sandy made no comment.

"Got a lot of foundation quarter in him, looks like."

The judges, finished with their observations, met in front of the horses, compared notes, then headed back toward the announcer's booth.

Newton took a deep breath, pushed her hat back even farther on her head. "Sure has me stumped," she sighed. "Something that might blow the lid off the equestrian industry. No ideas, huh?"

Sandy shook her head.

"What if you were to guess?"

"Look, Ms. Newton—"

"Abbe."

"All right, Abbe. Whatever Chet meant, he never said a word. Not to me."

Newton made a clicking noise with her tongue and teeth. "I guess we'll never know now that he's dead."

Sandy frowned.

Newton's face was no longer cute. The once friendly blue crescents were narrowed beneath a hooded probing glare. The springy little-girl curls no doubt covered scales; the rosy-lipped smile, curling subtly at the corners, hid a set of fangs. It was really the face of a rattlesnake.

"That's right. Because he's dead."

"I find that interesting." Newton grabbed the top of her hat, moved it back and forth over her scalp as though scratching an itch. "He took you into his trailer and he never said a word?"

Sandy recoiled slightly.

Newton bared her fangs, her pointed incisors glistening. "That's right, his trailer. Wanna see a picture I took?"

Without waiting for a reply, Newton clicked some buttons on her laptop, then turned the computer toward Sandy. A full-color photo filled the wide screen. It showed Chet and Sandy stepping up into his trailer, Chet holding the door open for her. "He told me he was going to talk to you about it, Ms. Cameron. Get your police advice. Don't you remember?"

The scene drifted through Sandy's mind like a phantasm. Stepping into the trailer, she had felt the immediate cooling relief of the air-conditioning. "Feels nice," she'd said.

"You know it." Chet was looking at her as he shut the door behind him—that slanting look of his. That killer look. There was something else in his eyes, though, which she couldn't quite identify. Sadness? Pain? Remorse? "You look great, by the way." He'd grinned, hiding whatever it was. "Nothing sexier than a pretty woman in chaps."

"Forget it, Chet. Doesn't work anymore." Sandy stepped over to the sofa in the pop-out wall, folded her arms across her chest with leveled eyes. Chet was wearing a multicolored striped shirt, the sleeves rolled up to the elbows, a pair of faded jeans, Olathe boots, and a sweat-lined straw Stetson pushed back off his tanned forehead. A man of rugged good looks, he reminded Sandy of the Marlboro Man. "What did you want to talk about?" she asked.

Chet put a hand to his chest in mock surprise. "You're not still mad at me because of the Sweetwater deal, are you?"

Sandy's expression did not change.

He grinned. "*Me* first? Okay," he said, checking his wristwatch. "Just a minute, though. It's time for my ten o'clock."

"Can't it wait?"

"You know it can't." Chet unbuttoned his shirt, grinning at her as he stepped into a small bathroom. "I'll be right with you," he said, rummaging around in his medical bag. "What do you think of the place?"

Sandy glanced around the trailer. "You've got the world by the tail." She picked up a *Western Horseman* that was opened on the sofa, flipped through it until she came to a full-page ad for Sorrel West Outfitters—a gorgeous blonde in western duds, making eyes at a hunky boy leading a horse. "All rancor aside, Chet, congrats on the Sorrel West deal. Should do well for you."

"Ain't complainin'."

She shook her head at the magazine ad. Neither models looked as if they'd never seen a horse before, much less ridden one. Didn't matter, the ad wasn't selling horses; it was selling sex in custom jeans. "Using you, I guess they're going for the professional appeal, huh?"

"That's right. Finally got somebody to dress me. Sure ruffled some feathers, though."

"Oh?"

Chet poked his head out of the bathroom. "You seen my insulin anywhere? Little bottle—you remember."

Sandy picked up a small bottle off the counter next to a box of Wheaties and read the label: "Insulin, 20 units per dose." It was about half-full. She handed it to him. "This it?"

"Ah, that's the baby." He poked a syringe needle into the rubber cap and drew back on the plunger. The syringe filled with clear liquid—a liquid that, injected three times daily, kept the Marlboro Man alive.

Sandy looked away as he rubbed alcohol over a spot on his stomach with a cotton ball. She flipped through the magazine, paused at an article featuring a horse clinic by Bud Nichols, then flipped the page over to a double-page spread, featuring Ideal's Bar Zahn Zee—Zee-Zee—Angelina Montoya's stallion. The left page was a full-bleed photo, Zee-Zee's perfectly shaped head turned toward the camera to reveal large expressive eyes. Truly a beautiful horse. He was standing at $3,500.

Sandy raised her eyebrows. Most show-worthy Western Pleasure stallions ranged anywhere from $1,000 a pop to $2,500. Then again, most stallions didn't have Zee-Zee's credentials. On the opposite page was a photo of Angelina, mounted on Zee-Zee, after her win at the World, two years ago. Chet was standing beside her. "You've done wonders with this horse, Chet," she said. "You ought to be proud."

Chet laughed. "Next thing you know they'll be wantin' to make a movie about me. Show the world what a real 'horse whisperer' looks like." There was an edge in his voice. There was something else in his voice, too—a note of regret, perhaps. It echoed what she'd seen earlier in his eyes.

"I mean it, Chet. You're a good trainer."

"You think?" Chet looked down at what he was doing, grunted a single note of contempt as he poised the needle over his abdomen. "Just shootin' blanks is all."

Just then Kate Bledsoe crashed into the trailer, glared at Chet's exposed stomach, then at Sandy. There were lightning bolts in her eyes.

"Twenty minutes later Chet's dead," Abbe Newton said, yanking Sandy back from her reverie.

Sandy blinked at her, her mind making a difficult transition back to the indoor arena.

Newton shrugged, a devilish smirk playing at the corners of her pursed lips. "Seems kinda peculiar to me. Chet's death," she clarified. "I'm thinkin' there might be a motive in it. You know . . . for murder."

Sandy narrowed her eyes. "Who told you he was murdered?"

More fangs. "He *was* murdered, wasn't he? Chet had info on something big. Somebody didn't want it gettin' out. Sounds like a motive to me, don't it you?"

Sandy did not respond.

"Well, it does me." Newton cocked her head to one side inquiringly, a reptile sizing up a rodent. "You sure he didn't mention anything to you?"

Sandy said nothing.

"In his trailer . . ."

Sandy adjusted her cap and stood.

". . . before he died." Newton grinned venomously.

"End of interview," Sandy said. "If you have any more questions about Chet's death, talk to the police." She turned and started to walk away.

Newton asked, "I don't suppose you ever heard of something called the Sweetwater Equestrian Estates, then?"

Sandy looked back at her sharply.

Newton raised her eyebrows. "So you *have*. What can you tell me about it? It's some real-estate development I gather."

"It's none of your business."

Newton stood, laughing, little sharp knives in her laugh. "Now, how did I know you were going to say that? I must be psychic."

"Try psychotic."

Newton's laughing mouth retracted into a small hard line; her baby blues hardening into flinty blades that cut across Sandy's face. "Is that right?" She sneered. "Well, according to a reputable source, you and Chet had an argument about it. Witness says you got pretty heated. Think that's what he wanted to talk to you about—the Sweetwater Estates development?"

Sandy stepped over the back of her seat and started out of the bleachers.

"I'll put that down as a 'No comment,'" Newton called out.

The sun was a white-hot poker, aimed at the back of Sandy's head as she headed across the dusty hardpan toward her truck.

Moments later, Newton was on her heels, shrugging her satchel onto her shoulder. "You don't like that angle, try this one," she said, huffing. "The way I hear it, you and Chet were the darlings of the industry until some pretty filly busted up your little rodeo. That's a cryin' shame. Horse tranquilizer, huh? That's cute. If it was me I'da split his skull with a tire iron."

Sandy kept walking.

Newton kept up with her, her satchel slapping against her thigh, the muffled sound of camera equipment and laptop rattling inside. "You can see how the wind might drift that way."

Sandy kept walking.

Newton let out a windy chortle. "Not many of us have a blowout with their ex-lovers a couple days before they're murdered."

Sandy wheeled angrily. "That's a lie."

Newton almost collided into her. She smiled, recoiling. Even in her high-heeled boots she only came up to Sandy's chin. It didn't make her any less dangerous. "I'm going to get to the bottom of this story, sweet pea," she said, all friendliness gone from her tone. "With or without your help. Chet Gundry was murdered and I think you're mixed up in it somehow."

Sandy stabbed a finger at her chest. "You think what you want—*sweet pea*. But if you print any of it I'll sue you for libel."

A sardonic chortle hissed in Newton's throat. "I'm always careful to print the whole truth and nothing but," she said, batting her lashes. "We've got a team of lawyers that haven't lost a libel suit yet."

Sandy glared at her a moment, then stalked away. She did not hear footsteps behind her, but she could feel the hot poker boring into her. Once reaching her truck, she looked back. Abbe Newton was still standing where Sandy had left her, satchel dumped on the ground, hat cocked back on her head, camera aimed in her direction.

Click, whir . . .

Chapter Eleven

Tom turned off the Antelope Valley Freeway at Sand Canyon. Sand Canyon was one of the more beautiful areas of Santa Clarita, a "rural-esque" strip of real estate from an older, gentler time in southern California that belied the fact that downtown LA was a mere forty-five-minute drive away. It had long been an equestrian community, quiet and remote; however, with the urban sprawl of the San Fernando Valley, people, mostly professional and movie-industry types, swept northward during the '80s and '90s into the coyote-infested canyons and valleys of Santa Clarita, swelling its population into the six figures. The homes along Sand and Iron Canyons reflected the wealth the owners brought with them. There were no streetlights there to wash out the stars at night; no subdivisions ruled with a T-square by some city planner. Instead, custom homes were set back from the oak-lined road on handsome lots, some with horses, most pushing seven-figure mortgages.

It was Sandy's neighborhood.

Tom wondered if she was at home. Wondered if he'd blown it with her earlier. Wondered if he might have handled it any better. He grunted inwardly. *There's always a better way.*

He passed a golf course on his left, then slowed to read the address on a mailbox, saw by the even numbers that the address he was seeking was on the other side of the road. He continued down the road another half mile, then, rounding a bend, he once again slowed to a crawl.

"This is it, Tommy," Dan said, indicating a series of six-inch-high black numbers mounted on a brass plaque set into a ten-foot-high stone monument on their right. Written over the plaque in brass rope was the name Fair Oaks Ranch. The monument had a twin on the opposite side of the drive, with massive black wrought-iron gates connecting them. A large letter *M* was set into each of the gates.

"I see it." Tom wheeled their vehicle into a gravel apron, pulled over to a call box on the left, and rolled down his window. He reached outside and pushed a red button on the box, hooked his arm on the window sill, and waited. No response. A warm wind blew dust across the drive in front of them. A ground squirrel scampered to the middle of the drive, rose onto its haunches and looked at the detectives, with quick jerks of its tail, then bounded back from whence it had come.

Dan laid his head back on the seat and closed his eyes. "Wake me up when it's time to go home."

Tom pushed the button a second time. Waiting, he glanced into his door mirror, noticed a red Monte Carlo with gray primer on the front left fender parked across the street behind them in a turnout shaded by a giant oak. Nothing unusual about that; Tom had seen cars parked along Sand Canyon many times before while driving to Sandy's house. Usually it was people picking up Latino day laborers, or Sunday afternoon drivers checking out the area, or drivers who were simply lost. What caught his attention now was the man behind the wheel. He was wearing a baseball cap and sunglasses, and was looking out the window at the Montoya ranch. There was something odd about the setup.

Tom was about to push the button a third time when a woman's voice came through the speaker: "May I help you?"

Tom identified himself, asked if Angelina Montoya was at home.

"She is busy right now. Maybe you come back later?"

Dan opened an eye. "Come back later. I like that."

Tom guessed by the woman's accent that she was either a Hispanic housekeeper or perhaps a relative of Angelina Montoya. The name Montoya was Spanish, after all. Tom knew that from reading

The Sun Also Rises in high school. He told the woman that he was on police business, and that he would not take up too much of Mrs. Montoya's time.

"*Policia?*"

"*Si, policia,*" Tom said. "*Donde esta Senora Montoya? Es muy importante.*"

"She is down at the barn," the woman said.

"*El establo? Gracias.*"

Dan slid a dubious look at Tom.

"What?" Tom said. "You never took Spanish in high school?"

"Not so's I'd remember any of it."

A buzzer sounded, followed by the electric whir of a motor. The massive gates swung slowly inward, Tom drove into the property. The tires made a grating sound as the detectives rolled up the smooth gravel drive on a slightly elevated grade. Two lines of towering pepper trees spread lacy withes over the drive, giving the approach the appearance of a leafy green tunnel. A three-rail white vinyl-clad wooden fence enclosed a grass field on the left, where horses were grazing. Through a clump of trees above the field Tom could see a large blue metal barn, riding arenas, round pen, corrals, and a couple outbuildings. No sign of a house just yet.

"Nice spread," Dan said, rousing. "Whaddya think a place like this goes for? Couple mill maybe?"

Tom made no comment. He was thinking about the man in the red Monte Carlo. There were no day laborers in the vicinity waiting to be hired. The man didn't appear to be a looky-loo (the car didn't fit the Sand Canyon profile—an SUV or sports car would be more fitting, one without bondo on the fender). If he was lost, he didn't appear to be looking at a map; he appeared to be casing the property. There was something definitely odd about the setup.

A pair of young horses galloped up to the fence and watched curiously as the detectives drove past. "I saw a horse in my neighborhood, once," Dan said. "No one riding it. Just the horse, bolting down the street. Big as life."

Tom looked at him.

Dan nodded sharply. "Craziest thing you ever saw. Minute later, here comes this jockey runnin' up the street, waving his arms—eyes big as moon pies. 'You seen my horse?' he shouts. 'Maybe I have, and maybe I haven't,' I says. 'What's his name?' 'Hoof-hearted,' says the jockey. 'Not me,' I says. 'Maybe it was the horse.'" Dan let out a belly laugh.

Tom shook his head, followed the drive up and around a bend where it opened into a wide gravel area, the barn and equestrian complex to the left. Situated on a gentle rise, about fifty yards beyond the barn, was the house. A large French Provincial job made of river rock, red used brick, and gray siding, maybe six or seven thousand square feet, stood amid stands of hardwood and evergreens. Monster oaks bracketed the house and an expanse of cross-cut lawn. Three gardeners were working the grounds with mowers and blowers.

Dan blew out a long low whistle. "Something tells me we're not in Burbank anymore, Toto."

Tom turned into the barn complex, where there was a bustle of activity. A Latino rider was working a horse in an open arena to the right. Latino stable boys raked corrals that ran off either side of the barn. One putted toward them on a John Deere Gator, hauling a load of manure. Tom waved him to stop. "*Donde esta* Angelina Montoya?" he asked.

The man slowed his vehicle to a stop. He had a wide friendly face that boasted a couple of silver teeth. "Angelina? *Si. Ella esta adentro con el caballo.*" He swung around in his seat, pointed toward the open bay doors of the barn. "*En el establo.*"

Tom looked, saw some vague outlines of people at the far end of the barn. "*Gracias,*" he said.

"*De nada.*" The man tipped his hat, flashed a silvery smile, and putted away.

Dan eyed the mounded load suspiciously as it rolled past his window, fanned his nose. "I hate horses."

Parked in front of the barn was a blue pickup truck with white compartments built in back. It looked like a veterinary truck. Tom wheeled their sedan next to it and parked.

•

The barn was the size of a light-aircraft hangar, maybe three hundred feet in length, two hundred fifty feet wide, with a vented ceiling rising maybe forty feet off the deck. Birds flew back and forth among the steel rafters. A sand-filled arena took up most of the middle section of the barn. A cement walk went around the arena perimeter, with a gooseneck pipe rail separating walking and riding areas. Stalls went around most of the perimeter; horses, inside the stalls, stamping their hooves. There must have been thirty or more horses. Past the arena at the far end of the barn was a paved area, with a large benchlike apparatus that stood in the middle. A woman and a man were huddled beside it, their backs to Tom and Dan. The detectives made their way along the cement walk toward them.

A brown-skinned boy raking fresh sawdust in one of the stalls looked up from his work as they passed, nodded at them.

Dan, looking at the thick sawdust bed in the stall, shook his head. "Horses got it better than I do."

"We can see if they got any openings for you."

The detectives stopped at the far end of the barn, just before the pipe rail curved around to the left to form the back end of the indoor arena. There were rooms that went along the back wall; tack rooms, by the look of them. A wash area, no doubt used to hose off horses, was to the right of these, next to the barn's rear entrance. Through the open doors, Tom could see horses walking in circles around a hot walker.

Dan was looking at something else, his eyes wide. "What is that thing?" he whispered, gesturing at the raised bench that held the man and woman's interest.

The thing that had Dan puzzled was a Twinkie-shaped padded leather bench about five feet long that was supported by a single metal pedestal. One end of the bench was slightly elevated, maybe five feet off the ground; the other end about six inches lower. It reminded Tom of a gymnast's vaulting bench.

The woman (Angelina Montoya, Tom presumed) and man were applying something to the lower end. Tom figured he'd wait until they were finished with their business before questioning her.

"They gonna ride it or what?" Dan whispered.

Just then the woman turned, gestured to a small wiry brown-skinned man standing by one of the stalls to the right of the detectives. "Okay, Miguel, we're ready," she said, her voice slightly echoey in the vast openness of the barn.

Miguel slid open the stall door and went inside.

It was then that the woman's eyes met Tom's. She stared at him for a long moment, frowned, then looked over at Dan, no doubt wondering who they were. She looked away as Miguel came out of the stall leading a horse. The horse, a dark brown muscled brute with four white socks and an S-shaped blaze on his forehead, emitted a low throaty whicker as he headed toward the giant Twinkie, his hooves flinting against the cement, his heavy, powerful shoulders and flanks rippling. He seemed very excited. Horses in other stalls snorted and stamped their feet. It all sounded very primal.

Miguel led the horse to the slightly lower end of the padded bench. As soon as he arrived there, the horse, without so much as a howdy do, dropped his nine iron, lifted himself up onto its hind legs and mounted the thing, his front legs straddling the elevated end.

Dan's eyes bugged. "You *see* that, Tommy?"

"Breeding dummy," Tom said. Sandy had talked about them, but this was the first time he'd ever actually seen one. "They're collecting semen."

Dan watched the stallion; eyes wild, neck arched, his flanks shuddering—the stallion's, not Dan's. "Breeding dummy, huh? Which one's the dummy?"

It was over in a flash. The horse dismounted, shuddered and shook his mane, no doubt thinking he'd made a fine conquest. Miguel held out his hand to steady him.

The other man removed a tube from the business end of the dummy, the tube maybe two feet in length, four inches wide, made out of some kind of latex material by the look of it. He held it up, removed what looked like a baby bottle and inspected its contents.

The woman inclined her head toward it and asked, "How'd we do, Vern?"

"Need to get it under a 'scope."

Dan looked at Tom, his eyes screwed up into a look of disgust.

"Good," the woman said, gestured to Miguel. "Take Billy to his stall, Miguel."

When Miguel saw Tom and Dan, he nodded with a smile, led the stallion back into the stall, removed the harness, slid the door shut, and hung the harness on a brass horseshoe beneath a wooden sign with the name Zhantastic Bonanza Billy written on it.

Dan seemed to be in a state of shock.

The detectives walked over to the man and woman. Dan slowed to a stop, his eyes transfixed on the woman, thoughts of horses and breeding dummies clearly eclipsed by her beauty.

She wore blue jeans and a clingy white T-shirt that revealed a terrific figure. With shoulder-length black hair and dark blue eyes set wide in a finely chiseled face, she reminded Tom of Elizabeth Taylor in her glory days. A fair-skinned stunner who was probably not of Spanish descent. The air was charged with her presence.

"Angelina Montoya?" Tom asked.

The woman looked at him, her eyes narrowing to a flinty blue. "Who are you? Who let you in here?"

Dan was suddenly catatonic. Smitten. His mouth slightly agape, one corner of which jerked upward into a kind of idiot grin, a series of nonsense syllables bubbled in his throat.

"Someone from the house." Tom showed his badge.

Angelina Montoya glanced at it; her face flushed, then hardened. She looked at Dan. Dan was a statue, the idiot grin carved in granite. She turned to the man with her. "Let me have that sample, Vern," she said, extending her hand. "I'll get it ready for shipment."

Vern looked to be in his early fifties, wore a white straw hat, khaki trousers, and a striped shirt. He had a blotchy red face, the kind that can't hold the sun, a round lumpy head with a thin comb-over, and eyes the color of battery acid. He was built stocky, but without defined musculature, like a block of window putty. Tom guessed he was Vern Wieder, Montoya's vet, based on the information he'd gotten from Wieder's office.

"You sure?" he asked.

"I'm sure." She took the latex tube and bottle, headed toward one of the rooms. "Are you here about Chet?" she asked Tom.

"That's right, Mrs. Montoya. We have a few questions, if you don't mind."

"Of course." She looked over her shoulder at Vern. "Wait a sec. Vern, before you go, could you take a picture of that mare's front right? You know the one."

"The gray?" He nodded. "Sure thing."

"Miguel will give you a hand."

Dan, rousing from his stupor, held up his hand as the man started to leave. "You wouldn't be Vern Wieder, by any chance, would you?"

The man looked at him, his eyes a pair of pale blue question marks. "Yes. Why?"

"We have a few questions for you, too."

Vern shot a quick look at Angelina Montoya, then back at Dan with an acid squint. "About what?"

"We're investigating the death of Chet Gundry," Dan said, a detective once again. "Won't take up too much of your time."

Wieder chuckled, made a shrug with his head and shoulders. "I don't know how I can help you."

"We won't know, either, until we've had a little chat," Dan said, a deadly grin spreading over his face. It was a grin that looked as though it had been cut with a razor, the right corner of his mouth curling upward like the point of a scimitar, one designed to cut, to slash through a suspect's confidence—his alibi. Make him squirm. It appeared to be having that very effect on Wieder. "Mind if I tag along?"

Wieder appeared to shrink several inches. "Suit yourself."

The two men headed toward the front of the barn, where the blue veterinary truck was parked, Dan still wearing his killer grin. Dan loved to enlighten possible suspects with the myriad possibilities of a case.

•

Tom followed Angelina Montoya into what he'd thought to be an office, a well-lit room located next to the wash area along the back wall. The room was around sixteen by twenty. It was cool, with two air-conditioner vents in the tongue-in-groove drop ceiling. The walls and ceiling were painted white, the floor was made of large, squeaky-clean white tiles, with smaller black diamond accents, presumably to break up the monotony. A sink was set into a white tile counter that went along the right wall, cabinets went above the sink. A microscope set on the counter, along with other equipment—stainless steel trays, tool sterilizer, plastic slide container—gave the room the look of a laboratory. Angelina Montoya walked over to the sink, set the tube and bottle down on the counter, and washed her hands.

Tom glanced over the rest of the room. Two stainless-steel-faced refrigerators took up most of the wall space on the left. A desk stood against the center wall opposite the door, a window above the desk, revealing a picturesque view of a portion of the house and gardens. Charts and calendars took up the wall space on either side of the window. A giant framed photo of a stallion hung on the wall over the sink, same photo Tom had seen in *Western Horseman*—Ideal's Bar Zhan Zee. Four white socks, S blaze on his forehead, packed solid with muscles. "That the horse we just saw?" he asked.

Angelina Montoya looked, her eyes glittering with admiration. "No," she said, taking a towel and drying her hands. "We're going to have to talk as I work. I've got to make the last UPS shipment." She glanced at him quickly. "Call me Angelina. Mrs. Montoya seems so—so old."

She was certainly not old looking; she looked to be in her late twenties, early thirties. Light coming through the window ignited violet flecks in her irises. Elizabeth Taylor in *Raintree County*. "All right, Angelina." Tom watched what she was doing.

She took an eyedropper, removed a drop of semen from the bottle and touched a glass slide with it. She placed the slide under the microscope.

"Pretty amazing process," he said. "You can just ship his semen like that." Angelina looked into the eyepiece, adjusted the focus. "What'll they think of next?"

Tom glanced out through the door at the breeding dummy. "Horse doesn't know the difference?"

She did not respond. Tom guessed she was busy watching little squiggly things playing rugby in the microscope. He waited.

She raised her head from the eyepiece, looked at Tom. "No, the horse doesn't know the difference. We take a sample from one of our mares in season and swab it around the AV."

"AV?"

"Artificial vagina." She held up the latex tube.

Tom raised his eyebrows.

Angelina laughed, walked over and opened a refrigerator, placed the baby bottle inside. "I can see you've never been around stock animals much."

"Nope. How long can you keep it refrigerated?"

"If we freeze it—indefinitely. We usually ship it overnight, though. Client's vet on the other end will thaw out the sample, then artificially inseminate the mare."

"Kind of takes all the fun out of it, don't you think?"

She looked at him.

"For the horse, I mean," Tom clarified. "Seems kind of clinical."

Angelina made a face, a scrunched-up face that still held its beauty. "Oh, I'm sure there will be a candlelight dinner before the big event," she said.

Tom allowed a smile.

She closed the refrigerator, walked back over to the sink, turned on a sink spigot and once again washed her hands. She held them there, water running over them, her expression growing serious. "What do you want to know about Chet?"

"What can you tell me?" Tom removed his notebook from his blazer pocket.

"He was a good man," she said, finally turning off the spigot. She shook off the excess water from her hands, reached for a towel on a wall peg and wiped them. "We're going to miss him around here."

"He was your trainer?"

"Yes. He was the best in the business. The best," she repeated, pausing reflectively. She hung up the towel on the peg, straightened its corners.

"How long did he work for you?"

She lowered her head, pursed her lips in thought. "Let me see. I guess he started training my horses about three years ago." She nodded, looked at Tom. "That's right. That was pretty much off and on, though. It wasn't until the last couple years that he trained them exclusively."

"You say off and on . . . you use other trainers before?"

"Oh, sure. Bud Nichols."

Tom frowned. "Bud Nichols?"

Angelina cocked her head. "Something wrong?"

"I don't know. Chet Gundry was murdered."

She blinked at him a couple of times, searched his eyes for

something—for a hint of a joke maybe. A smile groped around her pretty lips but didn't find a handhold. "Murdered? Are you sure?"

Tom nodded.

"How horrible." She leaned back against the counter, put her hand on the countertop to steady herself, and stared. She frowned at Tom. "You think Bud had something to do with it?"

"We're conducting an investigation. Right now the field is open."

Angelina Montoya scratched the base of her throat with a varnished fingernail, considering this, a puzzled look in her eyes. "I heard he had a heart attack. Something to do with his diabetes."

"That's correct. He suffered a grand mal seizure. Someone spiked his insulin with Xylazine."

The fingernail lifted off her throat. "Xylazine?"

"Horse tranquilizer," Tom said. "You wouldn't know anything about that, would you?"

She looked at him quickly, her eyes narrowing. "What do you mean?"

"We're asking the same question of everyone we talk to. Did you know that he had a heart condition?"

Her eyes rounded. "What kind of heart condition?"

"The walls of his aorta were weak. He never mentioned it to you?"

She shook her head. "No. Never. I only knew that he had diabetes." She smiled with a gentle shrug. "But pretty much everyone knew that, though. It kind of defined his life."

"It defined his death too."

She said nothing to that.

"Can you think of anyone who might've had it in for him?" Tom asked.

"No, of course not. Everyone liked Chet."

"Not quite everyone."

She blinked at him a couple of times, the glitter dimming in her eyes. "No, I suppose not," she said, again scratching her throat. "Not if you say he was murdered."

"No one comes to mind?"

"Sorry." She laughed incredulously. "I can't believe this."

"Now that you've lost your trainer, who do you have in mind to replace him?"

"Replace Chet?" She walked over to the counter, opened a cabinet door, and removed a UPS shipment box. It looked like a cold-storage container of some kind. Thermos, maybe. "I really haven't thought about it yet."

"I find that hard to believe. All these horses. It would've been my first thought."

Angelina studied him a moment. Then she dropped her eyes, scraped something off the counter tile with a fingernail, and wiped a palm over it. "I *did* think that," she admitted. "I didn't want to, but I did. It just seems so self-serving. Like a betrayal."

"It'd be a normal reaction. You've got a business to run."

"Yes, I suppose so." She glanced out the window, her eyes clouding. She stood looking out at something far beyond the house and manicured lawn. "I just can't get over it," she said quietly. "I keep wanting to pinch myself." She looked at Tom with a smile that might have been lovely but for the sadness it held.

Her eyes were moist, the light streaming in through the window firing a million highlights in her jet black hair—blues, purples, browns, even a few reds—soft shadow pools forming in the hollows of her high cheekbones. She was truly a beautiful woman. Tom wondered for a moment if there was something more between Angelina Montoya and Chet Gundry than strictly a professional relationship. "Any replacements in mind?" he repeated.

"You just don't replace Chet."

"Who, then?"

She wiped her hands, as if removing thoughts of Chet from them. "I'd like to get Bud, of course." She shook her head with a weak chuckle. "I don't think he'd come back, though."

"Why's that?"

"For one thing, he's got his own breeding line now. Good-looking horses." She shook her head at a thought. "No, Bud would never come back. We're too much rivals."

"He get his nose out of joint when Chet took over around here?"

She shrugged. "Maybe a little. He got over it. That was years ago, though." She looked at Tom with dark probing eyes. "You think Bud had something to do with it, don't you?"

"Was there an altercation between them?"

"You do. You think Bud killed Chet." She shook her head, dismissing it with a flip of her hand. "Chet and Bud were friends. They may've had differences of opinion on training techniques, but Bud would never hurt Chet. They were like brothers."

"Ever hear of Cain and Abel?"

The window light cut delicate fissures across Angelina's wrinkled forehead.

Tom said, "You mentioned they had differences in training techniques. What kind of differences?"

She shook her head slowly. "Not so much with the horses themselves but with their clients. The overall approach. Bud tends to belittle anyone who doesn't know as much as he does. Chet—" She paused, looked down at her hands, as if they held her thoughts. "Chet was more personal."

Watching her, Tom felt pretty sure that Gundry's loss was more than professional. "With his fillies, you mean."

Her eyes flickered, then sharpened. "I don't know what you mean by that, Detective. I said he was more personal, that's all."

"Were you and he involved? On more than a professional level, I mean."

Her cheeks colored red. Then her eyes flashed angrily. She sat down at the desk with her back to Tom, removed some papers from a drawer, and began writing on them. "I resent that, Detective. I'm a married woman."

Tom walked over to the desk. "So was my wife before she left me."

Angelina set the pen down, laid her hands flat on the desktop, palms down, stared at the desk for a moment, then looked up at him as though she were a grade school teacher about to correct him on a botched homework assignment. "Chet and I were friends," she said with an indignant edge. "That's all. He loved horses. We got along great. I'm going to miss him."

Tom saw her face change, her eyes suffuse with tears.

"Damn," she said, and reached for a tissue. "I don't know what I'm going to do."

No teacher ever broke down in front of Tom before. He gave her a moment. "Any other trainers beside Bud Nichols come to mind?"

She looked at him over the tissue.

"It could be important," Tom said.

She shrugged, blew her nose, then cleared the emotion from her throat. "I don't know . . . maybe Kate."

"Kate Bledsoe?"

She nodded, picked up the pen, looked at the tip briefly, and resumed writing. "We've discussed it in the past. She really wants to be a trainer full-time. I think she'd like to move on from her job."

"What's she do?"

"She's an RN."

"A nurse, huh?"

"Works at the Bethesda Medical Group. The one in Valencia." She gave her head a little shake. "She's quite devoted to her work," she added. Tom noticed a change in her tone; an edge of something that made him suspect another meaning. "I think she'd prefer working with horses, though." She smiled. "I can relate to that."

"How long ago did Kate discuss working for you?"

She made a circular motion with the pen. "We were just talking about it—couple weeks ago maybe."

"Oh? Can you remember what she said?"

"It was nothing big. Just casual talk. If Chet ever decides to go it on his own to let her know kind of thing." She ran the tip of the pen down an address book, stopped, then wrote the address down on a shipping label. Tom saw the address was some ranch up in Oregon. "Kate does well with Zee-Zee's babies. She's got one of her own now, you know."

Tom knew. He also knew that Kate had made no mention of wanting to work for Angelina Montoya.

"You were at the center yesterday morning?"

She nodded. "All day. I was in three events. Watched a couple others—see how my babies did." She smiled weakly. "Breeding brings out the maternal instinct, I suppose. Makes up for not having children."

Tom didn't want to go there; the loss of his unborn son two months ago was still painful to him. "Where were you around ten-fifteen?"

"Routine question?" she asked, forcing a smile. She frowned in thought. "Ten-fifteen. I think I was in a Western Pleasure class. Yes, I was. That's when he died, isn't it? I heard some sirens."

"What's going on here?" a man's voice growled.

Tom turned, felt the man standing in the doorway before he actually saw him. He was a big bruiser, maybe six-one, and probably weighed in at two-fifty. He was dark skinned, with short black hair slicked back to reveal a wide forehead, dark, wide-set black eyes, and a belligerent jaw and face that was horribly pockmarked. Dressed in a Ralph Lauren shirt, white slacks, and loafers, with a gold wristwatch and chain around his thick hairy neck, he didn't fit the image of a rancher; he looked more like a drug lord. There was something vaguely familiar about the man, but Tom couldn't think why.

Angelina perked when she saw him, stood and went over to his side. They didn't fit—at least to Tom's way of reckoning. She was beautiful; he looked like someone beat him with an ugly stick. The guy either had a great personality or was loaded. "Julian," she said, a giggle of surprise in her voice. "What are you doing here?"

Julian's eyes never left Tom's. "Can't find my car keys." He spoke with a heavy Spanish accent. "Who's this guy?"

Tom felt a prickling of testosterone in the room. "Detective Rigby," he said, feeling an immediate visceral dislike for the man. He was sure the feeling was mutual. "And you are? . . ."

"The one who pays the bills around here."

Angelina laughed, a nervous, bubbly laugh diffusing hostility. Tom got the feeling she'd done it before. "This is my husband, Julian," she said. "Detective Rigby is investigating Chet's death."

"Oh?" Montoya could have cared less, apparently. His small black eyes flicked down at his wife. "You seen my keys?"

"Yes, darling. I saw them earlier, right where you always leave them."

Montoya looked back at Tom with a flat dead stare. "Gundry, huh?"

"That's right. Someone murdered him."

"No kidding?"

Tom wasn't sure if he'd caught a flicker in Montoya's eyes. He was sure, however, that the 'lost keys' were just a ploy, that he'd really come down to check out the goings-on—a bull sniffing out potential challengers. "That's right," Tom said. "Any ideas on who might've done it?"

Montoya's eyes widened slightly. "You asking *me*?"

Angelina giggled, patted her husband's thick girth. "My husband's interests and mine are worlds apart," she said, covering for him. "I'm afraid he wouldn't be of much help. He doesn't know many of my horse friends. He supports my habit, though, don't you, darling?"

Montoya grunted. "Kitchen counter, you say?"

"In the little dish by the sink. Going to the hospital?"

"Uh-huh." Montoya pecked his wife on the forehead—*good puppy*—cast a warning glance at Tom before exiting the room. The room cleared of hostility.

Angelina stood in the doorway, watching Montoya making his way out of the barn, the look in her eyes giving away nothing of her feelings toward the man. There was nothing in them. They were neither hot nor cold. She could love him dearly, or hate him truly. Either way or down the middle. She feared him, though; that was certain.

Had to be loaded, Tom guessed.

Angelina turned deliberately, put her hands on her hips and looked Tom square in the eyes, then breezed her midnight blues over him as if she'd just now seen him for the first time. There was either something new in her eyes, or she was a different person, the other one having left with her husband. "Are you by any chance *Tom* Rigby?" she asked in a playful, scolding tone. "Sandy Cameron's Tom?"

"Guilty as charged." *At last tally,* he didn't say.

Angelina smiled, the violet flecks in her irises once again charged with glittering light. "I've heard all about you. Sandy has good taste."

Tom smiled politely. "Your husband's got to be doing pretty well to float this boat," he said, changing the subject. "What does he do?"

She eyeballed Tom a nanosecond longer, then crossed the room and once again sat down at the desk. She picked up the phone and pushed a series of numbers. "I'm so glad Sandy's feeling better," she said. "We were worried about her for a while there. I can't imagine. She should get out of that line of work."

"Your husband? . . ." Tom repeated.

She spoke into the receiver. "This is Angelina Montoya. I need a pickup. Semen shipment. Okay, I'll hold." She turned, looked at Tom inquiringly. "Julian? He's a surgeon."

"A surgeon?"

"You know—the kind that pokes around inside people." She smiled.

"Is that so?" *With a cattle prod, no doubt.* "Where does he work?"

"At the Bethesda Medical Group."

Tom frowned. "Does Kate Bledsoe work with your husband, by any chance?"

"Kate? For several years now," she said, her eyes probing him. "She's really quite good at what she does. Why do you ask?"

Once again Tom noticed a slight change in her tone, her smile masking an edge of bitterness perhaps. "Routine question."

Angelina held up her hand abruptly and spoke into the receiver. "Yes, I have a semen shipment ready for pickup."

Tom looked out of the door in time to see a gold convertible Mercedes 500 SL driving past the bay doors on the far side of the barn, past Dan and Vern Wieder. Montoya was at the wheel looking in his direction, and for a fleeting moment, even across the distance of the barn, Tom could read the hostility in his eyes.

●

Wieder's hands trembled like an addict's as he fiddled about in one of his truck's compartments. He seemed about ready to wet his pants. Dan had done a good job softening him up. Miguel was holding a gray horse to one side of the truck. Tom figured it was the mare with the foot concerns.

Jerking a thumb at the vet, Dan cocked an eye at Tom, and said, "Man here doesn't remember any conversation about federal offenses, Tommy."

"No?"

Wieder shook his head. "No, I told you."

"We have a witness that heard otherwise," Tom said.

Wieder dropped something, looked quickly at Tom. "Who?"

"Someone very reliable."

Wieder's red face reddened even more. "What'd she tell—?" The word caught in his throat.

"*She?* What makes you think the witness is a she?" Tom asked.

Beads of sweat suddenly glistened on Wieder's knobby pate. His half glasses slipped down his nose. He reminded Tom of a ripe casaba melon, freshly spritzed by the grocer to make it more appealing. It didn't help. "I don't know," Wieder said. "It just came out of my mouth." He pushed his glasses back up his nose and rummaged through a compartment.

"If you know something, Mr. Wieder, it would be best to come clean with it."

"I don't know what you're talking about," Wieder said, pulled out a small clear bottle from a compartment and set it down on a pull-out tray next to a bottle of alcohol. "I don't know about any federal offense nonsense."

"You weren't having a friendly chat with Gundry yesterday morning?"

Wieder flushed. "No."

"You're sure?"

Wieder picked up a syringe, dropped it, picked it up again. "I told you I didn't have any arguments with Chet."

"No, you didn't, Mr. Wieder. You told that to Detective Cameron."

Wieder's eyes froze. "Well, I'm telling you now," he said, lowering his chin an inch to view Tom over the tops of his glasses. "I didn't have an argument with Chet." He stuck a needle into the stopper and drew back on the plunger. "Now, if you don't mind. I'm busy."

Dan drifted over to the truck, hooked an elbow on one of the compartments. He trotted out the grin. "Man says he's too busy to answer a couple simple questions. Maybe a trip to the station would loosen his tongue."

Wieder looked sharply at him. His hands were shaking something fierce now.

"You seem a bit nervous," Dan said. "You drink a lot of coffee?"

Wieder cleared his throat and stepped over to the horse.

"You gotta watch that coffee," Dan said. "Give you gas from here to Sunday. They teach you that in vet school?"

Wieder swiped alcohol over the horse's shoulder with a wad of gauze.

Miguel was staring down at the lead rope in his hand.

Tom watched what Wieder was doing. "What's that you're giving the horse?"

Without looking at him, Wieder jabbed the syringe into a muscle, pushed in the plunger, and said, "Rompun." He removed the syringe, the horse shuddered.

"That another name for Xylazine?"

"That's right."

Tom shrugged. "That's what was used to kill Chet Gundry."

Wieder lowered the syringe and blinked; his pale blue eyes draining of all color. "Chet was m-murdered?"

"That's right. Killer used Xylazine. Same stuff you've got in your hands."

Wieder looked down at the bottle, fumbled and almost dropped it when the implication struck home. "I heard it was his diabetes," he said, the corner of his left eye twitching a rumba.

"You catch a bit of dust in your eye, Mr. Wieder?" Dan asked, peering closely. "Santa Anas can be murder this time of year. Just murder."

Wieder stepped quickly back to his truck, opened a compartment and dropped the Xylazine into it. Then he began picking up items and setting them down, not really looking at them but going through the motions as though he was searching for something. His mind and body appeared to be operating on separate planes. Finally he removed what looked like X-ray plates.

Dan cozied up to him. "You don't happen to know who killed Chet Gundry, do you? It'd save the taxpayers a lot of money if you did."

Wieder's face flushed bright red, then hardened with a shudder. "If you have any more questions," he said, "make an appointment through my office. I have work to do."

Dan looked over his shoulder at Tom, his eyebrows pinched inquiringly. "Was that a no?"

Tom shrugged. "Sounded like a no to me."

Dan's is head listed to one side. "Was that a no, Mr. Wieder?"

Wieder wasn't saying. "Are you going to arrest me?" he asked.

Dan studied him for a moment, slid a quick look at Tom. Tom gave his head a little shake. Dan smiled at Wieder's ear. "Not just yet. Later maybe."

"Then if you don't mind, I'd like to take a picture of this horse's foot." Wieder gestured with the X-ray plates.

"By all means."

The detectives got into their vehicle, drove back down the long gravel drive through the pepper trees. While they were waiting for the gate to complete its inward swing, Dan said, "He knows something."

Tom looked over at him.

"I thought he was gonna drop a load in his shorts when you told him Gundry was murdered," Dan said.

Tom drove through the gates and, turning left onto Sand Canyon, noticed that the red Monte Carlo was gone.

Chapter Twelve

"We talked about his professional life mostly," Abbe Newton said, forking the hat-hair out of a thatch of yellow curls in the horizontal dresser mirror. A red cowboy hat sat on the dresser beside the mirror. "His methods of training horses, mostly. What influences shaped his techniques—blah, blah, blah. It was a boring interview."

"A livewire like Gundry?"

Newton glanced at Tom's image in the mirror, looked back at what she was doing. She shrugged. "He was distracted."

"Oh?" Tom and Dan stood at the foot of the queen-sized bed. Newton was between them and the dresser, her back to them. It was a small room, typical for modest-rate hotels: bed to the right, uninspiring floral prints hanging on the wall over it; dresser and mirror to the left, with a television to the right of the mirror. Two club chairs bracketed a table lamp in the far-right corner, the fabric covering them complementing the drapes and color scheme of the room. A desk sat beneath a large window that opened onto a view of the Golden State Freeway; the traffic, six stories below, was still sluggish after the lunch crunch. "Any ideas why he might've been distracted?" Tom asked.

"Wasn't in the mood for talking, I guess." Newton forked her hair some more, checked her image, first one side and then the other. With freckles splattered over her face and a thin, compact body with just enough adipose tissue to make it interesting, she leaned more toward cute than pretty. She touched the glossy red lipstick at the corner of her mouth with a bare ring finger, correcting a smudge, then turned around and faced the detectives, crossing her arms over her chest. "Not with *me*, at any rate."

"Meaning—?"

She gave them a quick smile, looked from Tom to Dan, then back to Tom, a sharpness in her eyes that could cut through steel. Tom guessed she was assessing which one of them was the soft touch—good-cop, bad-cop kind of thing. Which one to put the moves on. "Can I expect a little *quid pro quo* here?" she asked Dan. Good choice. "I give you a little information, you let me know how the investigation is proceeding."

"That's not how it works," Tom said.

She furrowed her brow. "Come on, Dectective, you've got snitches. You grease their palms, they give you tips. Chet Gundry's death is big news. I just want a little information—nothing that would impede your investigation."

"What have you got to sell?"

A shade of a smile softened the corners of her hard red mouth. She went over to a small refrigerator, enclosed in the cabinets below the television, and opened it. "Nothing much," she said with a wink in her tone. "Just something that would blow the lid off the equestrian industry."

The detectives exchanged glances.

"Can I fix you fellas something?"

"No, thanks," Tom said.

Dan was eyeballing the complimentary bowl of fruit on the dresser.

"Help yourself, sweet pea," she said, reaching for a 7Up. "*Mi casa es su casa.*" She dumped a handful of ice into a plastic cup, closed the refrigerator door, then slid a roguish look at Tom as she crossed the room to one of the club chairs in the corner. She plopped down in it, cocked a leg over an armrest, and grinned. She'd set the hook pretty well and knew it.

Tom said, "All right, Ms. Newton, you've got our attention. Give."

"What do I get in return?" she asked, bouncing a booted foot up and down.

"We check out your lead. If it's good, we'll work something out. Now what's this about?"

Newton popped open the 7Up can and poured some of its contents into the cup. The ice popped and cracked. "He never told me," she said.

Tom and Dan exchanged dubious glances. Tom said, "Gundry's got a bomb in his pocket, tells you he's got it, but won't let you see it?"

"That's right. He said he had to clear it with a lady detective first," she said, eyeing Tom over her plastic cup as she took a sip. "Sandy Cameron," she added. "Name mean anything to you? She's with L.A. Sheriff's."

Tom said nothing.

Newton said, "According to her, he never told her."

"You spoke to her about it?"

"Not more'n an hour ago."

Newton had deep-set prowler's eyes, a bright blue intensity in them that appeared to be probing the back of his skull, looking to steal something.

Tom said, "But you don't believe her."

"She goes with him to his trailer and he doesn't tell her?" Newton held the cup between her thumb and middle finger, twirling her drink, the foot bouncing much slower. "Gimme a break," she chortled throatily.

Tom thought about his conversation with Sandy. She'd made no mention of industry-shattering bombs, only that Gundry wanted to get her advice on a police matter. It may have had nothing to do with the horse industry, of course. It may have had nothing to do with something involving a federal offense either. All of that was speculation.

Dan hiked up his trousers that had dipped a couple latitudes below the equator. "You've got nothing concrete then?"

She took another sip of her drink, slid another look at Tom over the plastic rim. Thief's eyes. She looked back at Dan. "Don't believe me?"

Dan shrugged his eyebrows. "Dead man gives you a lead and you got nothing to corroborate it."

She looked at the toe of her boot. "I got it on tape," she said.

"The interview with Gundry?"

She set her drink on the lamp stand, unhooked her leg, leaned over and, with the quick compact movements of a gymnast, opened a large black satchel beside her chair, and removed a digital palm recorder. Popping out the minitape, she held it between the tips of her fingers as though it were a cigarette. "Got it right here, sweet pea."

Dan stepped forward. "Mind if we make a copy?"

"Not a problem." As Dan reached for the tape she snapped it back into her palm with a grin. "If I can expect a little reciprocity. Reciprocity: that's a fancy word for 'You scratch my back, I'll scratch yours.'"

"Okay," Tom said. "If your information helps us break the case, you get first dibs."

"Fair enough." She handed Dan the tape, who then went over to the desk, removed an envelope, and placed the tape inside.

Tom flipped back in his notes to his meeting with Sandy. "Did Gundry mention any altercations he may've had that morning? Run-ins with people?"

"Run-ins?" She shook her head, once again leaned back in her chair, hooked her leg back over the armrest, and recommenced poking holes in the air with her toe. "Why?"

"Nothing that may've ruffled someone's feathers?"

"No. Why?"

"*After* we break the case, Ms. Newton."

She grunted, took a sip of her drink, again watching Tom over the plastic rim.

"Did Gundry mention his deal with Sorrel West Outfitters?"

"No."

"Any idea what the deal was worth?"

"I have no idea. You think it might be a motive?"

"No ideas, huh?"

She shot a look at Dan. Dan was idling about the room, one hand behind his back, a slightly amused look in his eyes, as though he was drifting through the Louvre, taking in points of interest. Tom caught him glancing into a trash can; no doubt looking for anything out of the ordinary: smoking gun, bloody knife, half-eaten candy bars.

"No ideas whatsoever," she said, looking back at Tom. "I can find out, though. Shoot—gotta be six figures or better. There was talk of television ads as well. That would definitely be a motive, wouldn't it?"

"Sorrel West is a good-sized company?"

"They've had a few financial setbacks in the past, but they seem to be on better footing now. Could be a player. You play the market, Detective?" she asked, a look in her eyes that Tom read for mischief.

Tom ignored the remark. "I hear that Bud Nichols may get the deal now."

Newton's foot froze midbounce. "Oh?"

"You didn't hear that?"

She shook her head, a flicker in her eyes that made Tom think otherwise. "I knew he was being considered for it." She recommenced kicking her foot. "If it's true, Bud deserves it. Not that Chet didn't—don't get me wrong. But I'd like to see Bud get ahead. With all he's been through."

Dan, peeling a banana he'd swiped out of the fruit bowl, ranged over to where Tom was standing. "Like what, for instance?"

She slid a look at him. "Find any clues, Detective?"

Dan took a bite of banana, grinned, then talked around the banana. "Tell us about Bud's woes."

"Bud's a bit of a hard-luck case," she said. "A few months back he lost Two For The Show to HYPP—his prize brood mare that gave birth to Mister Dobson. Mister D . . . his stallion that won the World," she clarified. "It was a major setback, as you can imagine. I hear he just lost another one, too. Another mare. Don't know if it was from HYPP, though." She shook her head. "It's a shame."

"What's HYPP?"

"Horse disease. Hyperkalemic periodic paralysis. You think Bud had something to do with Chet's death?"

Tom wrote it phonetically in his notebook.

Dan had a mouthful of banana, swallowed hard. "Horse disease, huh?"

Newton looked at him. It was clear from her scowl that she wasn't going to get an answer to her question. "Yeah, horse disease."

She lifted her leg off the armrest, brought it down swiftly, the momentum propelling her out of the club chair toward the desk, where she plopped down into the desk chair, flipped open a laptop, and pushed a button that brought the computer to life. "I wrote an article on it a few months ago." Manipulating an in-key mouse, she moved the cursor over a desktop icon, double-clicked, and waited. "Here it is," she said.

Tom and Dan bent forward and read over her shoulder.

" 'HYPP is a disease that is transmitted through the bloodline,' " she read. "Blah, blah, blah . . . 'causing muscle tremors which, in severe cases, can cause death—usually through heart attack.' Blah, blah, blah . . . 'came to light back in the seventies with Impressive'—World Champion quarter horse," she clarified to the two horse illiterates standing behind her. She scanned through the rest of it. "So on and so forth."

"May we have a copy of that?" Tom asked.

"Don't have a printer here, but I can e-mail it to you."

"We'd appreciate it," Dan said, removed a card from his wallet, and set it on her desk. "E-mail address is on the bottom."

Tom pinched his lower lip. "So the disease is transmitted through the bloodline?"

She swiveled around in her chair, hooked an elbow over the seat back and batted her lashes. "That's right, sweet pea. It's hereditary."

"Don't they have tests to screen for that kind of thing? You know, through DNA." He'd overheard Sandy talking to one of her horse buddies about it on the phone a few weeks ago. It was her horseshoer—Ozzie Something-or-other. He didn't pay much attention to their conversation. He had no interest in horses at the time. "It was required, I thought."

"Not for HYPP. DNA testing—sure. AQHA requires all breeding stock to be tested."

"Why is that?" Dan asked, tossing the banana peel into a trash receptacle beside the desk.

"To keep the riffraff from slipping into the bloodlines. Too bad they don't require it on humans." She grinned.

Tom smiled. "AQHA is—?"

"The American Quarter Horse Association."

Tom thought about it for a moment. "Feds don't have anything to do with the testing?"

"The feds?" She laughed. "What do they care about horses?

No, if you want to know if your horse has HYPP, you gotta check it out yourself."

"Someone might sell you a diseased horse and you wouldn't know it?"

"Ever hear of caveat emptor? Horse business is full of crooks. You wouldn't buy a used car without your mechanic checking it over first, would you?"

Tom frowned at a thought. "Bud Nichols is a world-class trainer—"

Newton held open a hand. "So how come he didn't have his horse checked when he bought her?"

"That's right."

"Not a whole lot was known about the disease until a few years back," she said. "Bud may not have known about it. Not many people did. You think he killed Chet, don't you?"

"This horse that died—who'd he buy it from?"

"Two For The Show? I have no idea. Not from Chet, though. I'd've heard about that." Newton looked at him speculatively. "Bud bought her five years ago, Detective. Since then he's built himself up a nice breeding stock—world contenders. It doesn't make sense."

"You said he just lost another one?"

"That's right. Another mare. Don't know if she had HYPP, though. Can't imagine Bud not checking her before he bought her. Once burned, you know."

Tom knew. He turned a page in his notebook. "Gundry look okay to you at your meeting yesterday morning?"

"He looked fine. Chet always looked fine. Here—wanna see?" She closed the HYPP file, double-clicked on another one. Moments later, the screen filled with rows of tiny photographic images.

Dan leaned forward. "You take these with a digital camera?"

"That's right. Hooked a USB line to my laptop, pushed a couple buttons and—voilà."

The images appeared to have been taken at the equestrian show—riders and horses in show gear, several crowd shots, horse and riders standing in front of a blue drape, holding ribbons and trophies.

Newton scrolled through several pages of images, stopped and clicked on one. Chet Gundry, sitting at a booth in the clubhouse, the date in the lower-right corner. Wednesday, June 10, 8:15 A.M. Two hours before the man's death. He was grinning at the camera.

"This from your meeting with him?" Tom asked.

She nodded. "Got some more." She minimized the image, double-clicked the cursor over another one, which now filled the screen. Gundry gazing out the window, a faraway expression on his face. "Looks like he's carrying the weight of the world on his shoulders, don't it?"

Tom leaned closer. *Yes, it did.*

Newton minimized it.

Dan indicated the screen. "What are these ones?"

"Those are from the day before," she said. She brought up image after image of Chet Gundry at the show—in the saddle, out of the saddle. Close-ups, medium shots. A day in the life of Chet Gundry, horse trainer. In one he was gesturing to a mounted Angelina Montoya, advising her, it appeared. In another he was surrounded by a crowd of admirers, mostly women. Chet Gundry, lady-killer. "Got any more of the morning he died?" Tom asked.

"Sure."

She brought up another page of images.

"Hold it." Tom pointed. "Can you enlarge that one?"

Newton did. The image of Sandy Cameron filled the screen. Dressed in show apparel, she was riding her horse Buster Brown in a practice arena. "She's beautiful, isn't she?" she said. "That's Sandy Cameron." Newton looked at Tom for a reaction.

Poker face.

She minimized the photo, enlarged another one that showed Sandy in front of the covered arena, talking with a man who looked familiar to Tom. Sandy, again wearing show apparel, was mounted. The man was standing with his boot up on a fence rail, his arms draped over the top one. He was wearing a blue ball cap. Something in the angle of the man's head, the cast in his eyes, gave Tom the impression he was a man with a chip on his shoulder.

"Who's that she's with?" he asked.

"Oh, you haven't met Bud? That's Bud Nichols."

Tom leaned closer, grunted. The trainer at the horse clinic. "I've seen him."

"Take a look at this one," Newton said. She enlarged a photo of Sandy stepping up into Chet Gundry's trailer, Gundry's hand touching her back.

Tom stared. Something went cold inside him.

Newton's eyes slithered toward him. "They were lovers, you know."

Tom ignored the comment, glanced down at the time and date in the lower-right corner. Wednesday, June 10. Twenty minutes before kick-off. "Why so many of her?" he asked.

"She's a subject that interests me."

Tom looked at her.

"I have my reasons," she said, her eyes narrowing to a darker blue truculence. "What are yours?"

Tom looked back at the photo.

Newton smiled. "Suit yourself, sweet pea." She watched Tom out of the corner of her eyes. "I get the idea you think she might've had something to do with Chet's death. Am I right?"

Tom said nothing.

She rattled the ice in her cup. "Maybe her and Bud in it together? Some dastardly love plot?"

Dan cleared his throat. "Can you e-mail those photos to us as well?"

Newton looked at him. "The whole file?"

"We promise not to publish them. Any way you can send them with the times and dates like you got there? It would be helpful."

She raised an eyebrow, then raised a finger. "I get first dibs on the story, right?"

"Absolutely."

Tom looked at another photograph. Sandy was sitting in the bleachers of the covered arena, looking at the camera, her face taut. The photo was taken about an hour ago. Tom could see something behind her eyes—pain maybe. He wasn't sure of its source. He wasn't sure of a lot of things.

"That girl's fighting some demons," Newton said. "Maybe it's because of her getting shot—I don't know. I do know one thing, though." She waited until she had both Tom's and Dan's undivided attention. "There was something going on between her and Chet. Something she's keeping almighty close to the vest. Does the name

Sweetwater Equestrian Estates ring a bell with either of you boys?"

Tom frowned.

Dan blinked.

Newton grinned like a snake. "Thought so. They had an argument about it, two days before he died," she said. "I got it from a reliable source. Don't know what it is just yet, but I find it kind of interesting."

So did Tom.

Chapter Thirteen

Tom and Dan sat in the cool of their office listening to the Gundry interview. The tape didn't give them any new information (certainly nothing more about the life and times of Chet Gundry), but it did corroborate what Abbe Newton had already told them: namely, that he seemed distracted. At times he was unresponsive to her questions, leaving dead air sections on the tape. On these occasions Newton had to reel him in. *C'mon, sweet pea, the party's over here. . . .* It was after the last of these reel-ins that Gundry mentioned he had information that would blow the lid off the equestrian industry. Quite a revelation if it were true. Newton pressed him for an explanation but he refused, said he needed to see a lady friend of his first. A cop. Whatever Gundry knew, or thought he knew, was a matter for speculation, for there was no hint of it on the tape. However, there was a note of sadness in his voice as the interview concluded. It was as though the world—*his* world—was coming to an end.

It did.

Happy trails.

Silence flooded the room as Dan turned off the recorder. Soon the sound of voices and typing wafted in from down the hall. Someone had a radio tuned to a soft rock station, James Taylor singing "Fire and Rain." The detectives sat staring down at the tape machine, each man entertained by his own thoughts. Not much to go on.

"Well, whaddya make of that, Tommy?" Dan, sans brown coat,

wiped beads of sweat off his forehead with the back of his hand, clasped his hands behind his head, and leaned back in his chair. There were dark circles the size of manhole covers under his arms. "Something sure was eating him."

Tom did not answer.

I've seen sunny days that I thought would never end. . . .

"I'd say we've got a motive for his murder."

Tom nodded absently. Could be. If Gundry had information that would blow the lid off the equestrian industry, maybe someone didn't want it blown.

"Wonder what it could be," Dan said. "What could be so earth-shattering about a bunch of horses?"

Tom had no idea, but his mind was on other things. He was thinking about the last part of the interview, Gundry saying, "I can't tell you right now. Got to see a lady friend of mine first. A cop." There was something in the way that he'd said "lady friend" that disturbed him. It was a different tone than he used in the rest of the interview. It was a tone of familiarity, of intimacy. "Of mine." Sandy was *his* lady friend. *His* cop.

". . . *sweet dreams and flying machines in pieces on the ground . . .*"

Once again, Tom felt a marly confluence of emotions churning deep inside his chest: anger, fear, despair. He bit his lower lip, as though willing it to stop. It didn't. When he broke from his thoughts Dan was looking across the desks.

"What is it, partner?"

"Nothing. Just thinking about the interview."

"You sure?"

Tom furrowed his brow. "Knock it off, Dan."

Dan, still looking at him, started to say something, but backed away. "You asked Sandy about that business, right? What Gundry said on the tape. She never told you what it was, right?"

"No."

"Never mentioned anything about the lid being blown off the horse biz?"

"No."

Dan shook his head at the bad luck of it all. He looked at Tom once more, his electric blue eyes probing. Then he unclasped his hands, brought his chair down with a thump and sat forward. "Best get to it," he said.

Tom agreed. He was tired of competing with a dead man.

They divided up the work. Dan reached into a box on the floor, took out a sheaf of papers that he'd collected from Gundry's house, and began arranging them in columns across his desktop. Tom took the stack of color photographs they'd downloaded from Newton's digital file out of the printer tray, and began pinning them up on the bulletin board.

For the next several minutes neither detective spoke. Dan, reading through his columns, crunched loudly on beer nuts (beer nuts were grist for the brain mill, he had often said, defending his affinity for them). Tom thought beer nuts smelled like dog kibble. He shook his head, leaned back against his desk, folded his arms across his chest and looked at the wall of photos.

Tom had arranged the photos chronologically, the first photo being shot two days before Gundry's death, the last one taken before their meeting with Newton about two hours ago. There were about three hundred photographs in all, twenty to a page. The images were each about an inch and a half long by an inch and a quarter wide, like those on a photographic proof sheet, some shot vertically, others horizontally.

Several of the shots were of trainers giving clinics—Bud Nichols, Chet Gundry, a woman trainer Tom didn't recognize. There were shots of horses and riders; shots of judges; shots of spectators at various events; as well as at the death scene, the EMT vehicle and police cruisers arriving and leaving. Tom imagined that it would take a considerable amount of editing for Newton to reduce the volume of images to a handful that would add visual interest to her story. Tom had a similar task, only he was working on a different kind of story. A mystery. He hoped that somewhere in the volume of photographs he might find clues that would reveal a killer.

He scratched vaguely behind his ear. That was speculation, of course; there might not be any clues at all in the photos. Gundry's death might be unrelated to the horse industry. It might be tied to an entirely different arena. That he was killed because of something he knew was also an assumption—a good assumption, but still an assumption.

Tom started back at the top.

"Here's something," Dan said, breaking a long silence. Got an investor backing out of the deal. A doctor. Emil Rickie. Office in Palmdale."

"What's that?" Tom was squinting at a photo he'd seen in Abbe Newton's hotel room: Gundry gesturing to a mounted Angelina Montoya.

Dan did not comment further; instead he made jabbing forays at the bag of beer nuts.

"Any way we can blow these images up?" Tom asked the bulletin board.

Crunch . . . crunch . . . crunch . . .

Tom looked back. Dan's searchlight was reflecting the overhead incandescent lights as he scowled down at a letter in his hands. "Dan?"

Dan looked up, his eyebrows twin blond arches. "You say something, Tommy?"

"Any way we can blow up these images? I'm going blind."

"Sure." Dan nodded, snagged a handful of beer nuts, popped a couple into his mouth and looked down at the letter. "Just read off the little numbers over each one and I'll type it into the computer," he said, reading, crunching. His face suddenly screwed up into a scowl and he fell silent.

Tom gave him a skeptical look. "The little numbers."

"Um-hmm." *Crunch, crunch . . .*

Tom could see that Dan's gristmill was in overdrive. He leaned back over his desk, opened the top drawer, and removed a magnifying glass. He held it over the photo of a group shot that included Gundry, Angelina Montoya, Vern Wieder, and a horse (Angelina's, by the look of it). Standing in the background, looking over at them, was a black man that Tom didn't recognize.

He stood back and shook his head. There were too many photos to wrap his mind around, so he decided to narrow his search to the photos taken on the actual day of Gundry's death.

There were five pages. The first photo was taken at 7:30 that morning—Angelina Montoya exercising her horse in a practice arena; the last one taken that night—some equestrian event in the covered arena. Dozens of photos in between. Still too many.

Tom narrowed his search even further. Grabbing a red marker from a pencil cup on his desk, he put a check mark on the photos preceding Gundry's death by two hours, stood back and looked them over.

According to witnesses, Gundry's death occurred at approximately 10:15. There were twenty-eight red-checked photos chronicling who was where and when, within two hours of Gundry's death. Abbe Netwon's interview took place in the clubhouse between 7:45 and 8:15. At 8:45, Bud Nichols, Gundry, and Vern Wieder were standing next to Wieder's blue truck, a horse to one side of it (Tom figured that Newton must have either gone with Gundry to continue her interview with him or had followed him). The shot of Sandy and Gundry walking toward his trailer was taken at 9:35. At 9:55 she exited the trailer. At 10:05, Kate Bledsoe and Angelina Montoya (now dressed in show attire) were mounted and entering the covered arena. The event itself accounted for an additional six photos, two of which featured Sandy. At 10:20, five minutes after Gundry's death, Bud Nichols and Sandy Cameron were talking by the covered arena, followed by one taken two minutes later of Sandy and Angelina. Great alibi for each of them if Gundry had been offed with a gun or knife—some weapon requiring the killer's actual presence. But he wasn't. The killer might have spiked his insulin hours, even days, before he injected himself with it. That meant that everyone had an alibi, and no one had an alibi.

There were other shots of Sandy, most of which he'd already seen in Newton's hotel room. But there were a few he had not seen. These were mostly candid shots—Sandy standing, walking, sitting on her horse. It was clear, based on the percentage of photos that Newton had taken of her, that Sandy was more than just a subject of casual interest. Tom held the magnifying glass over one of her pictures; saw from her expression that something was troubling her. *Fighting demons*, as Newton had observed. Was it because of her shooting (Tom knew she was suffering from posttraumatic stress syndrome) or because of something that Gundry had told her? The photo didn't tell him.

"Here's another one," Dan said. "This one's from a lawyer."

He crumpled the empty beer nuts bag, bounced it off the rim of his trash can, where it landed on the floor next to Tom's foot.

Tom ignored it, made another sweep of the lens over the red-checked images. He kept hoping that some hidden picture might suddenly, brilliantly, leap out of the scramble of images, like in one of those 3-D pictures. None did. But then Tom always had trouble with those pictures. He chalked it up to being too literal-minded—too left-brained. Sandy, on the other hand, could spot them right away. "You're trying too hard," she'd say. "You can't see the forest for the trees. You have to back away from it a bit. Not look at one thing too long."

Tom closed his eyes, rubbed the bridge of his nose. *Back away from it, Tom. Gain some perspective.*

He opened his eyes, his mind still foraging through a forest of thoughts, and found that he was staring at a group of photos just to the right of red-checked country. The actual death scene. Gundry lay flat on his back, surrounded by a crowd of gawkers, a police cruiser arriving on the scene. There were a couple of shots show-ing Kyle Platchett examining the body, his partner holding the crowd at bay. There were two of Tom, also examining the body. Shots of the body by itself. One photo showed the aged western star Dakota Smith, Dan Bolt standing beside him like an adoring puppy. There were shots of the EMT vehicle arriving, the ME stooping to examine the body, Tom and the ME conferring.

"Whaddya know," Dan said.

Tom kept staring at the photos, his mind a riot of disjointed thoughts. He looked once again at the shot of Kyle Platchett and frowned. It just occurred to him that Abbe Newton had been in the crowd the whole time, an invisible bird behind the camera lens, darting about the scene, collecting twigs of information, chroni-cling the days, hours, and minutes before and after the death of Chet Gundry. Horse whisperer. It would make a great story.

Tom dragged a hand over his face. It was almost as if the event had been staged for that very purpose. Would somebody kill for a good story? Perhaps if there were film rights attached.

"Tommy, you gotta listen to this."

Tom broke from his thoughts. "What's that? Got something?"

Dan was excited. "A bunch of investors jumping off Gundry like fleas off a wet dog."

"Investors?"

"Investors in the Sweetwater Estates development."

Tom glanced over his shoulder.

"Looks like a limited partnership going down in flames." Dan held up a stack of papers, slapped them back on his desk, and picked up the top one. "Here's one from an investment firm. Want me to read it?"

"Sure."

Dan read: " 'Because of recent losses in the stock market, and the failure of housing starts to gain this past quarter as we had hoped, we feel that we must back away from risky speculations at this time.' " He looked at Tom. "The others say pretty much the same thing; each one backing out for one reason or another. They're all addressed to Gundry."

Tom frowned.

"That's not all, listen to this." Dan leaned over and picked up an official-looking document off the floor. "Gundry and Max Cameron formed a partnership to develop Sweetwater Estates," he said. "To pull it off they needed six million dollars for a down against a twenty-million-dollar bank loan. Cameron put up three million of his own money as collateral—bought the land, apparently, and handled the city fees. Gundry needed to raise the additional three."

"So he formed a limited partnership."

Dan nodded. "Doctors, lawyers, investment firm, and so on. Here's the kicker, though." He glanced down to the next clause in the contract. "Ever heard of a key-man insurance policy?"

"Sure. Where they insure the top dog in a company."

"Top *dogs* in this case. Chet Gundry and guess who—?"

"Max Cameron."

"You said it. The contract states that Max Cameron and Chester Gundry each take out a three-million-dollar key-man policy on the other in case of death."

Once again Tom felt a sinking feeling in his stomach. The clock ticked. A bluesy Bonnie Rait song nuzzled into the quiet of their office.

Let's give them something to talk about. . . .

Dan reached into a side drawer, pulled out a toothpick, and began working a wedged bit of beer nut from his back molars. "Know what I'm thinkin', Tommy?"

Tom had a pretty good idea.

Dan held up a letter from one of Gundry's investors. "Gundry and Cameron were partners in the Sweetwater Estates deal. Gundry forms a limited partnership to raise his half of the down. But for one reason or another each of his investors back out, leaving him holding the bag."

"Leaving Max holding the bag, you mean?"

Dan nodded. "Stands to lose his half of the down if he can't come up with the additional three mil."

Tom shook his head. "That's an assumption. Maybe he's got a back-out deal with the bank."

Dan shrugged. "Possible. Doesn't need one, though, does he? Gundry died." He tossed the toothpick at the trash can and missed. "Insurance pays Max three mil to cover his end of the down. Scratch one partner, double your profits. Pretty neat deal."

Tom said nothing.

"I'm sorry, Tommy. Like it or not you gotta admit it's a strong motive."

Tom thought about it. *Sure. Okay.* "I can't see that blowing the lid off the horse industry, though."

Dan shrugged. "No, but who says the two are connected? That other business might be a wild goose. A red herring. This might be the real deal."

Tom felt a pain between his eyes. "Okay," he said rubbing the bridge of his nose. "Assuming we're on track here, how did Max spike Gundry's insulin bottle?"

Again Dan shrugged. "They're partners. Couldn't have been a secret that Gundry was diabetic, or that he had a bum ticker. Max could've gotten hold of one of his bottles on any one of their meetings, either at his house, or at Gundry's. Gundry's calendar indicated he'd met several times with him, didn't it? Last meeting, two days before he died. None scheduled for after his death. I find that real interesting."

Tom stood, looked at the photos of Gundry where he was being interviewed by Abbe Newton. The look on his face, the slump in his posture—*like the weight of the world on his shoulders.* He looked at the one of Sandy. Their expressions were like mirror images.

"There's another possibility," Dan said. He opened his notebook and flipped back a few pages. He knit his brows together.

"What?"

Dan stared levelly at Tom.

"Go on, say it."

Dan smoothed a hand back over his scalp. "Maybe he had some help." He shrugged sheepishly. "You got to look at it from all angles, Tommy."

Tom felt a surge of anger. "You think Sandy and her dad are in it together? That they conspired to commit murder?"

Another sheepish shrug. "I'm not saying anything." Dan put both of his hands on the edge of his desk, his arms straight out, as though to keep the desk from crowding him. "This whole business stinks," he said. He rotated a hand, showing a palm. "But you got to admit it jibes with what Newton said. Sandy and Gundry having an argument, two days before his death. Arguing about the Sweetwater deal."

"Arguing's a long way from murder."

"She had motive and opportunity. Don't forget her prints are on the bottle. It raises some questions."

"You're assuming she knows about the key-man insurance."

Dan conceded the point with a shrug. "We need to ask her—ask her dad."

Tom stood, paced back and forth in front of the photos. He stopped and stared at the photo of Gundry and Sandy stepping into his trailer. Twenty minutes before his death.

"I'm probably all wet on this," Dan said.

Tom said nothing.

"She probably knew nothing about it."

Tom said nothing.

"So Newton's got a lousy wit. Who knows what the argument was about? There might not've even been an argument."

"Give Max a call," Tom said quietly. "His number's in my Rolodex." He looked back at his partner, who was still gripping the edge of his desk with both hands. "Call him," he repeated.

Dan flipped through Tom's Rolodex until he found the number. He picked up his phone and dialed, eyeing Tom.

Tom looked back at the wall. He could hear Dan talking to Mrs. Cameron on the phone. He liked Sandy's mother. He liked her father, Max, as well, believed him to be a decent man, the kind of father he wished he'd had growing up. Tom never knew his real father; he'd run off when Tom was a small boy. A succession of stepfathers proved to young Tom that marriage was a loser's game. At eighteen he joined the Marines, because he liked their commitment to excellence. He also liked their motto—*Semper Fidelis*. Always Faithful. He vowed that if he ever married, it would be for life, for richer or for poorer, in sickness or in health. A vow he took seriously when he married Carolyn, not that it made any difference. It takes two to tango. Carolyn did not tango. With that Tom joined the other losers of the world.

Then Sandy appeared like an angel of light, reached into his soul and yanked out a mess of dirty laundry, washed it, swept him clean, painted the walls and rearranged the furniture. She gave him a new lease on life and charged him nothing for it, gave him a solid hope that two people could actually build something permanent together. A sunny little dream built on trust. On a commitment to excellence. *Semper Fidelis.*

"All set, Tommy," Dan said, cradling the phone. "The wife said Max was on his way home from a job site but that he'd be happy to meet with us."

Tom continued staring at the photo of Sandy and Gundry stepping into his trailer, feeling hope once again slipping through his fingers, the dream unraveling. He felt dirty inside. He felt like a traitor.

"You sure you're okay, Tommy? I can go it alone on this one."

"Let's go." Tom grabbed his coat and car keys, headed out the door without looking back.

Chapter Fourteen

Max and Connie Cameron lived in a single-story custom home, off Iron Canyon, not far from where their daughter, Sandy, lived. The house, with steep-pitched gabled rooflines, was situated handsomely on three acres of manicured lawn, a wide red brick drive winding up from the canyon road through majestic oaks, pines, and spruce, past tennis court and gazebo, green and white in the yellow afternoon glare. Stands of eucalyptus, sycamore, live oak, and evergreens screened views of neighboring homes, with copses of hardwood and fruits trees accenting focal planes from every quarter of the house. The home, a country ranch, with Cape Cod siding and dormers, had been featured in *Architectural Digest* two years earlier when the magazine did a spread on Cameron Construction and the man behind the company, Max Cameron, a real-estate entrepreneur who had built a nationwide reputation for designing and building first-class homes and commercial properties.

Tom wheeled around a wide brick-curbed center island, its landscaping bursting with gazaneas, petunias, irises, and white birch, and parked in front of the house. He had only been here once before, two weeks earlier, the occasion being the official meeting-the-parents dinner.

"Some digs," Dan said, observing the marble fountain in the center of the island, the seven-foot-high structure bedecked with frolicking sprites filling three tiers of baths with canted pitchers.

Birds splashed in each of them, their bright-colored wings flashing in the sun. "That fountain's bigger than our pool."

Tom looked at him without expression. "You have a pool?"

"Sure, the missus has been after me to blow it up for weeks now."

The detectives got out of their vehicle, walked up a wide flight of used-brick steps through the lacy shadow of an overspreading willow. Flower and shrub grottoes separated lawn and walk, their myriad colors affording eye feasts to anyone approaching the ten-foot-high double oak doors. Once there, Tom rang the bell, heard a deep welcoming intonation of chimes within the house. He stood holding his hands behind his back.

Dan fidgeted. Wealth made him nervous.

Moments later, hearing the sound of footsteps, Tom could see the silhouette of a woman approaching from inside the house. Viewing her squat round form, vague and distorted through the beveled glass ovals set in the doors, beautifully etched with floral designs, one got a sense of a living Picasso—*Woman Approaching Front Door.*

The oval on the right filled with human form, a pair of obsidian eyes set in a brown melon-shaped face peering out through the glass at the two visitors, like a curious grouper in a seaside aquarium. The eyes frowned, as though Tom and Dan were a couple of uninvited door-to-door salesmen, then opened wide.

The door opened, revealing a thickset middle-aged Latina wearing a pair of dark brown slacks and a black short-sleeved cotton blouse, two sizes too small for her heavy arms and bosom. "*Hola, Tomas!*"

Tom smiled. "*Buenos tardes*, Margarita."

Margarita was the Cameron's live-in chief, cook, and bottle washer. She smiled, her glistening black eyes charging with humor as she made a quick appraisal of Tom, as though she'd forgotten what he looked like since his last visit. "*Que tal?*"

"*Bien,*" Tom lied. Truth be told, he was dreading what lay ahead. "We are here to see Mr. Cameron."

"*Si*, he has just got home. He is expecting you." She brushed a smudge of flour on her cheeks with the powdery heel of her left hand, stood smiling up at Tom as she wiped her hands on a towel. She smelled like a bakery.

"May we come in?"

Margarita blushed. "*O, si*. Come in, please." She smiled at Dan, albeit with less gushiness. "You too."

Dan made some kind of deferential noise in his throat, gestured for Tom to precede him.

Tom wiped his feet on the coarse-hair welcome mat and stepped inside onto the hardwood floor of the wide, high-ceilinged foyer. Dan followed, glanced down at his worn wingtips and, likewise, wiped them on the mat.

The house was built solidly—white oak window sashes, the windows double-glazed, with wide floor and crown molding and wainscoting throughout, crystal chandeliers in foyer and formal dining room, polished brass sconces and appointments—a testament to the man who built it, Max Cameron.

From somewhere inside the house the sonorous Westminster chimes of a grandfather clock sounded the half hour. The chimes rang, their echoes sounding off the high walls, adding to an ambience of wealth.

Margarita held up a stubby index finger. "Please follow me, Señor Tom."

"Okay," Tom said.

Dan followed obediently, his eyes sweeping over the Lalique crystal and Giuseppe Armani porcelains gleaming from accent shelving. Directly ahead was a black marble-and-glass island that stood in the intersection of the house, hallways and rooms radiating outward. Surmounting the island was a magnificent Pietà, the supple textures of cloth and bone and muscle so lifelike it appeared as though the figures had only moments before been frozen in alabaster. Oils and watercolors filled the walls with color and beauty, bronzes adorned tabletops and pedestals.

Just then Connie Cameron stepped up into the hallway from the sunken living room, her face brightening at the sight of Tom as she stepped toward him with her arms extended.

"Tom." She took his hand with both of hers and smiled. "So good to see you. Come in, come in. I'll take it from here, Margarita," she said, still looking at Tom.

Margarita smiled, winked at Tom as she disappeared down the hall toward the kitchen.

Connie, still holding Tom's hand, gazed up into his face as though he were the only person in the room. "How are you?"

"Fine." He nodded weakly, could not look directly into her searching eyes. He nodded at Dan. "This is my partner."

She looked at Dan, extended a hand and smiled warmly. "Of course. We talked on the phone. Dan, wasn't it? Dan Bolt?"

"Yes, ma'am."

A beautiful woman in her early sixties, Tom could see where Sandy got her looks. Dressed in pastel green slacks and hunter green-and-white striped knit shirt, she stood about five-seven with a youthful figure that could still turn heads. Her eyes, clear and alert and of the same smoky blue-gray as the Wedgwood in her china cabinet, were framed by silvery blond hair that was pulled back loosely into a ponytail. "Max is expecting you," she said, faint lines radiating out from the corners of her eyes and mouth as she smiled.

Tom, noticing that Connie was barefoot, her toenails painted a soft peach, looked back into the foyer where there were several pairs of shoes. "Should we take off our shoes?"

Connie waved a hand through the air, made a dismissive expulsion of air through her lips as she started away. "This old floor?"

Tom looked down at his feet. This old floor appeared to be made of hand-rubbed cherry, and gave one the sensation of standing on a dining room table.

"Can I fix you men something?" Connie asked leading them past the large, kitchen that was now visible through a wide arch on their left. "Coffee? Sodas? Margarita's baking Tollhouse cookies."

Dan's nostrils actually flared, his head jerking toward the scent like a bloodhound. Tom was afraid he might start drooling. "No, thanks," he said. He just wanted to get the interview over with. "We won't be here long."

She looked at him quickly, a puzzled expression creasing her brow. "You wanted to see Max about Sweetwater Estates?"

"That's right."

"Isn't it strange about Chet dying?" she said, her face clouding as if she'd just remembered that awful business. "He was murdered?"

"Looks that way."

"How horrible. And you think Sweetwater might have something to do with it?"

"We're just looking at all the possibilities," Dan said.

She looked at Dan, then back at Tom, her expression thoughtful. "I see."

Tom wasn't sure she did.

They passed a gallery of family photos—the rogue's gallery, as Sandy called it—chronicling Sandy's and her brother's lives from infancy, to adolescence, on into early adulthood. Dan lifted his chin at one of six-year-old Sandy in T-shirt and bangs, mounted on a black-and-white pony, her jubilant smile revealing a gap where her two front teeth ought to be. Tom smiled humorlessly, looked ahead to an open door on the left that opened onto Max's study.

"Here we are, gentlemen," Connie said, an ironic grin edging into her tone. "Here's Max hard at work. I'll leave you men to your business," she said, glanced thoughtfully once more at Tom, then padded back down the hallway.

As the detectives walked into the study, Tom felt as though he'd entered the inner sanctum of an outdoorsman, a retreat from all things Woman.

It was a large room, maybe twenty by twenty-five, with blond maple wainscoting going along three walls and rising upward from rich base molding. The coffered ceiling was made of tongue-in-groove maple, with darker-stained beams. A built-in gun cabinet went along the right wall, likewise of maple, with custom rifles and shotguns, each resting upon dark green felt pads, gleaming behind beveled-glass doors that had pheasants and Irish setters etched in them. Directly ahead, a double set of French doors opened onto a brick patio, beyond which lay gently sloped grounds with groupings of conifers and oak and hardwood in the background. A huge rock fireplace, festooned with muskets and fishing rods resting upon cradles of deer hooves, took up most of the wall space on the left. Bookshelves filled the wall space on either side; the hearth, fronted by brass fenders and tools, was bracketed by heavy burgundy leather chairs. Elsewhere, Terry Redlin prints of ducks and grouse hung on the walls.

Dan was slack-jawed. Tom thought he heard a whimper of excitement warbling in his throat.

Max was seated behind a red shotgun-reloading press in the far-right corner of the room, the press mounted on a workbench that was pushed against the wall to the left of the gun cabinet. He pushed back from the bench and stood. "Gentlemen."

"Mr. Cameron," Tom said, stepping toward him.

Max Cameron's eyes blazed with metallic blue intensity as he shook Tom's hand. "Please call me Max," he said. "You must excuse my appearance. I just came in from the job site."

Wearing a cotton plaid shirt and blue jeans—his work clothes, Tom imagined—he stood at least six feet two (in a pair of work boots, Tom was pleased to see), carrying two hundred pounds or better on a solid frame. A square-jawed man oozing with tanned and weathered masculinity, he looked very much at home in this world of duck decoys, guns, and stacks of hunting magazines. "How are you doing, Tom?"

"Fine." Tom nodded.

Max smiled at Dan. "I remember you from the hospital," he said, shaking his hand. "When Sandy was shot," he added, in case Dan's memory didn't go back that far.

"I remember," Dan said, and remembered to close his mouth.

Max turned to Tom with an expansive grin. "When am I going to get you out on the range? Get you off that boat for a couple hours."

Tom smiled. "When I can get a break from work."

Max's eyes clouded momentarily. "Oh, yes, nasty business, work." He gestured to the brace of leather club chairs facing a large cherrywood desk. "Have a seat, gentlemen."

Tom felt a sudden tension in the room, didn't know if he was generating it or if Max was. "That's okay," he said, noticing a picture of Sandy and her brother on the desktop beside a green-shaded Churchill lamp. Sandy, wearing cap and gown, stood beside her grinning brother, Paul, a near copy of his father.

"Well, you don't mind if I sit, do you?" Max sat down at the bench without waiting for Tom's reply. "You fellas want a beer or something?"

Dan shook his head.

"No, thanks," Tom said, his eyes sweeping over the workbench that resembled something out of *Cabela*'s. Fly-tying equipment cluttered the far end, along with an assortment of feathers, colored thread, hooks. On the shelf behind the reloading press were books on upland game hunting, custom shotguns, rifles, ballistics tables. Beneath the shelf, pushed against the wall, were cloth bags containing shot—7½, and 8. Bird shot. There were also tins of powders, plastic bags of pink and yellow wads, primers and Winchester AA hulls; the component parts of a shotgun shell.

"I figure we can talk while I work," Max said. He set a red plastic hull—a twelve gauge by the look of it—in the circular turret of the reloading machine (in line with several hulls in progressive stages of completion), placed a pink wad into one of the hulls, pushed it down with a finger to seat it, and pulled the lever, the turret advancing several hulls counterclockwise to their next station. Two plastic tubes, each about a foot and a half in length and two inches wide, were mounted atop the machine; each tube containing shot or powder; the latter with tiny red flecks mixed in it. The powder and shot in their individual tubes lowered a measure as the lever was pulled, a primer clicked into place, a completed shell ejected from the machine down a metal chute and landed in a plastic tray, attached to the edge of the bench, containing other completed shells. "I need to work to get my mind off work."

Tom smiled lamely. "Reloading, huh?" It was a dumb question.

Max grinned. "Cost of shells, you know."

Tom nodded. Eyeing a magnificent Purdey in the gun cabinet, its English walnut stock and fine engraving on the lock and double barrels gleaming, he was certain that Max didn't need to reload shells to save money. He knew that that shotgun alone would cost more than he would earn in six months.

Max emptied the completed shells from the tray onto the bench top, his expression changing as he began placing them into an empty cardboard shell box. "Now, what's this about Sweetwater Estates?"

Tom looked at him. "Just a couple questions."

Max set a new hull into the turret. "Sad about Chet, huh? Sandy said you might call."

Tom nodded, put on his game face, flipped open his notepad. "Regarding your key-man insurance," he said. "Who else besides you knew about it?"

Max looked at him, a shadow crossing his brow so that the blue in his eyes became a gunmetal gray. "Can I ask why?"

"Gundry had a limited partnership."

"It had nothing to do with them," Max said, pulling down the lever. "It was a policy that Chet and I took out on each other. Standard business practice."

"Three million dollars?"

"For a twenty-million-dollar deal—sure."

"I see. Now that Gundry is dead, what will happen to Sweetwater Estates?"

"We've got to push forward. I can't afford to back out. Got a lot of money tied up in the venture. What are you getting at, Tom? You think the key-man insurance policy is a good motive for murder?"

Tom shrugged his eyebrows. "What was your relationship with Gundry like?"

"Didn't like him much."

"Oh?"

Max shook his head.

Dan shrugged his shoulders. "Why go into business with him, then?"

Max looked at him, looked back down at his bench, and picked up another hull. "I have business dealings with many people I don't like," he said. "I can't stand my lawyer but I've used him for over thirty years."

Tom frowned.

Max grinned at him. "Trust, Tom. Trust. I can excuse a shark for being a shark, but a wolf in sheep's clothing—" He shook his head. "He better not break a trust . . . not with me." He pulled down on the handle. A completed shell tumbled into the catch tray. "No excuse for that."

"Did Gundry break a trust with you?"

Max gave Tom a long hard look. "Because he was backing out of the Sweetwater deal?"

Tom nodded.

"No. It wasn't his fault. His investors got cold feet and backed out. I'm sure you know that if you've gone through his records."

Tom said nothing.

Dan started to say something.

"You're probably wondering what I'd do if Chet had backed out for other reasons," Max said.

Dan nodded.

Max reached for another hull, inspected its sides for stress cracks, blew into the opening, and then set it into the turret. "I would have sued him for breach of contract," he said, tapping another wad into place then pulling down the lever. "A man's word is his bond. It may not hold much water in some of your big corporations or in Washington, but with me there is no other basis for a relationship. Business or friendship."

"Did you know that Gundry was a diabetic?" Tom asked.

"He and I never discussed it, but yes, I knew about it. Sandy mentioned it once. I knew about his heart condition too." He grinned. "Save you the trouble of asking me."

Tom smiled.

Max stood, removed the plastic cap off the shot tube, placed a funnel into the opening and poured number-eight shot into it from one of the cloth bags under the shelf. The powder tube was filled halfway, so he left it. "I didn't kill him, if that's what you're driving at," he said, sitting down and placing a hull into the turret. "Insurance policy or no. Chet Gundry, even with his moral failings, was a man of his word. I consider his death a loss."

"Who else knew about your key-man policy?"

"My corporation knew about it." Max pulled down on the lever, releasing another completed shell into the tray. "Why do you ask?"

"You have a board, then?"

"That's right. We met last week to discuss Chet's pulling out of the deal."

"Who else is on the board?"

Max studied Tom for a moment, reticence in his eyes. "Why?"

"Routine question." Tom could see that Max didn't believe that for a moment.

"There are three of us," Max said. "My wife is president, Sandy is vice president and treasurer. I'm chairman of the board."

The detective exchanged looks.

Max looked at each of them. "We just discussed our options. Murder wasn't one of them." He chuckled, saw that his attempt at humor wasn't well received, then stood and placed his hands on his hips. His face tightened. "Do I need to contact my lawyer, Tom?" he asked, seriously. "I may not like him but he's the best shark in Los Angeles County."

Dan slid a doubtful look at Tom, nodded at Max. "That's your right, of course."

"Who needs to contact a lawyer?"

Tom turned around.

Sandy was standing in the doorway, her eyes narrowed. "What's going on here?" she demanded. "Dad?"

Max put up his hands. "It's all right, Sandy. We were just having a little chat."

"I heard what you were 'chatting' about."

Dan cleared his throat, closed his notebook. "That's all the questions for right now, Mr. Cameron. I'll wait for you by the car," he said to Tom.

•

Tom and Sandy left Dan eyeballing the water sprites in the fountain. Making their way along the side of the house on a curving footpath of sandstone, they came to the flagstone patio and swimming pool in the rear, star jasmine climbing up the overhang supports that shaded the patio and perfuming the hot air. Just below the pool was a koi pond, sculpted into the slope. Boulders and rocks going around the pool and pond made the two seem connected. Palms, African daisies, lily of the Nile, a spectrum of colors of flowers and groundcover gave everything the look of a tropical paradise, cooling the grounds.

"Whoever said we were arguing was making up stories," Sandy said, stepping onto a wooden bridge that curved gracefully over the pond. "We had a lively discussion. People can have lively discussions without it being an argument."

"What did you discuss?"

Sandy let her fingers trail over a handrail of thick white rope that looped through wooden piles. "I wanted to know why he was pulling out of the Sweetwater deal. He told me. That was the end of the discussion."

"His investors were pulling out?"

She nodded. "The real-estate market's gone a bit flat. Once one investor got wind that another was pulling out, they fell like dominoes."

Tom made a vague gesture with his hand. "Doesn't seem to warrant even a lively discussion."

"I thought Chet was giving up too soon," she said. "I told him he should try and get other investors. It was he, after all, who found the property."

It rang true. Or maybe it rang true because Tom wanted to believe it.

"It was a beautiful piece," Sandy continued. "Rolling hills, secluded. It even had a little live stream going through it. You don't find too many of those in southern California. It was a perfect setting for custom homes and riding stables. Chet thought it'd be a great place for us to—" She looked at Tom quickly, not completing the sentence.

Tom did. *Build your dream home together.* "Develop an equestrian community?"

"That's right." She gazed at him for a moment, her once bright hazel eyes becoming a pale gray-blue, the coral and driftwood flecks around the outer irises almost invisible, then averted her eyes from his. "Don't you see? It was me. I put them together. I took Dad out there and convinced him we ought to go for it."

"He went into it with his eyes open."

"Yes, but I feel responsible. Dad sank a ton of money into the project. Got the bank to loan us the balance. Everything seemed to be going great until Chet called last week and dropped the bomb. I couldn't believe it."

Tom's gaze drifted toward a gazebo festooned with grape ivy, standing off to one corner of the swimming pool, white against the lawn. It was where he and Sandy had sat after a delicious rack of lamb supper, enjoying drinks in the cool of the evening, Sandy assuring him of her parents' approval.

"Well, you know the rest," she said, a hint of bitterness edging into her tone. "Chet was whipped."

Tom waited a moment, then: "You didn't threaten him?"

Burnished color flashed in her eyes. "Did you get that from Abbe Newton?" She didn't wait for a reply, Tom's expression must have confirmed her suspicions. "It figures," she said, shaking her head. "I don't know what it is with that woman."

"She says she got it from a reliable source."

"She didn't happen to mention who it was, did she?" Her nails flicked against a bridge piling. "It isn't true, Tom."

"You knew about the key-man insurance?"

"Of course."

"And Gundry didn't tell you what it was that might blow the lid off the equestrian industry."

"He never said that to me. Newton said it. For all I know she made it up."

"Why would she do that?"

"Ask her. She's the one with all the answers." Sandy's face hardened. She looked like a female copy of her father. "You think I'm withholding something, don't you? You think I don't want you to know about this supposed bombshell of information that Chet had."

"I didn't say that."

"Maybe not with words, but I can see it in your eyes." She gave her head a little exasperated shake. "He didn't tell me, Tom. If he meant to tell me he didn't get the chance."

"Because Kate Bledsoe interrupted you."

"That's right. It had nothing to do with Sweetwater Estates, though, I can assure you." She turned away from him, gazed down at the pond, the sun casting a wide-looped net of mesmerizing light over the surface.

Tom watched a koi holding still in the shade of a water lily and listened to the quiet gurgle of water in the rocks for several moments. He could feel Sandy standing beside him, almost hear her mind at work.

"Have you talked with Vern Wieder yet?" she asked. "He's the one hiding something."

"A couple hours ago. At Angelina Montoya's place."

Sandy looked at him.

"Quite a spread," Tom said, forcing a smile. "She was collecting semen from one of her stallions. Bonanza Billy. Good-looking horse."

She continued looking at him, her expression serious, remote, and then the hope of a smile broke the corners of her mouth, as though it had just caught up to what Tom had said. "He's gorgeous. I don't know why she doesn't show him."

"He was quite impressive," Tom said to lighten the mood. He went on to describe the process. "Dan about fainted."

Sandy glanced thoughtfully at her hands. The mention of horses seemed to lift her out of a dark mood.

"Was there anything going on between them, do you think?" Tom asked. "Between Chet and Angelina?"

She looked at him. "Not that I'm aware of. They were good friends. Why?"

Tom shook his head from side to side slowly. "Just a hunch. A tone in her voice—I don't know. I get the feeling that her marriage is a bit shaky. I thought maybe . . ."

"Julian has a roving eye," Sandy interrupted, contempt edging back into her voice.

"Kate Bledsoe?"

"What makes you say her?"

"Angelina said something that made me think she might have a little side practice going with her boss."

"I wouldn't doubt it. Why Angelina doesn't put her foot down." Sandy grunted angrily, a condemnation of all philanderers. "I hate adultery. It violates the most sacred of trusts."

There it was again, "trust." Tom got the feeling there was more in her meaning than Julian's wayward eye. Without trust there is no basis for friendship, for business or for love—certainly for intimacy. *Why don't you trust me, Tom?*

He stood gazing blankly at the pond.

Sandy leaned back against the piling, folded her arms across her chest and looked sideways at him. "So what'd old Vern have to say?" she asked, changing the subject. "Something mysterious, I'm sure."

"We asked him if he knew anything about a federal offense."

"He denied it, of course."

Tom raised his eyebrows.

Sandy shook her head. "Well, he was lying. I heard what I heard. He and Chet were arguing about it, and I don't mean they were having any lively discussion, either."

"He seemed pretty shook up when we told him Gundry was murdered with Xylazine."

"Vern gets shook up if you say boo to him." Her eyes probed Tom's eyes, his mouth, the line of his jaw. "I expect Abbe Newton's got me tried and convicted."

Tom thumbed back in his notebook, and recapped the Newton interview: Bud Nichols's two dead mares, HYPP and DNA testing, Gundry's knowledge of something apparently earth-shattering. "She thinks Gundry's death has something to do with Sweetwater Estates."

A shade crossed Sandy's eyes—a breath of wind over water—and was gone. She turned, looked across the expanse of lawn at something, far beyond the bordering trees, Tom was sure. "I didn't do this, Tom," she said quietly. "Neither did my dad. You need to talk to Vern again. He—" She started to say something, dismissed it with a deprecating wave of her hand. "Talk to Vern."

Tom stepped closer to her and took her hand. "I'm just following leads, Sandy. No one's pointing fingers."

"No?" She removed her hand, held it with her other one, still gazing at the wall of trees, as though they were whispering a dark secret to her. "I think we ought to give each other a little space, don't you?"

She looked at him tentatively, a the once-hopeful smile struggling to form on her lips but failing. "Until this thing is settled," she added. Her eyes were flat, void of expression, a far-away cast in them as though she had taken leave of her body, gone off into the trees or beyond them.

Tom could already feel a space between them, a strange drifting of emotions similar to what he felt this morning at her house. Stepping back from her, as though to emphasize it, he felt that old hollowness chilling inside his chest. "Perhaps you're right," he said, folding his notebook into his coat pocket. Not knowing what to do with his hands, he let them fall limply to his sides.

The awkward silence that followed was broken by the sharp ringing of her cell phone. It seemed a fitting end to their discussion—to other things, perhaps. *Ringg.*

Next page.

Next chapter.

"This is Sandy," she said into the receiver. "Hi, Ronnie, what's up? No, I won't let Lieutenant Ubersahl know you told me. What's up?"

Tom knew that Ronnie was a deputy dispatcher at Sandy's station. He made a weak parting gesture with his hand, started to leave, but stopped when he heard:

"Who?" Sandy's eyes blazed with intense heat. "Are you serious? Thanks for the heads-up, Ronnie," she said, looking at her watch. "Be there in fifteen minutes." She was already heading off the bridge as she clipped her cell phone back onto her waist. "There's been another murder."

Before Tom could ask who the victim was his cell phone rang.

Chapter Fifteen

Agua Dulce. 4:33 P.M., Thursday

LASO black-and-white units crowded beneath dusty green pepper trees that shaded the southern border of Borden's Peppertree Ranch, a ten-acre riding and boarding facility nestled in the red hills of Agua Dulce. A dirt road wide enough to accommodate two-way traffic ran through the peppers, and described the southernmost boundary of the ranch. A dry wash ran along one side of the road, pipe corrals on the other. In these horses stood in the sun, heads lowered, hips cocked, seemingly oblivious to the sharp shade wedges cast by corrugated shed overhangs that would give them a bit of relief from the sticky, unforgiving heat. A team of LASO criminalists worked the crime scene, bagging, tagging, and photographing the length and breadth of the area. A coroner's wagon was parked in a broad turnout fifty feet up the road along with a couple of Burbank units. Heat radiated off the ground where the body of Vern Wieder lay beside the rear wheel of his truck, half his face and head missing, the result of a shotgun blast.

"Close range," Jorge Ortega, the coroner's deputy, said. Jorge was a small Hispanic man with sad brown eyes and hands that seemed too refined, the fingers too delicately tapered to belong to a man. "You will notice the GSR around the wound," he said, his voice conveying obvious empathy for the victim. Death, to Jorge, was the Great Injustice. Odd that he would choose this line of work; hospital or hospice work seemed more fitting. Perhaps, as Sandy once speculated, he felt that by studying death's causes and effects he might somehow discover a cure for it. "There is more here . . . and here," he said, indicating powder burns around the face, neck, and upper chest.

Sandy, stooped beside the body, nodded her head as she considered the GSR pattern. A gun discharge, whether small or large caliber, will leave a gunshot residue pattern on the target (or victim), if the target is within a certain distance from the muzzle of the gun; the closer the muzzle to the target, the tighter and more concentrated the pattern. Environment is a factor: indoor, outdoor; wind, no wind. In this case the shooter appeared to have been no more than a few feet away. "No defensive wounds?" she asked, looking at the hands and arms that normally would have been raised, instinctively, by the victim to shield him from assault, if he saw it coming.

Jorge shook his head sadly. "No."

Took him by surprise. Sandy didn't know what to make of that just yet. "Time of death?"

"Rigor hasn't started yet. No indication of lividity. I'd estimate an hour or so." Jorge let out a big sigh.

Sandy looked at Wieder's face, at the pale blue left eye staring disinterestedly at the dirt, and felt a clinical dispassion toward the gore. An hour fit the time established by the kid on the dirt bike who had discovered the body and made the 911 call. Wieder was wearing a red-and-white checked short-sleeved shirt, blue jeans, and work boots. Clutched in his right hand was a hypodermic. A bottle of Xylazine, already marked by a criminalist with a spot of orange paint, was lying in the dirt, three feet to the left of the body.

She looked over at the sorrel gelding that was found tied to the rear of Wieder's truck, where he had planned, presumably, to work on him. The horse, perhaps the only witness to the crime, was now tied to an empty pipe corral away from the immediate crime area, grazing contentedly among weedy thatches of grass. Too bad it wasn't Mister Ed.

Looking back at the body, Sandy guessed that Wieder was preparing to give the horse a tranquilizer when the killer surprised and shot him. She shook her head sadly. Poor Vern. Even with all of his annoying idiosyncrasies, he was still a human being that deserved to live.

She stood upright, looked at the position of the body in relation to the pattern of pellets stopped by Wieder's truck, which was immediately behind the body. The width of the pattern indicated that the killer was probably using either a full or modified choke on his shotgun. Nasty at close range.

"No sign of a spent shell?" she asked Greta Sandoval, a thin, hard-edged, dirty-blond criminalist going over Wieder's truck.

"Nope."

"How 'bout the wad?"

"Not yet."

Sandy chewed on her upper lip. If a rifle or pistol had been used, the "rifling" inside the barrel would have left signature imprints on the bullet that would help identify the weapon used. Shotguns, however, were smooth-bored. Without lands and grooves their barrels would leave no imprints on the shot load—the tiny BBs. A spent hull would reveal a gun's unique extractor marks on the edge of the brass part, as well as the strike imprint in the primer made by the firing pin. If no hull were found, then it was important to locate as many of the remaining component parts of the shot shell as possible—shot, propellant residue, wad. With these Ballistics could at least identify the shell manufacturer, if not the gun, to help build a file of circumstantial evidence. "Keep looking," she said. "Wad's gotta be around somewhere."

Greta nodded, disappeared behind the truck.

Sandy looked up the road, lowered her Brighton sunglasses over her eyes to cut the harsh June glare reflecting off the dirt road, dirty red in the afternoon sun. The kid who had made the 911 call was sitting on his dirt bike about twenty-five yards up the road in the shade of a drooping pepper tree, a few yards off to one side of a huddle of detectives. Tom and Dan were standing in the huddle, talking with Lieutenant Ubersahl and Lieutenant Stenton. Heads nodded, hands gestured, shoes scraped over the dirt. Men in council.

Sandy had a pretty good idea that they were discussing jurisdiction. Although Wieder was killed in L.A. County, forty-five minutes from beautiful downtown Burbank, his and Chet's murders were probably connected. Any first-week cadet, despite the different MOs, could see that two men who are connected by trade, by personal history, by an argument involving a federal offense, and who are murdered within thirty hours of each other, was too great a co-incidence to suppose otherwise. The case would probably go to Burbank.

As Sandy looked at Tom, she felt a queer mixture of emotions stirring in her breast, a breath of air over cooling embers. She wondered if that was what she was doing, cooling. It felt like it.

Tom was standing a little apart from the other men, connected yet disconnected to the group. He seemed alone, lonely perhaps, his head lowered in a kind of contemplation. His dark deep-set blue eyes were shaded by his brow. She knew his recent divorce made him edgy at times, untrusting; there were hints of it in a too-quick word, a doubtful look in his eyes, a tentative reach of his hand. Yet she knew that they were defenses, walls against pain, against vulner-ability. One part of her wanted to go over and hold him, feel his strong arms around him, laugh, kiss, laugh again as they had in Catalina, with abandon, like kids let loose early from school. The other part? She wasn't sure about the other part just yet. The other part was confused.

Just then Tom, as though hearing her thoughts, looked over at her, the sun catching his eyes beneath his dark brows and setting them ablaze. Tom could set the world ablaze with those eyes if he cared to. She smiled remotely—a weak effort, she knew—then looked away. Couldn't think about Tom right now; she needed to focus on the crime scene. The crime scene gave her focus, a wall against confusion.

"Found it," Greta said.

Sandy looked.

Greta, standing in the back of Wieder's truck, held up the pink plastic wad, pinched between two gloved fingers. "Blew up here. Looks like a twelve gauge."

"Good," Sandy said.

Looking up and down the road, running north and south along the dry wash, she thought through a couple possible scenarios. There was a clear field of vision southward, shade from the trees lying across the road. The north elevation curved around the ranch complex, and was obscured by a clump of manzanita shrubs. The killer may have hidden behind them, waiting for his moment. That meant he would have had to know that Wieder was going to be here working on a horse, or perhaps had followed him to the location. From the manzanitas he would have had to walk a distance of about seventy-five yards with a shotgun. Sandy chewed on her lip some more. Pretty hard to conceal a shotgun, unless it was one with a sawed-off barrel. She looked at the pellet pattern on Wieder's truck and ruled that out; a sawed-off—especially a twelve gauge— would have left a wider spread.

Another thought occurred to her. The killer might have driven up to Wieder, parked alongside him, using his vehicle to shield them from view of the ranch behind them, then walked around to the trunk (assuming there was a trunk), popped it open, pulled out a shotgun, and given Wieder a lead facial before he had time to react, then driven off in the direction he was heading. Plenty of egress opportunity.

She looked over to where a criminalist was making plaster casts of tire tracks. "Anything, Marty?" she asked.

Marty Madsen was a thin man with a balding pate that he shaved, compensating for his hairlessness with a thin goatee. "Doubt it. Most of this is decomposed granite, packed pretty hard. Be lucky to get a partial."

"Check behind those manzanita bushes over there," she said, indicating the shrubs in her first scenario.

"You got it."

She looked down at her feet, looked at the area beside the truck where there was evidence of horse activity on the road. "Get some casts of these horseshoe tracks, as well."

Marty looked at her.

Sandy gestured to the tied gelding. "We'll need to get imprints of the horse's feet."

Marty looked over at the horse, then blinked back at Sandy as though she had suddenly sprouted a third eye in the middle of her forehead. "You want me to print the *horse?*"

"All four hooves."

"Why?"

"Same reason you're making casts of tire treads. Killer may not've used a car to get here."

"Oh." He frowned, looked back at the gelding, his Adam's apple moving up then down his throat. "What if it kicks me?"

"Kick him back." She smiled.

Sandy looked beyond the pipe corrals on her left, saw a clutch of horse barns and arenas, sycamores, cottonwoods, and ash providing shade and screening. From where she stood she could just see a sheriff's deputy questioning a rider wearing a red ball cap in one of the sand arenas. Another deputy was questioning two teenage girls who were mucking out a corral. So far, the deputies were turning up goose eggs.

Just then Deputies Mark Kelso and Mark Weinman—the Mark Twains, as they were affectionately known in the station—walked down from the stables with a woman. An eyewitness, Sandy hoped. The deputies, first to arrive on the crime scene, were both bald and pink on top, buzzed around the ears, also pink, with laser blue eyes. By the look of their arms bulging against short-sleeves, they each must have lifted their combined body weights for breakfast. "This is the owner, Sandy," Kelso, the taller of the two, said, indicating the woman. "Mary Borden."

"Did you see what happened?" Sandy asked.

Borden shook her head. "No." She looked to be in her early fifties. Wearing faded jeans, a sun-bleached olive T-shirt and scuffed boots, she had an iron gray thatch of hair that looked as though she'd combed it with a mucking rake, and a leathery hide wrapped tightly around a frame that seemed hammered out of re-bar. Glancing down at the body, at the splash of blood around the head, she clucked her tongue, and said, "Poor Vern," without the slightest hint she'd meant it. She had a smoker's rasp and smelled like stale nicotine. "What a mess."

"How long have you known him?"

As Borden's keen gray eyes lifted upward, searching back in time, her fingers idly scratched a worn spot in her shirt between her loose breasts. "He's worked on my horses forever, it seems," she said. "Maybe ten, twelve years. You lose track of time."

Sandy nodded. "Did you hear anything?

"Yes, but I thought it was a backfire. Kids—" she said, indicating the one over by Tom and Dan with the dirt bike "—ride up and down the wash. I thought it was one of them. You get so you don't pay attention."

"No one was with him?"

"Vern? Not to my knowledge. He just shows up, works on a horse or two, then leaves. He's part of the scenery around here."

"Any idea when he showed up today?"

Borden planted a sharp fist on her hip, with the other pulled on a leathery lip. "No idea," she said, lifting a forefinger off her lip. "Unless he was working on one of my horses I wouldn't know."

"Who does that gelding belong to?" she asked, indicating the sorrel.

Borden looked. "That's Julie's. Julie Livermore—you know. The actress?"

Sandy recognized the name, couldn't remember any movies or television shows she'd been in. Agua Dulce was a way station for fallen stars; close enough to Hollywood to be near the old action, the occasional retrospective film festival, but far enough away to be affordable on declining residuals.

Borden, still eying the gelding, said, "Not much of a horse to look at, but he's a neat little jumper."

"Is Julie around today?"

"Haven't seen her. Like I said, Vern just shows up and works on whatever horses. Giving shots, you know. People set it up with him ahead of time."

"Can you think of anyone who'd want to kill him?"

Borden cast a sardonic eye at the body. "Vern?" She grunted, dug a finger in her left ear. "He wasn't exactly the life of the party around here—no more'n he is now." She grinned, showing stained teeth. "But he was tolerable. No, I can't think of anyone."

Sandy watched Jorge bag Vern's left hand. *But he was tolerable.* Quite an epitaph. Vern was not well liked. Sandy, in fact, had never cared for him. Tolerable? Yes, he was tolerable. But he was also hated, perhaps feared. The killer must have had a pretty strong motive to kill Vern in broad daylight, to risk being seen by any number of witnesses.

She glanced back up at the grounds. The rider with the red cap was now loping her horse. Brown-skinned stable hands ranged about the grounds, pushing wheelbarrow loads of manure, hosing off rubber mats. "People coming and going and no one sees a thing."

Borden shrugged, hooked a flattened pack of cigarettes out of a back pocket. "It's quite busy around here, as you can see."

"Where were you about an hour ago?"

"An hour ago?" Borden shook out a bent cigarette, clicked open a dull silver Zippo and lit it. "Probably talking with the shoer," she said, blowing a cloud of smoke over their heads.

Sandy looked at her. "What shoer?"

"Oz Ramsey."

Sandy's eyes widened, made another quick sweep of the stable areas. "Ozzie's here?"

"You know Ozzie?" Borden asked, pushing her cigarette works back down into her pocket. "He left right after he finished his business. I think he was heading over to the Cottonwood Equestrian Center. Said he had some horse there with a lame foot." Borden took a heavy pull on her cigarette.

Sandy frowned. "By any chance did you see Ozzie and Vern together?"

Borden barked a harsh cackle that precipitated a coughing spell, smoke hissing through her teeth. "If I did I would've run for cover," she said, coughing, and then clearing her throat. "Those two boys don't exactly see eye to eye."

Sandy thought about Ozzie's wife sitting at home in a wheelchair, watching the sun rising and setting on a world which she could no longer touch or feel or move about in freely. She could well understand Ozzie's rancor toward the man who had been the cause of it, could understand how, in a final act of frustration and rage, he might have picked up a shotgun and blown his head off.

The sound of approaching footsteps interrupted her thoughts. Looking, she saw Lieutenants Ubersahl and Stenton striding toward her, Ubersahl's howitzer gray eyes taking in the crime scene with a truculent sweep. A square-jawed and brick-shouldered man with a Marine Corps high-and-tight, he exuded a point-me-to-the-front machismo that often rankled Sandy. She didn't like men who were always trying to prove they were men, or that they weren't women. "Wrap it up, Detective," he growled, jerked his head at Stenton. "It's Burbank's now."

"But—"

"I said wrap it up."

Sandy gestured at Wieder's body. "I know this man."

"Whatever you know, give it to Burbank."

Sandy started to object, but was cut off by a blistering look. "You're still on convalescent leave, Detective. I don't want you touching this thing, is that understood?"

Without waiting for her reply, Ubersahl, followed by Stenton, strode up the road toward his unmarked sedan that was parked behind one of the black and whites.

"He's a sweetheart today," Mark Kelso said, shaking his pink head. His nose had blistered from the sun; there were white streaks along the sides of his nose where he had not rubbed all of the sunscreen lotion into the skin.

"He's always a sweetheart," Sandy said. She looked over at Tom, who was walking over to the dirt biker.

•

The boy, clothed in bright blue-and-white body armor and motorcycle boots, sat straddling a green Kawasaki KX250, his gloved hands resting on a blue, white, and gold helmet sitting on the tank. His dark brown eyes were as busy as a ferret's, alternately eyeballing Wieder's bloody shape and Sandy's curvy one. It was a toss-up which held more of his interest. Tom guessed Sandy's. Glancing at his notes, he said, "Let's see—Jesse, was it?"

The kid swung his head at Tom. "Huh? Oh . . . right. Jesse Nolan."

According to Tom's notes Jesse was fifteen, lived about a mile down the road, and was dirt-biking up and down the wash when he discovered Wieder's body. He seemed an intelligent kid, and a good witness, "Let's have it again. Everything you saw."

Jesse frowned. "Everything?"

"In case you forgot anything."

Jesse removed a glove, raked his grimy fingers through a sweat-plastered mat of strawberry blond hair. "Like I said, I was riding my bike in the wash. I saw this guy and a horse"—he nodded in Wieder's direction—"so I slowed down. The lady there"—he pointed to the crone talking with Sandy—"said she'd call the cops if I spooked any more horses. That's when I saw the red Monte Carlo, parked up the road there." He swung his head toward the stretch of road behind Tom and Dan.

Tom hooked a thumb over his shoulder. "Behind the manzanita bushes."

"I don't know what they're called. It was those bushes," he said, pointing at the manzanitas.

Dan, who had been busy opening a Snickers wrapper, asked, "You get a look at the plates?"

Jesse shook his head. "I didn't get a number. But they were original plates. Yellow on black."

Tom had noticed the plates when he spotted the Monte Carlo parked across the street from Montoya's, but unfortunately did not get the number either. "You didn't see anybody behind the wheel?"

"I was looking at the car. You don't see many of them around. It was a '70 or '71. A '71 I think. It had square fog lights."

Tom smiled. "You know your old cars pretty good."

"I like the old muscle cars."

Tom checked his notes. "You said you saw primer on the front left fender?"

Jesse nodded. "It's the kind of car you'd wanna fix up. They didn't make too many of them, I hear."

"No, they didn't."

Jesse shrugged, picked absently at an acne scab alongside his nose. "Like I said, I headed down the wash. A little bit later I came back—"

"About a half hour you said?"

"Right. The Monte Carlo was gone by then. Then I noticed a man layin' on the ground. I thought it was kinda weird—layin' in the dirt like that. I thought maybe the horse kicked him or something."

"Then what?"

"I came over and checked it out." Jesse nodded at Wieder's body, the coroner's deputy and his assistant still poking at it like a couple of chimps. "I could see right off he was dead. His head blown off like that. I called nine-one-one right away."

"On your cell phone?"

Jesse nodded, patting his fanny pack.

Tom checked his notes. The call was made at 3:45 P.M. Allowing for a half-hour window, the time of death occurred somewhere between 3:15 and 3:45, which corroborated the deputy coroner's initial assessment of the time of death. "I want you to think hard now," he said. "Earlier, when the Monte Carlo was still here, you didn't notice anyone talking to the dead man?"

Jesse, working a nail under the scab, raised his eyebrows. "There might've been someone, but like I said, I was looking at the Monte Carlo." He frowned, looked back at the Wieder's truck. "Wait a minute—"

"Remember something?"

"Yeah, wait a minute, I think there *was* someone, now that I think about it." Jesse stared, as if replaying the scene in his mind. "Yeah, there was. I couldn't see him very well because of the truck and the horse. They were standing behind them. There were *two* of them."

The detectives exchanged glances.

"You said *him*," Dan said. "Was it a man?"

Jesse blinked, doubt in his eyes. "I guess so. I'm not sure, though."

"Tall? Short? Black? White?"

"I don't know. Like I said, I couldn't see very well. He was wearing a baseball hat and sunglasses, though. I remember that much."

"What kind of a ball cap?"

Jesse shrugged. "A ball cap—I don't know. Like the one that babe over there's wearing," he said, pointing at Sandy.

She was wearing a blue Dodgers' cap. Tom said, "That *babe's* a police officer."

Jesse continued staring at her. "She's still a babe."

Dan took a bite of candy bar. "It was blue, then? The baseball cap?"

Jesse frowned. "Yeah, I'm pretty sure it was blue. But I wasn't looking at him. I was looking at *him*—the dead guy," he said, indicating Wieder with a nod, "only because he was working on a horse, and I didn't want to spook him." He put his hands on his helmet, looked up at Tom. "Can I go now? My dad's probably wondering where I am. I was supposed to mow the lawn this morning."

Tom smiled. "You're a little late," he said, patted the kid's shoulder. "Tell him the Burbank Police detained you, and that you were a big help." He handed the kid a business card. "If you think of anything else, give us a call, okay?"

Jesse looked at the card. "Okay. Sure." He put the card inside his helmet before placing it on his head. "You think that dude in the Monte Carlo killed him?"

"Hard to say."

The kid took one last look at Wieder's body, pushed the starter on his handgrip, shrugged on his glove, lowered his visor, and took off up the road.

One of the criminalists walked up to the detectives, a thin, bald man with a ratty goatee. His nametag read: Madsen. "I hear you fellas are taking over the show. Let us know if there's anything else we can do."

Tom fanned a thumb at the manzanita bushes. "I'd like some casts made around those bushes."

Madsen looked, beads of sweat rising on his high forehead. "Already on it. We're covering those other ones, too," he said, pointing at a tangle of shrubs bordering the wash. He pulled out a gray rag and mopped his brow and the top of his shaved head. "Hotter'n blazes out here."

"Firm grasp of the obvious," Dan said after he left, then indicated the approaching coroner's deputy with a nod. "Here comes Jorge. Looks like he just lost his mother, don't he?"

Jorge stopped, looked from Tom to Dan, back to Tom, his eyes a picture of great sorrow. He reminded Tom of a Latino Emmet Kelly. "Do you detectives need to look at the body again before I take it downtown?"

"He's all yours, Jorge," Tom said.

Jorge nodded, stood gazing at the detectives with his big sad eyes as though he expected them to say something, to commiserate with him, perhaps, over humanity's great loss. They didn't. So with a deprecating smile, Jorge shrugged his little rounded shoulders, let out a big sad sigh, turned and started back toward the body, his head bowed as though he were contemplating the end of the world.

Dan shook his head slowly back and forth, crumpled up the

candy wrapper and shoved it into his coat pocket. "Old Jorge takes 'em kinda personal, don't he?"

Tom ignored him. He glanced over at the manzanita bushes, his brow pinched in thought. "I saw a red '71 Monte Carlo in front of Montoya's earlier," he said. "Parked across the street."

Dan frowned.

"Primer on the front left fender," Tom said. "There was a man behind the wheel wearing a blue cap and sunglasses."

"Well, there you go. Musta been laying for him. Follows him here and rearranges his face with a load of birdshot."

Tom looked from the manzanita bushes to where one of the criminalists was outlining Wieder's body, a distance of about seventy-five, eighty yards. A long way to be carrying a shotgun in broad daylight. He pulled on his lower lip, looked beyond the blue vet truck to the shrubbery bordering the wash. Unless of course there was a third vehicle, one the kid didn't see.

"What're you thinkin', Tommy?"

Tom shook his head. "Nothin'. Just thinking."

"Like you said, it probably has something to do with a federal case they were arguing about. Maybe something to do with that Sweetwater deal."

"We got two different MOs."

Dan shrugged. "Don't mean it's a different killer."

"No, it doesn't." Tom looked over in Sandy's direction and their eyes met briefly; rather, his eyes and her sunglasses met briefly. She smiled, but Tom could see that it was out of politeness. He sighed.

"We're going to have to compare notes, Tommy. Best get started."

Tom started toward her. "Best."

Chapter Sixteen

Shadow Hills. Evening

A rattlesnake buzzed its tail angrily, warning Tom not to take another step forward. Tom recoiled instinctively before realizing that he and the snake were separated by the glass walls of a terrarium and that he was quite safe. Even so, he stepped back. Tom hated snakes, especially rattlesnakes, especially beefy western diamondbacks about four feet long with an attitude. The rattlesnake, apparently satisfied that Tom posed no immediate threat, retreated into coils of hostile silence, its forked tongue licking the air for scent.

"Will you look at this place, Tommy," Dan said, stepping warily through the next aisle in a large room that could only be described as a miniature zoo. "Guy was a kook."

"No contest," Tom said, moving down his own aisle.

The room, occupying the rear portion of Vern Wieder's Shadow Hills home, appeared to be a converted two-car garage. It was divided into sections by aisles made of long tables, placed end to end, with additional tables going around the four outer walls. Surmounting each aisle table were glass terrariums and cages, two deep, back to back, end to end, so that walking down a given aisle animal specimens could be viewed on either side. There were reptiles, amphibians, birds, small rodents, and arachnids. Birdcages hung from the open rafters, a spectrum of colorful wings and beaks, fluttering, squawking, chirping, screeching. Scaly skins wriggled and writhed. Tiny nails clicked against glass walls. The place reeked of sawdust, urine, and fecal material. As the detectives made their way through the aisles, dark feral eyes peered at them from a hundred shadowy niches.

The aisle that Tom had entered appeared dedicated to all manner of snakes—king, gopher, red racers, snakes that rattled, snakes that constricted; others that draped from spindly tree limbs. Occupying the last terrarium was a small but rather wicked-looking Mojave green, its eyes fixed on a white mouse huddled in a corner, the mouse seemingly oblivious to any danger as it scratched behind its pink ears with fast little strokes of its hind leg.

"Wonder when was the last time they were fed," Dan said, pausing to eye a great horned owl. Bones from little animals littered the cage floor.

Tom didn't know if he meant the animals in general or the cage of little white mice, huddled in a mass of shivering, multiplying fur beside the owl's cage. The owl, membranes of translucent skin lowering and opening over fixed yellow eyes, appeared to be following the progress of Dan's bald spot as he moved past the room's single large window set into the middle wall.

Dan made a sound of disgust. He was stepping warily through a row of arachnids—spiders, tarantulas, scorpions, centipedes—as though one of these might leap out at him when his head was turned. "This place gives me the heebie-jeebies."

Tom jumped when he felt something brush against his leg. It was a cat, one of a dozen or more that seemed to have a free reign in the house. He almost kicked it.

Hal Peters walked into the room. "Called the Animal Shelter. They're sending a truck over."

"Okay," Tom said, watching the dead slow progress of a gecko, gripping its way along a branch tentatively with tiny spatulate fingers.

Peters glanced around the room, shook his head. "Some kind of a nut, huh?"

"Chopped and channeled," Dan said, heading for the door. "You coming, Tommy?"

"Sure." Before exiting, Tom took one last look at the room. A flicker of movement caught his eye. Looking toward it, he saw that the rattlesnake had taken the mouse; the mouse's dangling pink tail and hind feet protruded from the snake's grinning mouth.

•

Wieder's office was sparse in comparison to the zoo room. It contained a desk pushed against the right wall, stacks of medical books taking up much of its surface. An unframed anatomical poster of a horse was pinned onto the wall over the desk. A burgundy-colored safe, about three feet high, stood to the right of the desk, a wood carving of a horse head sitting atop it. Both were covered with layers of dust. A floor-to-ceiling bookshelf took up most of the left wall, its shelves crammed with medical and animal books. Angled in the corner was a ratty green La-Z-Boy recliner and faux brass table lamp. A spectrum of multicolored cats lounged on the recliner, some sleeping, others flicking their tails, eyeing the detectives with disinterest.

Dan sneezed. He was allergic to cat dander. Blowing his nose, he scowled. "Lousy cats." Wearing latex gloves, he pulled back the desk chair, peered warily underneath for who-knows-what-might-be-lurking-there—cats, mice, something with scales. He opted to remain standing as he opened the top drawer and began sifting through its contents.

Tom went over to the safe and tried it. Locked. "Need to get a locksmith over here," he said.

"Here's something, Tommy," Dan said, handing Tom a slip of paper with four sets of numbers written on it. "Looks like a safe combination."

Tom tried the numbers. "Eureka," he said, opening the safe door. Inside were a revolver, a Rolex watch, and a manila envelope. The revolver, a Smith and Wesson .44 magnum, was loaded, the corroded shells in the cylinder indicating that it hadn't been fired in ages. The Rolex wasn't ticking.

Tom removed the envelope, carefully pried open the metal tabs, and peered inside. Photographs. He removed them and looked at each one. "Here we go."

Dan looked up from a stack of files. "Got something?"

Tom laid the photos across the desktop.

There were four color photos, each photo taken one after the other by the look of the subject matter. In the first photo Kate Bledsoe was sitting in the aft lounge of a large cabin cruiser, wearing white shorts and a striped T-shirt. The next three photos showed her undressing. Behind the wheel was the skipper, captain's cap perched jauntily on his head as he steered out of a marina (Marina del Rey, by the look of it) his eyes alternately marking the progress of an oncoming sloop as well as the unfolding drama taking shape behind him. Tom could just make out the arrogant smile curling over the pockmarked face.

Dan blew a long low whistle. "Man's got an interesting bedside manner."

"Doesn't he, though." Tom remembered now why Julian Montoya had seemed familiar to him; he'd seen him before at the marina. His boat, a sixty-foot Chris-Craft, was moored three docks down from Tom's slip.

Tom picked up the last photo and studied it. It appeared to have been taken with a telephoto lens; neither of the subjects apparently aware that they were on *Candid Camera*. Tom wondered how Wieder came to be in possession of the photos. Two possibilities came quickly to mind: either he took them or he hired someone else to take them. "Need to ask the FETs if anyone came across a camera."

"You thinking what I'm thinking, Tommy?"

"I'm thinking that Wieder has some incriminating photos that he keeps locked in his safe."

"Last I checked blackmail was a federal offense."

"It certainly is, Ollie." Tom flipped the photo over and saw the date that it was developed printed on back. "May twenty-ninth."

"Couple weeks ago. Interesting."

"Right about the time Bledsoe made inquiries about training Angelina Montoya's horses," Tom said.

"Yep. Two weeks before Gundry kicks off. Almost like she knew there was going to be a job opening."

Tom looked at him, both men obviously on the same page.

Dan said, "Curiouser and curiouser, don't you think?" He sneezed. "Let's get out of here before I start shooting cats."

•

The detectives sat at the small, round, dull yellow Formica-topped kitchen table, with a band of corrugated aluminum going around the edge, the sun setting through a dirty bay window that afforded a dingy view of the backyard that probably hadn't seen a lawn mower in years. Wieder no doubt kept his digs au natural to attract scaly critters. The neighbors probably loved Wieder. Probably one of them killed him.

Dan picked up one of the photos Tom had found in the safe. "Working for Montoya has its perks, I see." He set the photo back down, leaned back in his chair, interlacing his fingers behind his head, and gazed speculatively at the ceiling. "Try this one on for size, Tommy. Wieder lets Lover Boy know he's got incriminating photos of him and Bledsoe. Says he'll let his wife have a look-see if he don't cough up some coin. Montoya doesn't like being blackmailed, doesn't want to risk losing half his fortune over a fling with a nurse, so he hires the dude in the Monte Carlo to tail Wieder and whack him."

Tom was looking out the window at the rusting shell of an old, once-white Buick. "Hit man, huh?"

"Probably a whole lot cheaper than a divorce."

Tom thought about it. Hit man driving a red Monte Carlo? A muscle car. Too conspicuous for a hit man. "Why kill Gundry?"

"Wieder might've said something to him—don't ask me what or why. Maybe he was just letting him know that Bledsoe was two-timing him."

Tom looked at Dan. "Why kill him?"

Dan leaned forward, picked up another photo, studied it briefly before tossing it back onto the table. "Maybe Gundry says he's going to expose Montoya to his wife. That'd blow the deal for Wieder, so he tries to talk him out of it. You said Sandy overheard them arguing about a federal offense. Maybe that was it."

"You think Wieder killed Gundry to stop him from doing an end-run?"

Dan shrugged, scowled down at a cat that had followed them into the kitchen. "Beat it, cat. Could be," he said to Tom. "With Gundry out of the way he goes to Montoya with his little surprise. It backfires. Montoya has him whacked."

"Two killers?"

Dan shrugged. "Two MOs."

It was a possibility, of course. Killers tended to stick with tried-and-true methods of annihilating their fellow man. Why fix what ain't broke? Tom wrote in his notebook. "Assuming your hit-man theory, what if it wasn't Montoya that hired him? What if it was Bledsoe?"

Dan pursed his lips, picked up his pen and tapped it against his notebook. "Last I heard nurses don't generally make it into the Fortune Five Hundred. Hit men aren't cheap. Besides, what's she got that's worth blackmailing for?"

"Not her, Montoya."

Dan frowned.

"Sure," Tom said. "The trainer job. What if—like you said—Wieder blackmails Montoya for money. Montoya tells Bledsoe that Wieder is going to show the pics to his wife. Think about it. Bledsoe wants to train Angelina's horses. The photos wouldn't look too good on her résumé, would they? Wieder's a threat, so she hires the Monte Carlo to take him out."

Dan arched an eyebrow. "Could do."

Tom frowned at a thought.

Dan said: "What? It could work."

"Gundry."

"Right. What about him?"

"His murder was premeditated," Tom said, voicing his thoughts. "Somebody went to a lot of trouble to kill him. They set it up days—maybe weeks—ahead of time. Wieder's murder appeared to be more spontaneous. Spur of the moment."

Dan spread his hands, palms out. "Like I said, you might have two killers here. Someone kills Gundry for one reason. Someone else kills Wieder for another."

Tom glanced out at the old Buick, its faded roof a burnished color in the deepening sunset.

"They may not be connected, Tommy."

The detectives sat thinking about it, Dan watching an evidence technician dusting items inside the refrigerator, Tom once again considering the photos. "We're assuming Wieder showed one or both of them the photos," he said. "Big assumption."

Thin red cornrows creased Dan's forehead. "Why keep the photos locked up in a safe, then?"

Tom shrugged. "Insurance?"

"Ace in the hole?"

"Possibly. Maybe one of them had something on Wieder, something related to a federal offense. The photos were kept as a hedge against the wolves. You squeal on me, I squeal on you."

"Didn't work, did it?"

Tom thought about it. No, it didn't work, which supported the idea that Wieder hadn't shown them the photos. If not, why not? Why keep them at all?

Dan drew squiggly lines in his margins. "Here's an angle. What if it was Wieder who hired the Monte Carlo to take pictures for blackmail? Something backfires in their relationship and the guy whacks him."

"Trouble among thieves? Maybe." Tom ran his fingers through his hair, rubbed the back of his neck as he looked down at the photos. "Big flaw in all this, you know."

"Oh?"

"If Wieder was killed because of the photos, you'd think the killer would destroy them before we got hold of them. Wieder kept the safe combination in his desk. Didn't take you but a minute to find it."

Dan stared, his face a mask of bewilderment. "My brain hurts." He scribbled through his doodles, pushed back from the table, the chair legs barking over the grimy yellow-and-brown linoleum floor, and stood. "Think I'll box up Wieder's files, check them out back at the station. Maybe something will turn up. Any word on the autopsy?"

"It's scheduled for tomorrow morning. Think you can hitch a ride back to the station with one of the FETs?"

"No problem. Heading home?"

"I'm bushed."

"You and me both."

"I thought I'd swing by and have a few words with Bledsoe on the way," Tom said. "See if I can't get a rise out of her. You wouldn't happen to know the number for the Bethesda Medical Group, would you?"

Dan looked at him. "Bethesda Medical Group?"

"Yeah. That's where she works."

"Which one?"

"The one in Valencia. There's more than one?"

Dan flipped back a few pages in his notebook, found what he was looking for. "There's one out in Palmdale. Chet Gundry's doctor has an office there. Dr. Emil Rickie. I told you at the office."

Tom gave him a look. "When?"

"Today. Earlier. You were too busy dragging your nose over Newton's photos to hear me. Rickie was one of the investors that backed out of the Sweetwater Estates deal."

Tom narrowed his eyes. "Curiouser and curiouser."

"That's my line." Dan grinned, looked wearily down the hall. "Think I'll tidy up in the back, then blow." He left the kitchen, headed down the hall toward the office. He was followed by a couple of wicked-looking felines, tails vertical like periscopes. Tom heard him sneeze, followed by a couple of expletives.

Tom placed the photos back into the envelope, checked the time on his watch, and stood. It was getting late. He called Information, got the number for the Bethesda Medical Group in Valencia, and dialed it. The clinic was closed for the day. He looked up Kate Bledsoe's home number, got her answering machine after four rings. He figured she was probably at the horse show for an evening event. Maybe she was out murdering someone else. He went outside to his car and looked west at the last of the sunset, dark brown ugly smears made by smog and haze streaking through blood red layers, mirroring how he felt inside.

Chapter Seventeen

Burbank. 8:15 A.M., Friday

Tom made a call from his apartment to Dr. Emil Rickie's office in Palmdale, asked the supervising nurse if he could speak with the good doctor. She said with an adenoidal voice that he was busy with a patient at the moment, then asked if she could be of service. Tom identified himself, asked if she knew Dr. Julian Montoya. She did. Did she know Kate Bledsoe? Not personally, but her name was listed in the personnel file. Would the Valencia office have access to Chet Gundry's medical files? Every patient in the group was in the system. Tom thanked her, hung up the phone, and sat thinking about that.

•

Tom pulled his vehicle into the parking lot of the Bethesda Medical Group, a five-story glass-and-stucco edifice off McBean Parkway, nestled in the heart of Valencia's civic district. A diaphanous tatter of clouds drifted imperceptibly across a transparent sky, the first indication that the weather might be changing. Stepping out of his vehicle, Tom could smell and feel moisture in the air, the barometer dipping slightly. A tardy June gloom on its way.

He walked through the automatic doors on the ground floor into the sterile glare of incandescent lighting, wide wheelchair-friendly hallways, and sick people. Tom didn't like hospitals; the chances of catching something were too good. At least it was cool inside. He walked over to a wall directory located beside a bank of elevators where a Hispanic couple stood waiting. The man was coughing and wheezing and probably releasing a contagion of some foul disease into the air. Reading through the list of names on the directory, Tom saw that Dr. Julian Montoya's office was on the third floor. At the sound of a bell one of the elevator doors opened, the Hispanic couple stepped inside, the man blowing his nose then pushing a button. Tom opted to take the flight of stairs across the hall. Fewer germs in stairwells.

Tom took the steps two at a time, turned right as he reached the third floor, then made his way around a mezzanine terrace that overlooked the courtyard below. He turned right again into a wide corridor and read Family Medicine on a set of glass doors on the left. Beneath this was a list of several doctors' names. Montoya was one of them. Tom held the door open for an arthritic elderly woman with orange hair pushing a walker no faster than a turtle with shin splints. She smiled a thank-you. Tom returned her smile, then, having done his good deed for the day, entered the waiting room.

Behind the desk sat a heavyset black woman wearing medical whites, her shiny black hair pulled back into a severe bun. She was bent over a tabloid, and looked over her reading glasses at Tom as he stepped up to the desk. Her name tag read W. Robbins. "Is Dr. Montoya in?" Tom asked.

W. Robbins closed the magazine, as if to suggest she hadn't been reading it, mild annoyance in her smile. "He's not in today, honey. Did you schedule an appointment?"

"How about Kate Bledsoe?"

W. Robbins squared her heavy shoulders, folded her plump hands on the desk as though fortifying a defense. She drummed her fingers. "May I help you?" she asked, a sweetly menacing smile pushing into her ample cheeks.

Tom produced his badge. "It's important that I see her toot sweet."

She frowned at the ID, squinted up at Tom's face to verify that he wasn't a liar, then pushed heavily back from the desk, more than a little annoyance in her voice now. "I'll see if I can locate her."

"Thank you." Tom looked back into the room where a handful of sick people sat as far away from each other as possible. Meeting his eyes, an elderly black man resumed looking at the wall-mounted

TV; the woman beside him flipped a page in her magazine. A cadaverous white-haired man, host to who-knows-what disease, stared dully at the wall, his eyelids at half mast, no doubt contemplating the labyrinthine wonders of HMOs. Sitting next to an attractive Hispanic woman was a small boy with short black hair and a fierce cowlick. A green mucous rope throbbed down from a nostril and spread across his upper lip. He stared fiercely at Tom. Tom smiled, turned around as Kate Bledsoe entered the room and made a beeline toward him with short menacing strides, her eyes flashing.

She was wearing a powder blue short-sleeved polyester medical jacket, white pants, and white shoes, her hair tied back in a ponytail. She looked sanitized. "Something I can do for you, Detective?" she demanded in a harsh pinched whisper. "I'm working, as you can see."

"So am I, Ms. Bledsoe."

Bledsoe's eyes narrowed into slits of hostility. "I told you everything I know yesterday."

"Not quite everything." Tom smiled without humor.

She blinked at him, uncertainty surfacing in her flinty greens.

"We can talk here, if you like," Tom said. "Doesn't matter to me. If I were you I'd opt for a little privacy. I'm sure Julian gives you people breaks around here." Tom could almost see the wheels turning behind her eyes that so much reminded him of Oleander; a shrub poisonous to horses, deadly to humans.

She glanced quickly around the waiting room. The boy with the cowlick was still staring fiercely at Tom. Bledsoe leaned over the desk. "Tell Sue to cover for me for about ten minutes, okay, Wanda?"

Wanda, aka W. Robbins, cleared her throat, adjusted herself in her chair without taking her stony beads off Tom. "Will do, Kate."

Bledsoe made her way for the double glass doors.

Tom smiled at Wanda, got a withering scowl in return, and then followed Bledsoe out onto the terrace.

Bledsoe stopped beside a row of empty waiting chairs, remained standing, her arms akimbo, fisted knots planted firmly on her hips, a fresh storm of lightning bolts in her eyes. "Now what is this regarding?" she demanded.

Tom removed a photo from the envelope and handed it to her. "I have three more where that came from."

She blinked at the photo, her cheeks reddening. Her expression, though colored by modesty, read more alarm than surprise. Tom could not tell if she had seen the photo before. "Where'd you get this?"

"You don't know?"

"Should I?"

"Have you seen it before?"

"No. Why?"

"You're certain?"

"I think I'd know if I'd seen it before. You said you had others."

Tom made a vague gesture at the photo. "That one's the best. How long have you and Julian Montoya been playing doctor and patient?"

Renewed hostility eclipsed any residual modesty in her features. "I don't see that as any of your business."

"Oh, but it is, Ms. Bledsoe. It's a motive for murder."

Once again uncertainty surfaced in her eyes, doubt flickering around the hard green edges. "What are you talking about?"

"Where were you between three and four yesterday afternoon?"

Bledsoe frowned. "Is that important?"

"I'm asking the questions."

Bledsoe glared at him for several long moments, saw that Tom wasn't going to budge. "I don't see why I have to answer any more of these questions."

"You don't. Silence is golden. It also implies guilt."

She broke from his gaze, looked down at the photo in her hand. "Between three and four?"

"Yesterday afternoon."

She cocked a hip, fanned the photo in the air. "I was at the show," she said. "I was in a Trails Class. What's this got to do with Chet?"

"This isn't about Chet; it's about Vern Wieder."

"Vern?"

"He's been murdered."

She blinked. Tom heard a shuddering intake of wind in her throat, her hand rising to her mouth to stifle a gasp. It went well with the cocked hip. It was almost believable. "Vern?" She looked quickly at the photo, looked back at Tom. Her lower lip trembled. "Murdered?"

"You see something in the photo?"

Bledsoe gave her head a fast little shake. "No . . . I—"

"Do you own a shotgun?"

"A what?" She shook her head again, looked at the photo, back at Tom. "A shotgun? No—"

"Are you sure?"

"I hate guns. Someone killed Vern?"

Tom grinned humorlessly. "He's made his last house call. You said you were in a Trails Class yesterday. What is that? You go out on a trail or something?"

Bledsoe stared at a point on Tom's chin. "What? Oh . . . you take your horse through obstacles," she said absently. "Water, gates, poles on the ground—things like that. Plenty of people saw me; I can prove it."

"I'd like a list of names."

Bledsoe's eyes rose from his chin to the bridge of his nose. "You think I killed Vern?" she asked, alarm in her voice. "Why would I do it?"

"Was Vern Wieder blackmailing you?"

She held up the photo. "Because of this?"

Tom took the photo from her, glanced at it once more before slipping it back into the envelope. "Wouldn't do for Angelina to find out you were giving anatomy lessons to her husband, would it? She might not hire you to train her horses." He could see Bledsoe's jaw muscles flexing, then tighten as the implication sank home.

"Train her horses?"

"You talked to her about it a couple weeks ago. She told me. Why would you do that, since you knew that Chet Gundry—your boyfriend—had the job pretty well secured? Maybe you knew there was going to be an opening. That sooner or later he was going to drop dead."

Bledsoe shook her head. "No."

"You knew because you laced his insulin with Xylazine, didn't you?"

"No, I didn't."

"You said you didn't know about his heart condition. You had access to his medical files. You're a nurse. You're dating a man with diabetes and you never once take a look at his files? You're lying, Ms. Bledsoe."

Her face was as white as her pants. Her lip trembled some more. "No."

"Meanwhile, you got a tête-à-tête going with your boss, thinking maybe he'd put in a good word for you with the missus. Cover it from both angles."

"No. I—"

"Problem is, Wieder finds out about you two and threatens to blow your deal if Montoya doesn't cough up some hush money. Can't have that, so you give him a shotgun lobotomy."

Bledsoe's eyes rounded. Her face twisted into a fist, and then went to pieces. She covered it with her hands and burst into tears. "That's not what happened!"

"Tell me what happened."

"Nothing happened." She reached into her pocket for a tissue and blew her nose. "I don't know anything about any murders or blackmail. I don't. You have to believe me." She sobbed some more.

Tom watched her. When he had informed her of Gundry's death, a man with whom she'd been romantically involved, she reacted with cool, if not icy, indifference. Now she brings out the waterworks. "You knew about Gundry's heart condition, didn't you?"

She gave her head a fast little shake.

"C'mon, Ms. Bledsoe, do you expect me to believe that?"

She continued sobbing.

"You knew, didn't you?"

"No."

"Didn't you?"

She straight-armed two fists at the floor. "Yes!" she screeched. "Yes, I knew he had a heart condition!"

Bledsoe's voice bounced off the walls, echoed over the terrace, and fell three stories to the courtyard below. It never came back.

"There. I said it," she spat. She brought a hand up and glared at Tom over her tissue; highlights sparkling on the liquid red, white, and green surfaces of her eyes. "Now are you satisfied?"

"I'd like to know why you lied to me."

She wiped her nose. "I had to. If I told you I knew about his heart you'd think it was me that killed him."

"Did you?"

"No. I didn't. And I didn't kill Vern, either. I didn't kill anyone."

"Are you protecting someone Ms. Bledsoe?"

"What? Protecting? Why—" Her eyes blinked a couple times, then filled with fresh tears. "No."

"Julian Montoya, maybe?"

Her face twisted crazily. She seemed to fold inside her shoulders. "No!"

Tom watched her crying. It was a good show. Better than the first one. This show had plenty of face wringing, shoulder bouncing and blubbering, guaranteed to evoke any man's sympathy. Tom let it play for a minute. "Why didn't you tell me you had asked Angelina about training her horses?" he asked.

She looked at him over a tight fist. "I didn't think about it," she gurgled. "So what?"

"Didn't it occur to you that it might be a motive for murder?"

She shook her head, honked into her tissue. "No, I didn't," she said, turning off the spigot. "Honestly." Composing herself, she folded her arms across her chest, the tissue balled in a fist. "May I go now?" she asked, contempt edging back into her voice. "With Julian— With Dr. Montoya out, we are quite busy."

Tom studied her a moment. Her cool demeanor was back in place, a bit bedraggled but back in place; the emotional, waterworks part of her dried up and shed like a rattlesnake skin in Wieder's zoo. "That's all for now," he said.

Before she left she slanted her eyes down at the envelope in Tom's hand. "What are you going to do with those—plaster them all over your squad room?"

"They won't appear on the six o'clock news, if that's what you're concerned about." It wasn't, he knew. She wanted to know if he was going to show the photos to Angelina Montoya. He'd bet a month's salary on it.

She wetted her upper lip with the small pointed tip of her tongue. Licking the air for scent, Tom thought, her eyes just as deadly as a Mojave green's. "They don't prove anything, you know."

Tom shrugged. "I didn't say they did."

Her nails flicked against her arm.

"By the way, Ms. Bledsoe? Where *is* the good doctor today?"

"I wouldn't know." She gave Tom a drop-dead smile, wheeled, and stormed away.

Tom watched her until she disappeared around the corner. He tapped the envelope against his leg. If nothing else, the photos did prove one thing: they spooked her. Spooked her enough to commit murder? Maybe. Maybe not. If not, Tom suspected she knew who did.

Chapter Eighteen

Sandy opened her front door to find two uniformed sheriff's deputies standing on her porch: Frank Dutton, a stocky, craggy-faced man, and his partner, Tim Sturdevant, a taller, leaner man with hooded blue eyes and a thin, slightly aquiline nose. Both men were in their late thirties.

"Got the photos," Frank said, handing Sandy a thick manila envelope. "Hope you know what you're doing."

The envelope was heavy. "Thanks, guys," she said, cradling it in the crook of her arm. "I appreciate this very much. Did Burbank give you any trouble?"

Frank was looking at her legs. She was wearing a pair of white shorts and sleeveless lilac cotton blouse tied above her waist, her legs tanned and sleek with suntan oil.

"Frank?"

"Hmm? Oh—" He shook his head. "No. I told them that the department needed them to compare with the Wieder case. The spirit of cross-departmental cooperation—you know—"

"Good. If word gets back to Ubersahl I'll take the heat."

Frank shrugged. "What can he do, fire us?"

Sandy made a face. "Yes. And you know he would."

A clanking sound drew her gaze down to the street, where she saw a garbage truck approaching her house. It was an orange one this time, the name Waste Away printed on its high, steel-bulked sides. It was the company that came midweek to collect trash from her Dumpster that she filled with manure and grass clippings, a different company from the one collecting the regular trash. A thought occurred to her, a vague, watery shape rising through a mind fog.

"What is it, Sandy?" Frank asked. He looked over his shoulder at the truck, then back at Sandy. "Forget to take the trash out?"

She looked at the deputies. "You both were on the force when my brother was killed, weren't you?"

Frank asked, "Your brother?"

"Ten years ago."

"Sure, I was on the force." He turned to Tim. "You were too, weren't you?"

Tim nodded. "Twelve years now."

"Do either of you remember the case?"

Frank said, "Sure. It was just after I got back from working the jail. Ubersahl handled it."

"That's right," Tim agreed.

Sandy knew that. Lieutenant (then Sergeant) Ubersahl had been first to arrive at the parking lot of city hall where her brother lay crumpled in the driver's seat of his car, a single 9-mm bullet through his left temple. Sandy, away at Pepperdine studying law, returned home to a welter of police and media activity. Paul's death was big news. Newly elected to the Santa Clarita city council, the story made the front page of every Southland newspaper. People working in the civic complex were questioned, but no one saw anything. Because Paul's wallet and Rolex were taken, the police had ruled his death a robbery homicide. Local miscreants were rounded up and questioned, but let go for lack of evidence. Soon the fervor cooled, the story fell to the back page, and then dropped off entirely, landing in the department's open files, on top of a pile of other unsolved murders and crimes. Ghosts forgotten in cold tombs. Returning to school, Sandy switched her major to criminology, graduated with honors, then joined the Los Angeles Sheriff's Department. She would not forget.

"Do you remember any hoopla at the time involving the trash business?" she asked.

Frank frowned. "Trash? You mean as in—"

"Trash." She indicated the truck, now forking her Dumpster into its container amid a clangor of motor whines and clanking sounds. "Waste disposal."

"Not that I can recall." Frank looked at Tim. "You remember anything, Tim?"

Tim scratched alongside the long thin bridge of his nose. "Ten years ago, right?"

Sandy nodded.

The detectives frowned in thought for several moments. Tim brightened, looked at Frank. "You remember that dude with the baseball bat—"

"Baseball bat?"

"Yeah. Didn't that have to do with the trash business?" Tim backhanded Frank's shoulder. "Sure. You remember."

Frank pulled on his cratery chin. "Baseball bat . . . baseball bat."

"What baseball bat?" Sandy asked.

Tim worked his earlobe. "What was his name?"

Frank held up a finger, poked a hole in the air. "Yeah, wait a minute! The dude with the baseball bat."

Tim looked at him, expectantly. "Remember?"

"What dude with a baseball bat?" Sandy repeated.

"Rearranged some guy's kneecaps?" Frank asked Tim. They were facing each other now, as though Sandy wasn't there.

Tim nodded. "That's him. Smashed both his kneecaps."

"Who smashed his kneecaps?" Sandy asked, frustration mounting in her voice.

"Ten years ago . . . ten years ago . . ." Frank clucked his tongue.

"Might've been less," Tim said. "Nine maybe. His name's on the tip of my tongue—Larry, Lon—" He shook his head. "Nope, gone."

Sandy drummed a hip with her fingers.

Frank brightened with an epiphany. *"Louie!"*

Tim snapped his fingers. "That's it. The Louisville Slugger."

"Old Slugger," Frank said, looking back on it with some admiration. "Made all the papers. Went after some dude for horning in on his territory."

"That's the guy. The trash business, right?"

Sandy held up her hand. "Time out, guys. Will somebody please tell me who you're talking about?"

The deputies looked at her. "The Louisville Slugger," they said in unison.

"Hit a stand-up double," Frank grinned.

"Actually it was a fall-*down* double," Tim winked.

Sandy looked from one man to the other. "Does anyone remember Louie's real name?"

"Something Armenian, wasn't it, Frank?"

"I think so. Armenians rule the trash biz, you know? Get pretty tribal about it."

"Bunch of pig farmers," Tim said. "It's true," he added when Sandy gave him the eye. "They raised pigs when they came over from the old country. People used to pay 'em to eat their trash. Before long Armenians are hauling trash and making millions. Who'da thought?"

Sandy was in no mood for a history lesson. "Does this pig farmer happen to have a name?"

Tim nodded. "Denmarkian or something, wasn't it, Frank?"

"Abadjian."

Tim snapped his fingers. "That's it. Abadjian. Louis Abadjian."

Sandy grabbed the pen protruding from Frank's beige uniform shirt pocket. "Louis Abadjian?"

"Pretty sure that was his name. Case was dropped as I recall."

"The vic dropped the A and B charges," Tim said, and winked. "Guess he didn't want his bean knocked out of the park."

Sandy wrote the name on the envelope. "Who were the detectives that handled the case? Maybe I can talk to them."

Frank looked at Tim. "It was Ubersahl, wasn't it?"

Tim nodded. "That's right, It was Ubersahl."

Sandy looked at them.

Tim said, "Don't remember who his partner was, though. You, Frank?"

Frank scratched the side of his stubby nose. "Rocky-something-or-other." He looked at Sandy. "Think it might mean something?"

"I don't know," she said. "Just something I remembered."

Watching the garbage truck grinding up the street brought to mind a phone conversation she'd overheard between her brother and someone whose name she didn't hear. She was home on Christmas break. She remembered the occasion because it was one of the few times she'd ever seen her brother lose his temper. She had no idea what prompted the outburst other than that it had to do with the trash business. She thought nothing of it at the time. Paul was a crusader. He was constantly trying to right wrongs, "defending the widows and orphans." Sandy figured it was just one more in a long list of wrongs he intended to right once he got into office. He was killed a month later.

"You okay, Sandy?" Frank asked, pulling her from her thoughts.

The men stood looking at her, Frank wearing his big-brother expression.

"I'm fine," she said, truthfully. She didn't know if it was because of a new lead in her brother's case or if it was because Wieder's death had, strangely, forced her mental plumb back on center.

"That's good," Frank said. With nothing more to add, he looked up at the sky as if it suddenly occurred to him that it was up there. "Looks like some clouds heading in maybe."

Observing the sky, Tim pursed his lips, nodding.

With no further observations to make on the weather, Frank raised his eyebrows at Sandy. "Best get going," he said, nodded his head at the envelope in her hand. "Hope that helps."

"You never know. Once again, thanks guys."

Frank touched the side of his forehead with two fingers, made a final furtive visual sweep of her legs, then he and Tim headed down her front walk toward their cruiser. Frank looked up at Sandy once he reached the vehicle. "Rockwell," he said.

Sandy cupped an ear. "Rockwell?"

"Ned Rockwell. Ubersahl's partner. I just remembered."

"Thanks," Sandy said.

"No sweat." Frank climbed into the black-and-white and he and Tim drove away.

Sandy closed the door, allowing the sudden cool quiet of her home to envelope her, the clanking of the garbage truck a muted and diminishing percussion. She looked down at the envelope, read the name she'd written, and frowned. Nick Ivankovich used to say that she was "tilting at windmills." Perhaps he was right. A word remembered in an overheard phone conversation between her brother and an unknown caller ten years ago suggested that she was on a fool's errand. Chasing after the wind. Still, tilting at windmills or not, she knew she'd have to take a look into the Louisville Slugger file.

She padded into the kitchen, the smooth texture of the wooden floor cool on the soles of her bare feet, and opened the envelope. There were two smaller envelopes inside; one marked "Gundry Crime Scene," the other marked "Horse Show Photos."

She opened the crime-scene envelope and spread the photos over her granite counter. There were photos of Chet's trailer, of his body lying in the dirt. She picked up one of these, held it up to the light coming in through the kitchen window. She groaned. Such a waste, she thought, studying the features of a man she once cared very much about.

She set the photo down, picked up one of the interior of his trailer. In her mind she could see Chet standing by the bathroom door, his stomach bared as he prepared to inject himself, unwittingly, with a dose of Xylazine. "Just shootin' blanks," he'd said in response to her praise of his training skills. At the time she'd thought it an odd comment, since Chet was not known for self-deprecation. Normally he wore praise like a victorious Roman general, crowned with laurel. Seeing his face in her mind's eye, lines of concern creasing his brow, it was clear that he'd had other, more weighty matters on his mind. What were they? She could only speculate.

She grabbed a pad of paper and a pen by the phone, and wrote "Federal Crimes" across the top and underlined it. Beside it she added "crossing state lines" in parentheses. Beneath it she wrote: "Something that would blow the lid off the equestrian industry." She tapped the pad with her pen, thinking through a list of federal crimes.

First on the list was drug trafficking. Drugs and horses went back as far as there were drugs and horses, and money to be made with either. Owners might use steroids on their halter horses in order to muscle up chests and hips, prized points of conformation in halter classes. Others might sedate their horses in order to quiet them in the ring. She could believe drug abuse of Vern but not of Chet. Chet was as pure as the driven snow when it came to drugs, whether for human or animal use. Perhaps it was because of his diabetes, his respect for his own body transferring to a respect for all living things. Still, the drug angle was doubtful. With all the blood and urine testing going on now at big shows, how could anyone get away with it?

She thought about other possibilities—stolen goods, vehicles, bank robbery, counterfeiting, kidnapping, Internet fraud, racketeering—trying to imagine how any of these might involve horses. There were always horse thefts, of course; if one were transported across state lines, then it would constitute a federal crime.

She shook her head. Chet may have had his moral failings, but he was no horse thief. And although Vern was a man of dubious character, she couldn't imagine him involved with that, either. Besides, with current lip tattooing, microchip implants, even DNA testing, horse theft, particularly in the high-profile show world of quarter horses, was unlikely.

Sandy frowned at her list. Not one of the entries made sense. Counterfeiting? It used to happen all the time in crooked horse racing; one horse (a ringer) made to look like another one in order to qualify for a certain event. Horsenapping? She didn't know if such a thing would even fall in the federal crimes category. She glanced at a stack of bills on the counter. Letters cross state lines. She added "U.S. Mail" to the list, but had no idea how letters might blow the lid off the equestrian business, or how it might be a motive in two murders.

Frustrated, she scribbled in the margins, acknowledging that the murders might not have anything to do with a federal offense. They might be connected to Chet's Sorrel West deal, his "ruffled feathers" comment tipping her thoughts in that direction. She wrote "Sorrel West" below her list of federal crimes, wrote "ruffled feathers" beside it. The only person, to her knowledge, who might have gotten his nose out of joint was Bud Nichols. She wrote "Bud" on the page, drew circles around the name as she thought of that possibility. It didn't fit. Vern's death threw a wrench at it. Vern wasn't connected with the clothing deal, as far as she knew. She tapped her pen against the pad, picked up the phone, dialed Information, and got the number for Sorrel West Outfitters in Houston. She dialed the number.

A woman with a Texas accent answered. Sandy identified herself, asked to speak with someone regarding contracts. "That would be Sorrel Rose," the woman said. "She handles all the business deals."

"Sorrel, as in—"

"Sorrel West Outfitters, yes, ma'am."

"Can you put me through to her, please?"

"Can't do that, ma'am. She's out in L.A. at a horse show. I can give you her hotel, if you'd like."

"That would be helpful." Sandy wrote down the name of the hotel, its number and Sorrel Roses's suite number. "Thank you," she said, depressed the button on the cradle, waited a moment and then dialed the hotel number.

"Burbank Hilton," a man's voice said. "How may I direct your call?"

Sandy gave him the suite number and waited while he put her through. After several rings with no response, the man picked up and asked Sandy if she'd like to leave Ms. Rose a voice mail. She did. Sandy asked Sorrel Rose to contact her as soon as possible, left her cell phone number, then returned the phone to its cradle.

The grandfather clock sounded the quarter hour.

She looked over the crime-scene photos once more, tapped a photo with her pen. She realized, of course, that the murders might not be connected at all. Chet's murder was clearly premeditated. The killer was someone obviously cool and calculating, willing to wait hours, if not days, for Chet to get to the tainted bottle of insulin (that is, unless the killer knew he would use it that very morning). On the other hand, Vern was killed by a shotgun blast to the face. Nothing cool about that; the killer acted out of blood heat. There may have been premeditation involved (the killer had to know where and when he would be at that location); but there was little calmness and collectedness in the execution of the crime.

Sandy wrote "Two killers?" on the page, and thought about it. The different MOs certainly suggested the possibility.

The second envelope marked "Horse Show" contained photos that she hadn't asked for, the reason being that she didn't know that they existed. They were a series of show photos taken by Abbe Newton. At first Sandy didn't understand why they'd been sent over to her. Then seeing the shots of Chet, before and after death, the times when they were taken shown in the lower-right corners, she realized they provided valuable evidence of who was where and when at the time of his death. Tom must have gotten them from his interview with Newton. There was a rather good one of him talking with the coroner; his eyes a deep blue intensity; his "detective eyes" as she liked to tease him when he fell into his thinking mode.

Thoughts of their recent trip to Catalina eased through her mind, pleasant thoughts of sitting on the veranda of the little harbor bistro with Tom, the two of them holding hands as they watched the sunset lights flickering among the boats in the harbor—red, gold, turquoise highlights, the boat masts bobbing rhythmically among them. Then the distressing thoughts of the past couple of days overshadowed the tranquil scene like a sudden squall. "No," she said aloud, chasing them from her mind. "Can't allow any distractions."

Sandy took Newton's photos and spread them in left-to-right rows over her living room floor, allowing walking space between the rows, which she now did, pausing to study each one. Regardless of her distaste for Abbe Newton as a person, she was a good photographer. She had captured the horse show quite well, each of the events, the major players and horses, with plenty of background material to flesh it out. That there were far too many shots of herself led Sandy to believe that Newton was building, if not a circumstantial case against her, then a titillating intrigue about Chet Gundry's life and times. She shook her head. It would certainly be a work of fiction.

Sandy felt something soft and furry brush against her ankles. "There you are, Sylvie," she said. "Have you been sleeping?"

She stooped to scratch behind the kitty's ears, smiling tenderly, feeling genuine warmth toward her new cat. Appreciation for her little life. Perhaps it was a sign that she was getting better, that her flashbacks would mercifully recede into the mists of forgetfulness.

Sylvie bounded away, jarring one of the photos. As Sandy straightened it a detail she had not seen before caught her eye. She picked up the photo and stood. It was a group shot. Chet was on the far left. Beside him were Vern Wieder and Angelina Montoya, standing in front of Zee-Zee. The photo was taken two hours before Chet's death. What had caught Sandy's eye, however, was a black man standing in the background, about twenty feet to the right of the group. The man was standing by himself, fists balled on his hips, and his eyes, like burning coals, glowering at Vern.

Sandy's brows came together, pinching a dark thought. If looks could kill. "What do you make of that?" she said quietly. "Oz Ramsey."

She went over to her phone, thumbed through the address book next to it, found Ozzie's cell phone number in her address book and dialed it. After two rings, he picked up.

"Oz, it's Sandy."

"Hey, girl. What's up? That shoe hasn't come loose already."

"No, nothing like that. I was just wondering if we could get together? I have a couple questions I'd like to ask you."

"Questions?"

"Nothing big. Where are you?"

"Now? I'm on the southbound Golden State, heading toward the equestrian center. Got an emergency toenail filing." He chuckled. "Don't you love these big shows?"

Sandy smiled without humor. "Could I meet you there, maybe in an hour or so?"

"Sure. What's this about?" There was a note of wariness in his voice.

"Like I said, nothing big. What if I meet you at the clubhouse for lunch? Say around noon. My treat."

"Noon it is."

•

Sandy parked her truck in a space opposite the clubhouse. She'd changed out of her shorts into an outfit more conducive to horses: blue jeans and boots, peach-and-blue wide-striped T-shirt, and blue Dodgers cap, the bill shielding her eyes from the sun. She grabbed her purse and the envelope containing Abbe Newton's show pho-tos, got out of her truck and headed for the clubhouse.

There was no sign of Ozzie inside. She checked her watch. It was twelve straight up. Ozzie, ever prompt with his appointments, must have gotten detained. She went outside onto the patio, think-ing he might be waiting for her there. He wasn't. She was about to go back inside when she saw Bud Nichols at one of the far tables in the shade of a green umbrella, his back turned toward her. Sit-ting at the table with him was a woman Sandy did not recognize. She was laughing at something that Bud had apparently said.

Sandy walked over to the table. The woman, a heavyset red-head wearing custom jeans and a sleeveless white blouse printed with jaunty horseshoes, cowboy boots, and hats, looked to be in her mid to late forties. She was sitting back in her chair with her feet thrown up onto the table, showing off a pair of pointy-toed black-and-white boots, red roses stitched on the uppers. She was smoking, her shoulders and heavy bosom bouncing as the last of her laugh trailed off in a throaty chortle. Bud was stretched out in his chair, boots heel-on-toe, elbow hooked over the seat back, a can of Coors Light in his fist. His head shook slowly from side to side, as though he was shaking out the last bit of humor from his joke.

Sandy said, "Hey, Bud."

He turned, a grin still etched on his face until he saw who it was. His eyes flickered, darted to the woman with him, then back to Sandy. "Hey," he said. His expression struck Sandy as someone who'd gotten caught with his hand in the proverbial cookie jar.

Sandy nodded. "Hear about Vern?"

Bud nodded his head in apparent concern. "Yeah. Tough break."

"Tough break?" A flat tire is a tough break. Not getting a pro-motion is a tough break. "He was murdered, Bud."

"That's what I heard."

"My word," the redhead said turning to look at Sandy. "This sounds juicy."

The woman had a round pretty face, with eyes as blue as the turquoise stones in her bracelets and necklace, framed by too much blue and magenta mascara and slashes of rouge on her cheeks. A buckaroo hat with the crown creased down the middle toward the front kept a fireball of frizzy red hair from burning out of control. A plume of brightly colored peacock feathers fanned across the crown. She looked familiar.

"Bud, honey, ain't you gonna introduce me to your pretty friend?" the redhead said, her voice betraying a west Texas twang.

Bud swung his head around. "What's that? Oh." He indicated Sandy with a sharp chin thrust. "This is Sandy." He looked away.

The redhead frowned at the side of his head. "And—? Never mind." She stubbed out her cigarette, slanting an eye at Bud as she extended her hand to Sandy. "Numbskull here seems to've forgotten his manners." She flashed a rake of tiny teeth through glossy rootin'-tootin' red lipstick. "Call me Sorrel, honey. Sorrel Rose."

Sandy shook her hand, the grip firm like the set of her jaw. She knew she'd seen the woman's face before, but still couldn't place it. "Pleased to meet you. Sorrel Rose, of Sorrel West Outfitters?"

"That's right." The woman raised a glass of what looked and smelled like whiskey, and emptied into her mouth. "You hearda me?"

Bud's eyes flicked between the two women. "She's a police detective," he said, taking a swig of beer.

Sorrell's eyes widened in mock surprise. "Do tell. *Po*-leece, huh?"

Sandy smiled. " 'Fraid so."

"I don't believe it." Sorrel looked her over pretty good, one eye in a squint. "And I thought Texas had all the goddesses. Tell me you've done modeling before, honey." Without waiting for Sandy's reply, she turned to Bud. "Don't you think she'd fill out our fall line nicely, Bud?"

Bud smiled, the humor never reaching his eyes as he threw back the rest of his beer. "Gotta go," he said, and stood.

"Go? Go where?" Sorrel asked, affecting a wounded tone. "The party's just gettin' started."

"Gotta see a man about a horse," he said, reprising the humorless grin. Sandy couldn't tell if Bud had to go to the bathroom or if he actually needed to see a man about a horse. One thing was certain: he was making a fast exit.

"See you later, then? At the shoot?"

"Later." Bud started to walk away.

Sandy raised a finger. "Bud—?"

He looked back.

"Just for the record," she said. "Where were you between three and four yesterday?"

Bud frowned, then grinned. "Think I killed him?"

"Three and four?"

Sorrel waved a hand, dismissing the matter outright. "Why don't you remember, Bud, honey? You were showing me your stud. Out at your place," she added. She turned to Sandy. "Had 'im mount one of his breedin' dummies for me. Quite a show."

Bud looked at her, looked back at Sandy and made a gesture with his thumb, indicating that Sorrel had answered for him. "Gotta go," he said, and walked away.

"It's a shame about his new mare dying," Sandy said.

Sorrel looked at her quickly, the gloss on her lips dulled a mite.

Sandy angled her head inquiringly. "He didn't tell you? I'm sorry. One of his mares."

"No." Sorrel looked back at Bud walking away. "That's a shame," she said. Her eyes squinted with mischief. "Danged if you don't just love a cowboy in blue jeans." She started to laugh, but a smoker's hack chased it back into her throat.

Sandy waited until the woman had taken a sip of water. "May I join you?" she asked, putting her hand on a seat back.

Sorrel swung her boots off the table, sat forward and touched Sandy's hand. "By all means, honey. Have a seat," she said, indicating Bud's empty chair. "Sandy, was it?"

"That's right." Sandy sat down, set her purse and the envelope down on the table. "I left a message on your voice mail."

"On *my* voice mail?"

"I've got a couple questions, if you don't mind."

"Why, no, honey. 'Course not." Sorrel lit a cigarette, squinting at Sandy through a cloud of smoke as she slowly fanned out the match, the loose skin under her arm waving like turkey wattle. She tossed the match vaguely in the direction of a tin ashtray on the table and missed. "This about Chet?" She blew a streamer of smoke to one side, raised an empty glass to a waitress. "Gimme another Jack and water back, won't you, honey?" She looked at Sandy. "You want anything?"

Sandy shook her head.

"My treat, you sure?"

"I'm fine, thanks."

"Put a fire under that, will you, dear?" Sorrel said to the waitress, smiled sweetly, then looked back at Sandy, deep lines radiating out from her eyes and corners of her mouth as she smiled at her for several moments. "Chet told me about you."

"Oh?"

"Said you were prettier'n a spring colt. He was right."

Sandy ignored the comment. "When did you see him last?"

"Chet? Oh, dear. Let's see . . . couple few nights ago. Night before he died—whatever night that was. I get mixed up traveling." She pulled hard on her cigarette, shook her head at the blown smoke. "Can you believe it?—Chet dead. Helluva trainer."

"How well did you know him?"

"Chet'n me go way back."

The waitress brought a fresh tumbler of bourbon and a glass of water to the table.

Sorrel paid with a twenty. "Keep it, honey." She raised her drink in a wordless toast, extending her pinkie daintily. "Here's to spring colts," she said, drained half its contents, then chased it with a sip of water. She smiled. "I'm still on Houston time," she said, lifting the tumbler slightly. "We're just now warming up to happy hour."

Sandy smiled. Sorrel Rose was clearly someone who enjoyed herself. "Were you in Chet's trailer anytime before his death?"

Sorrel hesitated a moment, a subtle downturn in her perpetual smile as she rolled the end of her cigarette over the ashtray. She took another sip of bourbon, eyeing Sandy over the rim of her glass. "Think I killed him? Killed old Chet?"

"Since you asked—"

"Don't kid yourself, honey. You ain't here to swap recipes. You wanta know if I killed Chet. That vet feller too—what was his name?"

"Vern Wieder."

"Him too."

"Did you?"

Sorrel stubbed out her cigarette in the ashtray. "Like I said, me'n Bud were out at his place."

"Between three and four yesterday afternoon?"

"That's right. Convenient, huh?"

Sandy made no comment. "Were you in Chet's trailer at any time?" she repeated.

"Yes, I was. Like I said, we partied the night before he died."

"You were drinking?"

"Like a largemouth bass." She laughed, and then took a sip of her bourbon, wiped her mouth with a flick of her index finger.

"Jack Daniels, by any chance?"

"That's right. Why? D'I leave some in the bottle?" She chuckled throatily.

"Just you drinking?"

"Me'n Bud. Chet don't drink nothin' but bubble water. His diabetes, you know."

Sandy raised her eyebrows. "Bud was there too?"

"The three of us. Bud's a hoot. Why?"

Sandy did not answer. She turned her head in the direction Bud had gone.

"D'I say somethin' here, honey?" Sorrel asked seriously. "Chet had to tend to one of his horses . . . left Bud'n me to clean up. Did we leave something incriminating behind?" She smiled, sipped her drink. "Where're ya headed with this?"

Sandy looked at her. "Did the three of you talk business?"

"Sure. What else?"

"Did it have to do with the contract for the clothing line?"

"That's right. The fall line. I told the boys I was going to make up my mind at the show which one I was gonna give it to. One or t'other." Her eyes glowed with mischief. "Keep 'em guessin', you know."

Sandy frowned. "I was under the impression that Chet had the deal pretty well sewn up."

Sorrel played with her pack of cigarettes, lifting it an inch off the table, letting it fall as she studied Sandy's eyes. "D'e tell you that?"

"He didn't have the deal, then?"

Sorrel flicked the side of the pack with her middle finger, batting it in a tight circle. "I might've let the wind drift that way once or twice, but as far as I was concerned it's always been a horse race." She grinned, showing her tiny teeth. "I like a good race, don't you?"

"Not when one of the horses is murdered."

The grin came apart at the edges.

"Does the contract go to Bud now that Chet's dead?"

Sorrel was staring at a point over Sandy's shoulder, the luster gone out of her eyes. "What's that? The contract? Say, you don't think—?"

Sandy let Sorrel's mind connect the dots.

Sorrel flicked the pack once more, tapped out another cigarette and lit it. "You think Bud killed Chet?" She tossed the lit match at the ashtray. It bounced off the edge and lay burning on the ripple-glass tabletop. "You do, don't you?"

Sandy did not answer. She watched the match burn down to the end, finally extinguishing in a wisp of smoke. Chet was certain he'd gotten the deal. Bud may have been told the same thing. Pitting two men against each other, two men with enormous egos, may have been a good horse race, but Sorrel Rose might have unintentionally (or intentionally for that matter) tossed a lit match into a bucket of gasoline.

Sorrel was staring blankly at the smoke curling off her cigarette. She raised her eyes as several riders in sparkling show apparel rode past on their way to the next event, Angelina Montoya and her stallion trailing the long line.

"Beautiful horse," Sandy said, observing Zee-Zee. "It's a shame Chet isn't here to see him. He's a sure bet to take the World again this year—"

"What's that?" Sorrel looked at Sandy, then looked over at the line of horses and chortled sardonically. "Zee-Zee? Ain't no such thing as a sure bet in the horse business, honey."

"No, I suppose not. Especially now with Chet out of the way."

Sorrel smiled benignly, lifting the pack of cigarettes, then dropping it.

Just then Oz Ramsey walked across the patio from the direction of the stables. He did not look in Sandy's direction. He entered the clubhouse, and Sandy could see him inside through the windows looking for her. The hostess came up to him. He said something to her, she pointed outside, he looked out and saw Sandy.

Sandy waved, held up a finger to wait inside. She stood. "It's been interesting, Sorrel. Gotta go."

Sorrel affected another wounded look. "You ain't gonna leave me here by my lonesome, are you?"

"Plenty of cowboys in the area. Lots of blue jeans."

Sorrel smiled, glanced into the clubhouse at Ozzie. "You probably gotta beat 'em away with a stick, don't you?" She threw back the last of her drink. "I mean it about you modeling for me, honey."

Sandy started to leave but turned back and smiled, a vague, curious smile. "By the way, how did you know that Vern Wieder was a veterinarian? I never mentioned it."

Sorrel blinked, pursed her lips as she shook her head. "Danged if I know. Bud musta said something." She picked up her glass but saw that it was empty, empty like the expression on her face.

•

They were sitting in the same booth that Sandy and Tom had occupied two days earlier. Ozzie was eating a club sandwich and sipping iced tea. He looked beat. "What were you doing at the Borden ranch?" Sandy asked, picking at a taco salad.

Ozzie sprinkled salt onto his turkey, watching Sandy with friendly, but warm, eyes. "Borden's? Workin' a couple of horses," he said. "I'm there a couple times a month. Why? This about Vern?"

Sandy nodded. "Couple times a month?"

"Sure, couple three times or so. I don't know. A horse throws a shoe or something, I come out." Ozzie took a sip of tea, set the glass down in a circle of water.

"Is Vern usually at the ranch on the same days you're there?"

"I don't keep track of his schedule," he said, an edge of bitterness in his voice.

"You've never seen him there?"

"I've seen him. I just ignore him. What're you gettin' at?"

Sandy removed the group photo from the envelope and slid it across the table. Ozzie picked it up. "What's this?" His face darkened. "Who took this?"

"That's not important." She nodded at the photo. "Doesn't look like you're ignoring him there, does it?"

Ozzie studied the photo. After several moments, he set the photo down and said quietly, "You know I got reason to do him harm."

"You had motive and opportunity, Oz. What time did you leave the Borden ranch?"

"I don't know. Three-fifteen, three-thirty. Sometime around then."

"It wasn't later?"

Ozzie's eyes flickered. "It might've been, I don't know. I don't keep track of the time."

Sandy frowned at that. She pushed her salad around with her fork. "After you left the ranch you came straight here?"

"Straight here." Ozzie nodded. "Ask Angelina, she can vouch for me. She had me look at Zee-Zee's foot." He looked steadily at Sandy. "Ask her," he repeated then broke gaze. He looked out the window for several moments, staring, a faraway cast in his dark eyes. He shook his head slowly. "You know I thought about killin' him. He was scum."

"Did you kill him, Oz?"

He looked across the table at her. "No. No I didn't, Sandy. You got to believe me."

Sandy tried to read his eyes, read some hint of truth; instead, she saw only a reflection of pain in them, his wife's pain and suffering, the lost dreams of a woman who would not be able to bear children, the rage of a man torn by the consequences of a senseless blunder. "I want to believe you, Oz," she said.

She took the photo and slid it back into the envelope. "You didn't hear anything yesterday afternoon—a gunshot, maybe?"

"A gunshot?" Ozzie shook his head, looked down at his glass and made tight figure eights with it in the water circle. "Can't remember. If I did I wouldn't've taken note of it. People shoot along the wash all the time. Lotta quail."

"Quail season doesn't open until October."

Ozzie shrugged. "Maybe just shootin' crows, then. I used to shoot 'em when I was a kid. Them an' jays."

"What'd you shoot them with?"

"Twenty-two mostly. Winchester pump." A smile flickered at the corners of his wide mouth. "My peepaw gave it to me. Grand-dad," he clarified, allowing the smile to flourish.

Sandy smiled back. "Do you own a shotgun, Oz?"

He looked up from his glass. "Sure. Who doesn't?"

"What gauge?"

"Twelve." He grinned. "Can't hit a barn with anything smaller. That all you wanted to ask me?"

"That's all, Oz."

"Okay. Gotta go anyway," he said, glancing at his wristwatch. "Make my rounds." He drummed the tabletop with his palms, slid out of the booth and looked down at Sandy. He hiked up his shoulders, nodded a smile, then walked out of the clubhouse.

Sandy sat alone in the booth with dark thoughts. Ozzie, more than any of her friends, had a motive to see Vern dead. He also had opportunity. He was at the Borden ranch around the same time that the murder took place. Further, he knew precisely what time he was there, and when he left. Ozzie was the most time-conscientious far-rier she'd ever met. It would have been a simple thing for him to pull up next to Vern's truck on his way out, kill him, and then leave with-out anyone the wiser. But could he have done it? Ozzie was a gentle soul, a man who smiled easily. Sandy looked out of the window and saw Ozzie walking toward his parked truck. She knew that even gentle souls can be driven to violence, if they are desperate enough.

Chapter Nineteen

"What can you tell me about the pellets, Fitz?" Tom asked Detective Robert Fitzgerald, a wiry-built mick with short-cropped red hair and round, melancholy blue eyes, poet's eyes. Tom and Dan were in the Burbank station lab with him, a long clinical-looking room down the hall from the detective wing. There were cabinets and refrigerators and several long white tables with forensic apparatus on them. Two field evidence technicians, a sandy-haired man with a pair of glasses perched on top of his head and a woman with a brown pageboy, were at the far end of the room peering into microscopes.

Fitz, holding a petri dish that contained several pellets found at the Wieder crime scene, rotated his hand on his wrist so that the pellets rolled around in the dish like a puzzle game. "I weighed them with the ones the ME took from Wieder's body."

"And?"

"A little under an ounce, give or take a pellet or two. The truck stopped most of what got past Wieder. We might've missed a few strays."

Tom took the petri dish and eyed the pellets. "Little under an ounce, huh? Look like seven-and-a-halfs maybe."

"Number eights. Just got the report back from ballistics."

"Eights, huh?" Tom had been hoping they weren't eights. "What about the wad?"

"Winchester. Twelve gauge. But you knew that already."

Tom frowned. "Winchester, huh?" He set the petri dish on a bench. "Got anything on the GSR yet?"

"Should have the chem analysis in a couple of days. I can tell you this, though, the killer was using Remington powder. Red Dot," he clarified. "Found tiny unburned red flakes in the vic's clothing. Winchester uses ball powder."

Tom looked at him. "Winchester wad and Remington powder?"

Fitz nodded. "The killer used a reload."

Tom and Dan exchanged looks; each knew what the other was thinking. A factory-made shell—say Winchester—would have used Winchester powder, hulls, primers and wads; likewise with Remington or some other manufacturer. That the wad was made by Winchester and the powder by Remington pointed the finger at a custom reload. The killer rolled his own. "Thanks, Fitz, you've been a big help."

Fitz opened his poet's eyes as if pondering the ending to a sad couplet. "Why so glum, then?"

Tom pinched the bridge of his nose, rubbing it as he headed for the door without saying a word. Dan followed.

"Wasn't Max Cameron reloading with number eights, Tommy?"

Tom nodded.

"Did you notice what kind of wads he was using?"

Tom shook his head. "He was using Red Dot powder, though."

The detectives continued down the hall in silence. Entering their office, Tom stood looking at Abbe Newton's tiny photographs still pinned to the bulletin board.

Dan continued around to his desk. Neither detective spoke for several moments. "Ounce of eight shot is a pretty common load," Dan said. "Especially for southern Cal. Not much call for the bigger stuff."

Tom continued looking at the photos. A quail hunter might use the slightly larger number seven and a half, adding an additional eighth of an ounce to the load for more punch. An ounce of number-eight shot was a light load, the kind used mostly by skeet and trap shooters. The kind used to kill Vern Wieder.

"I know lots of guys that reload, Tommy."

Tom looked over at Dan. Wieder's files were spread over his desk. "Got anything there?" he asked.

Dan shook his head. "His personal stuff is pretty normal. No outstanding debts, other than his mortgage." He lifted a newspaper clipping out of a box on the floor, handed it to Tom. "I did find this, though."

Tom read the headline: " 'High Dollar Horses, Mules for Drug Lords.' What's this?"

"Pretty weird stuff. Drug traffickers stuffed balloons of cocaine into—get this—a mare's uterus."

Tom frowned.

"That's right," Dan said. "A woman bought a mare from a ranch in Mexico and had it transported to Texas. Someone in Mexico loaded her up with balloons. A vet on the Texas end removed them before the new owner took possession of the horse. Neat little trick, huh?"

"A horse for a mule."

Dan's expression revealed that he knew what Tom was thinking: federal offense. "It's eight-year-old news, Tommy."

Tom looked at a faded color photo of one of the defendants indicted by the feds: a redheaded woman named Sonny Weston, horse trader out of Houston. She was wearing a cowboy hat with feathers sprouting from its hatband. The article stated that although it was her horse that was used to transport the drugs, there was insufficient evidence to prove that she had knowledge of any foul play. None of those indicted in the roundup implicated Weston. The charges against her were dropped.

"Don't ask me why it's in Wieder's effects, Tommy. Maybe he knew the vet who removed the balloons."

"Yea, maybe." Tom slipped the clipping into his pocket. "I'm gonna make a copy of this."

"Think Wieder and Gundry could've been mixed up in something like that?"

Tom could not say. Eight years ago was a long time. It *was* old news.

He turned his attention back to the wall of horse-show photos. Making yet another sweep he hoped that something might jump out at him, point the finger of guilt at someone other than Max Cameron. "Nothing back from Martinez yet?" he asked. Sergeant Martinez, a ten-year man who handled the auto theft detail, was doing a DMV search of all 1971 Monte Carlos registered in Los Angeles County.

"Lemme check." Dan picked up his phone and dialed. "Hey, Martinez—Dan Bolt." He made a face at the receiver. "I know it's only been twelve hours. Quit flirtin' with Carmelita and get on the stick, okay?" Martinez said something. "Yeah, well, he didn't catch the plates, okay?"

Tom looked up from what he was doing.

"They're original plates, what more do you want?" Dan told Martinez to check with GM on the vehicle ID numbers—see how many Monte Carlos they might have shipped to Los Angeles. A simple DMV check should handle it. Martinez said something. "No, I don't think you're a moron," Dan said. "You're a lousy wetback who thinks all the girls in the office are in love with him."

Dan rolled his eyes at Tom. He listened, frowned. "What? No, I don't want in on the lousy pool. Lakers don't stand a chance against the Spurs. They're a bunch of geriatrics, Martinez, give it up." He hung up the phone. "Lousy Martinez."

Tom had stopped listening. He grabbed the magnifying glass off his desktop and poised it over a photo. He saw something there.

"Got something, Tommy?"

"Don't know." Tom moved to another photo and held the magnifying glass over it. He grunted.

"What is it?"

Tom said nothing. He moved in on another photo, then another one.

"Do I have to hold my breath until you tell me what you're doing?"

Tom unpinned three sheets from the bulletin board, walked over to Dan's desk, and spread them out. He circled four photographs with a red marker. "Can you blow these up?"

"If you tell me why first."

Tom stabbed a photo with his finger. "Look at it. Notice anything?"

Dan took the magnifying glass from Tom. He shrugged. "I see Angelina Montoya riding a horse."

Tom pointed. "Look at these."

"Angelina riding a horse," Dan said, looking at each of the red-circled photos. "Angelina talking to Gundry and Wieder. Angelina walking a horse."

"Look in the bleachers."

Dan looked, shook his head. "Yeah, so?"

"You don't see the man with the sunglasses." Tom pointed. "Here, here, here . . . here. There's more of him on the wall, but these are the best."

Dan looked.

"The photos were taken on different days . . . same man in the bleachers. Notice how he's looking at Angelina."

Dan squinted at an image, grunted. "Will you looky there. Wearing a blue baseball cap and everything. Sure got the beads on her, don't he?"

"It's the guy in the red Monte Carlo."

•

Angelina Montoya was removing a silver saddle from her horse as Tom approached her combo RV and horse trailer. The trailer was parked in the day lot of the Cottonwood Equestrian Center. The saddle gleamed in the sun as Angelina put it on a free-standing saddle rack. So did Angelina. She was dressed in purple and black show apparel: black hat and chaps; purple knit shirt that clung to her shapely figure. Rhinestones swirling over her breasts, cuffs, and hat band; her black hair tied in back with a purple ribbon matching her shirt.

"Another win, huh?" Tom said, noting the blue ribbon tonguing off the horse's bridle.

Angelina turned to face him, the violet flecks in her blue eyes coming alive as she saw who it was. "Tom Rigby. Detective," she added with a radiant smile that revealed pretty white teeth framed in a glossy red bow. Tom could well understand her husband's jealous eye, and why he might have had her tailed (assuming he hired the man in the red Monte Carlo).

"Your housekeeper told me where to find you," he said.

"What a pleasant surprise." She glanced beyond him, as though she expected to see someone with him. "No Sandy?"

"I'm here on business. Do you have a minute?"

Her smile flattened. "Is this about Chet or Vern?"

"You've heard about Wieder's murder then?"

"It's all over the center," she said, shaking her head sadly. "What a terrible thing." She removed the saddle pad, placed it bottom up on top of the saddle.

"I need to ask you where you were yesterday afternoon," Tom said.

She tilted her head, a frown of incredulity pinching her dark eyebrows together.

"We're asking everyone who knew the victim," Tom said.

"Yes, of course. What time?"

"Between three-fifteen and three-forty-five."

Angelina pursed her lips, looked over at Miguel brushing down her horse. "I was either here or at home," she said. "I had an event around then, but I couldn't tell you when it started. During these shows I'm pretty useless as far as time goes."

"You were in an event yesterday afternoon?"

"Trails Class. You can check with the registrar. They'd know for sure what time. It was around that time, though. Midafternoon."

Tom intended to check on his way out. He removed several blown-up photos from the envelope he had brought with him. "I was wondering if you might help me with something."

Angelina waved a hand at him. "Not out here, it's much too hot." She turned to Miguel, who was turning on a spigot. "Miguel, after you give Zee-Zee a bath, could you take him over to the hotwalker? Wrap his front right leg like you did yesterday. Don't want it swelling."

"*Si.*" Miguel nodded, watched Tom as he hosed the horse's flank.

Angelina smiled at Tom, her eyes glittering as she gestured with her hand. "Shall we go inside? It's cooler."

It was. The layout was similar to Chet Gundry's (there probably weren't too many variations, given the space constraints); however, her trailer was more plush than his. It contained a small kitchen and dinette area to the right in a pop-out section, a bathroom, and a sleeping area over the gooseneck, cream-colored leather sofa and chair, and real oak appointments. It smelled new, luxury-car new, the smell of leather and money and the scent of a beautiful rich young woman wafting through it. "Would you like something cold to drink?" Angelina asked, stepping over to the refrigerator. "A beer, maybe?"

Tom shook his head. "No, thanks."

"I've got Perrier," she said pouring one for herself.

"No, thanks." Tom placed a photo on the dinette table.

Angelina came over and stood beside him, glass in hand. He could smell her perfume, an elegant scent with a sensual hint of musk (fifty dollars an ounce more than Kate Bledsoe's probably), mixed with the smell of horse on her clothes and hair that was actually appealing. She smelled a lot like Sandy, in fact. "Could you look at this photo, Mrs. Montoya?"

"Only if you call me Angelina," she said, a scolding tone in her voice.

"Angelina." Tom pointed at the man with the sunglasses. "Do you recognize this man?"

She leaned forward to get a better look. "No. Should I?"

"He's looking at you."

"Lots of men look at me." She smiled.

Tom couldn't tell if she was being flirty, conceited, or just candid. He placed another photo on the table. It was a photo of Angelina and Sandy riding in the practice arena. "What about this one?"

She looked at it. "I've always said that Sandy should go into the movies. She's so beautiful, don't you think?" She slapped his hand playfully. "Of course you do."

Tom nodded his head at the photograph. "The man with the sunglasses."

"Oh, right. The man with the sunglasses." She looked more closely at the photo, shook her head. "Never seen him before. Sandy sits a good horse, don't you think?"

Tom had no idea what sitting a good horse meant, didn't care at the moment. He put two more photos on the table, leaving the one of her husband with Kate Bledsoe in the envelope. He didn't think it necessary at the moment to show it to her. She studied the photos a few seconds, picked one of them up and frowned. "See something?" Tom asked.

"Oz Ramsey."

"The man with the sunglasses?"

"No, this man," she said, pointing at a black man. "Ozzie. The one who looks like he's got his nose out of joint. He's my shoer." She brought the photo closer to her eyes and smiled. "It's a good one of Zee-Zee, don't you think?"

"Look at the man with the sunglasses."

She did. "Sorry." She set the photo down on the table. "Who is he, some sort of underworld character?"

"You've never seen him before at your house? Talking with your husband, perhaps?"

"My husband?"

Tom figured it was as good a time as any to drop the bomb. "What was your relationship like with Chet Gundry?"

"He was my trainer. You know that."

"Nothing more?"

She looked at him seriously. "I told you before that I am—"

"A married woman. I know. You're still a woman . . . a beautiful one, I might add. Chet was a good-looking man."

She continued looking at him, something cooking behind her eyes.

"I have to ask," he said. "It's important."

"You think Julian hired Mr. Sunglasses to spy on me?"

"I have no idea. He was watching your house the other day."

Angelina's face clouded, a smile of incredulity tugging at the corners of her mouth. She laughed suddenly; a gay, fluttery warble that ended in a question mark. "And you think he was watching *me*?" She picked up the photo again and looked at it. "Like some greasy peeper in a detective movie?"

"Something like that," Tom nodded. "Assuming that your husband hired him. If he did then he probably knows if there was anything going on between you and Chet. Was there?"

"I don't believe it," she said, a warble once again fluttering in her throat. "Julian wouldn't."

"Wouldn't he?"

Angelina's laugh caught in her throat, her smile flattened. He would, apparently.

"Were you and Chet intimate, Angelina?"

She looked at him bleakly, glanced once more at the photo, then set it down on the table. She sat down in the dinette sofa, picked up the group photo and stared at it a couple moments, her expression growing wistful. "I suppose it doesn't matter anymore now, does it?" she said, resignation in her voice. "Chet and I were friends—best friends."

"And? . . ."

"He was a lot of fun." She smiled thoughtfully. "He made me laugh." She took a sip of her drink, held the glass over the table for several moments, then set it down gently. "We could talk about anything. We shared a common goal: breeding a line of horses that was second to none. A bloodline that they would write about in generations to come. Chet knew which horses to breed, which ones to avoid. With his knowledge of horses and my resources, we were well on our way to building something together. A dynasty."

"Sounds pretty intimate to me," Tom said.

She flicked her eyes at him, then frowned at a thought, angrily it seemed, a smile rising through it. A tear leaked down her cheek. She wiped it with the side of her finger with the elegance of a ballet dancer. She stood quickly, walked over to the freezer, opened it and removed a couple of ice cubes.

"Did you love him?" Tom asked.

Angelina plopped the ice into her drink, walked back to the dinette. The ice cracked.

"It doesn't have to go beyond these walls," he said.

She laughed the emotion out of her throat, looked up at him through her long lashes. "There is always someone listening, Detective," she said. She took a sip of her drink. "Yes, I loved him. Is that what you wanted to hear? I loved Chet in ways I could never love Julian. But there was only one indiscretion—you have to believe me. Just one. It was a moment of weakness. Or strength," she added with a reflective smile. "Does it seem wicked to you?"

"I'm not here to pass moral judgment."

Angelina looked at him for a moment longer—gauging his

sincerity, Tom guessed—then gazed out the window as Miguel walked past it leading her horse. A smile fluttered over her lips. "I'm not a loose woman," she said, her tone suggesting that she might be trying to convince herself rather than Tom.

Tom believed her. As beautiful as she was, she seemed to care more about the world of horses than the world of men. "Did your husband know about you and Chet?"

She shook her head. "I don't know how he could. Not even Chet knew about it until a couple of weeks ago. We were discreet," she added, looking Tom square in the eyes. "Julian was off on one of his business trips to Catalina. Chet and I were training hard for the show. It just happened. Why do you ask?"

"Do you think your husband is capable of murder?"

A shade crossed Angelina's pretty brow. "You think he might've killed Chet?"

"Jealously is an old motive."

"It's absurd." She waved a dismissive hand. "No. Absolutely not. Julian may be a bit rough around the edges, but he would never hurt anyone. He's a doctor. He heals people."

"Doctors kill diseases to save lives. Maybe he thought that in order to save his marriage—"

"Absolutely absurd," she snapped. Angelina's eyes blazed at Tom. "I can't accept it. I won't." She looked down at the group photo, edged it over the others, squaring their corners with her fingertips. "And he wouldn't go hiring any snoop in sunglasses to follow me, either. Besides," she said, her voice cooling, "your jealousy theory doesn't explain Vern. I never looked twice at him."

"Did he ever look twice at you?"

She looked up at him.

Tom could almost see the thought forming in her mind, a glimmer of doubt flickering in her rounding violet eyes. He let it percolate there. "Your husband goes on these Catalina trips often?"

"Catalina?" Angelina seemed to awaken from a dream. "He has a boat," she said, then made an ironic face. "He thinks if he takes his doctor buddies out he can write it off."

"His doctor buddies, huh?" Tom wondered if she knew about his nurse buddies. He collected the photos, slid them back into the envelope beside the one of her husband and Kate Bledsoe. "Do you know where your husband was yesterday between three and four?"

"When Vern was killed?"

Tom nodded.

She shrugged. "Thursday afternoons he's usually at work."

"Usually?"

"Unless he has surgery. He'd be at the hospital then."

"Henry Mayo?"

"That's right."

"Where is he now?"

Angelina took a sip of her drink. "Let's see . . . on Friday afternoons he golfs. Saturdays and Sundays he's usually playing on his boat. Tuesday and Friday evenings he goes shooting at the club. What day is today?"

"Golf."

She smiled.

Tom was suddenly interested in Tuesday and Friday evenings. "What kind of shooting does your husband do?"

"I have no idea." She shook her head doubtfully. "The shooting kind. He belongs to the Silverado Gun Club, if that's any help."

Tom knew the place. It was a trap and skeet club for the hoity-toity—celebrities, investment bankers, professional types. "I assume your husband owns a shotgun?"

"He has lots of guns. Shotguns are the big ones, right?"

"That's right, the big ones."

"I think he has some of those. I don't go into his study much. That's his world. I have mine." A shade of sadness seemed to cross over her smile. One bed, two people, worlds apart.

"Would you know if he reloads his own shells?" Tom asked.

Angelina wrinkled her forehead. "I don't know what you mean."

"People reload their spent shells and hulls—make their own ammunition. It's a hobby. It also saves money."

She shook her head. "Julian doesn't do that, not that I'm aware of. Why do you ask?"

Tom let it slide. "Where does your husband usually golf?"

"Heritage Oaks. It's off Sand Canyon."

"I know it." Tom had golfed there a couple of times, but it, like the gun club, was too blue-blood for his blue-collar salary. "Do you know what time he usually tees off?"

"Sometime after lunch, I think," she said. "That's when he usually goes—him and his doctor buddies. They go there to talk medicine—so Julian says." She made another face, an attempt at resurrecting the smile. "Mention a hangnail and it's a write-off."

Tom nodded his head. He checked his watch, stepped over to the door, put his hand on the round pewter doorknob and looked back. "Just one more question. Have you ever bought any horses in Mexico? Mares, perhaps?"

Angelina's head bobbled as if he'd slapped her. "Are you kidding? Mexico? Who knows what you'd get. I wouldn't dare."

"Would Chet?"

"Not on his life."

Tom and Angelina's eyes were locked, the implication hanging in the air between them. Tom let it hang.

"Why would you ask that?" she asked, walking over him. "Do you think it might have something to do with his death?"

"Just a routine question," he said, turning the doorknob. "Thank you for your time, Angelina."

"Not at all." She touched his arm, pinning him there while a thought segued into her eyes. "You're wrong about Julian, Detective."

"Probably." Tom nodded a farewell, then stepped down from the trailer into the sudden merciless heat. Even so, he was glad to be out in the open. Angelina, with her beauty, the smell of her perfume in the close confines of the trailer, made him feel slightly claustrophobic. As he started to walk away he looked back.

She stood framed in the doorway, her show chaps accenting the curve of her waist and hip as she leaned against the jamb with her right shoulder, sparkling like a sky full of diamonds. She smiled, made a little wave with her fingers, sadness once again clouding her pretty eyes.

A lonely woman, Tom thought as he walked away. All the beauty and money and horses in the world wouldn't change that fact.

•

The Heritage Oaks parking lot was filled to capacity as Tom parked his Bronco in a newly vacated space. He cut the engine, looked over at the tenth tee where two golfers had just hit their balls. Two o'clock on a Friday afternoon and nobody was working; everyone was scheming ways to bilk Uncle Sam. Not a bad idea. Maybe if Tom interrogated suspects on his boat he could write off his sailing expenses. He grabbed the envelope on the seat next to him, got out of his vehicle, and made his way to the clubhouse.

The clubhouse was large, with high-beamed ceilings, lots of wood paneling and plenty of windows affording views of fairways, greens, and small lakes that were great for ducks but lousy for golfers. The slate entryway gave way to plush gray-and-hunter-green carpeting as Tom entered the dining and bar rooms. Several of the tables were occupied by golfers and people who had just come to the club to enjoy the scenery. There was no sign of Montoya.

Tom went down a short wide-open flight of wide carpeted stairs into the pro shop. A young athletically built man wearing a forest green Heritage Oaks club shirt was demonstrating a driver to a couple golfers by one of several club displays. Standing at the door leading outside was an elderly gent with clipboard in hand. He looked to be in his early seventies, and wore a crisp white-haired flattop. He looked ex-military. His face, arms, and hands were deeply tanned. Tom figured he was the starter, walked over and asked him what time Montoya teed off. The starter—Ray, according to his name tag—looked dubiously at him.

Tom flashed his badge.

Ray eyed it with the careful scrutiny of a desk sergeant, flipped a page back on his clipboard, reading the list while making a humming noise deep in his throat. "Is there some kind of trouble?"

"Time?"

"His foursome teed off at twelve-thirty," Ray said, then checked his watch. "Should be rounding out the eighth hole about now."

"Who else was in the foursome?"

Ray read three names: Wong, Washington, Bleimer.

Tom wrote them down. "Thank you," he said, left Ray pulling on his lower lip.

Tom went up into the lounge, sat down at the bar and ordered a Heineken. He looked out at the ninth green. Three women were putting, one holding the flag while the other two holed out. They looked sporty in their short vented skirts and colorful golf shirts and sun visors. Tom's cell phone rang. It was Dan.

"Good news, Tommy. We found our man."

"What man?"

"The dude in the red Monte Carlo. The vehicle is registered to a Calvin Litton."

"Litton?"

"It's our man, Tommy. We cross-checked his driver's license with Newton's photo blowups. No question. It's Calvin Litton."

Tom wrote the name down.

"Got a Fresno address, Dan said."

"Kind of far from home, wouldn't you say?"

"That ain't all. Did a background check on him. Get this; he used to be a private dick in Fresno until the DA there yanked his ticket."

"Yeah?"

"Excessive use of force. Woman hired him to tail her husband, claimed he was cheating on her. He was, apparently. Litton caught them in a no-tell motel, an altercation ensued between Litton and the man, shots were fired. Litton blew his head off. Claims it was self-defense."

"He didn't use a shotgun by any chance."

"Forty-four. Still . . ."

Tom thought about it as he took a sip of beer. "Good work, Dan. Give Martinez an attaboy."

"His head won't fit through doors."

"It doesn't fit now."

"That's true. What'd Mrs. Montoya have to say?"

Tom told him. "She was riding in an event at the time Wieder was killed."

"You believe her?"

"I checked with the registrar at the center." Tom looked out of the windows and saw two carts moving up the ninth fairway. Montoya was in one of the carts. "Gotta go, Dan."

•

Tom stood in the shade of a giant oak where Montoya and his party had parked their carts. He was looking at the green, bright in the sun, where the golfers were lining up their putts. One was black, one Asian, one white, and Montoya who was brown. They looked like a miniature United Nations. Each man putted, his ball making a hollow plunk as it dropped into the hole. Montoya replaced the flag and the men walked off the green, talking golf.

Montoya was wearing a pastel turquoise knit golf shirt over light blue-green slacks; the knit shirt emphasizing his big shoulders and thick hairy forearms. When he saw Tom he broke stride, his face froze. "What are you doing here?" he growled.

"I have some questions, Mr. Montoya, if you don't mind."

Montoya looked at him with belligerent dark brown eyes. The chest hair boiling over his open V-collar seemed to crackle with testosterone. "I mind."

"I still have some questions."

The United Nations contingent looked at Tom, then at Montoya, the men smiling uncertainly. "What's up, Julian?" the white man asked. "Who's this guy?"

"I'm the police," Tom said, showing his badge. "Why don't you fellas go wash a couple of balls while I talk with your pal here."

The men blinked at Tom, blinked at Montoya, and then drifted toward their carts.

Montoya brushed past Tom like a minor annoyance, shoved his club into his bag in the rear of the second cart. "I'm busy."

Tom was getting tired of the line.

Montoya walked around the cart and sat sideways on the green vinyl seat, grabbed the scorecard and stubby pencil clipped to the dash.

Tom had an urge to add a couple more strokes to his score, maybe subtract a couple of teeth while he was at it. "I think you'll want to hear what I have to say," he said, holding up the envelope in his hand.

Montoya scribbled down his score; his big hand smothering

the pencil. "Whatever you got in that envelope doesn't concern me," he said. "You get a five, Wes?" he asked the white guy sitting next to him. Wes nodded. Montoya wrote down his score, clipped the card and pencil back on the dash.

Tom removed the boat photo, clipped it over the scorecard. "Don't forget to add this to your scorecard, Tiger."

Montoya glared at the photo. He lifted his foot off the accelerator pedal, unclipped the photo and held it in his gloved hand so Wes couldn't see it.

"What you got there, Julian?" Wes asked.

"Nothing." Montoya got out of the cart. "You take the wheel, Wes. I'll catch up to you up at the next tee."

Wes looked dubiously at Tom, then followed the cart with the other two men in it onto the cart path, their electric motors whining into the distance.

Montoya's eyes became small and mean and as black as obsidian, brown veins lacing the dead white corneas. He jabbed his finger at the photo. "Where'd you get this?"

Tom ignored him. "Do you own a shotgun?"

"A shotgun?"

"Big gun. Goes boom-boom."

Montoya stared at him levelly. "Lots of people own shotguns. It's not a crime."

"Blowing people's heads off with them is."

Montoya shrugged his big shoulders. "What's that to me?"

"Someone used one on Vern Wieder."

"Yeah?" Montoya clucked his tongue. "People got to be careful where they stick their heads." He chuckled and started away.

Tom and Montoya were walking up the cart path toward the parking lot, the clubhouse above them on their left. Montoya's cleats drummed against the asphalt. "Was he blackmailing you?" Tom asked.

Montoya held up the photo. "This?"

"That's right. We found it in his effects." Tom took the photo and put it back into the envelope.

"Think I killed him because of a photo?"

"It's an interesting photo. I don't think your wife would understand, do you?"

"You show it to her?"

"Not yet. I might."

Montoya looked at him; his eyes flicked to the envelope, then looked straight ahead. Tom could almost feel Montoya's mind on the photo as they walked around the front of the clubhouse toward the tenth tee. "Do you know anyone who owns a red Monte Carlo?" Tom asked.

"No."

"It was parked out in front of your house the other day."

"Imagine that, a red Monte Carlo." Montoya continued around the path, walked onto a bridge that, spanning the road separating the front and back nine, dropped down onto the tenth tee. The United Nations contingent was up on the tee making practice swings. They looked over as Montoya walked up to his cart.

"Know anyone named Calvin Litton?" Tom asked.

Montoya fiddled in his golf bag, zipping and unzipping pockets.

"Here's what he looks like." Tom showed him a photo of Litton.

"Don't know him."

"You didn't look—here."

Montoya's eyes jerked to the photo, back to Tom. "Still don't know him. He play golf here?"

"You didn't hire him to keep an eye on your wife maybe?"

Montoya appeared not to have heard the question. Tom repeated it. Montoya selected a wood from his bag, gripped it first with his gloved hand, then added the other. "Leave my wife out of this," he said, his voice suddenly low.

Tom slid the photo of Litton back into the envelope. "She's a beautiful woman. I can see where a guy might want to keep an eye on her."

A dark crimson flushed above Montoya's shirt collar. He raised the club two feet off the ground, its head pointed at Tom's kneecaps. "I told you—"

"You get friendly with that club and I'll guarantee you a new handicap," Tom said evenly.

The two men stood looking at each other; Montoya's small dark eyes a fixed but calculating belligerency. After a few tense moments he lowered the club with a huff of wind, clipped off the head of a dandelion with a short chop. "I told you I don't know any Litton," he said, took a ball out of his bag and started to walk up onto the tee.

Tom held up a hand in front of Montoya's chest. "Not so fast."

Montoya looked down at Tom's hand, color flushing again around his collar.

Tom said, "I understand you work for the Bethesda Medical Group. I find that interesting. Chet Gundry was a patient there."

Montoya raised his thick eyebrows. "You don't say?"

"You would've had access to his medical records."

"You think?"

"You'd know about his heart condition."

Montoya's eyes rounded in mock surprise. "Is that what he had . . . a heart condition?" He stepped past Tom's hand, clucked his tongue as he headed up to the tee.

Tom remained by the cart. "By the way, Mr. Montoya, where were you yesterday afternoon between three and four?"

Montoya placed his ball on a tee, stood back and looked down the fairway gripping his club. The United Nations contingent looked at Tom, then back at Montoya, who took a couple practice swings. The Asian said something to the white guy.

"Maybe you didn't hear me," Tom said.

Montoya addressed his ball, shifting his weight from foot to foot, glancing down fairway, lifting the club head, then settling it. "I was at work," he said, glancing once more down the fairway, then, fixing his eye on the ball, he brought the club back and swung it through the ball with a whack. The hit sounded flat, like he'd connected with the outside of the clubface. The men all stood shielding their eyes, watching the ball slice high and away into the rough.

The black man shook his head. "Take a mulligan, Julian."

•

Tom sat in his car thinking about Montoya's face when he'd shown him Litton's photo. He knew him. Why deny it? Was Litton a hit man? A keyhole peeper like Dan said? A skeleton in Montoya's closet? The possibilities were endless. There was the possibility, of course, that Litton might not have anything at all to do with Gundry's and Wieder's deaths. Montoya might have hired him to keep an eye on his wife, and that was the end of it. Tom considered the possibility that Angelina might have hired Litton to watch her husband, but that didn't jibe with the Newton photos.

He thought about the photo of Montoya and Bledsoe. It sure got a rise out of him, didn't it? Definitely a cause for divorce, if Angelina were made aware of them. A nasty business all around. Maybe it was blackmail after all. Blackmail is a federal offense. Wieder blackmails Montoya with the photo; Montoya has him whacked, despite his wife's denials that he could do such a thing. If it was blackmail, how did Gundry fit into it? Maybe he didn't. Maybe he was killed for an altogether different reason. Two MOs. Two motives. Two killers.

Tom shook his head. No matter how he lined up on the ball, he'd shank it into the rough. *Take a mulligan, please.* He was about to call Montoya's office to verify his alibi when his cell phone rang. It was Dan.

"Bad news, Tommy."

Tom set himself for it.

"Max Cameron." Dan told him the latest.

Tom cursed.

"I'm headed over there now," Dan said. "You need directions?"

"I know where it is." Tom folded the cell phone onto his coat pocket. He sat staring out the windshield for several long, sinking moments, his hands on the wheel, wishing he could just chuck it all, drive down to the marina, get on his boat and sail away. He turned on the ignition, put her in gear and drove out of the parking lot, feeling numb. He forgot all about Montoya.

Chapter Twenty

Sandy stepped into her house with bags of groceries, toed the door closed behind her, then walked through the mud room into her kitchen where she placed the bags on the counter. She put the groceries away in the refrigerator and in the pantry, saw the blinking red light on her answering machine. She ignored it. She did not want any distractions at the moment. She had seen another garbage truck on her way home and it made her think of her brother, Paul.

She kicked off her boots, padded down the hall in her stocking feet and went into her office, sat down at her desk by the window through which shuttered light came in and spread a gray June gloom over the walls and furniture. She turned on her computer, waited a few moments for the desktop to appear on the monitor, then double-clicked on the search engine icon.

Sylvie prowled languidly into the room. She looked as though she had been sleeping.

"Hey, there," Sandy said. The rekindled warmth she had recently felt for the kitten was still there. She scratched behind her ears. "Did you miss me?"

The cat purred, then curled up in her tail on the rust-colored Berber. Sandy smiled, looked at the monitor. She was on line. She pulled up the LASO home page, typed in her access code, and within moments was admitted into the station database. She linked over to Case Files, typed "Louis Abadjian" in the search window. Moments later his file came up.

There wasn't much to it, just a couple of paragraphs describing an altercation between two Armenians, Louis Abadjian and Miklos Djansezian, waste disposal entrepreneurs. Sergeant Pete Ubersahl and Detective Ned Rockwell had filed the report. According to the report, they were first on the scene in an upscale Valencia neighborhood, where they found Abadjian standing over Djansezian with a baseball bat, the latter crumpled in the grass holding his knees. Witnesses at the scene told the detectives that Abadjian had smashed Djansezian's kneecaps with the bat. According to one witness (Cheryl Talbot, thirty-six), there had been other such altercations, but without violence. When questioned, Abadjian stated emphatically that Djansezian had fallen down a flight of stairs; further, Abadjian had been hitting balls to a few neighborhood kids. Since it wasn't his neighborhood, and since there were neither kids nor a baseball in view at the time, and since there was only a single step leading up to the victim's porch, the detectives surmised that the witnesses had probably come closer to the facts. Regardless, Djansezian refused to file charges against Louis Abadjian (dubbed the Louisville Slugger in the report), and that was the end of it.

Sandy felt a little disappointed. She couldn't imagine how a territorial dispute between two Armenians, ten years ago, could have had anything to do with her brother's murder. It probably didn't. There was the possible trash connection (she had overheard her brother talking about the trash business on the phone), but that might be purely coincidental.

She thought about Pete Ubersahl, Old High and Uptight. He had never once in all the years she had known him mentioned the case, or his former partner, Ned Rockwell. In fact, she'd never even heard the name until Frank and Tim mentioned it. It was nothing unusual. The Los Angeles County Sheriff's Organization was huge. Officers came and went, often without fanfare. Sandy figured that Rockwell had either transferred to another department before she arrived at the station or had retired. An old cop put out to pasture, soon forgotten.

Sandy downloaded Rockwell's service file, but as she read through it an altogether different picture emerged. He hadn't transferred, he hadn't retired; after fifteen years of distinguished service, he was killed in a shootout in Palmdale. He and his partner, Sgt. Pete Ubersahl, were working narcotics at the time. Moving on a tip on the whereabouts of a methamphetamine lab, the detectives pulled into an empty lot, where three well-armed Latinos appeared to be waiting in ambush. Rockwell took three 9-mm slugs in the chest, but managed to return fire and kill one of his assailants. Rockwell died at the scene. One of the other killers was a notorious gangster by the name of Francisco "Cisco" Alejandro; he and the third ambusher were both felled by Ubersahl. Both Ubersahl and Rockwell were awarded citations, the latter posthumously.

What Sandy read next caused her to frown at her monitor: the shootout had occurred three days after her brother's death. She looked out the window of her office, a strange, almost preternatural tingling prickling along her spine.

Three days.

Her brother had not yet been buried.

Sandy looked up the ballistics report and found that the slugs taken from Rockwell's chest did not match the one taken from her brother's head. She scratched the side of her nose in thought. Two MOs. Two killers. One case closed, the other relegated to the Open Files. One involved a drug bust gone terribly bad, the other a robbery homicide. Throw in a tribal dispute about trash, and what did she have? On the surface there was no reason to suspect that the cases were linked at all. Yet another windmill? Maybe. But the fact that Pete Ubersahl had been at each of the three scenes tilted her thoughts in that direction.

"What do you make of that?" she said to her kitten.

Sylvie, sleeping soundly behind her, made no comment.

Sandy stood, still feeling a sense of wonder as she walked into her kitchen and made a glass of iced tea. She thought of a possible plan of investigation, one that would not arouse Ubersahl's suspicions. Not an easy task, considering that Ubersahl appeared to be everywhere at the same time—Ubiquitous Ubersahl—his fingers in every pie.

The blinking red light on her answering machine pulled her gaze toward it. Sipping her drink, she hit Play. There was one message. It was from Kate Bledsoe. "I know we haven't exactly been the best of friends," Kate's voice said, "but I think I might need your help."

Sandy set her glass down on the counter, her brother's case

once again sliding to the back burner. Kate went on to say that she needed to talk to Sandy as soon as possible about a matter that might require her police expertise. She gave three numbers where she might be reached. "Thank you, Sandy. I appreciate it."

Click.

Sandy hit Replay, listened again to the message; this time parsing the words and the tone. There was a sense of urgency in Kate's voice, of fear perhaps. Something had her spooked.

Something that might require her police expertise.

Feeling a sense of déjà vu, Sandy dialed Kate's home number, waited four rings, then got her answering machine. She left a message, gave two additional numbers where she might be reached, and disconnected the line. She dialed Kate's work number. Her supervisor said she had failed to show up—not like Kate at all. Her cell phone was out of service. *Terrific.* Three strikes and you're out. Sandy felt a premonition of danger.

Just then her telephone rang. She picked up the receiver. "Kate?"

"It's me, Sandy." *Dad.*

"Oh, sorry, Dad. I was expecting another call. What's up?" She listened, frowned suddenly at her countertop. "I don't believe it," she groaned wearily. "No, don't call Wilson. If you lawyer up it might be perceived as an admission of guilt." She listened. "I'm on my way over there right now. Don't worry, Dad, I'll be right over. Fifteen minutes." She hung up the phone, shook her head.

"What in the world is Tom thinking?" she said, reaching for her car keys.

Chapter Twenty-One

Tom drove his Bronco down a rutted washboard road that wound through the northern hills of Agua Dulce, and finally came to a sign that read Sweetwater Estates, Cameron Construction. Max Cameron, General Contractor. The road opened into a wide valley split by a stony creek that snaked from one end to the other, bulging in the middle where Caterpillar tractors appeared to be digging out a lake. The hills on either side of the valley were burlap brown and rocky, dotted with sage, scrub oaks, and manzanita. The yucca was still in bloom with thousands of pale yellow torches—Lord's candles—tonguing up over the hills. Huge rocks pushed up through the soil that was reddish in color. There was a wild tart scent breezing through Tom's open windows as he pulled next to a white F-150 and parked. Dan and Max Cameron were standing by the truck. Max did not look pleased.

Tom got out of his vehicle, nodded a curt greeting. "Dan. Mr. Cameron."

"I'm not saying anything until Sandy gets here," Max said, fixing a hard eye on Tom to underscore the point. He looked up the road that Tom had just driven down.

Dan shrugged at Tom.

"We just have a couple of questions," Tom said.

Max continued looking up the road. "Not until Sandy gets here."

Tom noticed a set of grading plans spread over the hood of Max's truck, weighted down with a ball peen hammer and a crescent wrench. He looked at the earthmovers grading pads. Based on the plans in Chet Gundry's office, he guessed where the clubhouse and other facilities would eventually stand. He could see why Sandy liked it so much. "Looks like things are moving along nicely."

If Max had heard him he gave no indication of it.

"Here she comes," Dan said, nodding up the road.

Sandy's truck rumbled toward them, a cloud of red dust rising behind it, like a desert storm. The men waited until she parked.

Seeing Sandy walking toward them, her hair an insouciant mane bouncing around her shoulders, her hazel eyes clear and sharply focused beneath sweeps of long black lashes, Tom felt as though he was always seeing her for the first time.

"What's going on here, Tom?" she said angrily, planting her fists on her lovely hips.

Tom cleared his throat. "We need to ask your father a few questions."

"About Vern's lawsuit?"

"That's right."

"His claim on the property is bogus."

"Totally," Max nodded.

"Vern's deal was with Chet," Sandy said.

"With his limited partnership, not with me," Max said, apparently feeling the freedom now to speak. "I had no dealings with him. When he pulled out of the deal the partnership went with him."

"When Chet pulled out of the deal," Sandy clarified.

"That's right—Chet." Max stabbed the hood of his truck with his finger. "He's got no claim."

"Wieder thought otherwise," Dan said. "He filed a *lis pendis* with the courts."

Max put up his hands, waved them from side to side. "He had no grounds to do that. My deal was with Gundry, no one else."

Tom looked from Max to Sandy, then back to Max. "According to his records, he put up a hundred thousand . . ."

"Which was returned to him."

". . . to secure a foothold in the development."

"Like I said," Max said, "our deal was with Gundry's limited partnership, not with any individuals in it. If Wieder had a beef, it was with Gundry."

"And now they're both dead."

Max's face tightened, the muscles in his jaw moved, then locked. He glanced quickly at Sandy, then back at Tom. "I can see how that might look," he said, dragging a callused hand over his scalp, "but it's got nothing to do with me or what's going on here."

Tom watched an earthmover rolling, big-wheeled, over a section of ground, dark smoke belching from its stack. "Lot of money tied up here."

"*My* money."

"Three million of which is coming from the key-man insurance," Dan said.

"That's right."

"A court battle could put a stop to work."

A shovel-faced man in a white Cameron construction truck drove up to Max and leaned a leathery elbow out the window. "Got a couple questions about the clubhouse pad, Max."

Max waved him off. "I'll be with you in a minute, Cory." The man nodded, eyed Tom and Dan as he drove away. Max said to Tom: "Does it look like we're stopped?"

Tom knew that Max Cameron was a well-respected man in the Santa Clarita community, well connected with the city council, the power brokers. He was wealthy, used to getting his own way in matters of real-estate development. He knew that in most communities, money talks, dead men don't, especially ones without heirs to pursue lawsuits. "Two men connected to this development have been murdered, Mr. Cameron. I find that a little peculiar, don't you?"

"Peculiar?"

Sandy raised her eyebrows. "Do you really think my father had something to do with their deaths?"

Tom continued looking at Max. "You tell me. The first man had a three-million-dollar key-man policy taken out on him by you. That's three million to secure your down. The second man threatened to put a halt to your development. Both men are lying in the morgue, the second man's head blown half off by a shot-gun."

Max's steel blue eyes flickered.

"That's right," Tom said. "Shotgun. Twelve-gauge. Whoever killed him used the same shot you were using in your reloads. Number eights."

Max gave his head a little shake. "Most trap shooters do."

"What kind of wads do you use?"

"Wads?" Max's tanned forehead wrinkled into a frown. "Depends on what hulls I'm loading. Winchester Double-A's mostly."

"Do you ever use any other kind?"

"Sure."

"What kind?"

Sandy stepped forward with an indignant chop of her hand. "He said he was using Winchesters, Tom."

Tom did not look at her. "Ever mix brands? Hulls and wads?"

Max thought about it. "Not usually. Maybe I have, but not lately. I know they do out at the gun club."

Tom frowned.

Dan raised his eyebrows.

Max nodded. "Sure. They mix hulls and wads all the time. They buy wads in bulk, then load 'em into hulls they collect off the line."

"There you go, Tom," Sandy said. "You need to be asking around the club."

Tom looked at her, thinking about it. Nothing would have prevented Max from buying a couple boxes of reloads from the club, if nothing else for the hulls. He looked back at Max, feeling heartsick for what he was about to ask. "Where were you yesterday between three-fifteen and a quarter to four?"

"Three-fifteen?" Max looked at Sandy.

She shook her head in frustration, raised her hands. "Go ahead and tell him, Dad. You've got nothing to hide."

"Let's see." Max looked down at his feet. "I had some errands to run—city stuff. Sometime after lunch, I know. Yes." He looked back at Tom. "Between three-fifteen and a quarter till I was back here. Plenty of men around to verify it."

Tom looked over the job site—tractors digging, earthmovers grading, workmen and inspectors crawling like ants over a new mound. People coming and going. The Borden ranch where Wieder was killed was about ten minutes away; someone could easily slip away for a half hour or so and not be missed. "Do you know anyone who owns a red Monte Carlo?"

"A red Monte Carlo?" Max shook his head. "Can't say that I do."

"Haven't seen one around the site lately?" Dan asked.

"No, I haven't. Is it important?"

"It could be."

"Someone saw a red Monte Carlo parked near where Vern Was killed," Sandy said. "They think he might've had something to do with Vern's murder."

"His name's Calvin Litton," Tom said.

Max looked at him. "Why are you talking to me, then? Why aren't you out looking for this Litton fellow?"

"Good question," Sandy said, folding her arms across her chest. "Do you think my dad hired this guy, Tom? Hired him to kill Chet and Vern?"

Max looked at Sandy incredulously, a smile jerking cautiously over his lips. "A *hit* man? Well, that's nuts." He looked at Tom as if he'd told an off-color joke. "You think I hired a hit man?"

"We didn't say that, Mr. Cameron," Tom said, again feeling the cold isolation of a traitor. "We're just trolling."

"A hit man?" Max laughed at Sandy.

Sandy was staring glumly at the ground, shaking her head back and forth.

A dark red color flushed suddenly over Max's face. He turned and faced Tom, his eyes burning. "I don't believe it. A hit man." He reached over and yanked the plans off the hood, but the wrench and hammer anchoring them came with them and clattered to the ground.

Tom started to pick them up.

"I got 'em," Max said gruffly. He bent down and picked up the tools and tossed them into the truckbed with a jarring clatter. "You got any more questions, Detective?" he said, rolling up the plans. "I've got work to do."

Tom looked grimly at Dan.

Dan shook his head no.

"That should do it," Tom said, knowing that he had offended a man that he admired. He started to shake Max's hand—maybe dam up the breach a little—but thought the better of it. "Sorry we have to put you through this."

Max looked at him steadily, his steel gray eyes an implacable bright intensity. "I didn't kill them," he said evenly. "I don't kill people. You ask any one of the men around here and they'll tell you where I was." He continued rolling up the plans, chuckling disgustedly. "Hit man."

Tom looked over at Sandy, who was gazing at the hills. Then he and Dan walked over to Dan's vehicle without a word.

"Whaddya think, Tommy?"

Tom looked over the job site.

"He could've done it," Dan said. "He was here and then again, he might not have been here. He could've got the shells from the club."

Tom said nothing.

"He could've hired Litton."

"I'm not buying it."

"Because of Sandy?"

Tom turned his head with a sharp glare.

Dan put his hand on Tom's shoulder and squeezed. "I'm your partner, Tommy. You've lost a bit of perspective here. Was me, you'd say the same thing."

Tom glanced back at Sandy and her dad. Max was tapping the plans against the side of his truck as he said something to Sandy. "You wanna nose around here a bit, Dan? Maybe somebody saw the Monte Carlo. Maybe somebody knows Litton."

"No problem. I'll check with the city as well. I turn up anything, I know how to reach you." Dan squeezed Tom's shoulder once more, got into his car, and rolled down the window. "For what it's worth, Tommy, I think he's clean."

Tom said nothing. He walked back to Sandy. She was standing watching her dad drive away toward the clubhouse pad, her arms still folded across her chest. She would not look at Tom. "We need to talk," he said.

Then she looked at him, all the hurt and anger rising to the surface of her eyes in a mist of color. "Fine. Talk."

"Not here. Let's get out of the heat."

"There's a little pizza shop in town." Without waiting for his reply she turned and walked back to her truck.

●

Agua Dulce is a tiny bedroom community with western-style storefronts, hitch rails and boardwalks, a stone's throw from picturesque Vasquez Rocks. There are no traffic lights or streetlights or sidewalks busy with people; there is only a two-lane road bisecting a clutch of stores and small businesses that comprise the hub of the town. Tom and Sandy sat in a shaded corner booth, neither one looking at the other as a vacant-eyed girl with a black-and-purple scab of hair and a pierced lip took their orders. Tom could tell that Sandy had been holding her emotions in check since leaving the job site. Then:

"You honestly think my father killed—?" Sandy looked quickly at the girl drifting vaguely back to the counter, lowered her voice to a fierce whisper. "You really think he killed Vern Wieder?"

"Look at it from our perspective," Tom said. "Your father had both motive and opportunity. You have to admit—"

She held up her hand as though halting traffic. She looked out the window on her left, gave her head a little shake. "Do you have any other leads, or is my father the prime suspect? He *is* notorious, you know. Bodies dropping around him like flies. Got his picture in all the post offices."

"Sandy."

"I don't believe this." She would not look at him. "My father the killer," she said, her voice throaty with emotion. "Why not question my mother while you're at it? She cheats at solitaire."

Tom could see a metamorphosis taking place on her face, her eyes blinking away the sarcasm and anger as she gazed steadily at him. There was only hurt in them now. "I'm really sorry, Sandy," he said. "I don't know how else to go about this."

Sandy's eyes misted, then she frowned, apparently chasing back tears.

Tom reached across the table and took her hand as he had done at her parents' house. And as she had done there, she withdrew it, sitting upright as the girl brought their drinks. The girl smiled emptily, her mind apparently in another universe. She left a slip on the table and drifted back to the counter as though moving through a dream.

Sandy sipped her drink through a straw. "Okay, Tom," she said, coolly. "So what did you want to talk about?"

"Can we try and leave the personal stuff out of it?"

She looked at him coldly. "Sure. That's fine," she said, jabbing the straw up and down through the ice cubes. "Nothing personal. Just two detectives going over a case."

Tom rolled his glass between his hands. "That's right, two cops," he said evenly. "For starters, I don't think your father killed anyone."

She laughed. "You deduced that since we left the job site? That's pretty good, Detective."

Tom stared across the table.

She held up a hand. "Sorry. I forgot. Nothing personal." She took a sip of her drink, jabbed the ice cubes some more. "Okay then, if it wasn't Daddy dearest, then who?"

Tom gave her everything he had on Calvin Litton, his Fresno address, that he was a private detective, a bedroom peeper who killed a man with a .44 magnum and had his license jerked by the Fresno DA. He described the photos Newton had taken of Angelina Montoya at several equestrian events, Litton in several of them, watching her from the bleachers. He told her how he'd seen the red Monte Carlo parked outside Montoya's estate, explained his earlier suspicions that Julian Montoya might have hired Litton to tail his wife, then maybe had him kill Gundry for sleeping with her. It was a clinical briefing, without varnish.

Sandy had listened quietly, sipping her drink. "Chet and Angelina were sleeping together? Who told you that?"

"Angelina. She said she had one indiscretion with him." Tom briefed her on his meeting with Angelina earlier.

"I'll have to give that some thought." Sandy looked down at her hands, then back at Tom. "Adultery is a pretty strong motive for murder. But you don't think so now?"

"Wieder doesn't figure."

Sandy screwed her mouth into a wry twist. "No, I can't see Vern sleeping with anyone but his rattlesnakes."

"You know about those, huh?"

"Who doesn't? Julian *is* a jealous man, Tom. I've seen him get pretty worked up over men looking at Angelina. I could see him hiring a watchdog. Killing Chet? . . ." She shook her head doubtfully. "I don't know. How do you figure Wieder, then?"

Tom showed her the photo of Montoya and Kate Bledsoe on his boat.

Sandy turned the photo in the light. "Good old Kate," she said. Looking at Montoya behind the wheel, she chuckled sardonically. "I see it's okay for the gander but not for the goose. That's Julian for you. Well, they deserve each other." She handed the photo back to Tom. "You think Wieder was blackmailing him?"

"Possibly."

Sandy frowned. "Julian kills Chet for sleeping with his wife. Has plenty of time and opportunity to set that up. Then Wieder lets him know that he has the goods on his indiscretions with Kate . . . offs him on impulse. Is that the idea?"

"Or has him killed." Tom nodded. "Yes, something like that."

Sandy looked sideways in thought. "Wouldn't Julian make sure he had the pictures and negatives in his possession before he killed him?"

"We thought of that, too," Tom said, his tone suggesting doubt. "We didn't find any negatives."

"No negatives, huh?" Sandy swirled the ice with her straw. "You know Angelina might've hired Litton—ever think of that?"

Tom looked at her.

"Think about it, Tom. Maybe she suspected what was going on between Julian and Kate—hired Litton to keep an eye on them."

Tom shook his head. "Newton's show photos suggest that Angelina was the subject. Besides, how did Wieder get the photos?"

Sandy stared at him a few moments, a shadow drawing over her face. She looked down at her drink, her brows pinched in thought. "I can see why you might suspect my dad. He's a much neater package, isn't he?"

Tom said nothing, finally took a sip of his drink, feeling it cooling down his parched throat. He briefed Sandy on his interview with Kate Bledsoe.

"I just got a message from her on my machine," Sandy said. "Kate," she clarified, meeting his eyes. The chasm between them had either closed or had been momentarily forgotten. They were two detectives working a case. "Get this. She wants to talk to me about a matter that requires my police expertise."

Tom set his glass down on the table. "Seriously."

"As a heart attack."

"It has a familiar ring to it, don't you think?"

"I'll say."

"No ideas what it was about?"

She shook her head. "I've left messages for her to call me, but I've not heard back from her. She appears to have dropped off the radar."

Tom looked out the window at an old cob driving by in an orange Kubota tractor, its bucket raised high. The man waved at a woman crossing the street. Agua Dulce was a friendly little town.

"Something else, Tom. It may be nothing, but it's been bugging me. I talked to Bud Nichols the other day and he told me he hadn't met with Sorrel Rose for a couple of weeks. I saw both of them earlier at lunch. Rose told me that she and Bud met in Chet's trailer the night before he died." She waited a moment for Tom to assimilate the news. "He lied, Tom."

He pursed his lips.

"I think something's going on there," Sandy said. "I mean, why would he lie? Unless he didn't want me to know that he and Rose met."

"Who is Sorrel Rose?"

"She's the owner of Sorrel West Outfitters—the clothing line that wanted to use Chet in its ads. Wants to use Bud, too, I guess."

Tom thought about it. "Chet told you someone got their feathers ruffled in the deal, didn't he? You think maybe this Rose gal was playing two ends against the middle? Bud didn't like that so he blew out the competition."

Sandy shrugged. "That, or maybe Chet said something to her that ruffled *her* feathers. Maybe that's what Chet meant. She wears one of those hats with a lot of feathers in the hatband," she clarified. "I never cared much for the style, myself. But then she's a Texan."

"Rose is a Texan?"

"Down to her bootheels. Her company is located in Houston."

"Houston, huh?" Tom thought about something. "This hat with the feathers, does it have a crease that goes down the middle?"

She lifted her head inquiringly. "What if it does?"

Tom patted his coat pocket, remembering the news clipping that he'd forgotten to copy. "She have red hair by any chance?"

"Flaming."

Tom got out the clipping, unfolded it, and slid it across the table. "Like this, maybe?"

Sandy looked at the color photo in the clipping. "That's her. She looks a bit older than this photo, but that's her. That's Sorrel Rose. Where'd you get this?"

"Wieder's effects. You said you met with her?"

"Her and Bud this afternoon. Why?"

"Her name is Sonny Weston."

"*What*? Let me see that." She looked more closely at the photo, then read the headline: "'High Dollar Horses, Mules for Drug Lords.'" She frowned. "I remember this story," she said, reading through it. "It was big news in all the horse magazines."

"Would you say that it rocked the horse industry?"

Their eyes met. "Seven-point-two on the Richter," Sandy said. She tapped the photo of Sonny/Sorrel. "Sonny Weston, huh? I knew I'd seen her face somewhere before." She handed the clipping back to Tom. "You found this in Wieder's effects?"

"Uh-huh." Tom folded the clipping back into his pocket. "Using mares to transport drugs across the border would qualify as a federal offense, wouldn't it?"

Sandy's eyes jerked open. "Tom!" She grabbed her purse and slid out of the booth. "We need to go see a man about a horse!"

Chapter Twenty-Two

Vasquez Rocks, the flotsam of some gargantuan hydro-seismic up-
heaval in ages past, jutted violently against the late afternoon sky.
Thick veins of basalt, shale, and red-brown conglomerates sand-
wiched between alternating layers of sandstone formed huge slanting tables of rock almost perpendicular to the earth, boggling the
theories of Old earth geologists, inspiring nature lovers and navel
gazers, as well as providing dramatic backdrops for Hollywood film
directors ever since the days of Tom Mix. The sun, low in the sky,
cast its slanting light on the rocks, causing them to glow a blood red
like hell's own kitchen.

Reining his horse down through a twisting coyote trail in the
rocks, in much the same way that the bandit Tiburcio Vasquez may
have done a century and a half earlier, Bud Nichols galloped over
the flats to a lonely pepper tree and swung out of the saddle into
the waiting arms of a slinky blonde.

The blonde, dressed in a cropped T-shirt, a pair of low-slung
jeans that looked as if they'd been airbrushed onto her body, and a
pair of red fandango boots, looked dreamily into Bud's eyes.
"There's only one thing that looks better than a cowboy wearing
Sorrel West clothes," she purred.

Nichols, wearing a pair of custom blue jeans, a colorful print
shirt, and black hat, grinned like he'd just robbed a bank. "And
what might that be, darlin'?"

She undid his top shirt button, looking up at him with wicked brown eyes. "I'll give you three guesses." She smiled, stepped up onto her toes, and gave him a steamy kiss.

"Cut!" a little bald man in a director's chair shouted. Wearing a bush jacket, shorts, and hiking boots, the director of the commercial looked like a bug on safari. "Beautiful! Beautiful!" he shouted through a megaphone. "Let's do another one."

The moment the director yelled "Cut!" the blonde spun away from Nichols and stood, hands on hips, glaring at the director. "Eww," she whined, wiping her mouth. "Does he have to chew tobacco?"

Tom and Sandy were standing in a small crowd of onlookers composed mostly of film crew. "No chemistry," she whispered in Tom's ear.

Tom smiled. It was the first joke she'd made since the start of the case. "No?"

Sandy shook her head. "Flat." She moved her hand parallel to the ground, palm down, to suggest just how flat.

Sorrel Rose was sitting next to the director in a green canvas director's chair, her back to Tom and Sandy. She had a drink in her fist. A woman with a long-billed faded yellow cap and sunglasses came over to the director with a script and chewed on his ear.

"Just one more," the director said, clapping his hands. "Quickly now! Quickly! We haven't much light."

The film crew made adjustments to lights, cameras, and sound apparatus. A makeup girl with magenta hair pinned back in a loose swirl rushed over to the blonde and repaired her lipstick. Nichols swung onto his horse and reined it back toward the rocks. At the director's "Action!" he rode back down through the rocks, as before, then galloped over to the waiting blonde, her expression suddenly alive and sexy before the camera. They both seemed unreal in the intense artificial lights, like phantasms. There were six more takes.

Sandy made sotto voce asides to Tom, giving each take a verbal thumbs-up or -down. Tom smiled each time, watching her out of the corner of his eyes with the growing hope that it might be all right again between them.

Finally the director told everyone to prepare for the next scene. The blonde, ignoring everyone but her image in a handheld mirror, was having her cheekbones dusted and her hair primped for the umpteenth time. Nichols stood alone under the lights, holding his horse. He looked as though he was standing on a train platform with his bags, the train having just left the station without him.

"Shall we go over and cheer him up?" Sandy said.

Tom gestured with his hand. "After you."

They walked over to Nichols. Nichols was tying his horse to a hitch rail. "Got a minute, Mr. Nichols?" Tom asked. "We've got a few questions."

Nichols turned his head, saw Tom standing next to Sandy. "Who are you?"

Tom flashed his badge. "Detective Rigby."

Nichols looked from Tom to Sandy, then back to Tom. His makeup was on pretty thick. He looked muddy in the bright lights. "I've got a scene to do," he said.

"You'll have plenty of time to get back into character." Tom grinned.

Nichols eyed Tom a moment longer, his eyes darkening, then looked at Sandy. "What's this about?"

Sandy took the lead. "You lied to me yesterday, Bud. Your meeting with Sorrel Rose?"

"What are you talking about?"

"You said you hadn't met with Rose for a couple of weeks. She told me you met in Chet's trailer the night before he died."

A tight wooden smile jerked in Nichols's mouth. Tom guessed he was afraid of cracking his face. "You got your panties in a bind over that?"

"This is a murder investigation, Bud. You could be charged with obstruction."

Nichols stared at her, shifted his eyes to Tom, leaned stiffly to one side and spat in the dirt. "Okay, so it was a mistake," he said, wiping his lips with delicate flicks of his forefinger. "I thought if I told you we'd met you'd think I had something to do with Chet's death."

"Did you?"

"What would be my motive." Nichols jerked his head toward the film set. ". . . *this*?"

"Lot of people would die to get a break in the movie business. Some might even kill."

"This ain't the movies. I'm hustling shirts."

"How long have you had this deal in place?" Tom asked. "It couldn't have happened overnight."

Nichols shrugged. "A couple weeks now."

"Chet thought he had the deal," Sandy said.

"I can't speak to that. Maybe he thought he did, I can't say. You'll have to ask Sorrel. She's sittin' right over there." He hooked a thumb. Rose was watching them from her director's chair, holding her drink between her fingers. She had just lit up a cigarette. "I think she had both of us in mind, to tell you the truth."

"Kind of convenient that Chet just up and got himself murdered."

Nichols looked at Tom. "I signed the contract the night before he died. Signed it right in his trailer. Why would I kill him?"

Tom watched his eyes. The corners were tight, maybe because of his makeup. Tom still felt that he was trying to hide something. "I understand you lost a couple of horses in the past few months," he said. "Lost one just a couple weeks back."

Nichols's eyes flickered. He looked down at a stinkbug picking its way over the dirt, stretched out his chin and loosed a lipful onto its shiny black back. The beetle, understandably ticked off, aimed its pointy rear end into the air and emitted a foul odor. There was a slight warm breeze blowing up from the southwest that kept the smell at bay, so no one moved. "What of it?" Nichols asked, wiping his lower lip clean of brown spittle.

"The mare just up and died?"

"That's right."

"How'd it die?"

"Heart gave out. I've got the death certificate if you need it."

"The one that Vern made out for you," Sandy said.

"That's right," he said evenly.

Tom shook his head skeptically. "Heart gave out, just like that."

"Just like that. I've got to get set for my next scene." Nichols started to walk away.

Tom put up his hand. "Just a second, sport. You didn't happen to buy the mare from someone in Mexico, did you?"

Nichols looked at him. "No."

"Where'd you buy her from?"

"Someone local."

"Who?"

Nichols laughed. He broke from Tom's gaze, looked beyond the rocks to the mountains in the distance. The lowering sun cast reddish bronze shadows on the side of his muddy face. Tom could see his cheek muscles twitching.

"I'm sure you have a bill of sale," Tom said. "You wouldn't mind us taking a look at it, would you?"

"What's that?" Bud swung his head back at Tom, his eyes a bit dazed. "The bill of sale? I threw it away." He frowned, thinking about it. "I did. I threw it away after the mare died. Why keep it?"

"I would think you'd keep it for tax purposes. It'd be a write-off, I would think."

Beneath the hot lights Tom could see a single thick bead of sweat breaking through his makeup, glistening, then trickle down his cheek. Nichols touched it with a fingertip.

"You're not a very good liar," Tom said.

Nichols shook his head with a stuttery laugh. His joints seemed to come unhinged, roll around, and then lock into place: hip cocked, right foot forward, elbows back, thumbs hooked into his back pockets, a hard look back in his eyes. "I'm not lying," he said, shifting his eyes from Tom to Sandy. "I got nothing to lie about."

Tom looked at him steadily.

"I don't," Nichols said angrily. He unhooked his left thumb, rubbed the palm of his hand on his shiny new jeans, and then re-hooked the thumb.

"Did you kill Chet Gundry?"

Another bead of sweat traveled down the muddy path made by the first one. "No, I didn't."

"Did you kill Vern Wieder?"

Nichols shot a hard look at Sandy. "What's going on here? I don't have to answer these questions."

"Was that a yes or a no?" Tom asked. "Better call makeup. Your face is running."

Nichols swiped his fingers over his cheek, making a muddy smear.

Just then Sorrel Rose walked over to them, drink in one hand, waving a cigarette out in front of her with the other as though clearing a path through gnats. "You were terrific, Bud honey," she boomed, trailing a ribbon of smoke. She clapped a hand on Nichols's shoulder. "Wasn't he terrific?"

"Great chemistry," Sandy said, eyeing the two of them.

Rose laughed throatily. "Don't you know it?" She looked at Tom, looked him over from head to toe. "Who's your handsome friend? He don't ride horses by any chance, does he?"

"This is Detective Tom Rigby," Sandy said.

"You don't say. Another po-*leece*man." Rose gave him a second look-over, slower this time, grinning like an alligator. "You shore would look good in a pair of my jeans, honey."

Tom got the feeling Rose's entrance had been timed to prevent Nichols from saying something incriminating. She was about a minute late. "And what's your name?" he asked politely.

"Rose. Sorrel Rose." She touched a curl at her temple. "On account of my fiery locks."

Tom smiled, his eyes sweeping up from the red roses in her pointy black-and-white boots, over her too-tight jeans, to her flabby arms that she ought to have had more sense to cover, sweeping over her pretty round face with fire-engine red lips and blue eyes the color of twilight, twinkling with mischief, and on up to her white hat, creased down the middle of the crown, the band lined with feathers. "You remind me of someone," he said.

"Oh?" Rose's eyes twinkled warily. Still grinning, she said, "The police, huh?" She looked from Tom to Sandy. "Is there a problem here?" she asked, her tone flattening. "We've got a permit for the park."

Nichols was looking down at the ground, moving a toe over the dirt.

"We were wondering where your star here bought his mare, Miss Weston," Tom said. "Maybe you can help us."

Nichols looked up quickly.

Rose narrowed her eyes, the big Texas smile revealing small predator teeth. "The name's Rose."

Tom laughed. "Did I just call you Weston? I'm sorry. You just remind me of someone with that name. You know how you get a name fixed in your mind."

Rose said nothing, but flicked the end of her cigarette with her thumb.

Tom leaned forward and peered at Rose with a stubborn grin, tilted his head from side to side. "I swear you could be her twin." He grunted an ironic note, turned to Sandy. "Don't you think she looks like her?"

"The one mixed up with the feds a few years back?"

"That's right . . . Sonny Weston. I was just reading about her in the papers. That 'Mares for Mules' scandal. Rose here's a dead ringer for her, don't you think?"

Sandy pinched her lower lip, made a show of looking over Rose's features. "She's a bit older, of course. But you might have something, Tom."

Rose took a drag of her cigarette, stepped on it with her toe. "I don't like your friends, Bud honey," she said, blowing out a cloud of smoke. "You've another scene to do."

"Your scene can wait," Tom said, his tone abruptly changing. "We have a little script of our own we'd like to run by you first. The story has two villains—Little Red Riding Hood and the Big Bad Wolf." He grinned. "As the story goes, Red and Wolf buy a mare down in Mexico. Mare's carrying a little bundle, only she's not pregnant. She's carrying balloons."

Rose touched Nichols's arm. "Let's go."

"You haven't heard the best part," Tom said. "The balloons are full of drugs—cocaine, maybe. They're stuffed inside the mare's uterus. Wild, huh? Problem is one of them bursts and the mare dies from an overdose. Not a problem. Red and Wolf are in cahoots with a crooked vet named Humpty Dumpty, who rules it a heart attack. Humpty delivers the remaining balloons and everyone is in the pink. Everyone except the mare, of course. How does it sound so far, Bud honey?"

Rose shook her head. "Don't say a word, Bud."

Nichols made a noise in his throat.

"Wait till you hear the plot twist," Tom said. "The hero of the story—Jack Be Nimble—finds out about the setup. Maybe Red approached him at one time, but Jack turned her down and threatened to tell Mother Goose." Tom fanned a thumb at Sandy. "Can't have that, so Red and Wolf spike his Kool-Aid."

Nichols was looking down at his feet, shaking his head slowly back and forth.

"Here's where the plot thickens." Tom grinned some more. "Humpty almost loses his breakfast when one of the King's men"—he jerked a thumb at himself—"tells him that the hero's been murdered. Murder isn't part of Humpty's game plan, apparently, but—rotten egg that he is—he gets greedy and wants his slice of the pie fattened. Figures he's got it coming. What he gets is a load of birdshot and a side order of scrambled eggs. Red and Wolf go on to make millions hustling shirts."

Tom gestured with his hand. "Bit of a downer, I'll admit, but hey—so are the jokers in the cast."

Nichols looked up at Tom, his eyes cold and deadly. Sweat had trickled down from his hat and formed muddy rivulets in his face makeup, which he ignored. "I'd like to see you prove any of it."

"We will."

"Let's go, Bud," Rose said, taking Nichols by the arm. She glared at Tom. "You come up with any more fairy tales, cowboy, trot them by my lawyer first. Meanwhile, sit on it and rotate. How's that for a plot twist?" Rose flashed her small pointed teeth. She and Nichols headed back to the set.

Watching them, Sandy said, "Quite a performance, Tom."

Tom made a so-so gesture with his hand.

Rose sat down beside the director, leaned over and said something to him and laughed. Bud Nichols went over to the makeup girl to have his face repaired. He would not look in their direction.

"It doesn't figure, Bud being mixed up in this," Sandy said. "He's got a good thing with his breeding."

"The lure of easy money is a fierce competitor."

"What about Rose? Her company seems to be doing well. Why jeopardize that?"

"Abbe Newton mentioned that it had some financial setbacks in the past, but was on stronger footing now." Tom let Sandy fill in the blanks.

"Yes, but murder."

"It fits." Tom laid it out for her. If Nichols and Rose were running drugs from Mexico they had motive and opportunity. Gundry might have gotten wind of it and threatened to blow the whistle. Rose and Nichols were both in Gundry's trailer the night before he died; either one of them could have spiked his insulin. It fit Gundry's argument with Wieder about a federal offense. It fit Wieder's sudden case of nerves when Tom told him that Gundry was murdered. If he got greedy a shotgun blast to the face took care of it. Nichols was the triggerman, most likely, Rose providing him with a cozy alibi. Nichols usually wore a blue ball cap. The kid who'd discovered Wieder's body said he saw someone talking to Wieder wearing a blue ball cap. It fit. It was no fairy tale.

"How do we prove it?" Sandy asked. "By now the mare's probably at the cannery—that or cremated. They would've seen to that right away. No hope for an autopsy."

Tom looked at her.

Sandy gave her shoulders a little shrug. "We got nothing that will stand up in court."

The southwesterly breeze had died. Tom looked down at the stinkbug, its hind end still shooting the moon. "Let's go," he said. "This place smells."

They walked toward their vehicles, the rocks a rusty red in the waning light. Looking back at the film set, Tom could see Nichols seated on his horse in the lights above the crowd. "I'll shake a few trees down at the Department of Agriculture," he said. "Someone had to let the horse through."

"Someone on the take, you mean."

"Most likely. But we'll at least know who to squeeze."

"Who's to say someone didn't just ride the mare over the border in the dead of night?"

Tom hadn't thought of that. Given the porous nature of the California/Mexico border it was certainly a possibility. With tens of thousands of illegals swarming into the state every year for the freebies and overwhelming an understaffed Border Patrol, the occasional mare bearing gifts could easily slip across the border unnoticed. "We'll still check with the D of A," he said. "We might get lucky."

"I don't believe in luck, Tom," Sandy said, her eyes as clear and full of light and as beautiful as ever he'd seen them. They seemed to be probing him. "If you want something bad enough, you have to work at it hard. There are no shortcuts."

Tom felt that there was more to her words than simple police procedure. "No, there aren't," he said. He started to reach for her hand when his cell phone rang. It was Dan.

"We got a floater, Tommy."

Chapter Twenty-Three

Tom and Sandy were standing next to Dan Bolt by a stream that wound through the Placerita Nature Center. Calvin Litton was laid out before them, belly-up and spreadeagled on a plastic tarp spread over the rocky bank. He was not wearing his blue ball cap or sunglasses. He had been floating facedown in a pool made by a cottonwood snag. He didn't look too good. His face was as white as a dead fish belly and peppered with tiny dark dots. His lips a dull robin's egg blue, his right eye a watery vagueness, half-open and bulging. The left eye was missing. A thin man, maybe one sixty-five, one seventy, with stringy salt-and-pepper hair, he was wearing faded blue jeans, black Converse sneakers, a dirty white T-shirt with an STP logo on the pocket. The sun was already behind the hills, but there was still plenty of light to see that someone had taken off the top of the left side of his head with either a shotgun or a cement mixer.

"Any defensive wounds?" Tom asked.

Dan shook his head. "He wasn't expecting it," he said. "Hundred and twenty bucks in his wallet, so we can rule out robbery."

"Same as Wieder."

"Yep. Found a camera in the glove box. We'll have the film developed." Dan shrugged. "Might turn up something."

"Any sign of the wad?"

"We're still looking topside."

Tom looked up the embankment that rose steeply from the river bottom to the road. He could just see the flashing glow of police cruisers that marked the crime scene above. He couldn't see the cruisers, nor could he see Litton's red Monte Carlo, but he could tell by the muffled voices that there was quite a lot of activity up there. A forensic team composed of LASO criminalists and Burbank Field Evidence Technicians was combing the hillside, picking their way in overlapping sweeps. It was steep and rough going. Every so often someone would lose his footing. "Watch out for snakes," a man's voice said.

Tom said, "So the killer pops Litton topside, then dumps the body over the edge. Body rolls down the embankment and does a header into the stream."

"Looks like it," Dan said.

"We find bodies along here all the time," Sandy said. "Placerita Canyon connects Sand Canyon to the Antelope Freeway. Easy to ditch a body."

Tom looked down the length of the valley thick with scrub oaks, yucca, and junipers. Stands of big cottonwoods crowded along the stream amid tangles of mustard weed and sage. A haven for dead bodies.

Sandy was looking at the cattails around the snag pool. "Body might've stayed here for days, undiscovered."

Tom looked over at a man and woman, about thirty yards away, giving a statement to a sheriff's deputy. "They the ones who found him?"

Dan nodded. "That's them. Mr. and Ms. Tree-huggers."

Sandy turned her head. "Popeye's taking their statement."

"Popeye?"

"Al Dremmel. Everyone calls him Popeye."

Dan looked down the trail leading up from the nature center, where the vehicles were parked. The center was about a half mile away. "Here comes Phil. Walks like he's got hemorrhoids, don't he?"

The coroner and his young black cornrowed assistant made their way toward them past a police line where deputies were holding back a few adventurous newshounds, already onto the scent. They were carrying equipment, Carlton listing to one side from the weight of his bag. He was out of breath. He set his bag down, put his hands on his hips, and straightened his back. "I'm getting too old for this crap," he said. "The killer could've been a little more considerate—dumped the body on the side of the road up there maybe." He glanced down at the body without interest.

Dan grinned. "We could put the word out to have all killers drop the bodies off at the morgue."

"That would be nice." Carlton noticed Sandy. "I thought you were on convalescent leave."

She smiled. "I can't stay away."

"I wish I could." Carlton, emitting a weary groan, stooped to examine the body. His knees popped.

Tom and Sandy walked over to the man and woman who had discovered the body. Dan stayed behind with Carlton. "What've we got, Popeye?" Sandy asked the deputy.

Deputy Dremmel, wearing a beige short-sleeved uniform shirt, olive green trousers and baseball-type cap, was writing in his notebook. He looked at Sandy. "Hey, Sandy. You on this one?"

She shook her head. "I'm just a ride-along. Detective Rigby is handling the case."

The men exchanged nods. Tom could see why Dremmel was nicknamed Popeye. He was a medium-height thin man with wiry biceps, thick forearms and big hands, and he had a bit of a squint in one eye. He looked like Popeye. He briefed Tom on the basics.

Mr. Tree-hugger's name was Rivers; Ms. Tree-hugger's name was Bridges. Tom had Popeye repeat their names, thinking he'd misunderstood. He hadn't. Rivers was wearing hiking shorts, boots and an Earth Now T-shirt. A floppy bush hat shielded his eyes. He was holding a pair of binoculars and a notebook. Bridges was dressed similarly, only she had thin, ratty blond hair pulled back into a ponytail, wore round, wire-framed spectacles, and by the look of things had probably not worn a bra in twenty years. She was also holding binoculars. They were each shouldering rucksacks.

"Getting kind of late for bird watching, isn't it?" Tom asked.

"We were on our way back from the falls," Rivers said, gesturing upstream.

Tom followed his point.

"About a mile upstream," Rivers said. "It's beautiful up there, man."

"I see. And on your way back you just happened upon the dead man?"

"That's right."

"Kind of hard to see from the path here."

Rivers looked over at the body. "We had stopped to look at a rather colorful specimen of a *Phrynosoma calidiarum,* when I saw something caught in the stream—in that snag," he said, pointing.

From where Tom was standing he could just see Carlton and his assistant going over the body; Dan was watching them, popping handfuls of beer nuts into his mouth. "I see," he said, looked back at Rivers.

"It looked weird," Rivers said, "so I went over and that's when I saw it was a dead man."

"You could tell that just looking at him."

"He was facedown in the water. A crow was sitting on his head. I figured he was dead."

"A crow."

"Sitting on his head—you know." Rivers tapped the palm of his hand with a forefinger. "I thought I should maybe do something—maybe administer CPR or something. Then I saw his head. I shooed the bird away."

"And you called nine-one-one."

"That's right. We stayed here until the police arrived."

According to Popeye the call had come in at 7:43 P.M. Tom looked at the woman. She was standing with her arms folded across her chest, staring absently at a lichen-covered rock. She seemed a bit put off by the whole business: murdered human beings apparently not near as interesting as live fungus. "Can you think of anything else?" Tom asked her.

Bridges looked up, shook her head, then looked back down at the fungus.

Tom looked at Sandy. "You got any questions?"

"Can't think of any."

"Okay." To Popeye: "Make sure you get it all down."

Popeye nodded curtly. "Will do."

Walking back, Tom asked, "You know what a Phrynosoma whadyacallit is?"

Sandy smiled. "Horned toad."

Tom lifted his head. "Ah."

Carlton was examining the gauge on the liver probe protruding from Litton's side. "What've we got, Phil?" Tom asked.

"You mean other than the obvious?"

"How about the time of death?"

"Hard to say."

"Guestimates?"

"Seeing as how he's been in the water blowing bubbles, it's hard to pinpoint it accurately." Carlton shrugged. "Two, three hours, maybe—give or take."

"That would put it sometime this afternoon," Dan said. "Sometime between four and five."

"Give or take," Carlton repeated, looked up at a circling news copter, the lancing red sun flashing on its fuselage. "We need to get the body airlifted. I sure ain't gonna carry him out of here."

Dan made the call.

Tom and Sandy stood looking down at the liver probe. "How do you square this with Nichols and Rose?" he asked her.

Sandy shook her head. "Maybe he was their distributor. Somebody had to move the stuff."

"That's what I'm thinking."

She looked at him.

"It makes sense," Tom said, once again feeling her eyes probing him. In truth, his suspicion that Sandy's father might have killed Litton to tidy things up fit the scenario, too. He just didn't want to think about it at the moment.

Dan clipped his cell phone onto his hip. "Chopper's on its way. What are you two lovebirds twittering about?"

Tom briefed Dan on their meeting with Bud Nichols and Sorrel Rose, the various scenarios of drug trafficking, distribution, and possible motives for Gundry's and Wieder's murder. Litton was a new wrinkle, but the drug-trafficking angle still worked.

Two ideas were kicked around. The first: Litton might have been part of their distribution, working alone or with a partner or partners. Montoya's name was suggested since he was a doctor and might have a network in place to unload drug shipments. That Litton had been seen outside his home suggested a connection between the two men. The second: Litton might not have had anything to do with Rose and Nichols at all. Not initially, at least. His involvement could have come after he had witnessed Wieder's murder at the Borden ranch. Sensing an avenue for financial gain, a way to horn in on a lucrative opportunity, he might have put the touch on the killer. If so, it had been a bad career move.

Dan was not convinced. The two different MOs still bothered him. The photograph of Julian Montoya and Kate Bledsoe on his boat still bothered him. The fact that they were found in Wieder's safe still bothered him. Litton spying on Angelina Montoya still bothered him. Dan spread his hands. "Like I said, Tommy. I think we may have two killers here. Somebody popped Gundry for one reason. Somebody else popped Wieder and Litton for another."

Tom rubbed the back of his neck. It was a possibility, of course. Add that to all the other possibilities. The case was lousy with possibilities. He looked wearily at Sandy. She was staring thoughtfully at the ground. Something was on her mind. Tom had an idea what it was, but asked anyway, "Got any thoughts, Sandy?"

She looked at him quickly, her eyes clearing. "No. Just thinking."

Tom left it alone. He glanced up at the sky, as though there were even more possibilities floating somewhere over their heads. It was getting dark. Bats were hunting along the stream.

"Hey, Tom!" a man's voice called out.

Tom looked up the embankment.

Hal Peters waved his arm for them to come up. "Got something."

Chapter Twenty-Four

The detectives were standing beside the red Monte Carlo parked in a turnout on Placerita Canyon Road. It was lighter and a few degrees warmer up on the road than it had been down by the stream. The north side of the turnout was shielded by a mound of cut-out earth; the road on the south end was partially obscured by a clot of scrub oaks. It was fairly secluded. Police cruisers and technicians' wagons were parked at either end of the turnout, their lights flashing. A couple of LASO uniforms kept a growing snarl of reporters and motorist spectators at bay.

Tom frowned down at a plastic baggie he held in his hands. Inside the baggie was a three-by-five-inch sheet of pale yellow notepaper that had been crumpled. There was writing on it. "Montoya, huh?"

"Do tell," Dan said.

"Found the sheet crumpled under the front seat of the Monte Carlo," Hal Peters said. He was wearing a navy blue windbreaker with Field Evidence Technician printed in large white letters across the back, its sleeves too short for his orangutan arms. "I flattened it out so you could read it."

Tom squinted. Montoya's name, barely decipherable but legible, was scribbled across the top, and beneath it a bit of scribble that was impossible to read. He turned the baggie in the light to remove the sheen off its reflective surface. "Any idea what this chicken scrawl is?"

Peters shook his head. "We'll get the handwriting experts on it."

"Maybe Montoya wrote it," Dan said. He grinned. "Doctor's have lousy handwriting."

Peters's expression said no. "Paper came from a notepad attached to his dash. Must've scribbled it while he was driving."

"Looks like a capital C, Tom," Sandy said, leaning close to Tom to get a better look. Her shoulder touched his. Then her fingers touched the top of his hand, pushing it lightly to adjust the angle of the note. Tom felt a bit of electricity shoot up through his arm from the point of her touch. He looked out of the corner of his eyes and could see the side of her face, the light on her cheekbones and in her hair glowing wonderfully, the scent of her perfume faint on a wisp of cooling air.

"May I see it?" Sandy asked.

"Sure." Tom handed her the baggie, still watching her admitingly.

She moved to one side, stood adjusting the note in the fading light.

Tom looked out over the valley at the far hills, dark in shadow. The sun was well below the hills and he could see the bats now and then crazy against the clear, cooling, darkening sky. The note was a good lead.

"Montoya could've popped him after his golf game," Dan said. "Dumped his body into the river, hoping maybe nobody'd find it for a couple days or so. The water'd throw a curve ball at the time of death—he'd know that, being a doctor. It'd give him plenty of room to fudge an alibi, if need be." He shrugged. "One thing's for sure, it ties them together."

Tom thought about that. "It proves that Litton knew Montoya," he said. "It doesn't prove that Montoya knew Litton."

Dan frowned at Peters. "Some people you can never please."

Peters stood long-armed, big hands to his sides, thumbs along the seams of his trousers, with no expression. He was looking at Sandy deciphering the note.

Tom walked to the rear of the Monte Carlo, pulled on his lower lip as he looked over the area. Litton's blue ball cap, marked by a thin metal rod in the ground with a small orange flag attached, was lying upside down in the dirt a few feet behind the driver's side door. The left side of it was torn up pretty good. There were darks spatters of blood on the underside of the bill, and inside the crown, along with a pulpy dark red mass. Colored flags marked the range of the blast, red for blood, white for bone and brain tissue.

Another orange flag drew his attention farther up the road. The sunglasses were dangling from a sage bush growing along the edge of the embankment about twenty feet behind the Monte Carlo. The left lens was missing. There was a single hole the size of a tiny BB in the right lens. Tom guessed it had been made by a number-eight shot. The flag marking the sunglasses formed a line with the ball cap and a third red-colored flag located a couple feet forward of the front left fender of the Monte Carlo that indicated where Litton had likely been standing when killed.

"Carl's Jr.," Sandy said.

Tom looked over at her. He walked back.

"Carl's Jr.," she repeated. Sandy showed Tom the note, pointing. "This is definitely a capital C. And here you have a squiggle and then an L and a bit of a squiggle. This is a J with a squiggle tail. Has to be Carl's Jr."

"A squiggle tail, huh," Tom said, teasing.

"There's a Carl's a couple miles down the road," Sandy said, ignoring him. She was all business. "It's on the corner of Sierra and Placerita."

"Could be a meet, Tommy," Dan said. "Montoya called him and set it up."

"The note could've been written anytime," Tom said. "There's no time stamp on it."

Dan thought about that. He turned to Hal Peters. "Was there a cell phone in the Monte Carlo?"

Peters nodded. "Got it in my wagon."

"Good. I'll have Martinez pull his phone records—see who he's been talking to over the past couple of days. See if any of the calls link to Litton's approximate time of death."

Tom nodded. "Good idea."

Dan made the call.

"I think Dan may have something, Tom," Sandy said.

"How does this sound? Montoya calls Litton, tells him to meet him at the Carl's Jr. They do. It's too crowded for the kind of business Montoya has in mind, so he leads him up the road here to a nice secluded spot."

Tom gestured at the ground with an open palm. "Why not just set up the meet here?"

"Didn't you say that Litton was from Fresno? The Carl's is an easy place to find. It's right off the freeway."

Dan clicked shut his cell phone. "Makes sense, Tommy. Litton follows Montoya up the road and parks behind him. When he steps out of his vehicle, thinking he's going to conduct business, Montoya gives him an unexpected freebie."

Tom looked at the Monte Carlo. The driver's side door was open, as if Litton had stepped out for some reason—to have words with the killer, like Dan suggested—then walked to the front. The splash of blood and body tissue on the hood and windshield, coupled with a lack of defensive wounds on the body, suggested an ambush. Litton had not seen it coming.

"All right, let's run with it," Tom said. "Let's pay Montoya a visit—find out where he went after his golf game this afternoon."

Dan flipped open his phone and punched in some numbers. "I'll call his office."

"Find out where Montoya was yesterday between three and four," Tom said. "I'd like to know if he was at the office when Wieder was killed. He said he was."

Dan nodded, spoke into his phone.

Tom turned to Peters. "What else've we got, Hal?"

"Here's where the body fell," Peters said, pointing at the red flag marking a dark sticky scab in the dirt beside the front left fender.

Tom had already guessed that.

"The killer pushed him over the side where those weeds are smashed," Peters said. "There are blood splatters too."

"Any footprints?" Tom asked.

Peters shook his head. "Nothing we can make a cast of. We do have a pretty good tire track, though. Just one. Pickup truck, I'd guess. Maybe a large SUV."

Tom looked down at the south end of the turnout where a criminalist was making plaster casts. "Any idea on the make?"

"Not yet," Peters said. "We'll know more once we've made some tread comparisons."

Tom could feel Sandy standing beside him.

"That narrows it down to about a few hundred thousand possibilities," she said, a slight flutter in her voice. "Just about everybody I know drives a pickup or an SUV."

Tom thought about that. Everyone, that is, except Julian Montoya. Montoya drove a Mercedes coupe; at least he did the last time he saw him driving. "Okay," he said, scratching the back of his neck.

One of the technicians, a heavyset black man with a shaved head that gleamed in the sunset walked over to them from behind the Monte Carlo. His name was Lucius Johnson. He was holding something small, pink, and plastic in his gloved hand. "Found the wad. In some bushes over the side. Wind took it. Maybe a crow."

Tom looked at it. It was a Remington, same kind as the one found at the Wieder crime scene. His eyes went quickly to Sandy, who was staring at the wad. Her expression had sharpened. Tom could almost read her thoughts. "Pretty common wad," he said.

She lifted her eyes at him.

"Whoever killed Wieder likely killed Litton," he said. "It still works with our earlier scenario. Rose and Nichols may have killed Gundry to shut him up. Montoya may have killed Wieder and Litton for reasons of his own. He may've killed all three of them. Nothing definite here."

Sandy smiled remotely, her mouth small and pensive. "Sure."

Dan snapped shut his cell phone, clipped it onto his waist. "Montoya's office was closed," he said, "but I got his exchange. Lady said she didn't know where he was yesterday between three and four. The exchange only keeps track of him after hours. Right now he's at the gun club. Silverado."

"That's where his wife said he'd be," Tom said. "No way to confirm his alibi yesterday?"

Dan shrugged. "We could track down one of his nurses, I guess."

"Kate Bledsoe," Sandy said. "Let me give her another call." She dug out her cell phone from her purse, stepped away from the group to make the call.

Dan planted his fists on his thick waist. "Golfing, shooting. These doctors sure got it tough, huh?"

Tom was thinking about the time of Litton's death. Montoya could easily have finished up his round of golf, set up a meet with Litton, killed him, then driven across town to the gun club to establish an alibi. Gundry's time of death was a no-brainer. Montoya could have laced his insulin anytime, been halfway around the world when he dropped. Montoya's whereabouts at the time of Wieder's death was still in question, even though he'd said he was in the office at the time of the murder. Tom kicked himself for not immediately calling his office earlier. If he had, then he'd know for certain if Montoya had had the opportunity to kill all three men. Right now, all they had were two definites, a maybe, and a motive for each killing that was built on speculation. Add these to a truckload of existing possibilities.

Sandy walked back, shaking her head. "No soap. Bledsoe's dropped off the radar. I'll keep trying."

"All right," Tom said. To Peters: "Let us know if you turn up anything on the casts, Hal. I want to nail this tight before we go to the DA."

"Will do." Peters walked off with Johnson.

Tom looked at Sandy and smiled. "We'll get him."

She said nothing.

Just then two unmarked sedans, one dark blue, the other nondescript brown, were allowed to pass through the police line by one of the uniforms. Lieutenant Stenton was in the first vehicle, Lieutenant Ubersahl was in the second. Both men slowed as they drove past where the detectives were standing, looked over at them, then continued up the road behind the other police vehicles to park. A swarm of reporters raced to intercept them.

"Looks like the brass have arrived for their photo op," Dan said, starting up the road toward his own vehicle.

Tom followed, stopped, and looked back at Sandy, who had not moved. Once again, she was staring at the ground. Something was definitely on her mind. "Sandy, aren't you coming?" he asked.

Sandy looked up, shook her head. "Better take a rain check, Tom." She nodded up the road. The two lieutenants were walking toward them. Ubersahl looked angry, which was nothing new.

Tom figured Ubersahl wore skivvies that were too tight for him. Sandy said, "I have a feeling I'm in for a tongue-lashing."

"We were on a date."

She made a face. "Is that what this was?"

"We're just getting started," he said, smiling a smile that, although not out of the woods just yet, had risen easily to his face. "You haven't seen a date."

Sandy shook her head, that guileless smile of hers spreading over her lovely mouth. "I need to talk to the nice lieutenant anyway. We'll connect tomorrow."

"You sure?"

"I'm sure."

"All right, then." Tom stood looking at her. Her eyes were startlingly clear in the silvery gloaming and, once again, he felt the old hope swell in his chest. "We'll grab a bite to eat somewhere," he said, wanting to take her in his arms and kiss her. "Maybe take a little sail up the coast."

"That would be lovely. Dan is looking at you funny."

"What else is new?"

Chapter Twenty-Five

Tom was standing outside the starter's window of the Silverado Gun Club. It was dark and there were colored spotlights lighting the clubhouse overlooking the field that was also illuminated and littered with broken clays like the aftermath of a battle. The hills, surrounded by oaks, were dark beyond the reach of light, and everything caught in the glare had a slightly surreal wasteland appearance. Looking out at the shooters in the bright artificial illumination seemed very much like watching a ballgame at night, only they were shooting trap. There were shooters—mostly men, but there were a few women also—standing along a guardrail behind the trap line awaiting their turn. Many were wearing club patches on their shooting vests and hats. Wooden racks of guns stood behind them, their breeches open. Boys sat behind each of the trap lines in high chairs like lifeguards, keeping score and releasing clay birds electronically from the squat cement houses positioned in front of the shooters. It was quite noisy and the acrid smell of gunpowder hung on the cool still night air like a low-level fog.

"I haven't seen him," the starter inside the window said. "Did you try inside at the bar?"

"I'm trying you," Tom said, glancing at the man's name tag, "Charlie."

"He's probably in at the bar." Charlie chuckled nervously, adjusted the smudgy red Winchester ball cap back on his head to reveal a longish crop of graying blond hair. His eyes had the rheumy look of an alcoholic. "It's pretty busy out here, as you can see." Charlie was clearly uneasy talking to police. He looked to be of the Vietnam War vintage—fifty-something—his discomfort no doubt a carryover from his peace-loving antiestablishment days.

"Yes, I can see that," Tom said. He looked down through the window at a schedule pad opened on the inside counter. "I see Montoya's name. What time's he supposed to shoot?"

Charlie dragged a knuckled hand over a patchy stubble on his gaunt face. "He's not up for another ten minutes. You might want to check out the bar."

"I'll just wait out here." Tom smiled.

Charlie nodded, chuckling uneasily. "Sure, whatever you want."

Tom, leaning his elbow on the window counter, looked out at the nearest apron as a man called out "Pull," watched the fluorescent orange clay disc sail away from the house on a radical slant, spinning like a Frisbee, catching air, lifting a foot then shatter an instant after the report of the gun. He could see the pink shot wad falling short onto the hillside littered with broken clays.

Dan came out through the double doors of the clubhouse and walked over to the window. "No sign of him inside."

"Any Mercedes in the parking lot?"

Dan shook his head. "No gold Five Hundreds. Plenty of pickups, though. Maybe we ought to arrest everybody." He looked at Charlie in the window, narrowed an eye (Dan did not like antiestablishment types), then looked out at the shooters and sighed. "Makes you want to get the old Wingmaster out of mothballs, eh, Tommy?"

A silver-haired Asian man wearing yellow shooter's glasses and crisp beige shooting jacket walked up to the window. Tom gestured at the window, indicating that he wasn't in line. The shooter nodded, stepped forward and ordered two boxes of shells. "Reloads," he added. "Number eights."

Dan smiled knowingly.

Charlie swiveled around on his stool, took two boxes off the shelves behind him, swiveled back and pushed them through the window. The shooter paid for the shells and left.

Tom and Dan stepped back to the window. "You sell reloads here, I see," Tom said.

Charlie nodded. "Sure."

"Load them here?"

"Sure. Saves money." He chuckled for no apparent reason.

Dan asked, "What components do you use?"

Charlie looked at him. "Components?"

"As in components . . . wads, hulls, powder." He grinned.

Charlie frowned. "Different kinds. Winchester, Remington, Peters. Whatever we collect off the line."

Tom asked, "Do you ever mix and match—use say a Remington wad in a Winchester hull?"

"All the time."

The detectives gazed at him steadily like a couple of cheetahs.

"What?" Charlie looked from Tom to Dan. "What'd I say?" He chuckled some more. "We've never had any mishaps."

"Does Montoya bring his own shells, or does he buy yours?" Tom asked.

Charlie pinched his lower lip. "Most of the club shooters load their own. Sometimes they run out and buy ours. Here comes George." A stocky man with a big gut pushed out of the clubhouse, took a long pull from a can of Budweiser, and slapped his stomach like he was proud of it. "George ought to know; he's on Julian's team. Hey, George!"

Fat gut squinted over at him.

Charlie waved. "You seen Julian, George?"

George saw Tom and Dan, aimed his belly and followed it over to the window. He was wearing black jeans, a garish lime green knit shirt that didn't quite cover his stomach, and a khaki shooter's vest with lots of club patches. "What's up, Charlie?" he asked, his eyes not leaving Tom and Dan.

"These men are looking for Julian. They're detectives."

"Oh?" George took a final pull from his beer can, eyeing the detectives over the aluminum rim, his left eye narrowing over his slightly flattened nose that had probably been broken more than once. He crushed the can into a dull blue sheet-metal trash receptacle below the window. "Police, huh? You boys have some identification, I suppose?"

Tom showed his badge.

George leaned forward and took his time reading it. "A sergeant, huh? I knew a sergeant in the army once. A real jerk." George was one of those citizens who got their jollies acting tough around policemen. It could well explain the nose job.

"Have you seen Julian Montoya?" Tom asked.

"What do you boys want with him? He forget to pay a traffic ticket or something?" George snickered at Charlie.

Charlie was looking at Tom.

"Have you seen him?" Tom repeated evenly.

"I thought maybe he was inside," Charlie interposed quickly. "At the bar maybe." Charlie seemed a little anxious that he might have aided and abetted a possible altercation.

George's eyes went from Tom to Dan, back to Tom. He smiled, showing his cruddy dental work. "Sorry, boys." He obviously liked saying "boys." "Haven't seen him."

Tom wanted to work on the nose a couple more rounds.

Just then the double doors of the clubhouse swung open and Julian Montoya walked out smoking a cigar about a yard long. He stopped, threw his broad shoulders back and looked around the patio, the look on his face suggesting that he expected everybody in the area to stop what they were doing and take note of his entrance. He puffed on his cigar a few moments, watching the shooters.

Tom said, "Haven't seen him, huh?"

George brought his hand up to his mouth in mock surprise. "Oh, you meant *that* Julian Montoya." He snickered, jerked a thumb as he headed down toward the line. "Sure, he's right behind me."

"Funny man," Dan said.

Montoya, rolling the cigar contentedly in his mouth, walked heavily over to the window carrying a fine Beretta over-and-under, broken over the crook of his thick left arm. He was wearing a sleeveless shooting jacket over a powder blue knit shirt, gray khakis and boots, shooter's cap and glasses.

Dan caught Tom's eyes, jerked his eyebrows at Montoya's shooter's cap.

Tom nodded and said, "We'd like a word with you, Mr. Montoya."

Montoya slapped his right hand down on the counter, the corners of a couple of bills showing beneath meaty fingers, and pushed the bills through the window. "Two rounds, Charlie. Give me a couple boxes of shells while you're at it."

Charlie swept away the bills. "Number eights?"

Montoya nodded, puffing on his cigar; a Double Corona by the look and smell of it.

Charlie glanced once more at Tom before swiveling around on his stool.

Montoya turned slowly to face the detectives on his left, using his free hand on the counter as a pivot. He had wide-set bull eyes—dark as roasted coffee beans, round, hard, and mean. When his eyes met Tom's they hardened further into stony black nuts behind the clear yellow lenses of his glasses. "This is getting annoying," he growled through an exhale of smoke.

"You don't say," Dan said with a half grin.

Montoya did not look at him. He was looking at Tom, his head slightly elevated to show the under-jaw muscles of his thick neck working as he puffed on his cigar. He took the cigar between his thumb and first two fingers, looked at the tip, held it out to one side and tapped the ash with his third finger, his pinkie extended, then returned the cigar to his mouth with a throaty laugh.

Charlie stacked the shell boxes on the counter, pushed them through the window. Montoya, chuckling smoke through his teeth, slid them off the counter and steadied them against his chest as he walked down toward one of the gun racks, trailing cigar smoke.

The detectives followed him.

"You see that blue shooter's cap he's wearing?" Dan asked.

Tom nodded.

Montoya set the shells on top of the wooden gun rack, set the Beretta down in one of the empty slots, took a puff of his cigar as he cocked an arrogant brow at the detectives. "You jokers want something?"

Dan laughed. "Did you hear that, Tommy? We're jokers."

Dan and Montoya were about the same height and build, only Dan was squishier looking. "I've got some jokes you've never heard, sparky," he said. "Any of them too complicated for you, I can explain the punch lines, okay?"

Montoya's expression flattened. The glare of overhead lights cast his small bull's eyes deep in the shadow of his bill and showed the cruel acne craters in his heavy face, giving him a craggy, yellow-brown, menacing look. "Punch lines, huh?"

"That's right, sparky. The ol' one-two."

Montoya tongued the cigar to the side of his mouth and planted his fists on his waist. They looked the size of cantaloupes. Tom could not imagine hands that size holding scalpel or sutures. He could imagine them pummeling someone's face to a bloody pulp, though. Montoya chuckled throatily some more.

"He's a real laughing boy, Tommy."

Montoya, still chuckling, took the cigar out of his mouth and, with pinkie once again extended daintily, set it down on the edge of the gun rack beside the boxes of shells. He removed his shooting glasses.

Dan grinned.

Beer-gut George swaggered over with two of his buddies. His buddies were both pretty good-sized, but a couple decades past worrying anyone. "You okay, Julian?" George asked, stepping next to Tom.

"Butt out," Tom said.

A sneer curled over George's upper lip. "I don't have—"

Tom jabbed a finger into his chest. "I said butt out, champ!"

George almost tripped over his heels going backward. He raised his hands defensively. "Okay, okay." To Julian: "You need anything, you let us know, okay? We'll be right over here." George and his buddies stood a short distance away by the guardrail, George making wisecracks to the others. George was a real prince.

Tom stepped between Montoya and Dan, holding up his hand. "Mr. Montoya, this can go easy or hard. Your choice."

Montoya had not taken his eyes off Dan, but Tom could see a calculation taking place on his wide brown face. He may have been mean as a boar, but he was also intelligent. A dangerous combination.

Montoya stared at Dan a couple moments longer, grunted, then took his cigar off the gun rack. "I told you everything earlier."

"Not quite everything," Tom said. "You said you didn't know Calvin Litton."

Montoya leveled his eyes at Tom. "I don't."

"No? How is it we found a note with your name in his car?"

Montoya's eyes flickered, crawled away from Tom momentarily to examine the tip of his cigar, then jumped back full of fight. He jabbed the cigar back into his teeth. "My address is in the phone book. Anybody could've written it down."

"This anybody happens to be missing half his head. Someone splattered it all over his windshield."

The cigar dipped.

"We fished your buddy Litton out of the wash along Placerita Canyon," Dan said. "I hear they dump a lot of bodies there. Placerita . . . that's just a couple miles from where you live, isn't it?"

Montoya looked at him. "I told you I don't know anyone named Litton."

"No idea why he was carrying your name around," Tom said.

"He likes my name. Maybe he wants to name his kids after me."

"Is that so?" Tom said, ignoring a look from Dan. "Where were you between four and five this afternoon?"

"Is that when this guy I'm supposed to know was killed?"

"Answer the question."

Montoya's face flushed, his small mean eyes pinching into narrow slits. "You think you can come here and ask questions? You think you can just harass people? This is a respectable place. I have friends here. The mayor shoots here."

"Give him a call," Tom said. "Tell him to meet us down at our clubhouse. We have plenty of private rooms where we can talk." The two men stood looking at each other, Montoya rolling his cigar slowly between his thick wet lips. "What's it going to be, Montoya?"

Once again Tom could see a calculation taking place in his eyes.

"I was at home," Montoya growled. "I went home to change after my golf game."

"Anyone see you?"

"My housekeeper."

"You're sure about the time?"

"I asked her to make love with me on the kitchen table. Check it out, hot shot. I said I needed an alibi in case some idiot who likes my name got his head blown off between four and five." He grinned. Montoya was a real funny man.

"Nuts to this," Dan said, shaking his head. Dan wanted to haul Montoya downtown. Tom thought he'd give him one more chance to cooperate.

"Do you know Bud Nichols?" he asked.

"Who?"

"Bud Nichols. Horse trainer. Runs with Sorrel Rose."

"You find my name in his car too?"

"Do you know him?"

"Not personally."

"How, then?"

Montoya twirled his cigar some more, puffing. "I might've seen him around my place," he said, blowing a cloud of smoke over their heads. He looked out at the field as a group of shooters walked back from the line. "Nichols, you say? Yeah, I've seen him. Not for a while, though. Who's the other one?"

"Sorrel Rose."

"Sorrel Rose, huh?"

"You might know her as Sonny Weston."

"Never heard of her. She some kind of cop groupie? I hear they got cop groupies."

Dan, ignoring the remark, said, "You wouldn't know anything about smuggling drugs up from Mexico."

Montoya looked at him. "Drugs?"

"That's right, sparky. Using horses. Mares. A couple of solid citizens—like yourself—hide balloons in horse uteruses and run 'em over the border. Chet Gundry maybe found out about the setup and threatened to go to the police. They kill him. Wieder squeezes for a bigger cut, so they kill him too—probably hired Litton to do it, so they could establish an alibi. Litton was a loose cannon, so they take his head off with a load of number-eight shot. Same kinda load you're using right now. Get the picture?"

Montoya stared at him dully, his eyelids lowered almost sleepily as he looked at the tip of his cigar. "You're crazy."

Charlie's voice came through the loudspeaker, announcing the names of the next team of shooters. "That's all you get," Montoya said. "Any more questions, you talk to my lawyer." He took one of the boxes of shells, opened the top and side flaps and bent them back, flattening them along the sides of the box, then placed the box, shells exposed, in a leather pouch belted around his waist.

"You said you were at your office yesterday between three and four," Tom said. "Give me the name of someone who can verify it."

Montoya shook his head derisively. "You want me to do your job too, huh? I pay your salary and you want me to do your job. That's pretty good."

"Ready, Julian?" George called out.

George and three other shooters were walking out to the line, their guns broken over their arms. "Be right there," Montoya said, picked up his gun and hooked it over his arm.

Tom held up his hand. "Not just yet."

Montoya turned his head. "Talk to my lawyer."

"Do you own a pickup truck?"

"I own lots of cars," Montoya said, putting his shooter's glasses back onto his face. "I work for a living."

"Is that what you do?"

Montoya, chuckling, puffing on his Double Corona, walked heavily down toward the rail, passed through the gate, then walked out onto the apron to join the others at the line. Each of the shooters stood abreast of one another, at one of five positions on the line, the boy climbing into the high chair behind them. George turned his head and said something to Montoya that made him laugh. Montoya slid a look back at Tom, chambered a shell, then, clicking shut his gun, turned back facing the cement house, brought the gun up to his shoulder, leaned forward on his left foot, and said, "Pull!"

The phosphorescent orange clay disk just cleared the trap house and disintegrated in a puff of smoke, the spent pink wad drifting to the ground like a worn-out shuttlecock.

The detectives stood by the gun rack watching the shooters.

"He knows something, Tommy," Dan said, fishing a Baby Ruth out of his pocket.

"Yeah."

The detectives headed back to their vehicle, hearing behind them the intermittent reports of shotgun fire.

Chapter Twenty-Six

Sandy awoke at six-thirty in the morning. Cool slanting sunlight filtered through diaphanous sheers into the bedroom; the patio trees, trembling in a slight breeze, making nervous patterns on the walls. Sandy blinked thoughtfully at them. She had slept solidly and without dreams, and she felt the complete, satisfying, languid freshness that comes after a good night's sleep. There had been no attacks. It was the first time since the shooting. She smiled.

She wondered how Tom and Dan had made out last night with Montoya. She had never cared for the man; he was jealous, hot-tempered, and verbally abusive at times. She couldn't imagine what Angelina saw in him; they seemed so unequally yoked. She was beautiful, and he—well, he was not at all attractive. But then, love was blind, wasn't it? Julian might have other qualities hidden beneath his gruff exterior that only Angelina could see, qualities that outshone his ugliness. Maybe love was not blind but merely nearsighted.

Shifting her thoughts, Sandy couldn't see how Calvin Litton had anything to do with Rose and Nichols, unless, as they had discussed last night, he was some kind of distributor. That was possible, of course, given his checkered past. Perhaps he and Montoya handled one end of the transaction—the distribution—while Rose and Nichols handled the acquisition of goods.

Sandy shook her head. It seemed a bit farfetched. It would certainly qualify as a federal offense, and it would most definitely rock the equestrian industry. Still, the scenario that worked without frayed edges was the Sweetwater Estates deal. In that scenario her father hired a hit man to kill his business partner for a three million dollar insurance policy, then killed Wieder to rid the ointment of a troublesome fly. Finally, he killed the hit man to make it neat and tidy. Her father had motive and opportunity to kill each of the three men. She knew that Tom had had that very scenario in mind last night at the river. She could see it in his eyes.

Sylvie pattered up from the bottom corner of the bed and purred in Sandy's face. "I agree, Sylvie," she said, scratching behind the kitty's ears. "Enough of that. What do you say we go fix some breakfast?"

Sylvie leaped off the bed and disappeared.

Sandy swung her feet out of the covers, sat upright on the edge of her bed, and stretched. It felt good to stretch, first one arm and then the other, grabbing fistfuls of the morning. Then padding down the hall in her nightie, feeling the house cool and bright in early morning freshness, she went into the kitchen, poured kibble into a bowl, set it down on the floor, then washed out the French press and made a pot of coffee. She heard Sylvie batting a rubber ball down the hall, its tiny bell tinkling.

Cup in hand, Sandy stepped down into the living room, mindful of the rows of photographs still spread over the carpet. She sat down on her sofa, drew up her feet, clicked on the television and channel-surfed the local news. Litton's death made all the top stories; not because he was anyone important per se but because his death, coupled with the deaths of Chet Gundry and Vern Wieder, suggested that a serial killer might be on the loose. The media loves a serial killer. Who's next? Stay tuned!

The coverage showed the body of Calvin Litton being airlifted above Placerita Canyon, an aerial shot showing the road stalled with police cruisers, fire engines, and looky-loo traffic. The on-site reporter, a stunning bright-eyed brunette named Vickie Trumbo, stood before a crowd of onlookers speculating on the connection of Litton's death with the other recent deaths. Insets of Chet Gundry and Vern Wieder appeared in the upper-right corner of the screen as their names were mentioned. The coverage then dissolved to a two-shot of Lieutenants Ubersahl and Stenton, Stenton giving Trumbo a brief statement. Ubersahl glaring at the camera.

Sandy switched off the television. What a boob. Her conversation with him last night did not go well. She'd asked him about the Louisville Slugger case, asked if he had ever considered a connection between it and the death of her brother. His response had been a crisp "Let the dead bury the dead," then he'd stalked away. Sandy did not think it prudent at the time to ask about the death of his partner, Ned Rockwell, not without doing a little behind-the-scenes investigating first.

Sandy took a sip of coffee, gazing absently at the Civil War bronze on her coffee table when the doorbell rang. She frowned at the grandfather clock—7:10. She stood, cup in hand, and headed for the front door, wondering who could be visiting her at this hour. *Her mother?* She had come over nearly every day since the shooting, but usually later in the morning. *Tom?* That would be nice.

Setting the cup down on the kitchen counter, she felt a breeze on her legs, looked down and saw that she was still in her nightie. She grabbed a windbreaker from the hall closet, shrugged it on, and looked out through the tiny brass peep hole in the front door.

Kate Bledsoe was standing on her porch, her head turned away in profile. She was looking down the street.

Sandy raised her eyebrows. Kate Bledsoe was a surprise. Feeling a slight tremor of apprehension in her chest, she placed her hand on the brass handle, unlocked the dead bolt, and opened the door. "Kate."

Kate, still looking down the street, whirled as if startled from a distracting thought. "Oh . . . Hi," she said, her face clearing. A smile jumped brokenly over her lips, like a kid playing hopscotch. "I called yesterday," she added, as though that would explain everything.

"Yes, I know." Sandy forced a smile. *Good morning to you, too, Kate.*

Kate stood looking at her, holding her hands as though she didn't want them to escape. Her eyes were red and taut around the dark green irises. She didn't look as though she'd slept much. "I didn't know who else to come to," she said with an airy flutter in her voice. "I hope it's not too early."

Sandy reprised the smile. "Won't you come in?" She glanced

down the street, saw nothing of interest but a line of oak trees defining a bend in the road, then closed the door behind her.

Kate's boots sounded hollowly over the wood floor as she walked through the foyer. She stood with her back to Sandy, looking over the fixtures in the living room—the prints, the Crow war shield, the silver saddle in the far corner. The inseams and seat of her jeans were sweat-stained with dirt and horsehair, as though she had been recently riding bareback. She smelled of horse. Her hair was a mess. It looked windblown. "Nice place," she said, her voice still an airy fluttering.

Sandy knew she'd said it just to say something.

Kate walked over to the trophy case against the right wall, leaned forward with her hands behind her back, her right hand gripping her left thumb like a vice. "All your buckles. Look how far they go back." She frowned at several photos on the wall. "I never knew you won so much."

Sandy didn't know if she should take it as a compliment or an insult. Kate wasn't acting her normal acerbic self. "Buster's been a good horse," Sandy said, again marveling that Kate Bledsoe was in her home.

Kate was looking at a recent photo of Buster. "He's a good-looking gelding, isn't he? I'm thinking of cutting Jewel, did I tell you?"

"No, you didn't." Sandy was confused. "Why? I thought you were breeding him. All your magazine ads."

"Not anymore." Kate stepped sideways along the wall, perusing the photos. "His sperm count's been way down. Just shooting blanks lately." She giggled. "I thought it best to geld him."

"I'm sorry to hear that."

Kate shrugged it off. "It might settle him in the ring." She walked over to the counter. "I'd really like to win the World this year."

Sandy forced another smile. She knew Kate didn't have a snowball's chance in H-E-Double hockey-sticks, with Angelina's Zee-Zee and Bud's Mister Dobson winning everything. "Can I get you something to drink?" she asked. "Cup of coffee, maybe? Orange juice?"

Kate shook her head. She stood smiling at Sandy with a tight twist in one corner of her mouth, like she'd OD'd on Botox. She placed her hands, palms down, on the granite countertop, smoothing them over the surface. Her fingernails were dirty. She seemed embarrassed, though not about the nails. There was something reticent in her eyes.

Sandy knew she wanted to say something, but guessed she didn't know where to begin. Either that or she was playing a mind game. "You wanted to talk to me about something, Kate? Something involving a police matter."

Bledsoe's hands skidded to a halt. "I should've come to you earlier."

"You're here now." Sandy indicated a counter stool. "Have a seat. Sure I can't get you anything? I'm making some toast."

Kate shook her head, glanced at what Sandy was doing. "Oh, maybe I'll have a piece of toast, since you're already making some."

"Wheat okay?" Kate did not respond. Sandy popped two slices of bread into the toaster oven.

Kate remained standing beside the counter. "You're the only one I could think of coming to," she said, following it with a little shrug of her shoulders. She made a quick sharp sweep of Sandy's appearance, eyes down and up but seeing everything and nothing in a glance. She clearly had something on her mind.

Still, Sandy felt slightly self-conscious wearing a windbreaker with her bare legs showing beneath it.

Kate looked away, then looked back, the corners of her mouth jerking outward in an attempt to smile. "We haven't exactly been friends."

Sandy smiled humorlessly. "I called your numbers yesterday," she said, taking a sip of coffee. "Your supervisor said you failed to come in to work."

Kate resumed smoothing her palms over the countertop. "I went riding."

"All night?"

Kate giggled incredulously. "I guess I did. You ever do that? Just go riding. I don't even know where I went."

Sandy knew the place well. She had gone there several times herself in the past two months. "What's on your mind, Kate?"

Once again Kate's hand froze, her eyes locked, then watered.

"I'm scared," she said. Her face twisted sideways. She clutched it. Racking sobs jerked in her throat. "I don't know what to do," she said, her voice full of emotion. "I should've said something yesterday when Detective Rigby showed me that photo." She pinched tears from her red eyes.

Sandy handed her a tissue. "Tell me about the photo."

"There's a photo of me and Julian." Kate dabbed beneath her eyes with the tissue. "We're on his boat." She giggled throatily. "I'm not wearing any clothes. Can you believe it?"

Sandy smiled benignly. "You and Julian are having an affair?"

"We *were* but not anymore." Kate fingered her thumbnail. "It was dumb."

"And now you're afraid Angelina's going to find out about it? Maybe not want to hire you to replace Chet?"

Kate was staring absently at a point over Sandy's left shoulder.

"Kate, are you afraid she might not want to hire you to be her trainer?"

Kate continued working her thumbnail, continued staring. "I heard Chet and Julian arguing on the phone."

"Chet?"

"It was at the clinic. I had just walked into Julian's office and I could hear him arguing. I knew it was Chet."

"What were they arguing about?"

"Angelina. Julian found out Chet and her were sleeping together. He said he was going to blow his head off."

Sandy set her cup down. "You heard him say that?"

Kate nodded vaguely. "With a shotgun. He's Spanish," she added, as though it would make everything clearer.

"Chet was killed with Xylazine."

"I know, but Vern was killed with a shotgun. That's when I remembered what he said to Chet. What Julian said, I mean. He threatened Chet two days before he was killed." Kate looked at Sandy expectantly. "I figured Julian had something to do with it."

"What does any of this have to do with the photo of you on the boat?"

Kate shrugged. "I figured if Julian was the killer, then the police would think I had something to do with it too."

"Because of the photo."

"Right."

"And you think that because you and Chet were also seeing each other the police might think you killed him."

"Right."

"Killed Vern too."

Kate nodded.

"Because of the photo."

"Yes."

The toaster bell dinged.

"I see." Sandy frowned. *What a wicked little world we live in.* She buttered the toast, slid one over to Kate on a paper towel. Her story was a bit convoluted, but Sandy got the gist. At least she thought she got the gist. It was guilt by association. Whether Sandy believed her or not was another matter. "Was Vern blackmailing Julian with the photo?" Sandy asked, taking a bite of toast.

Kate looked down at hers, picked it up, then set it down without taking a bite. "I didn't know about the photo until yesterday. Now that I think of it, though, I'm sure that's what he was doing. Julian's been kind of edgy lately."

"How so?"

"I don't know. Edgy. He'll fly off the handle at nothing. Something's eating him."

"His wife and Chet perhaps?"

Kate looked at her. "Maybe. I think there's more going on, though. Those photos, maybe."

"You think it was Vern blackmailing him."

Kate fingered the crust of her toast. "Why else would he have taken them?"

"To blackmail *you* perhaps."

"Me?" Kate barked out a laugh. "Why would he want to blackmail me? I don't have any money."

"Money isn't the only thing men want." Sandy took a sip of coffee, allowing the thought to percolate.

Kate's eyes narrowed. "Vern never made advances toward me," she said, screwing up her face into a look of disgust. "Can you see me with Vern?"

Sandy reprised the benign smile. "Yesterday when Detective Rigby showed you the photo of you and Julian on the boat, you thought that Vern was maybe using it to blackmail Julian. You think that Julian killed him, but first killed Chet for having an affair with his wife, is that it?"

Kate nodded.

"Bit of a double standard, don't you think?"

Kate shrugged. "Men."

Sandy said nothing to that. "And now you're afraid that the police will somehow connect you to the murders and arrest you?"

"*Arrest* me?" Kate looked stunned. "Haven't you heard what I've been saying? I wish they *would* arrest me. At least I'd be safe."

Sandy gave her head a little baffled shake. "I'm sorry, Kate, I'm confused. What are you afraid of then?"

"Julian. I'm afraid of Julian. I think he's going to kill me now."

"Why would he kill you?"

"I was standing in the doorway when he threatened Chet. After he said it he looked over at me. I acted like I just came in, but I could tell he knew I heard him. I could see it in his eyes. I'm a witness."

"I see." Sandy thought about that. "And even though he knew you'd heard him, you think he went ahead and killed Chet and Vern anyway?"

Kate nodded.

"And now you think Julian might come after you?"

"Yes."

Sandy watched her eyes. Whether or not it made any sense, Kate seemed to believe it. "People often say threatening things in the heat of the moment but don't follow through."

"You don't know Julian. He's—"

"Spanish. I know. Did he ever mention that he was being blackmailed by Vern?"

"No."

"Then you really don't have any actual proof that he killed them, do you?"

"Who else could've done it?"

Sandy looked evenly at Kate over the edge of her cup.

Kate fidgeted with her toast, angled her head inquiringly. "*What?* You don't think *I* did it." She laughed incredulously. "I came over here. Why would I kill them?"

Sandy said nothing.

"You really think I did it?"

Sandy set her cup down on the counter. "I think you need some sleep."

"Sleep?" Kate made a rasping noise in her throat. "That's a joke. Who can sleep with all this going on?" She pushed her toast back and forth with short stabs of her fingertips. "I can't eat or sleep. I haven't been to the office. I dropped out of the show, in case you were wondering." Her eyes watered. "I get the feeling I'm being followed—like somebody's watching me all the time. Some crazy with a gun. Do you ever feel that way—somebody watching you?"

In Sandy's mind an image of a face appeared, surfacing in a dark pool, the face, vague and watery, rising behind a gun, green slits of madness leering over its gleaming blued surface as the knuckle whitened. She heard a gutteral sound rattling in the back of the killer's throat and prepared herself for the jolt. But it never came. Instead, the face submerged back into the murky depths of the pool, its voice muted, a terror that had no fangs. "Not lately," she said. She handed Kate another tissue. "Do you know a man named Calvin Litton?"

"Calvin Litton?" She dabbed her eyes. "I don't think so."

"He drives a red Monte Carlo."

Kate's eyes drifted over the tissue toward Sandy. "A red Monte Carlo?"

"It's an older car. A bit of a hot rod with gray primer on the front left fender."

Kate blew her nose. "Sorry."

"Try to think."

Kate shook her head, cleaned each of her nostrils. "What's this about Litton?"

"He was murdered sometime last night."

Kate shivered. She rubbed her arms, looking intently at Sandy. "Last night?"

"While you were out riding."

"Sorry. Is he someone important?"

"He might be. His name doesn't ring a bell?"

"Sorry." Kate looked away, clutched the tissue in a fist. "What should I do?"

"You should tell the police everything you've told me."

Kate blinked at Sandy. "Do you think I should?"

"You wanted my advice. That's my advice."

Kate looked down at the paper towel on which her toast sat, tearing the edges with her fingers. She seemed far away in her thoughts.

"It would look better if you called them," Sandy said.

Kate jumped back from wherever she had gone. "Better? Yes, of course." She checked her watch. "I need to get going."

"You can make the call from here if you want."

Kate shook her head. "I need to go home and feed my horses. They probably think I died." She chuckled lamely. "I'll call from home."

"Suit yourself." Sandy walked her to the door. As Kate stepped out onto the porch she immediately looked down the street as she had done earlier. There was no one that Sandy could see. "Is there something the matter?" she asked.

"What? No. It's nothing."

"Did you expect to see one of your crazies with a gun?"

Kate shook her head with a dismissive laugh, patted her pockets. "No. It was just Ozzie. These murders have me a little jumpy—where are my keys?"

"Ozzie?"

"He was following me up Sand Canyon. I thought maybe he was coming over here to work on your horse or something. He must've turned into Angelina's. Here they are." She held up her keys.

The women stood looking at each other.

"Gotta go," Kate said, gave Sandy a quick meaningless smile, and started down the bricked front walk to her red pickup. It was a Chevy, Sandy noticed; the tires fairly new. New enough to leave a good set of tracks. Kate stopped, looked back over her shoulder. "You were just joking about me killing them, right?"

"Get some sleep. Call the police first, though."

"Right." Kate stared. "Maybe we can go riding sometime." Without waiting for Sandy's reply, she continued down to her truck.

Sandy watched her. Kate had a good figure, worked it well when she walked, whether she was doing so consciously or not. She may not have had much money, but she had plenty else of what men were after. Sandy wondered if it might be a motive for blackmail, perhaps even murder. One thing was certain; she was back up on the radar.

Kate drove away without looking back.

●

Sandy closed the door quietly behind her, stood for a moment in the sudden startling quiet that closed around her. It was as though a wind had whipped up suddenly, thrashed about in the trees like a spoiled child, then died just as suddenly, leaving bits of leaves and debris scattered over the ground in its quiet aftermath.

Sandy removed her windbreaker, tossed it over the seat back of the nearest bar stool, then walked around the counter into the kitchen. She finished eating her toast, drank the rest of her coffee, then cleaned up the breakfast mess. Kate had not touched her toast.

Sandy collected dirty dishes from the sink and put them into the dishwasher. She was thinking about their conversation, wondering why Vern might have taken the photos of Kate and Julian Montoya on his boat. Kate's scenario of blackmail and murder seemed a little screwy. Pieces were missing. For example, how did Litton fit into the puzzle? Montoya had a motive to kill Vern; he also had a motive to kill Chet. Blackmail and jealousy are powerful motivators. But she could not fit Litton into the puzzle—unless, of course, there were two killers. Dan had said it last night.

Kate could have killed Chet for reasons of her own (the trainer job at Angelina's). Being his lover, she certainly had opportunity. Being a registered nurse, spiking his insulin with Xylazine would have been child's play. Montoya could have killed Vern for reasons already stated. A shotgun would definitely fit his modus operandi; it was a weapon of impulse and rage. Montoya was characterized by both of these. There were other possibilities.

Sandy was fairly certain that Bud Nichols and Sorrel Rose were running drugs up from Mexico using mares for mules. Montoya and Litton might have been on the distribution end of the deal.

That scenario also worked with Kate and Litton. Kate certainly knew the drug business; the legal drug business, to be sure, but she could also have contacts into various illegal markets. Perhaps Litton was one of those contacts. If that was the case, then the photo of Kate and Montoya was irrelevant. A red herring. Kate could have lured Litton up Placerita Canyon, consummated their business with a shotgun blast, and then driven off in her truck.

Sandy started the dishwasher. The machine hummed, colored lights blinked on, water splashed. Then again, it might be the three of them in it together: Montoya, Kate, and Litton. If so, the photo would once again be relevant. It would connect two of the players, potentially dangerous to either one. It sure had Kate spooked, enough for her to break character and ask for Sandy's advice (assuming that that was what she was doing). It may have been just a ruse to turn suspicion away from her; hide in the open, as it were.

Sandy frowned. There were still more possibilities—too many possibilities, each with its own motives, opportunities, and overlapping scenarios. Chet could have been killed by Vern, who might have been killed by Litton, who might have been killed by . . . fill in the blank.

She shook her head in frustration. Too many blanks. Like this case. So far, she was coming up with goose eggs for ideas. Shooting blanks, like Kate's stallion.

She picked up the phone, started dialing Tom's number. If he and Dan met with Montoya last night it might shed some light on her thinking. She smiled. Truth be told, she really just wanted to hear his voice.

She stopped dialing.

She blinked a couple times. Then her eyes locked, fixed in a distant gaze.

Somewhere in a faraway place a dishwasher thrashed mutedly; a faint rubber tinkling made its way down a hallway; a single fly beat furiously against a kitchen window, the sounds of each weaving into a single diminishing whine.

Something Kate said.

Sandy lowered the receiver away from her ear, allowing it to drift, forgotten, in midair. It was just a thought. A thought unformed and fragile. An inchoate shape forming in her mind upon a brittle armature, as yet without articulation of muscle and tissue and a course of blood. There was enough of it, however, to send a chill over her arms.

She looked over at the front door, as though it framed the thought, and felt the chill prickling along the base of her neck. She hung up the phone gently in its cradle for fear that any sudden noise might shatter the delicate thought. "Shooting blanks," she said into the awful stillness. "Isn't that what he had said, too?"

A series of mental puzzle pieces began to link together: little ones, then bigger ones, one after the other falling into place. A magazine spread. An argument about a federal offense. Ruffled feathers. Shooting blanks. It began to make sense what he meant by those words and why he'd said them—the thought giving shape to a motive.

It had to do with a horse.

Sandy's scalp tingled with wave after wave of chills.

She hurried back to her office, sat down at her L-shaped desk and, with a nudge of her mouse, roused the computer out of its sleep mode. She double-clicked on her search engine icon. Waiting for the home page to open, she thought back over the past several days, picking up a word here, a phrase there. Something Tom had said. Something Chet had said. A photograph that tied it all together.

The photo.

Sandy pushed away from the desk, went quickly back into the living room, and returned with the photo. She sat at the desk staring at it, the thought, clearer now, articulating both an opportunity as well as the face of a killer.

One killer.

"That could be it," she said, feeling the guarded excitement of one on the brink of discovery, cautious, yet growing steadily more confident that she had at last found the missing piece of the puzzle.

"Yes," she said. "It fits."

The horse is sterile.

All she needed now was the proof.

She typed "American Quarter Horse Association" into the search window, waited until the AQHA home page downloaded, then linked over to the stallion report. She typed in her member

ID and PIN number, waited, then typed in the name Zhantastic
Bonanza Billy. Moments later, her suspicions were confirmed: according to AQHA, no such animal existed; or if it did, it was not a
registered quarter horse.

Sandy almost giggled.

She picked up her office phone, dialed the number on the Web
site. After three rings a woman with a yodelly Texas accent answered. Sandy identified herself as a police officer, gave her badge
number, then asked the woman if there had been DNA testing on
the stallion in question.

"Hold on, ma'am, let me check." Moments later the woman
came back on the line. "Sorry. We have no record of any DNA
testing on that animal."

"Are you sure?"

"Yes, ma'am, I'm sure."

"This is very important."

"I'm sure it is, ma'am. That horse is not registered with
AQHA, and there is no record of any DNA testing. May I be of
further help?"

Sandy could imagine the woman's eyes rolling on the other
end. She gave her the name of another horse and waited. Moments
later, the woman, brighter now, said, "Oh, sure, got the DNA report right here. What do you need to know?"

Sandy asked the woman to fax her the report, gave her number, thanked her, then hung up the phone and picked up the photo.
She took several measured breaths to slow down her heart rate, her
scalp vibrating as all the pieces and loose ends came together in her
mind. She had a pretty good idea who the killer was, knew the motives behind the deaths of three men. Chet was going to spill the
beans on their game, a game that certainly qualified as a federal offense. Vern Wieder simply got greedy. She made an educated guess
about Cal Litton, but she was pretty sure about him, too.

One killer, one motive. A messy cover-up.

It was all there in the photo.

She picked up the photo and gazed at it hollowly. She felt the
thick blade of emotions churning deep inside her—sadness and
anger and hurt—slowly filling up the great emptiness that was her
chest. She shook her head. *Why? How could you do such a thing?*

No one answered.

Sandy set the photo down on the desk, reached for the phone, then, seeing something in the photo, picked it up again and stared. She felt a sudden, weighty hush in the room, an awful quiet poised on the brink of discovered knowledge. The air felt suddenly charged with transcendent horror, as though angels and devils, locked in immortal combat, had just crashed into her room amid a fluttering of wings. There was something in the background of the photo that she had seen before but dismissed foolishly. Once again she felt a tingling at the base of her scalp, a bony finger dragging a nail lightly across her neck.

She felt the blood drain from her head. "Dear God, no!"

Sandy jumped back from her desk, knocking her chair over backward as she ran out of the office and up the hall into the kitchen. Sylvie bolted out of her path, her tail spiked erect. Rounding the counter, Sandy grabbed her purse on her way to the garage door, almost made it outside when she realized she was still wearing only a nightie.

"Ah!" she growled. Stripping, she ran back around the counter and down the hall into her bedroom, threw on a T-shirt and, run-hopping back up the hall, shrugging into her jeans as she once again grabbed her purse and sped out of the house in her bare feet.

Sandy didn't remember getting into her truck or even starting it or cranking it into reverse. She did have a vague impression of a metallic jolt, of tinkling glass and her trash canister skittering sideways in her rearview mirror as she backed out onto the street with a squeal of tires and smoke. Her mind was fixed on the photograph. On the man in the background.

Ozzie!

She remembered what Kate said.

Racing down the street, she dialed Tom's number—*Dear God, make him be there.* He picked up on the second ring.

"*Tom*—thank God! I think I know who the killer is." He started to say something but she cut him off. "Don't talk. Listen," she said, then laid it out for him, driving crazy fast down Sand Canyon.

"You have proof?"

She told him.

He whistled. "Sounds like a federal offense to me."

"You bet it's a federal offense," she said, swerving around a beat-up gardener's pickup truck moving dead slow, speeding to pass, then cutting back sharply to avoid an oncoming SUV. A horn blared. "It'll blow the lid off the equestrian industry, don't you think?"

Tom agreed. "Definitely got probable cause for an arrest warrant."

"Get one. I'm on my way over there now."

"Sandy, no! Wait for backup!"

"There's no time. If I'm right one of my friends is in grave danger!"

Tom was still protesting as she tossed the phone onto the seat and punched the accelerator.

Chapter Twenty-Seven

Sandy swung her truck into Montoya's drive. The black iron gates were closed. She reached out her window and stabbed the call button, drummed her fingers on the steering wheel as she waited. "C'mon, c'mon." She was about to crash through the gates when:

"Montoya's residence." It was the housekeeper's voice.

"It's Sandy Cameron. Open the gate. It's an emergency."

"Who?"

"Sandy Cameron—Angelina's friend."

"Sandy—Oh, *si*. What emergency?"

"Open the gate or I'm going to crash through it!"

"*Que?*"

"Hurry!"

The gate began to swing open, slowly, obstinately it seemed. "C'mon."

Sandy drummed the steering wheel some more, leaning forward against the wheel as though to hurry the gate. She edged her vehicle forward, forward with the opening gates, punched the accelerator when she thought she had clearance, but cracked her right wing mirror against the gate frame.

She sped up the driveway through the dull green hollow of pepper trees, a cloud of dust boiling in her rearview mirror, horses bucking and kicking in the field at the speed and shock of her approach, fear mounting in Sandy's chest.

She swung left toward the barn, gravel plinking inside her wheel wells as she accelerated. Ozzie's truck was parked next to

Angelina's. Ozzie and Angelina were standing next to the vehicles in the shade of one of several giant cottonwoods, Angelina's arm resting on the driver's side edge of her truck bed. They appeared to be talking. Both their heads turned at her approach.

"Thank God," Sandy said.

She hit the brakes, skidded sideways in the gravel as her tires lost purchase, threw the gear lever into park with a grinding crunch; dust billowing back over her truck. She swung the door open, left it bouncing on its hinges as she jumped out, drawing her service revolver and pointing it at the ground in front of her feet. "Get away from her, Ozzie."

Ozzie looked at Sandy's bare feet, looked at the pistol in her hands, then flashed an uncertain grin as he adjusted the dull blue ball cap on his head. "You're joking, right?"

"No joke, Oz," Sandy said. She stepped gingerly forward on the balls of her feet, feeling the gravel digging into her tender soles. "Step away from the truck, Angelina."

Angelina's eyes widened, shifted quickly into the truck bed. The tailgate was lowered and, from her approach, Sandy could see a long cylindrical object lying on the bed, wrapped in a blanket, the heel of something wooden and shiny and wicked exposed. Angelina reached for it.

Sandy pointed her gun at Angelina's chest. "Don't do it, Angelina," she said, stepping closer. "It's over."

Ozzie looked over at Angelina, saw what her hand was reaching for, and jumped back. "Whoa, girl!"

Sandy pulled back on the hammer of her revolver. She didn't need to—it was a double-action Smith—but she did it to underscore her resolve. "I mean it, Angelina. Don't touch that shotgun. I don't want to hurt you."

Angelina's hand clasped the butt of the shotgun, a metamorphosis contorting her face into an expression Sandy had not seen before on her friend—her mouth drawing downward at the corners, twisting into a dark ugliness, her brows pinching together into a feral scowl. Something crazy in the eyes, framed in a jet black luster of hair, shaded by the bill of a Blue Angels baseball cap. It was the face of a killer.

A killer with a gun.

Sandy felt a shuddering chill. She fought it back as she stepped forward, sighting along her barrel. She applied pressure to the trigger, enough to whiten her knuckle.

Something changed in Angelina's eyes—a flicker of light finding a toehold in the dark recesses of her brow, a twitch of humor forming creases at the corners of her eyes. She lifted her hand from the shotgun, her face clearing of hostility. Rose spots bloomed on her cheeks. She shrugged her shoulders, a smile flourishing. "Sandy, what is this?"

Sandy gestured with her pistol. "Face the truck, Angelina. Spread your hands and feet."

Angelina continued to smile, shaking her head in apparent bewilderment. "I haven't done anything wrong."

"You murdered three men. Turn around and face the truck."

Angelina did so in stages; first one foot, then the other, her body turning with it, all the while smiling at Ozzie as though there had been some terrible misunderstanding that she would soon clear up. She placed her hands on the rim of the truck bed.

Ozzie stood, gape-mouthed and wide-eyed, looking back and forth at both Angelina and Sandy.

Sandy stepped quickly behind Angelina, holding the muzzle of her gun between Angelina's shoulder blades as she kicked out first one leg and then the other to offset her balance, and patted her down.

Angelina turned her head back slightly, a laugh fluttered out of her throat. "Sandy, this is silly."

"Hands behind your head," Sandy said. To Ozzie: "You'll find a pair of handcuffs in my purse."

Ozzie's eyes went from Angelina to Sandy holding the gun. He looked about as confused as a man at a bridal shower.

"Get the cuffs, Ozzie. In my truck."

Ozzie brought Sandy the handcuffs. "You sure about this?" he asked, his voice pinched up a couple of notches.

"I'm sure." Sandy shoved her revolver down the front waistline of her jeans, cuffed Angelina's left wrist, then brought the other one down behind her back and secured it. "Angelina Montoya, I'm arresting you for the murders of Chet Gundry, Vern Wieder, and Calvin Litton." She recited Miranda.

Angelina turned and faced Sandy, stood for a moment gazing steadily at her, the corners of her mouth flicking upward into a smile of incredulity. She leaned back against her truck. "Do you really think I could kill them, Sandy? I thought we were friends."

"I did too."

Once again Angelina shook her head in apparent disbelief. "This is ridiculous," she laughed.

Ozzie, was struggling to take it all in. "She killed Chet and Vern?"

Sandy nodded. "And Calvin Litton. She was probably going to kill you, too, Ozzie."

His eyes showed white around the brown irises. "*Me?* Why me?"

"Why don't you tell him, Angelina?"

Angelina stared at her for several long moments, still smiling, then blew out a throaty grunt of contempt and looked away at the horses grazing in the tall grass.

"If you don't want to tell him, then I will," Sandy said, and proceeded to lay out the story.

It had to do with a horse.

It had to do with a woman's lust for an empire.

It had to do with a man's blackmail and greed. A deadly combination of the lust of the flesh, lust of the eyes, and the pride of life.

The stuff of murder.

●

Angelina was sitting in a green canvas-backed folding chair beside the barn in the shade of a giant cottonwood, still looking through the white-railed fence at the field of horses. She sat quietly with her knees together, feet drawn back primly, her hands cuffed behind her upright back, a slightly furtive cast in her eyes. Other than that she didn't seem bothered at all by her circumstances; she seemed resigned to them.

Sandy and Ozzie were standing to one side of her, Sandy still in her bare feet with the handle of her revolver hooked out the front of her jeans. She was waiting for the sound of sirens as she briefed Ozzie.

"Chet had come to me with a question about a police matter," she said. "Something that would apparently 'rock the equestrian industry.'"

Ozzie listened intently, his big hands resting on his hips.

They'd gone into his trailer to get out of the heat. Waiting while Chet looked for his insulin bottle, Sandy had thumbed through a recent copy of *Western Horseman*, and stopped to admire Angelina's double-page spread featuring Ideal's Zahn Bar Zee, winner of the World two years earlier. She had commended Chet for his superb training, but his response had been a deprecating "Just shootin' blanks," which had surprised her. Chet was not usually given to humility. He was about to administer his midmorning injection when he'd made the comment, so she'd thought that he was making a joke about it. "He wasn't, though," Sandy said. "He was talking about Zee-Zee."

"Angelina's horse?"

"That's right, Oz. In that one cryptic remark Chet had revealed the whole show." Sandy turned and faced Angelina. "Zee-Zee's sterile, isn't he?"

Shadow patterns made by the cottonwood flickered over Angelina's face, and in her eyes a dance of light and shadow. Words weren't a part of the dance, apparently.

"A simple vet check of his sperm count will verify it," Sandy said. "My guess is that he went sterile years ago. Sometime before the American Quarter Horse Association started requiring DNA samples for stallions. That would put it sometime back in the early nineties, wouldn't it, Angelina?"

Angelina wouldn't say. She seemed to have withdrawn into a semicatatonic state. Her face was impassive and distant, drained of emotion, except for the corners of her mouth, which curled upward strangely into a kind of lunatic smile.

"That's when the cover-up began," Sandy said.

"How do you know Zee-Zee's sterile?" Ozzie asked.

"Something Kate said."

"Kate Bledsoe?"

"She told me she was going to have her stallion cut because he had gone sterile. 'Shooting blanks,' she said."

"The same thing Chet said."

Sandy nodded. "It made me wonder why he'd said it. So I reconstructed the scene in his trailer, listening carefully to the flow of our conversation—my comments, his responses—the context for each. The voice inflections. I realized that he wasn't being self-deprecating at all. He was talking about Zee-Zee. Zee-Zee was shooting blanks. He was sterile. That's what Chet was telling me."

Ozzie pursed his lips. "There's nothing criminal about that. Nothing that would rock the equestrian industry."

Sandy agreed, adding, "Certainly nothing that would rise to the level of a federal offense."

Ozzie stared at a point about a yard in front of his nose.

"Chet and Vern were arguing about a federal offense that morning," Sandy explained. "Chet was doing most of the talking—Vern just shaking his head and kicking dirt. When I asked him about it later, he went out of his way to deny it. At the time I thought that he was just being Vern—compulsive, as usual. But once it occurred to me that maybe Zee-Zee had gone sterile, it made me wonder if the two were connected—Zee Zee's sterility and their argument about a federal offense."

Ozzie looked at Sandy expectantly.

"They are," she said.

"How?"

"Bonanza Billy."

That sailed right over Ozzie's head.

"When the police came here the other day to question Angelina, she was breeding one of her stallions. When Detective Rigby and I met later, he went into great detail describing the breeding dummy and semen shipment. He was fascinated by the process." Sandy waited a moment, then: "The truly fascinating part is that she was breeding Bonanza Billy."

Ozzie gestured outward with large callused hands. "What's the big deal about that? Billy's one of Zee-Zee's babies."

"That's just it, Oz. That's the big deal. How could she breed Billy when AQHA has no record of him?"

Ozzie made a face.

"She never registered him," Sandy explained. "She never sent in a DNA sample—at least not under his name. According to the American Quarter Horse Association, Bonanza Billy doesn't exist."

Sandy gave Ozzie a moment for the penny to drop. It didn't. She asked: "How can a horse that is sterile sire a herd of champion babies?"

"He can't."

"He can if he has a surrogate sperm donor. A ghost horse that no one can see—one close enough to him genetically to almost be his twin."

Ozzie was back staring at the point in front of his nose. After a couple of puzzled moments his mouth fell slowly open; his eyes brightened. "Bonanza Billy."

Sandy nodded. "Bonanza Billy."

"The son is the father."

"In a manner of speaking, yes. Once the American Quarter Horse Association started requiring stallions to be tested, Angelina sent in Billy's DNA sample under Zee-Zee's name. AQHA took it at face value. Why wouldn't they? As far as they were concerned Billy *was* Zee-Zee—on paper at least. All of 'Zee-Zee's babies' winning big shows were actually sired by Billy. A simple DNA comparison of both horses will prove it."

Ozzie blew out a low whistle. "That would certainly rock the horse world, wouldn't it?"

"Off the Richter scale."

Ozzie's expression was an admixture of amazement, incredulity, and perhaps even a little anger. Angelina had been his friend, too. She had betrayed that friendship, and killed one of his friends. The loss was evident on his face. "You said it was a federal offense."

Sandy nodded. "If you ship falsified semen across state lines it is. It's interstate fraud. Detective Rigby told me that she was sending a shipment to Oregon. I'd say that qualifies, wouldn't you?"

Ozzie nodded thoughtfully.

Sandy addressed Angelina. "You must've had your little scam going for years," she said. "People thinking they were buying Zee-Zee's semen when it was really Bonanza Billy's. It didn't matter though, did it? His babies were winning. Everyone thought they had a piece of the great Ideal's Bar Zhan Zee. A legend. They were happy, you were happy. You raised Zee-Zee's stud fees through the roof. No one was the wiser; that is, not until Chet caught wind of it."

Angelina's eyes, no longer furtive, gazed unblinking at her horses that were now lined along the white fence; the lunatic smile locked into place giving her the appearance of a mannequin smiling mindlessly at nothing.

"How'd she keep it from him for so long?" Ozzie asked. "He was over here every day."

"It must have been difficult," Sandy said. "Still, Chet was responsible for Zee-Zee's training program. Angelina handled his breeding. They were separate enterprises. Chet trained in the mornings; Angelina usually bred her horses in the afternoon. He might've walked in on her one afternoon, slipped past the property gates unannounced like the Burbank detectives had done, and caught her breeding Billy. Being her trainer, he would've known that Billy had never set foot in a show ring. It might've started him thinking. Asking questions."

"Like why would she breed a horse that she had never shown?"

"Exactly," Sandy said, feeling a pang of remorse. Had she not been so distracted with her own inner turmoil, she might have asked questions sooner and learned the truth. It might have saved Vern's life. Saved Cal Litton's life, as well, men whose faces, she was certain, would haunt her for a long time.

"Think Chet looked up Billy's registry like you did?" Ozzie asked.

Sandy raised her eyebrows speculatively. "Possibly." To Angelina: "He confronted you about it, didn't he?"

No response.

"It would have been the end of a world-class breeding empire," Sandy continued. "A scandal—your picture in all the horse magazines and trade papers. It would've meant years in federal prison. Is that when you decided to seduce him?"

Angelina stared vacantly at the horses, her smile flattening into a small tight line.

"You told Detective Rigby that you and Chet had slept together," Sandy said. "An 'indiscretion' you called it. I wonder if it wasn't something more. Perhaps you thought you could bring him into the scam—seal it in bed, as it were. It didn't work, though, did it?"

Angelina said nothing.

"Chet may've been loose with his morals, but he was a man of integrity," Sandy said. "Suddenly he found himself caught between a friend and something he knew was very wrong. That's what he wanted to talk to me about that morning. He probably wanted to find out what kind of jail time you'd face if he turned you in. It was tearing him apart. I could see it in his eyes. I didn't know what it was then, but I know now. Vern was trying to talk Chet out of it, but he was going to turn you in. So you killed him."

"You killed Chet, Angelina," Sandy repeated, angrily now. "You killed our friend. You got hold of one of his insulin bottles, filled it with Xylazine and killed him. Later, you sneaked back into his trailer with a key you'd probably duplicated and refilled the bottle with insulin, hoping to cover your tracks. Pretty bold. But then your whole scam was bold, wasn't it?"

Angelina sat frozen in her seat, her mouth parted slightly, showing the gleaming edges of her teeth as she stared without emotion. She was making a soft clicking noise with her tongue.

Sandy felt an urge to slap her. "You and Vern were in it together, weren't you? You couldn't make your scheme work without him. You needed his signature on the semen reports to verify each shipment, sperm count, and so on. It probably wasn't too difficult getting him on board. Vern was greedy. Which brings us to why you killed him."

Ozzie shook his head.

"Vern may've been a snake but he was no murderer," Sandy continued. "He got real jumpy when Detective Rigby told him that the killer had spiked Chet's insulin with Xylazine. I imagine Vern knew, or at least suspected, that Angelina was behind it. She may have even said something to him—'We're in this together' kind of thing. But rather than go to the police, maybe plead a lesser offense, he probably demanded a bigger slice of the pie. Threatened to blackmail her, maybe. Bad move."

Ozzie kept shaking his head in disbelief.

"Vern was no longer an asset," Sandy said. "He was suddenly a liability. A threat. Angelina followed him over to the Borden ranch that very afternoon and blew his head off."

Ozzie looked over at the shotgun, still lying wrapped in a blanket in the truck bed, as though he'd forgotten its recent significance. "You think?"

Sandy nodded. "It probably belongs to Julian," she said, adlibbing a scenario. "My guess is to point the finger at him, in case the investigation got too close to home. A couple days ago she hinted that their marriage was on the skids. Maybe she thought that if evidence swung his way—away from her—he'd get indicted, maybe convicted, and go away for a long time. She'd have grounds for divorce, maybe secure a hefty settlement that would preserve her breeding empire."

"A shotgun would be hard to trace," Ozzie said. "She'd need to come up with something more incriminating."

"She did, Oz. The police found some revealing photographs of Julian and Kate in Vern's effects." To Angelina: "You knew about those, didn't you, Angelina? It was you who took them. You suspected that Julian was having an affair with someone. You said as much to me the other day. So you followed him to the marina and took the photos as evidence of his infidelity. You planted them in Vern's house. You probably thought that if the police found them there they would think he was blackmailing your husband . . . give him a motive to kill him. That's just what they suspected, too."

Ozzie wasn't convinced.

"I'm afraid it's true, Oz. She even had an alibi in place if she needed it. According to Detective Rigby, she was registered in a Trails class at the time of the murder. I'm sure she was. But I'll bet when we ask the judges they'll say that she was a no-show. It wouldn't matter; she'd still have enough to establish reasonable doubt. With people coming and going—with events happening one after the other—who can pinpoint where anyone is at a given time? She could've slipped away, murdered Vern, planted the photos, then come back and shown her face around."

"I saw her when I got back from the Borden ranch," Ozzie said.

"That's right, Oz, you told me."

Ozzie was frowning at Angelina. "She was putting an ice pack on Zee-Zee's leg . . . asked if I'd take a look at it."

"I'm sure she mentioned it to others as well," Sandy said. "The alibi would've worked too, except for one problem. There was a witness to the murder."

"Calvin Litton?"

"Uh-huh. Julian no doubt hired him to keep an eye on her." Sandy faced Angelina. "You didn't know about him until Detective Rigby told you, did you?"

Angelina gave no indication that she'd heard the question. She was rocking back and forth in her chair slowly, barely perceptibly, still making a soft clicking with her tongue as though putting an invisible horse through its gaits.

Sandy shook her head in disgust. "That must've come as quite a shock, realizing that there was someone who might've witnessed you killing Vern. Did he contact you? Or did you contact him?"

No response.

"We found a note in Litton's car," Sandy clarified to Ozzie. "He'd written that he was supposed to meet a Montoya at the Carl's Jr. We thought he meant Julian. But it was Angelina. She probably promised to pay him a pot full of money for his silence. Triple what Julian was paying him maybe. Quadruple. It didn't matter. She had no intention of paying him a nickel. She planned to buy his silence with a load of bird shot."

"Can you prove that?" Ozzie asked.

"Her phone records will tell us if and when they talked. My guess is she called him right after Detective Rigby left her trailer yesterday. He'd told her that Litton had likely witnessed Wieder's murder, which I'm sure threw quite a scare into her." Sandy gestured at Angelina's truck. "We also got a clean tire cast at the crime scene that I'm positive will match her truck. It's circumstantial, but that, along with everything else, should give the DA a solid case."

Ozzie removed his cap, scratched the back of his scalp. "What she want to kill me for? I didn't witness no murder."

"No, but she thought you'd overhead a conversation she was having with Chet and Vern at the show. One that would have incriminated her."

Ozzie slapped the cap back on his head with big brown question marks for eyes.

"It was the photo, wasn't it, Angelina?" Sandy asked, facing her. "The one of you, Chet, and Vern standing next to Zee-Zee."

Ozzie shook his head, clearly at a loss.

"You're in the photo, Oz," Sandy said. "The one you showed me at the clubhouse yesterday, right before the Western Pleasure class. When Detective Rigby showed it to Angelina she saw you in the background. She made a comment about your nose being out of joint, but that's not what she was thinking. She was wondering how much you'd heard of their conversation."

"What conversation?" Ozzie looked at Angelina, then back at Sandy.

"You didn't overhear what they were saying?"

Ozzie shook his head back and forth slowly. "Nothing that comes to mind."

"I don't think Angelina was willing to take the risk that something might. It's my guess that she and Vern were probably trying one last time to talk Chet out of going to the police . . . of going to me. After the class she asked if I'd seen Chet that morning. She wanted to know if he'd said anything to me yet. If he had, I'd've been on her hit list too. Why are you here, Oz?"

Ozzie shrugged. "Angelina called me up and told me she had this horse she wanted to buy. Some ranch out in Lancaster. She wanted me to look at it—check its feet to see if it was sound."

"That's something I don't think you would've ever found out."

The housekeeper, a squat round Latina in her mid-thirties, had come down from the house and was standing beside Miguel and two other stable hands in the open bay doors of the barn. They were all looking wide-eyed at Angelina in handcuffs, talking to each other in fast Spanish. They turned their heads toward the street as sirens mounted in the distance.

"Best go open the gates, Carmen," Sandy said to the housekeeper.

Carmen looked at her, looked quickly at Angelina, as though to verify that there had been some misunderstanding, a joke maybe. A gringo joke that didn't translate well. Getting no response, she shook her hands as if shaking excess water from them and headed back up to the house, her eyes wide in horror.

Sandy said, "That about cover it, Angelina? Who were you going to kill next . . . Abbe Newton?"

Angelina's eyes were a flat waterless stare, without depth or life, as she continued rocking to a gait that only she could feel. Sandy wasn't sure if she'd heard a word she'd said.

"Newton took the picture," Sandy said to evoke a response out of her. It didn't.

Sandy looked down at the entrance to the property, where Tom and Dan, along with three black-and-whites, had just rolled up to the gates; their lights flashing, the high-low wail of sirens lowering to a throaty growl. The horses bolted away from the fence in a thunder of hooves and flinging clods.

"Why, Angelina?" Sandy asked. It was a question that needed to be asked. The great Why. Why do people kill? Why do they steal? Why do husbands cheat on their wives, wives their husbands? Why break any of God's commandments? "You have all the money in the world," she said. "You had Bonanza Billy to start a new line with. A world champion line. Look at how his babies are doing."

Angelina's eyes, so beautifully shaped and colored the deepest night shades of blue and violet, seemed to flicker to life out of a deep sleep, then fix shimmering in a blaze of yellow sunlight that lanced through the overhead leaves. She straightened in her chair, lifted her head slightly, tilting it a little to one side, her mouth parted just enough to allow a shallow breath of wind to rush into it before choking to a halt in the back of her throat. It was as though she were sitting alone in an empty museum, straight backed, feet together, both hands clutching a purse on her knees as she gazed at a masterpiece that took her breath away. The strange smile once again lifted the corners of her mouth. It was a faintly shadowed, cryptic smile. A Mona Lisa smile. She was watching the horses running and kicking as the police vehicles wheeled up the drive through the pepper trees, the colts dashing stilt-leggedly after their mothers.

"Zee-Zee sure throws good-looking colts, doesn't he?" Angelina said, breaking a long silence. There was a bit of girlish lilt in her voice, her voice coming back from a long hollow-walled dream. "Some fine-looking colts."

Sandy felt a chill. Rubbing her arms, she looked over at Ozzie. Ozzie was glaring shock-eyed at Angelina. "But those are B—" The name caught in his throat, as everything became suddenly clear. He saw the whole show in her eyes.

Chapter Twenty-Eight

They were sailing up the coast to Malibu. Tom knew a good seafood restaurant across from the pier where he wanted to take Sandy for a quiet candlelit dinner. There was a steady southwesterly wind blowing, making foamy caps on the waves. The sun, probing the ocean depths, showed all of its colors, from light turquoise, flickering with phosphorescent flecks of copper and gold and reds, to a dark cobalt blue, to benthic murkiness as the sun lost its reach. There were a good many boats on the water, power and sail; a few driving before the wind had their spinnakers out. Looking to starboard, the hills were green with all of the cities of the coast bright and cheerful, the sun, far out to sea, flashing on tiny invisible windows, and giving everything a rich golden hue. Tom thought that cities looked better from the sea; they had a clean and tamed look about them as they nestled contentedly in the bosomy hills. Crime did not exist from this perspective; neither did the madding crush of industry, nor the raging clangor of automobiles, crowding, belching noxious fumes into the air; neither did sinner or saint exist, or stars rising and falling through a pyrite glitter of dreams. There was only the clean snap of sails, the air a saline tartness in all the splash and freedom of the sea, and the company of a beautiful woman.

Sandy was wearing a bright yellow windbreaker with white trim over a striped green-and-white T-shirt and shorts, her legs tanned and oiled a honey glaze all the way down to her toes. Her hair was pulled back loosely into a wide linen bow the same color as the green in her shirt, with white polka dots in it. She was sitting on a cushioned blue canvas seat on the port side of the boat, beside Tom, her eyes fixed on the horizon; the sunset, casting burnished light upon the waves, reflected in them. "Have you heard anything more about Bud Nichols and Sorrel Rose?" she asked.

"The FBI is building a case," Tom said, making a steering correction. He was wearing a blue-and-white striped boatneck shirt over navy trunks, docksiders, and a green ball cap with an R.L. Winston Rod Co. logo in front to keep the last of the sun out of his eyes. "Looks like their point man down at the border is going to turn." He grinned. "Maybe Nichols can introduce horse breeding at Victorville. At least there won't be any ruffled feathers up there. They'll all be wearing the same outfit." He winced inwardly as soon as he'd said it.

If Sandy had heard him she made no comment. She was looking at a slow-moving cruise ship, high on the water like an island of glass, heading south to Mexico.

Tom felt bad for having made the joke; Nichols, after all, had been one of her friends. She'd need to testify against him, and against Angelina Montoya, which he was sure was weighing on her mind. "I didn't mean that crack about Nichols," he said. "It was dumb."

Sandy smiled, still looking out to sea. "It's hard to believe," she said, a sadness in her voice. "It's like the world coming apart at the seams."

"The world? . . ." Tom suddenly could see the faces of Chet Gundry, Vern Wieder, and Calvin Litton rising before him, one after the other, like a spectral parade: one grinning at him; one with half his face missing; the third, facedown in a pool of water, a crow tapping his head. He could see them leading Angelina Montoya to the police cruiser, a slightly lunatic cast in her eyes as she muttered something unintelligible—something to do with a horse. A lousy horse. He knew he would see their faces again from time to time, that part of it never really went away. Not even the sea would cleanse it entirely. "We stitched up a little corner of it," he said.

"Did we?"

Hearing a slight luffing of sails, Tom made another steering correction, turned the wheel away from the wind and, as he came about, felt the sails fill with air, the deck up-tilting as the sails pulled the forty-two-foot Downeaster on a starboard reach. He could feel the quartering wind on his back. "It was a good bust," he said.

Sandy said nothing at first, turned her head in profile, the wind blowing long sun-bleached strands of coppery blond hair free of her bow and over her face, "So Julian hired Calvin Litton after all?"

Tom nodded. "His office phone records show that he'd made a couple calls to Litton's Fresno address. We developed the negatives we found in Litton's camera. They were all of Angelina. There's no doubt he hired him. We also found the negatives of Julian and Kate Bledsoe in Angelina's camera. She took them, all right. Planted them in Vern Wieder's house like you said."

"The DA isn't going to prosecute Julian for obstruction?"

Tom shook his head. "I don't think he knew anything about the murders until we told him about Litton's death at the gun club. I think he had a pretty good idea then what his wife was up to, but not before. He had his distractions."

Sandy seemed distracted too. She looked back at the ship growing small on the horizon, the sun flashing on a thousand portholes no larger than pinpricks.

"I saw him the other day at the marina," Tom said. "He was taking his boat to Catalina. Guess who with?"

Sandy gave her head a little shake.

"Kate Bledsoe."

Sandy turned her head and faced Tom, held her hair back from the wind as she said, "So Kate goes home with all the marbles."

"Love is blind, as they say."

She shook her head. "Nearsighted."

She had said it with a half smile, as though the word referenced a past remark that Tom was not privy to. He suspected it was a private joke. "I'm not nearsighted," he said, smiling. "Have I told you today that you were beautiful?"

"I don't know, have you?"

"You're beautiful. Would you like me to say it again? You're beautiful, and who cares about the world. This boat is our world and there are only the two of us."

She looked at him, studying him, then, smiling that wonderful guileless smile of hers, released her hair to the wind, looked off to port with a faraway gaze back in her eyes. She looked like a blond figurehead.

Tom watched her, allowing the sails and the wind and the splashing of the waves to fill the silence. It had been a week since the arrest, and it was once again good and solid between them. He did not bring up the business about her father, nor did she. It had never happened. Neither of them wanted to spoil the good ground gained between them. Over the past few days he'd catch her looking out the window as they were driving along the coast, the top down on her BMW Roadster, the warm, sea-washed California wind in their faces; or staring out at the mountains from her back patio, listening to the lonesome cry of quail in the sage; or sitting out on a restaurant terrace, people walking by on the wide bricked tree-shaded sidewalks, Sandy not seeing them but watching the sun setting beyond the gleaming Burbank skyline. Always she had the same faraway cast in her eyes. It was as though she were contemplating distant worlds, worlds unknown to mortals, far beyond the reach of sight and sound, world's where fiery seraphs trod tremblingly upon holy courts, where there were visions far too lofty to articulate with human tongue. The imagery was a bit lofty for Tom but it was how she made him feel then, and watching her now. He was almost afraid to interrupt her thoughts. "What are you thinking?" he asked.

She did not answer.

"Sandy?"

She looked at him quickly, her eyes seeing him but her mind still a great distance away, then really seeing him, her eyes clearing with a knowing twinkle. "Thinking?"

"You were a million miles away."

"Was I?" She frowned, and then smiled down at her legs, smoothing her hands over them. "I suppose I was."

She leaned over and kissed him, then her mouth suddenly alive with emotion as she kissed him again.

"What was that for?" he asked.

"Does there have to be a reason?"

"No," he said, his voice thick with feeling. "You didn't tell me what you were thinking."

She smiled wistfully. Then taking his hand in hers, holding it as though she would never let it go, she looked back off to port, her eyes once again settling on some distant point. The cruise ship was a motionless glint of light in a vast and shimmering universe. After a few moments, she said, "What do you know about the trash business, Tom?"